The PENNY JORDAN Collection

TITLES IN THIS SERIES

CAMPAIGN FOR LOVING

CAMPAIGN FOR LOVING

BY

PENNY JORDAN

MILLS & BOON LIMITED
Eton House, 18–24 Paradise Road
Richmond, Surrey TW9 1SR

First published in Great Britain 1984 by Mills & Boon Limited

© Penny Jordan 1984

Australian copyright 1984
Philippine copyright 1984
Reprinted 1984
This edition 1988

ISBN 0 263 76070 7

Set in Monophoto Plantin 11 on 11½ pt
19-0488-45510

Printed and bound in Great Britain by Cox & Wyman Ltd, Reading

CHAPTER ONE

As she unlocked the door of her Mini, Jaime glanced quickly at her watch, expelling a faint sigh of relief. Three o'clock. She still had plenty of time to pick up her three-year old-daughter, Fern, from playschool.

At first, when her mother had suggested she move back to Dorset, she had been dubious. She and Blake had lived in London during the brief eighteen months of their marriage and she had been reluctant to move away. Now she could acknowledge that her reluctance had stemmed from her hope that Blake would come looking for her and beg her to go back to him. For a girl of twenty-three she had been extremely naive, she thought sardonically. The unflattering alacrity with which Blake had accepted the challenge she had flung at him in the heat of her tempestuous outburst ought to have warned her, but it hadn't. It had taken Suzy Monteith to do that. Suzy had worked with Blake on the *Globe*'s Foreign Affairs team for several years and Blake had never made any secret of the fact that they had at one time been lovers. Suzy had never liked her Jaime realised with the benefit of hindsight, and no doubt she had thoroughly enjoyed telling her of her husband's request to his editor that he be sent abroad to cover the war in El Salvador, only twenty-four hours after she had accused him of putting his job before his marriage, more or less giving him an ultimatum to choose between her and working for the *Globe*.

Suzy had called round on the pretext of inviting them both to a party she was giving. But Jaime hadn't even waited for Blake to come home that evening, she had simply packed her things and gone round to a friend's flat where she had stayed for two weeks, willing Blake to appear and beg her to come back to him.

Of course he hadn't done and by then she had known that the possibility that she might be pregnant was a certainty. She had written to him then, an angry bitter letter to which he didn't reply, making it obvious that he didn't want her or their child—she had offered him a choice and he had made one—excluding her completely from his life. Her pregnancy had wrapped her in an anaesthetising shawl which numbed all pain. Blake's letters she returned unopened, accepting her mother's suggestion that she return home simply because she had no means of supporting herself, and was was determined not to accept any money from Blake. He hadn't wanted a child—he had made that more than clear to her. His lifestyle could barely accommodate a wife, never mind the responsibility of children, and that had been another subject for contention between them.

The truth was that they should never have married, Jaime thought as she manoeuvred her car down the bumpy lane that led from the old school hall she used for her dance and exercise studio to the village. And it was her fault that they had married. All Blake had wanted was an affair—but she had been naive and very much in love. When he discovered that she was still a virgin he had given in to the subtle pressure she had put on him and, within six months of meeting, they had been married.

Right from the start she had known that she wasn't really equipped to enter Blake's world. Shy and rather retiring by nature, she had gone to London at the urgings of a schoolfriend and her mother, and although she quite enjoyed her job as a secretary in a busy advertising agency, she had never really lost her longing for the peace and relative simplicity of the village she had grown up in. She had met Blake at a party, flattered and slightly bemused that he should single her out for attention. She knew she wasn't exactly unattractive but she had lived in London long enough by then to realise that London males expected more than a heart-shaped face, deep blue eyes, black hair and a willow-slim body. They wanted women who could converse with them on their own level, sharp witty women who didn't blush and fumble awkwardly; women who were as sophisticated and worldly as they were themselves.

She had recognised Blake instantly from a current affairs television programme he had participated in, but the effect of his lean, sun-tanned features and his air of cool cynicism were far more devastating in real life than they were on the television screen. She had had the impression that his green eyes were laughing at her, but when, seconds later, they roved her body with a sensual appraisal that was almost a physical caress, she hadn't been able to hide her response from him. Blake! Even now, just thinking about him made her pulses race and her mouth go dry. He had been, at first, a patient and then a very passionate lover, drawing her out of her shell of shy reserve, teaching her to please him and find joy in her own pleasure. As befitted a man who lived on the edge of danger, he brought excitement and challenge into her life, but she was constantly worried that she would never be enough for him; that after a while her inability to meet him as an equal would lead him to grow bored with her. Before their marriage he had dated sophisticated, glamorous women, and Jaime had always secretly compared herself to them and found herself wanting. If she hadn't blurted out to him that she loved him and that he would be her first lover, would he still have wanted to marry her?

'He married you because that was the only way he could get you into bed,' Suzy had told her tauntingly, 'but you'll never keep him—he's bored already. You see, Blake's like that. When he wants something, he goes after it single-mindedly, that's what makes him such a good reporter. He wanted *you* because you were a challenge. . . .'

And she, instead of trying to understand him, had begged him to give up his job and find another one that would mean less travel. That had been the cause of their final row. . . . Perhaps, because her own father had died when she was so young, she had always cherished in her mind a clear picture of what she wanted her life to be, and that picture contained herself, her husband and their two children, living cosily in a village very like the one she had been brought up in; a safe, secure little world, a universe away from Blake's lifestyle.

People thought she had got over him and her marriage to him. She talked openly to Fern about her father; she answered whatever questions people asked her, but only she knew the truth. She still loved Blake as desperately now as she had done the day she left him. But at least in the intervening four years she had achieved some maturity, she reflected as she brought her Mini to a halt outside the playschool building. At least she had finally accepted that Blake had the right to make his own decisions about his career and his life, but that didn't stop her regretting her folly in leaving him. If she had stayed, perhaps they could have worked something out ... perhaps. . . . Angrily, she dragged her mind away from the past. Blake had made it more than clear how much he regretted their marriage. He had never even asked to see Fern. He hadn't wanted a child and, although he had offered to support them financially, he had made no attempt to get to know his daughter.

Charles had told her she ought to get a divorce. She had known Charles Thomson since her schooldays, and she knew, without any conceit, that he would marry her tomorrow if she gave him any encouragement. It was ironic that Charles was tailormade to fit her childhood image of the perfect husband and father, but he was as exciting as cold rice pudding, and her body, which had been awakened and tutored by Blake's, instinctively repudiated him as a lover.

She knew why she had never bothered to get a divorce. She had no wish to marry again, but what about Blake? Was it just that he had never had the time between assignments to bring their marriage to a formal end, or was it simply that, having married once, he had no intention of repeating his mistake? Unlike her, Blake did not seem to lack congenial companions of the opposite sex. Over the years, she had seen him featured in several newspaper photographs as the escort of glamorous women.

'Mummy . . . Mummy. . . .'

The impatient and reproving voice of her daughter checked her thoughts. Fern was all Blake's child. She had her father's unruly, dark brown hair and his green eyes. And her personality held echoes of Blake's as well. A pragmatic, intelligent child, she sometimes gave Jaime the uncomfortable feeling that their roles were reversed and that she was the child. She even seemed to accept her own lack of a father. She had seen his photograph and knew that he lived and worked in London, but seemed to accept that his life lay apart from theirs.

'. . . and Mrs Childs told us a story. . . but I

knew it wasn't real. Frogs can't turn into princes, not really. . . .'

Jaime glanced into her daughter's scornful green eyes and sighed. She herself had been at least ten before she had finally and reluctantly abandoned fairy stories.

'You're daydreaming again . . .' the small firm voice accused. 'Granny says you've always got your head up in the clouds. . . .'

When Jaime repeated this comment to her mother later in the evening when Fern was in bed, Sarah Cummings laughed. Married at eighteen, a mother at nineteen, she was, in Jaime's view, far too young-looking and vigorous to be anyone's grandmother. A partner in a thriving antique business in the local market town her mother had the knack of drawing people to her, 'Jaime reflected watching her. Her once fair hair was tinged with grey now, but she still had the same youthful figure she had always had, and she still seemed to radiate that special sort of energy that Jaime always associated with her.

'Fern's like me,' her mother commented pragmatically, 'a down-to-earth Taurean. . . .'

'Umm, I was thinking today how like Blake she is. . . .'

'Don't tell me you're worrying about her lack of father again,' Sarah said drily, correctly interpreting her remark. 'Well, if you're thinking of marrying Charles to provide her with one, I shouldn't bother. She's already running rings round him.'

That Charles found it difficult to talk to her

young daughter Jaime already knew. An only child himself, he was always uneasy in Fern's presence and she seemed to know it and take advantage of his awkwardness.

'You're not worrying about the studio, are you?' Sara asked her daughter, noticing the frown pleating her fair skin. 'I thought it was just about beginning to pay its way.'

'Yes, it is.' At first on her return to her home Jaime had been wholly dependent on her mother, but once Fern had started playschool, she had trained in exercise and dance, and then, when she was qualified, she had opened her own school which was beginning to get an excellent reputation locally. She was fortunate in being able to rent a now-empty school hall at a very reasonable cost, and the knowledge that she had achieved something for herself through her effort and skill had boosted her self-confidence. Because she always looked so calm and self-possessed, few people guessed at the deep sense of inadequacy she suffered from. Indeed, it was only since she had left Blake that she had come to terms with it herself.

'So, what's worrying you?' her mother probed.

'Charles came to see me today. He's heard that Caroline means to sell the Abbey to a property developer and that it's going to be knocked down and a housing estate built.'

'Mmm . . . I shouldn't think she'll be able to go ahead with the sale. The Abbey is a listed building, you know.'

'And Caroline can be very determined.'

Jaime had gone to school with Caroline Travers, although they had never been good friends. Caroline's father had made a fortune in industry and had bought the Abbey and retired there. Caroline had inherited quite a substantial sum from him on his death, but she was a lady with very expensive tastes and she had never liked the Abbey.

'Charles wants me to go round and have a word with her—try to persuade her to reconsider. . . .'

'Why doesn't he go himself?' Sarah asked forthrightly. 'Really, the man is a fool. I honestly believe he's terrified that Caroline would seduce him.'

Jaime grinned at her mother's percipience. 'He did say that he thought the initial approach would be better coming from me—a "woman to woman appeal",' Jaime quoted.

'"Woman to man eater" doesn't he mean?' her mother quipped. 'Really, Charles is impossible. I don't know why you bother with him.'

'Because he's an old friend and he's my solicitor. . . .'

'And he's also a very safe wall to hide behind. Jaime, you're twenty-six, and a very attractive woman, but you behave as though you've voluntarily gone into purdah. . . .'

'You were even younger when you were widowed. . . .'

'Yes, but I didn't eschew all male company because of it. . . .'

'But you've never remarried.'

'No, because I preferred being single. You

don't. You need marriage, Jaime, I never did. I was too independent to commit myself to the sort of relationship marriage was in my day. I loved your father and I missed him terribly, but I didn't live like a nun the way you do. Blake. . . .'

'I don't want to talk about him. . . .'

Jaime turned away, hoping that her face wouldn't betray her. Her mother didn't know that she still loved Blake, and every time she mentioned him, Jaime retreated from the conversation like a flower curling protectively back on itself. Her mother had liked Blake. They had got on well together, chatting with an ease that had left her envious when she heard Blake's deep laughter mingling with her mother's. She had been jealous of the ease with which they became at home with one another, just as she had been jealous of anyone who got close to her husband. It was no wonder he had lost his temper with her, she reflected as she went into the kitchen on the pretext of wanting a drink. When she thought about it, it was a miracle he had stayed with her so long as he had. No man likes jealous scenes, and on occasions she had behaved like a spoiled child, demanding more and more of his time and attention because of her deep-rooted insecurity, her inability to believe that he loved and needed her with the same intensity with which she loved and needed him. She had created an atmosphere which must have been claustrophobic, driving him away from her in her frantic attempts to keep him with her. No one would ever know how much she regretted her behaviour, or how much she longed for a second chance, she thought as she reached automatically for the coffee. Her mother thought the subject of Blake was taboo because she hated him. That was what she had claimed when she first came home, driven to say so because she couldn't admit the truth, and she had never corrected that misconception.

When Charles commiserated with her about her marriage she had to grit her teeth to stop herself from telling him the truth—that the faults were all on her side. There had hardly been a night in the three years since Fern's birth when she hadn't longed for Blake's presence, and yet she couldn't regret Fern who had, in her way, been the reason for that final argument. Knowing that she might be pregnant, and that her pregnancy had been the result of her deliberate carelessness, she had panicked when Blake had declared quite firmly that he didn't want children. But what was the use of raking over the past?

'Perhaps you're right,' she said to her mother when she carried the coffee tray back into the small sitting room. 'Perhaps I ought to tell Charles to start divorce proceedings.'

Because she was bending over the tray, she missed the brief frown that touched her mother's forehead, and when she looked up it was gone, the older woman's face enviably serene.

'Charles is organising a committee to formally protest against any plans to pull down the Abbey,' Jaime told her mother. 'He wants me to be the secretary.'

'Will you do it?'

'Umm, I think so. It's a beautiful old building.'

'Talking of beautiful old buildings, I've booked my holiday at last. Ten days in Rome, in a month's time.'

'You mean that Henry is actually letting you go on your own?'

Henry Oliver was her mother's partner in the antique business, and had been her faithful admirer for as long as Jaime could remember.

'That's one of the advantages of being independent,' Sarah pointed out with a smile. 'I don't *have* to ask him.'

A week later, carefully noting down the minutes of the meeting Charles had called to discuss ways and means of preventing the Abbey from being destroyed, Jaime pushed a wayward strand of dark curling hair out of her eyes.

'You look about sixteen, poring over that notebook,' an admiring male voice whispered in her ear. 'How about letting me take you out for dinner when this is over?'

'No thanks, Paul.'

Paul Davis was their local celebrity, the Managing Director of their local radio station. He was also married, although he made no attempt to hide his many affairs from his wife.

'Spoilsport.'

Jaime returned her attention to the meeting. Charles was speaking, and she groaned inwardly, knowing his propensity for long and dull speeches. Fern was with Mrs Widdows next door, as Sarah Cummings was also out that evening, and Jaime had promised that she would be back by eight. It was seven now. Paul Davis was also glancing at his watch, and when Charles paused he made full use of the opportunity to stand up and bring the meeting to a rather abrupt halt. Charles looked pained and flustered. 'Rather like an irritated St Bernard,' Jaime thought watching him.

'I hadn't finished speaking,' he complained to Jaime in aggrieved accents later. 'Have you been to see Caroline yet?'

'No, I'll go tomorrow. But she and I were never friends, Charles, and I don't think an approach from me will do the slightest good.'

'Perhaps not, but at least she'd know that we mean to do something. It is a listed building after all. . . .'

Jaime thought of other listed buildings which had become piles of rubble in dubious circumstances, but said nothing—if she didn't leave soon, she'd be late for Fern.

Her route took her past the entrance to the Abbey. As she drove past, a car was turning in at the gates, and she caught a glimpse of a male outline before the car disappeared. One of Caroline's lovers? If so, this man must be rather more wealthy than they usually were. He had been driving a menacing-looking black Ferrari.

'No . . . look, you do it this way. . . .' Fern's clear, high-pitched voice reached her as she knocked on Mrs Widdows' door.

'I was just showing Mrs Widdows how to make a house,' she explained when she saw Jaime. 'A man telephoned after you'd gone out and asked to speak to Granny. He asked me what my name was, and I told him. He was nice.'

It was rare for Fern to make any comment on other adults, but as her mother was out Jamie was unable to question her about the unknown male who had won her daughter's approval.

It was perhaps cowardly of her to take Fern with her the following afternoon when she finally plucked up the courage to go and see Caroline, but Charles had telephoned in the morning, insisting that she go, and having Fern with her gave her something else to worry about other than the coming interview.

Caroline had never liked her; Jaime knew that they were worlds apart for all the similarity in their ages. Caroline had come to her wedding, and she could vividly remember the predatory look in her eyes when she saw Blake. There must be very few women immune to Blake's wholly male, sexual aura. During their brief marriage she had soon come to recognise the look in other women's eyes which said that they were imagining him as their lover. It had driven her into paroxysms of jealous insecurity. How could Blake genuinely prefer her to these sexy, assured women?

As it was a pleasant day she had elected to walk to the Abbey, her decision in no way connected with the fact that walking would delay the inevitable confrontation with Caroline, she taunted herself as she fastened Fern's sandals.

One day her daughter was going to be an extremely attractive woman, and when she was Jaime was determined that she would have far more self-confidence than she had ever had.

'I like this green dress,' Fern told her complacently. 'It's my favourite.'

'It matches your eyes,' Jaime told her. 'Are you ready?'

'Yes, I like your dress too, Mummy.'

It had been a present from her mother the previous year. It was quite simple, white crinkle cotton, with shoe-string straps and an A-line skirt, the ideal dress for a hot, sunny afternoon. Her skin tanned well and the white fabric showed off her smooth golden arms and shoulders. She had taken more care than usual with her make-up and hair. When she looked happy, her eyes glowed like sapphires, Blake had once told her, and he had bought her a sapphire engagement ring to match them. She still had it, but could not wear it because of the memories it brought with it. She felt her heart contract with pain and regret.

Fern was an entertaining companion, chattering away at her side as they headed for the Abbey, Jaime matching her steps to her daughter's slower ones.

'It's a very big house, isn't it?' Fern commented when they turned into the drive, 'but I think I like Granny's cottage best.'

Fern moved with a natural grace Jaime noticed, watching her daughter, unaware that her lithe delicacy had been inherited from her. Jaime had always enjoyed dancing. The discipline of teaching others, of helping them and watching their own appreciation grow with ability gave her an intense feeling of satisfaction. Fern tugged on her hand as she bent to examine a clump of ragged robin, and not for the first time Jaime gave mental thanks for the fact that her daughter had such an equable and sunny temperament. Fern would never suffer as she had done from an excess of sensitivity and over-emotionalism. 'You're too hard on yourself,' her mother always said when she voiced this fact. 'You have many things to recommend yourself, Jaime, you just don't realise it.' It sometimes seemed to Jaime that her mother had been trying to bolster her self-confidence all her life, but she had just never possessed the sturdy independence which characterised both her mother and her daughter.

The Abbey loomed before them, grey and ivy-coloured. Although not a beautiful house, it possessed a mellow air of continuity that had always appealed to Jaime. It had once been an Abbey, although little of the original building remained. It had been rebuilt during the reign of Charles the Second and, although Caroline complained that she found the panelled downstairs rooms gloomy and depressing, Jaime loved them.

Mrs March, Caroline's housekeeper, answered the door, beaming at Fern, who responded with a happy grin of her own.

'Why don't I take her into the kitchen and give her some of my home-made gingerbread?' she suggested, not realising that she was depriving Jaime of the emotional support she felt she needed. 'Miss Caroline's in the drawing room,' she added.

No doubt Mrs March knew quite well why she was here, Jaime reflected, watching her daughter follow the housekeeper without a backward glance. The panelling had been removed from the drawing room by Caroline's father, but the graceful stucco ceiling remained, and the Adam fireplace added by a Georgian owner. Caroline had completely refurnished the house when she inherited it. Personally, Jaime loathed the cold starkness of the modern Italian furniture she had chosen, but there was no doubt that it made a stunning setting for her startling beauty. Dark red hair framed her face in an aureole of curls, the leather trousers and silk blouse she was wearing being a soft khaki colour which emphasised her colouring. As always, she was immaculately made-up. She had played at modelling when she first left school and had picked up enough tips to achieve what always seemed to Jaime to be an effortlessly glamorous look. She reminded Jaime of the women who had pursued Blake, both before and after their marriage. Brittle, expensive, beautiful predators who lived by their own rules. Women she could never hope to compete with. 'Why bother?' her mother had once said lightly when she had tried to confide her fears to her. Blake had chosen to marry *her*, but she had never been able to rid herself of the conviction that, somehow, she had coerced him into marriage and that had been something she hadn't been able to tell her mother. She had been too deeply ashamed to admit to her that she didn't have the strength to be as independent as Sarah was. She had always felt that, secretly, she must have been a disappointment to her mother; that although she had never shown or expressed any impatience, there must have been some. 'You underestimate yourself too much Jaime.' That was what she had always said, and Jaime would have been surprised if she had known that, far from comparing her with Caroline to her own discredit, most people would have found far more appeal in her own natural beauty and quiet intelligence than in Caroline's showy, pushy manners.

'Well, well if it isn't Miss Goody Two Shoes,' Caroline mocked. The nickname was a throw-back to their schooldays, and Jaime managed to hold back the humiliating scald of colour she could feel rising up under her skin.

'No need to ask what you're doing here,' Caroline continued tauntingly. 'But what happened to the cavalry?'

'If you mean Charles, he's had to go to Dorchester to a meeting,' Jaime responded evenly. 'Caroline, surely it can't be true that you intend to sell the Abbey to a developer?'

'Why not?' Caroline asked carelessly, 'After all, it's mine to do with as I choose.' Without inviting Jaime to sit down, she drifted elegantly over to one of the uncomfortable-looking modern chairs, crossing her legs at the ankle, sure of herself as a woman in a way that Jaime felt she could never emulate.

'But it is a listed building,' Jaime reminded her quietly. Caroline shrugged. 'So what. . . . If you feel so strongly about it, you can always put in a more attractive bid. The current one is £250,000.' She laughed unpleasantly at Jaime's expression.

The sound of Fern's excited voice interrupted Jaime's thought flow. She could see her daughter in the garden, walking towards the French windows, chattering animatedly to the man at her side.

Jaime's heart seemed to do a somersault and then stop beating as she stared disbelievingly at the dark head bent towards her daughter's. She started to shake, her sight blurring, the two heads of dark brown hair so similar that they merged into one. Caroline got up and opened the French doors.

'Blake, darling, there you are. I thought you were writing. . . .' There was malice in her eyes as she directed a contemptuous look at Jaime's white face. 'You seem to have given poor Jaime rather a shock, didn't you let her know you were coming?'

As she watched the dark, hawklike profile of her husband turn in her direction, Jaime struggled to retain some composure.

'Jaime and I aren't exactly on intimate terms these days.' The indifferent tone of his voice, the cool aloofness in his green eyes, both combined to increase Jaime's feeling of nausea. She could scarcely believe that this handsome distant man had once possessed her body; had fathered her child.

'I agree.'

'Umm, it seems hard to believe that you were ever that,' Caroline drawled, 'but of course there is Fern.'

Fern! Trying to control the shudders of shocked reaction coursing through her, Jaime looked into her daughter's shining eyes.

'This is my Daddy,' she told Jaime importantly, 'I found him in the garden. He was looking at some flowers. I told him my name and he said that he was my Daddy.'

'Fern, it's time to go home.' How weak and faint her voice sounded. 'Go and say thank you to Mrs Marsh for your gingerbread and then we'll go.'

'I'm sorry about the interruption, Blake,' she heard Caroline apologising as she hurried Fern away. 'It's Mrs Marsh's fault, she should never have let the child loose in the garden.'

Blake's response was an indistinct blur that Jaime didn't stay to hear. Why should she? She already knew how Blake viewed his daughter; in much the same light as he did his wife; as an encumbrance he would prefer to do without.

CHAPTER TWO

'YES, staying up at the Abbey he is . . . writing a book or supposed to be. . . .' The voice faded away as Jaime entered the small post office and her face burned as she recognised who they were talking about. It was as impossible to ignore Blake's presence in the vicinity as it was the sympathetic glances that seemed to follow her everywhere she went these days. Even at the studio she was aware of the faint air of sympathetic concern that surrounded her.

'It's horrible,' she complained to her mother that night. 'I feel as though I'm being treated as the victim of an incurable disease.'

'It's only because people don't want to hurt you,' Sarah sympathised. 'If you talk to them openly about it, they'll soon accept the situation.'

'Why on earth did Blake have to come here?'

'Presumably for the reason Caroline gave you. He needs somewhere to write.'

'Or because he wants to flaunt his affair with Caroline in front of me.'

'Why should he want to do that?' Her mother's glance was calmly shrewd. 'You haven't seen him for four years, and if he wanted to have an affair with Caroline, there's nothing to stop him, although I doubt that she's his type.'

'But why should he need somewhere to

write. . .?' Frustration edged up under her voice, giving it a husky note of impatience.

'Jaime, I know as little about his motives as you do yourself. If you really want answers to all these questions, you must ask him yourself.'

'But to tell Fern that he's her father!' Why must her mother always be so reasonable and fair-minded? Why couldn't she simply side with her without question? Her impartiality was frustrating and, in some strange sense, vaguely threatening.

'He is her father,' Sarah pointed out mildly. 'One of your criticisms of him has always been his lack of interest in her. Try to be consistent, Jaime, my love. What do you want of the man? Or is he just to be a whipping post?'

'I don't believe for one moment that he's come down here simply for Fern's sake.'

'Jaime, I really can't see the point in discussing him with you while you stay in this frame of mind. I can understand why seeing him should shock and even upset you, but for Fern's sake you must try to set aside your own dislike of him, and remember that he *is* her father. Must he be damned for ever, because you quarrelled with him?' she asked quizzically. 'Perhaps he's changed, people do you know,' she said softly. 'Don't rush to meet trouble head on, Jaime. I personally can't believe for one moment that Blake is staying with Caroline simply because he wishes to flaunt any relationship they might have in front of you. He isn't that type of man. Now, I'm going shopping this afternoon. I need to restock my wardrobe for Rome, but I should be back for tea.'

On Wednesday afternoons Jaime closed the studio and usually spent the afternoon with Fern. She had just collected her from playschool and was making a drink when she heard a car stopping outside. Her mother's cottage was the middle one of a row of three with a long front garden and a pleasant, sheltered back one. The kitchen-dining room in which Jaime was standing had windows at either end, and her heart skittered to a standstill as she saw Blake unfold his lean frame from the low-slung black Ferrari she had seen entering the Abbey's drive earlier in the week, and unlock the garden gate.

'Mummy, you're daydreaming again,' Fern criticised sternly. She wanted to run but where was there to run to? And besides, she had left that sort of childish reaction behind her when she left London.

As she opened the door to him, he seemed to tower menacingly over her, dark and forbidding, his jean-clad figure familiar and yet totally alien. He had always affected her in this way; the maleness in him calling out to her deeply feminine core so that her pulse rate quickened and her stomach ached.

'Sensible of you,' he commented when she let him in. His eyes were derisive as he added, 'Knowing you as I do, I half expected to have to break the door down to get in. You always did have a taste for the dramatic.'

'Not to say farcical,' Jaime agreed, watching

the faint surprise replace the derision. 'We do have a back door,' she pointed out, 'and it is open.'

'We have to talk.'

'Do we? I can't think what about.'

'Well, there's Fern for starters.'

'Oh, yes. Of course.' It was her turn to sound derisive. 'Forgive me for not recognising your concern for your daughter straight away, won't you?'

'You know the reason I haven't shown any interest in her before.' His voice was clipped, and if she had not known better she could have imagined there was a trace of angry pain in it.

'What, besides Fern, brings you down here?'

'You heard what Caroline said. I need the peace and quiet to write.'

'A new departure isn't it? You always seemed to manage quite well at the flat.'

'With you for inspiration?' His mouth twisted. 'They were articles, this is a novel—my third to be exact.'

Her heart missed a beat and then hammered painfully. It hurt much more than she could say that there had been such drastic developments in his life and that she had known nothing about them.

'I started the first one just after you left me, after I got back from El Salvador.'

She didn't want to talk about the past. It held far too many unhappy memories. Fern heard their voices and came running out of the kitchen, launching herself at Blake with unabashed enthusiasm. 'Daddy. . . .'

'I'd like to take her out for the afternoon.'

'No ... Wednesday is the only afternoon I have her all to myself.'

'Then come with us.' It was a subtle challenge, reminding her of the many other challenges he had given her in the past and the often childish manner in which she had reacted to them. Fern's smile widened and Jaime knew that if she refused the little girl would be disappointed.

'Very well,' she agreed coolly, suppressing wry amusement as she saw disbelief flicker briefly in Blake's eyes. Had he expected her to refuse? She shrugged aside the thought. What did it matter what he had expected? She wasn't going to leave Fern alone with him, at least not until she knew why he was making this attempt to get to know his daughter. Nor was she going to allow him to provoke her as he had done in the past. With a slight start, she realised she was experiencing none of the tongue-tied anxiety she had previously felt in his presence. Somehow the gulf she had always felt between them seemed to have narrowed, and she no longer stood so much in awe of him. Not that she underestimated him for one moment. Fern was already showing incipient signs of being dazzled by him and her heart ached for her daughter, the pain followed by a fierce wave of protective mother love. Blake would never hurt Fern the way he had hurt her.

'How about the New Forest?' Blake suggested blandly. Jaime bit her lip. They had once spent a weekend there shortly after they were married. Blake had overruled her protests at dinner and, as a consequence, she had drunk rather more wine than was her normal habit. Later, alone together in their room, he had made full use of her intoxicated state to coax from her a physical response to his lovemaking which still held a vivid place in her memories.

'Fine,' she responded lightly. 'Fern will love the ponies.'

He glanced at his watch. 'Well, if we're going to make it there and back in the day, we'd better start out soon.'

He was right, but Jaime suppressed a mental sigh. She had looked forward to a little time on her own from which to draw enough strength to face the prospect of the rest of the afternoon with him.

Fern accepted his presence with her normal placid good sense, although she did comment to Jaime, thankfully while Blake was out of earshot, 'I like my Daddy; he's much nicer than Charles isn't he?'

It didn't take long to get ready. Blake waited for them in the sitting room, commenting admiringly on Fern's new pale pink boilersuit when they rejoined him, although it was on Jaime's slim shape in her faded jeans and soft T-shirt that his eyes lingered.

'I hear you've opened a dance studio,' he remarked, as he opened the front door for them, 'and that it's doing very well.'

'Surprised?' Her voice sounded nastily bitter.

'Why should I be? I always knew you had it in you to make your own way in life, Jaime. That air of helpless desperation is very deceptive. You've made it more than clear to me that you want neither my emotional nor financial support.'

As they were walking down the garden path, Charles' Ford drew up outside, Charles himself emerging from inside it, his eyes going from Jaime to Blake and then back again. Charles had met Blake at the wedding and, as he came towards them, Jaime could almost see the questions hovering on his lips.

'Templeton,' Charles greeted Blake stiffly. 'Quite a surprise.' He looked at Jaime as he spoke, his face taut with disapproval. 'I suppose you're here to discuss the divorce.' His gaze switched back to Blake and Jaime felt her heart lurch precariously. Of course! Stupidly that was something she hadn't thought about. Did Blake want to institute divorce proceedings? If so, he need hardly discuss them with her. They had been separated for longer than the statutory period necessary for an uncontested divorce. 'I'm Jaime's solicitor, and the right thing to do would have been for yours to get in touch with me,' Charles was saying stuffily. 'In fact, your divorce will be quite a simple procedure. . . .'

'Always supposing we want one.' Blake's drawl was calm but something about the way he spoke warned Jaime that he was annoyed. Why? Because Charles had pre-empted him?

'And besides, what makes you think we're discussing divorce? We could be contemplating a reconciliation.'

If she hadn't been so stunned, Jaime might

almost have laughed at Charles's expression. His eyes met hers, but before she could answer the question in them, Blake's hand was on her arm, guiding her towards the car. He opened the door and helped Fern into the back, never once releasing Jaime's arm from his grip.

When he finally put the Ferrari in gear and drove away, Charles was still standing mute, watching them.

'Uncle Charles looked like one of the goldfish at playschool,' Fern commented, watching him, as they drove off. Blake's laughter released Jaime from her stupefied incredulity . . . 'Why did you say that to him?' she demanded angrily. 'Why did you intimate that we might be considering a reconciliation?'

The powerful shoulders shrugged, his profile turning briefly towards her. 'Why not?' he asked blandly. 'It's as likely to be true as his comment about a divorce. At least on my side. Are *you* contemplating divorce proceedings?'

'Are you?'

He made a small, exasperated sound in the back of his throat. 'You know damn well if I was, you'd be the first person to know about them— via me, not some solicitor. The only reason I can think of for divorcing you would be because I wanted to marry someone else. As that doesn't apply, I'm quite happy with the present status quo. Apart from anything else, it acts as a pretty good deterrent.'

'You mean it gives you the freedom to have affairs without giving any commitment,' Jaime commented bitterly.

'It gives you exactly the same freedoms,' Blake pointed out. 'Why was Thomson coming to see you?'

His abrupt change of subject startled her for a moment. For some reason he obviously didn't want to talk about a divorce between them. But then, as he had so cynically commented, he had no reason to divorce her. He had the best of both worlds; the protective status of marriage, and the freedom of a single man.

'Charles? Oh, I expect he wanted to know how I got on at the Abbey.'

'Ah, yes, Caroline waxed most indignant after you'd gone about your plans to stop her selling the place.'

'Not to stop her selling it, it's the fact that she's planning to sell it to a property developer, who will probably pull it down, that we're objecting to.'

'It's a listed building, isn't it?'

'Yes, but when did that stop anyone?'

'You're letting your imagination run away with you. Always a fault of yours. You always did enjoy painting the blackest picture possible.'

They drove some miles in silence before Fern piped up with several questions. Blake answered her with a calm assurance that Jamie found surprising, listening to him tailoring his replies so that the three-year-old would find them easily comprehensible. This was a side of him she had never seen before. Perhaps her mother was right. Perhaps, where Fern was concerned, he had had a change of heart and genuinely wanted to get to know his daughter. How would she be able to cope if Blake came back into her life as Fern's part-time father? She had learned today it was easier to cope with never seeing him than with these brief exchanges, excruciatingly painful after the intimacy she had once shared with him.

With Blake's powerful Ferrari it seemed no time at all before they reached the outskirts of the Forest. Fern laughed excitedly when the powerful car splashed through one of the fords, the jolting throwing Jaime against Blake's hard shoulder. One hand left the wheel as he steadied her, his fingers resting against her body just below the full curve of her breast. She jerked convulsively against his touch as though it burned, watching the mocking arch of his eyebrows.

'Once when you did that it was because you couldn't wait for me to make love to you,' he murmured softly, watching her.

The way she had craved his lovemaking almost as though it were a drug was one of the things that sickened Jaime most about her behaviour during their brief marriage, and, in a way, his physical possession of her *had* been a drug. In his arms, she could forget all her doubts and insecurities and convince herself that he loved her as much as she loved him.

'Now, it's because I can't endure the thought of you doing so,' she responded crisply, hoping that he couldn't tell that she was lying. The proximity of him brought back memories she would much rather have suppressed. She had been shy and naive when they first met, but that had not stopped her from responding to Blake's lovemaking with an ardency that had surprised her. If he turned to her now and took her in his arms—suppressing the acutely erotic images tormenting her, she shook her head, and turned round to talk to Fern.

Blake brought the car to a halt in one of the small clearings. Half a dozen mares and foals grazed peacefuly several yards away, Fern's eyes widening with delight when she saw them. Jaime had taken the precaution of bringing a bag of stale bread with her, and Blake took it from her, demonstrating to Fern how to offer it to the ponies. When one finally deigned to take the bread from her small quivering palm, her serious little face was suffused with an expression of pure bliss.

Jaime caught Blake looking at her, something approaching pain darkening his eyes. An emotion stirred inside her, refusing to be quelled, and just for a moment, she gave in to the urge to make believe that they were a contented family unit; that she and Blake were still together.

'She's very much your child,' she said softly to Blake, acting instinctively, wanting to banish the look of pain in his eyes.

'Physically, yes, but in other ways she reminds me of your mother. She's very self-sufficient. Don't look at me like that,' he added sardonically. 'I've no intention of trying to deny paternity. Even if she didn't look like me, I'd still know she was my child. You were so physically responsive to me, there couldn't have been anyone else.'

Jaime's face burned at the implications of his remark, and trying to change the subject, she demanded curtly, 'Why have you come to Frampton, Blake? I don't believe it was simply because you want to get to know Fern. Especially as you're staying with Caroline.'

'In point of fact, I'm not staying with her. I'm renting a cottage from her. The old Lodge—I didn't even know it belonged to her until I answered the "ad" for it in *The Times*.'

'Are you saying you did come to Frampton purely because of Fern?'

Some of her anxiety must have shown in her face because he said lazily, 'I'm not going to attempt to wrest her from your maternal arms, if that's what's worrying you, but she *is* my child. . . .'

'A child you never wanted me to conceive,' Jaime reminded him hotly, glad that Fern was still engrossed in the ponies. 'She's three years old, Blake. . . .'

'Which means she and I have three years to catch up on. You say she's at playschool during the day. How about if I pick her up in the afternoon and have her with me until tea time?'

It was plain that she wasn't going to get an explanation for his change of attitude towards Fern, and Jaime sighed, knowing the impossibility of getting Blake to talk about something when he didn't want to. Part of her wanted to demand that he went away and left them alone, but did she have the right to deprive both Fern and Blake himself of their natural relationship?

'She is my child, Jaime. . . .'

'I'll have to think about it.'

His mouth curled sardonically, 'Well, when you have done, come and give me your decision. I'll wait until Friday.'

'Two days!'

'It's long enough, I seem to recall you made an even bigger one in two hours—that's how long it took you to decide to run out of our marriage, wasn't it?'

Jaime didn't know what he was talking about. Two hours! She had waited two long weeks for him to come looking for her and take her home, but he had left the country two days after their quarrel, without making the slightest attempt to get in touch with her.

'I think it's time we went back,' she said shakily. 'It's getting close to Fern's bedtime.'

'Same old Jaime,' Blake taunted mockingly. 'Always ignoring the unpleasant.'

They arrived back in the village several hours later with Fern asleep in the back of the car. Before Jaime could protest, Blake lifted the sleeping child out and carried her to the house. Her mother opened the door to them, and smiled at Blake without surprise.

'If you tell me which room she's in I'll take her up,' Blake drawled. Fern looked so right and at home in his arms that Jaime had to fight against the desire to cry. In sleep her tough independent daughter looked unfamiliarly vulnerable.

'You go up and show Blake the way,' Sarah suggested, 'I'll put the kettle on. Charles came round to see if you were back,' she added, answering Jaime's unspoken question. 'He told me you'd gone out with Blake.'

The cottage had only three bedrooms, but the third had been split to provide a small bathroom and a tiny room which could only be reached through Jaime's bedroom. She saw Blake glance mockingly at her single bed as she indicated the small room which was Fern's.

'Very nunlike,' he commented, as he carefully placed Fern on her bed. 'I imagine your dates must find it frustrating if they ever get this far, to find you're almost sharing a room with your daughter.'

'There's always their bedrooms,' Jaime pointed out, angry at his mocking assumption that she lived the life of a nun, even if it was true. She doubted that he was any monk, and it galled her that he should assume that her life was bereft of the sexual involvement he no doubt had a surfeit of.

Just for a moment, his eyes seemed to darken, his mouth compressing.

'I'll just slip Fern's dress off. You go down, I won't be long.'

'I'll wait for you.' There was an old rocking chair in her room in which she used to sit when she was feeding Fern, and he walked over to it, setting it in motion with his foot. His presence in her bedroom made Jaime feel acutely uncomfortable, and her fingers fumbled over Fern's small buttons. The little girl stirred, but didn't wake, and at last she was tucked up.

'Thank you for taking us out,' Jaime said formally, as she rejoined Blake in her own room.

'So very polite ... but you always were that, weren't you, Jaime? So polite and correct. The only place I could get to the real Jaime was in bed; it was the only place you ever lost your inhibitions.' He laughed when he saw her expression, his fingers suddenly and surprisingly curling round her wrist. 'Ah, Jaime, aren't you going to thank me in the traditional manner? Like this,' he added huskily when she frowned.

His seeking mouth found hers before she could move away, the warm, intimate pressure of it, transporting her to another world, her lips softening and responding before she could even think about rejecting him. Her eyes widened and darkened, her fingers clutching convulsively at the thin fabric of his shirt to hold herself upright. 'Ah, Jaime, this at least was always good, wasn't it?'

Blake's husky voice seemed to weave a spell around her, her mind and body acquiescing almost instantly to his unspoken commands. When his mouth left hers, she arched her throat, instinctively giving him access to the vulnerable skin his lips were seeking. Tiny frissons of reaction shivered across her flesh, a small moan suppressed in her throat as Blake's delicately thorough exploration triggered off feelings she thought had gone for ever. His teeth found the lobe of her ear and tugged on it gently, her fingers automatically curling into the thick springyness of his hair, her body unconsciously moulding itself to him.

'Jaime.' His hands slid down her body, lingering against the curves of her breasts, the pressure of his mouth gradually increasing as it moved across her skin, teasing tormenting kisses against her trembling lips, his tongue stroking their vulnerable contours until they parted in soft invitation.

She was lost, drowning in a warm, lapping sea that called out a siren song to her senses. Everything she had ever wanted or would want was here within her reach. Her fingers sought for and found the space between Blake's shirt buttons, feverishly stroking the silky dark hairs that shadowed his chest. She felt the sudden compression of his muscles as his mouth lifted from hers and dizzyingly and bewilderingly she was free.

'Your mother just called us.' Amusement danced in his eyes. 'Poor Jaime,' he taunted, 'despite all your attempts to hide it, you still respond to me physically, don't you?'

'How can I help doing?' Miraculously her voice sounded much calmer than she had expected. 'You were the one who first taught my body the meaning of physical pleasure. . . .'

'The first? Meaning there've been others since?' His eyes were almost black, glittering with a savage anger she couldn't understand.

'But Thomson isn't one of them, is he?' he tormented. 'He looks at you the way a dog eyes a particularly juicy and unobtainable bone.'

'My relationship with Charles has nothing to do with you,' Jaime choked out. 'Nothing at all.'

'No? Aren't you forgetting something?' He picked up her left hand and raised it until she was looking at the narrow gold wedding ring she still wore. 'You are still my wife, Jaime.'

'That can soon be changed,' she responded, goaded into making the declaration. Didn't he know how much he was hurting her with his careless lovemaking that stirred her body into an acutely painful response, and his equally careless assumption that she was still his for the taking, as though he had looked into her heart and seen the foolish love for him that still lived there. 'I can quite easily get an uncontested divorce. We've been separated long enough.'

'An uncontested divorce requires a separation of two years without any marital relations between the divorcing couple.'

'Meaning . . .' She was shivering all over now, wondering if Blake really meant the threat hidden in his dulcet comment.

'Meaning that just at the moment it suits me to remain a married man, and moreover that I intend to remain a married man, and that I'm fully prepared to take whatever steps are necessary to ensure that I do so.'

He saw her expression and smiled derisively.

'While you've been busy with your life, Jaime, I've been busy with mine. My first two books have been extremely successful in the States, and I'm now a comparatively wealthy man. A healthy bank balance makes a man appealing husband material. I have no intention of being trapped into a marriage it will cost a great deal to extricate myself from and, while I remain married to you, that won't happen.'

'Unless of course I decide to sue you for alimony.'

'Coming from the woman who's refused to accept a penny support from me for the last four years, that's hardly likely is it? I think we'd better go downstairs before your mother puts the wrong interpretation on our absence, don't you?'

When he left half an hour later, Blake turned to Jaime in the privacy of the cottage door and said, 'Remember, you've got two days to come to a decision about Fern. You know where to find me, Jaime, and if you don't, I'll have to come looking for you.'

CHAPTER THREE

THE next two days were hectic ones for Jaime, and she should have found that she simply didn't have time to think about Blake, instead of which he seemed to occupy her thoughts to the detriment of what she ought to have been worrying about. Sarah was busy preparing for her holiday, and Jaime herself had taken on a new assistant, a young girl from the village who had just left school and who, she thought, showed considerable promise. An interview with her accountant in Dorchester confirmed her own view that the studio was making good progress and becoming a modest success. Her accountant was in his late twenties and single, and made no secret of the fact that he found her attractive.

'It's a pleasure just to watch you walk,' he commented as they left the restaurant where he had taken her for lunch. 'I'd love to see you dance.'

Forestalling the invitation she sensed hovering, Jaime took her leave of him. On the drive back to Frampton, her mind was not on the studio and the success she had made of it, but on Blake. Time was running out. Tomorrow was Friday—the day of decision. She had talked the matter over with her mother, and as she had expected Sarah had been in favour of Blake's suggestion.

'He is Fern's father, no matter how much you personally may resent the fact,' she had pointed out calmly, adding, 'Sometimes, Jaime, I think you hate him so much now because you resent how much you once loved him.'

Once! What would her mother say if she knew that, far from hating Blake, she was still painfully in love with him? Perhaps if she did tell her, Sarah would understand why she found the thought of seeing more of him, albeit on Fern's behalf, so very distressing. It required a physical effort not to fling herself into his arms, not to beg him to take her back. As she stopped the car in front of her mother's cottage she acknowledged that she couldn't put off meeting him for ever. This afternoon, before she collected Fern from playschool, she would go and see Blake.

Her mother was out when Jaime walked into the cottage. After making herself a cup of coffee and then prowling restlessly round the small kitchen, she realised that, until she had got the interview with Blake out of the way, she would not be able to settle. Before she could change her mind, she picked up her car keys and opened the front door. It was only when she opened the car door that she realised she was still wearing the outfit she had worn to Dorchester, a soft pink silk dress her mother had bought her in Bath, its sleek lines emphasising the fluid grace of her body, her long dark hair a cloud of curls on her shoulders. She shrugged mentally as she slid into the Mini. Far from giving her the confidence to face Blake, in some subtle way the dress made her feel more vulnerable than she would have done in her normal jeans, but it was too late to go back and change now.

Blake's powerful Ferrari was parked outside the Lodge. Stopping alongside it, Jaime tried to quell the urgent thudding of her pulse. The cottage door stood open, and she approached it hesitantly, knocking briefly on the door. When there was no response, she unconsciously exhaled in soft relief. Blake obviously wasn't in. On the point of returning to her car, she caught the sound of tearing paper, followed by a muffled curse. The study door was flung open and Blake emerged, pushing irate fingers through tousled dark brown hair.

'Jaime!'

'If I've come at a bad time, I can always come back.' Why did she have to sound so nervous? Her eyes shifted apprehensively from the frown on his face, her gaze skittering wildly over the exposed column of his throat and the tanned flesh of his chest where his shirt was unbuttoned. He was wearing a pair of faded, tight jeans, and it required a conscious effort for her to drag her eyes away from the twin columns of his thighs, as she tried to blot out the memory of how it had felt to have the powerful reality of his naked body against hers. A dull surge of colour consumed her body, and she turned away quickly, hoping he wouldn't guess how desperately hungry she was for the sight and feel of him. With Blake making love had been a feast of all the senses and each one of hers now responded to his proximity.

'If I'm interrupting . . .' she hesitated half way to the door, and Blake grimaced saying, 'You're not interrupting anything apart from a monumental writer's block—something I haven't suffered from before with my other two. Come on in. It will be more comfortable to talk in here than standing out in the hall.'

Numbly she followed him into the small study. The settee and chairs had been pushed to one side to make room for a large desk and chair. An electric typewriter sat on the desk, sheaves of paper surrounding it.

'I didn't know you'd written anything other than newspaper articles.'

'You wouldn't, would you?' Blake agreed sardonically. 'I wrote my first book when I came back from El Salvador.'

Almost automatically, Jaime moved across to the typewriter. A half-finished sheet was rolled into the carriage.

'Wait there, I'll go and make us both a cup of coffee, I won't be long. . . .'

'There's no need to bother.' She said it stiffly, anxious to get their interview over and done with.

'Maybe not to you, but I haven't had a break yet today. Wait here.'

When he was gone, she studied the bookshelves behind her, recognising many of Blake's books from the flat they had shared. How long was he planning to stay in Frampton? How long did it take to write a book? She really had no idea. She picked up a novel she had read the previous summer in the paperback version, letting it drop from nerveless fingers when she saw Blake's face staring back at her from the dust cover. Blake had written this. She remembered how much the book had moved her; how she had felt for the sardonic hero; the power of the intensely passionate love scenes. As she bent to pick the book up she dislodged some of the papers from the desk. Down on her hands and knees she started to gather up the typewritten pages, her movements stilling as she started automatically to read.

The words seemed to leap off the pages to meet her, so tormentingly erotic that she could feel her body's response to them. What she was reading was a love scene that reminded her so vividly of how it had been when she and Blake made love that she felt that Blake had almost walked into her mind.

She was still kneeling beside the desk, the papers clutched in one tense hand when Blake walked back into the room carrying two mugs of coffee.

'You've written about *us*.' Her voice was accusatory and disbelieving. The previous books Blake had written, had they been self-biographical too?

'A writer uses his own experiences,' Blake told her emotionlessly, 'but you're not a naive twenty-year old any more, Jaime, you must know that this kind of sexual experience is common to the majority of the adult population, although I will admit that the adrenalin of our rows did help fuel my first few hundred pages. Perhaps that's why I'm having this mental block now—perhaps I need sexual stimulation to release me from it. . . .'

'I'm sure you don't have to go far to find any,' Jaime said coldly, thinking of Caroline. . . .

'Not far at all,' Blake agreed softly, watching her with a narrow-eyed stare that reminded her of a jungle cat stalking its prey. 'How pleasant to find we're in agreement for once.' He put down the mugs of coffee, his hands sliding beneath her arms as he bent to pull her upwards. 'Or is it just that you've suddenly realised what you've missed? Thomson doesn't strike me as much of a lover . . . I need you Jamie.' He jerked her into his arms, cutting off her automatic protest with the hard warmth of his mouth.

Her first instinctive thought that this couldn't possibly be happening was swamped by the effect Blake had on her senses. The musky familiar scent of him inflamed the hunger she could feel pulsing through her, her fingers instinctively finding their way beneath his shirt to stroke over his skin, exploring the tautness of muscle and bone.

'Jaime,' he breathed her name against her mouth, her lips parting to welcome him. When his teeth nibbled tenderly at the soft, inner flesh of her bottom lip, she moaned in pleasure, arching herself against him.

'Cool, distant Jamie,' Blake muttered hoarsely, releasing her mouth to taste the warm skin of her throat. 'When I make love to you, it's like watching you melt in my arms.'

Her fingernails raked protestingly along his back, so wrapped up in the pleasure he was giving her that she was barely aware of him releasing her zip until she felt his fingers tracing her spine and she shuddered in delicious response. Blake! Dear God, how she loved him.

'Jaime.'

She was lost in an intensely pleasurable dream from which she never wanted to wake, and the sound of Blake's voice echoed like a warning bell she didn't want to hear. She silenced it by turning her head and pressing her mouth feverishly to his, feeling the pent-up longing she had suppressed all the time they had been apart take over and dominate her actions.

When Blake lifted her and carried her over to the settee she felt only a fierce joy at being in his arms, sliding out of her dress with an abandon that normally would have shocked her. Her dancer's body curved lithely into his arms, arching hungrily toward him as his mouth left hers to trace a downward path along her jaw, lingering deliberately on the vulnerable spot behind her ear before moving downward with tantalising slowness, along the curve of her throat, pausing against the pulse that thudded at its base, lingering there until she cried out a soft protest, her pliant lips raining soft, delirious kisses over Blake's face, her hands running feverishly over his body.

'Jaime, make love to me.'

Behind the dark glitter of Blake's eyes she could see a passion that matched her own, a fierce intensity that swept aside the final barriers. His fingers trembled oddly against her skin, as he lay back pulling her down on top of him.

'Jaime.' He strung a line of tender kisses along her breasts where they met the barrier of her lacy bra, and then returned to stroke his tongue along the same line. Her nipples burgeoned into life, pushing tautly against the fragile lace, a husky moan leaving her throat as Blake's tongue pushed past the lace barrier, stroking the curve of her breast, igniting a burning coil of pleasure that seemed to reach out and engulf every part of her body. As tense feverishness possessed her, sensations which were familiar and yet strange, flooded to every nerve ending. Her fingertips stroked Blake's skin, her mouth tasting the warm salt of his throat as she inhaled the male musky scent of his body.

His hands gripped her waist and slid down to her hips, holding her against the male outline of his body, the fabric of his jeans rough against the tender skin of her thighs and stomach. Her briefs and bra were barriers she no longer wanted between them, and she stroked her tongue moistly along Blake's skin trying to convey to him without words what she wanted.

His hoarse moan of pleasure rasped against her ear. His eyes were closed; the thick fan of dark lashes making him seem unusually vulnerable, the hard line of his mouth relaxed and almost tender. Jaime traced it with her fingernail, supporting herself with her free hand, watching his lips part and his white teeth nibble on her finger, strong fingers closing round her wrist, forcing her palm against his open mouth. 'Two can play at that game,' he murmured softly, the caress of his tongue against her vulnerable skin making her shudder with a pleasure that threatened to break over her in drowning waves when he took her fingers in his mouth and sucked them gently.

His erotic stimulation of her senses demanded a response she was powerless to refuse. His skin tasted faintly salty beneath the slow exploration of her lips, her tongue slowly circling one flat male nipple until she felt the responsive shudder jerking through Blake's body, his fingers curling into her hair as he muttered a husky imprecation and pulled her away saying hoarsely, 'Let's see how you like being teased like that.'

She was still wearing her bra and the moist probing of his tongue beneath its fragile barrier was an incitement her body couldn't ignore.

It wasn't just teasing! It was torture to feel his tongue brushing so close to the aching peak of her breast and then withdrawing, and Jaime didn't think she could have borne it, if she hadn't been aware that his fingers were slowly, barely a centimetre at a time, drawing back the lacy covering until she could feel his fingertips grazing against her nipple.

'Blake. . . .' His name was a tormented protest on her lips, her eyes feverish with a desire she couldn't hide.

'Ah, ha, so you don't like it when the boot's on the other foot, do you.' He reversed their position, and now she was lying on her side almost beneath him, her fingers curling into the smooth muscles of his back. He raised his head to study her for a second and then lowered it again. A long slow shudder rippled through Jaime when, with one hand, he pulled the lacy bra free of her breast while the other dealt efficiently with the clasp at the back, freeing her tumescent nipples to his avid gaze. Strangely enough she felt none of the shame or embarrassment she had so often experienced during their marraige, when he had managed to arouse her to the point where nothing mattered save the ultimate culmination of his lovemaking, and her body arched instinctively upwards, the desire-swollen curves of her breasts rising and falling swiftly with the rapidity of her breathing.

As though unable to resist their temptation, Blake lowered his head. His hand cupped one breast whilst his tongue circled the nipple of the other, somewhat unsteadily; the aroused weight of him pressing Jaime back against the settee, her thighs parting automatically to cradle the male power of him.

She heard Blake groan and the tenor of their lovemaking which he had controlled suddenly changed, a dark tide of colour sweeping over his face as his mouth closed over the nipple his tongue had been stroking, subjecting it to a roughly urgent suckling that sent fierce spears of pleasure lacing through Jaime's body.

Almost delirious with pleasure, she was aware of Blake's hand on her thigh and her body shuddered in anticipation. At the same moment, she heard his voice in her ear, and his words were like a cold shock of reality as he muttered, 'If I'm still suffering from a mental block after this, I'll. . . .'

He broke off as Jaime tensed, repudiation in every stiff line of her body.

'What's the matter?'

She forced herself to look into his frowning face, praying that he couldn't read her thoughts; that he knew just how incredibly stupid she had been. For a moment she had actually believed that it was possible to turn back the clock; that it was possible for him to love her as she loved him. Now she felt sick with shame and shock, unable to believe the reality of her own actions.

'Fern,' she heard herself say sickly in an unfamiliar voice, 'I must go and pick her up. I don't like being late. . . .'

'I remember,' Blake said derisively. 'You always used to refuse to make love in the morning because you thought it might make you late for work. . . .'

'Not always. . . .' She pulled away from him, groping for her clothes, hoping he wouldn't guess the real reason for her scarlet face.

'I wonder what dear Charles would say if he knew what just happened?'

'Nothing happened,' Jaime said fiercely, not wanting to admit to herself that if Blake hadn't spoken when he had she would still be in his arms and their lovemaking would have been much closer to completion and, worse still, her body ached intolerably because it wasn't.

'Does he know how hungry you are for love, Jaime? So hungry that you'd even let a man you hate make love to you?'

'Does Caroline know that you make love just to get copy for your books?' she challenged back.

His mouth hardened, his eyes as dark and cold as flint. 'I never like to refuse a lady,' he mocked, watching the vivid colour run up over her skin, 'especially when that lady's already the mother of my child. We still haven't talked about Fern.'

'I . . .' She couldn't come back here and talk calmly to him, not in the room where she had so nearly forgotten all the hardwon lessons of the last few years and begged him to make love to her, as she had begged him without words so many times in the past.

'I've got to go to London for a few days,' Blake interrupted before she could speak. 'I'll come and see you when I get back. We'll talk about it then.' He bent his head briefly before she could move, brushing his lips against hers. 'I can taste my skin on your mouth,' he told her softly. 'How many men have made love to you since you left me, Jaime? One . . . two?' His eyes narrowed cruelly. 'I'd take a bet that it was none. . . .'

'I have to go.' She was out of the room before he could say any more, shocked that he could speak so tormentingly to her.

She was still shaking when she got out of her car at the playschool. Fern, fortunately, didn't seem to notice anything amiss, and Jaime was glad to discover that her mother was still out when she got back to the cottage. Settling Fern down with a drink and something to eat, she hurried into the bathroom, stripping off her clothes and standing under the harsh sting of the

shower until she was sure that she had washed
her body completely free of the clinging scent of
Blake's; only then did she dry herself and dress
again, but although she might have washed her
body free of the scent of him, nothing could
cleanse her mind of the mental images it insisted
on relentlessly parading before her; Blake's body,
sleek and supple, his skin taut and firm beneath
her finger tips. The way he touched her body and
her acutely abandoned response to him. But what
was most agonising of all was the knowledge that
he had simply made love to her because she
happened to be there, and that any woman would
have served his purpose equally well. Would the
way she had responded to him be faithfully
recorded in his book? She shuddered, glad to
hear her mother's key in the door forcing her to
abandon her unprofitable thoughts.

There was a meeting in the village school that
night to discuss Caroline's plans to sell off the
Abbey. Jaime was late setting out for it, and she
rounded the bend by the Abbey gates just in time
to see Blake's Ferrari emerging. Blake was
driving, Caroline seated in the passenger seat, the
brief play of her own headlights revealing
Caroline's shoulders and the expensive evening
gown she was wearing.

White-hot, searing jealousy poured moltenly
through her veins. She wanted to stop the car and
drag Caroline away from Blake.

What was happening to her? She was losing all
sense of pride and reality. It was no concern of
hers any more whom Blake chose to date. She

had always known that he hadn't spent their years apart living the life of a monk, but that was before he had held her in his arms and made her body ache for the fulfilment of his lovemaking.

She drove the remainder of the way to the village in a dull daze. The meeting was well-attended and a week ago she would have been wholly absorbed in their fight against the destruction of the Abbey. Now it was all she could do to drag her mind off Blake and on to the speakers.

Charles spoke first, rather pedantically, and there was muted clapping when he had finished. Other speakers followed, and then it was her task to go round collecting names for the petition they were organising. Someone had suggested that the appropriate government department ought to be contacted and, as the meeting reached its more informal stage, heated discussions broke out as to the right things to do.

'Caroline came to see me this morning,' Charles informed Jaime as she stood at his side. 'It seems your ex-husband is encouraging her to go ahead with the sale.'

'Blake? But why should he do that?'

'Perhaps he wants to help her spend the money she'll make out of it,' Charles suggested nastily, 'after all, for an out-of-work reporter. . . .'

'He isn't out of work. He's working on a novel.' How quickly she sprang to Blake's defence. Her reaction to Charles' comment mortified her.

'It didn't take him long to get you back under

his spell, did it?' Charles wasn't pleased, she could tell by the angry glitter in his eyes. 'You're a fool, Jaime, if you're taken in by all that reconciliation talk. He doesn't want you any more now than he did four years ago. He was quite willing for you to leave him them—remember? I suppose it amuses him to play dog-in-the-manger, but he'll soon lose interest in the game once he's got you where he wants you. Why don't you divorce him? You know how I feel about you. . . .' Charles' voice thickened over the last few words, and Jaime was hard put not to let him see the shudder of rejection they aroused. She liked Charles as a friend, but as a lover. . . . Never! Her body instantly signalled its revulsion at the thought, repudiating the idea of Charles' love-making as much as it had welcomed that of Blake's.

She didn't need Charles to warn her that Blake felt nothing for her, but that didn't alter the way she felt about him.

She drove slowly home after the meeting, answering her mother's questions absently.

'Surely Charles can't be the reason for this lack of concentration,' Sarah teased mildly. 'You're miles away. . . .'

'I was thinking about the Abbey,' Jaime lied. 'Did you get everything you wanted this afternoon?'

'Most of it. Did you sort things out with Blake?'

'Umm, sort of.' She turned away quickly, hoping her mother wouldn't notice the guilty flush of colour staining her face. 'Did you know he was MacMillan Henderson?'

'No, I didn't. I seem to remember you saying how much you enjoyed his book though.'

'That was before I knew he was Blake.'

She heard her mother laugh, and realised how childishly petulant her remark had sounded. 'He used us . . . me . . .' she tried to explain, fighting to conceal her pain.

'He used his own experiences is what I think you're trying to say,' Sarah responded mildly, 'which is surely quite reasonable. Where Blake's concerned, you seem to delight in wearing blinkers, Jaime, and I can't help wishing you'd swap them occasionally for those rose-coloured glasses through which you view Charles.'

'There's no comparison between them.'

'No,' her mother agreed drily, 'I would have thought not, but you don't seem to have any problems in making one. I think I'll have an early night,' she added. 'Only a couple of days now until we leave.'

'We?' Jaime picked up on the small slip immediately.

'Henry has decided to come with me. He can't get anyone else to look after the shop, so he's decided we might as well close it down for a fortnight.'

'Henry's going with you?' Jaime was frankly astonished. Her mother had determinedly kept her suitor at bay for the best part of the last fifteen years at least, so why the sudden suggestion of capitulation.

'Why?'

'Perhaps I've seen what celibacy has done to you,' Sarah responded wryly, not pretending not to understand the question. She watched Jaime colour brilliantly and added in a softer tone, 'Or perhaps it's just that I've realised that I'm a woman in her forties, with a grown-up daughter and a grandchild, who's lucky enough to have a male acquaintance who makes no secret of the fact that he finds her desirable.'

Jaime eyed her mother narrowly, wondering for the first time whether she and Henry might already be lovers. If so, they had been extremely discreet. Summoning a smile, she said impishly, 'Well, if that's the case, I hope you make the most of it—if you don't, I might try and lure Henry away from you myself; he's a very attractive man.'

'Yes, isn't he?' It was said in such a complacent, self-satisfied way that both of them burst out laughing. As she prepared for bed, Jaime wondered why it had taken her so long to realise that her mother was a woman too, with needs and desires of her own. Was it because her own senses still aroused from Blake's brief lovemaking were more attuned to vibrations she had previously shut herself away from? Where was Blake now? Making love to Caroline? She shuddered with a chill that had nothing to do with the soft evening air wafting in through her bedroom window.

CHAPTER FOUR

'AND stretch ... and breathe ... and rest. ...' Jaime exhaled evenly, allowing her own body to relax in obedience to the instructions she had given her pupils.

If the old school had one drawback as an exercise studio, it was its lack of showering and changing facilities, she reflected ten minutes later, when the last of her advanced class had driven away. The advanced class had been her last one for the day. Today, for the first time, some of her intermediate pupils had graduated to it, and it gave her a warm glow of accomplishment to see them there.

Sally, her assistant, had left early because of a dental appointment, and so Jaime was on her own. As she always did before she left the school she went round checking windows and doors. Frampton wasn't a village where rowdy youngsters went on the rampage and destroyed property in an excess of boredom and youthful resentment, but her years in London had taught her to be careful.

She had just finished her checks when she felt a frisson of awareness race down her spine. Even before she turned round, she knew she wasn't alone, although there was nothing familiar about the heavy, thickset man standing by the open door.

For no logical reason Jaime felt fear pound through her. The man could be the son or husband of one of her pupils, but some deeply rooted atavistic instinct told her that he wasn't, and for all that he lounged carelessly against the wall by the door, she sensed that any attempt on her part to simply walk through the door would be quickly foiled.

'Who . . . who are you, and what do you want?'

How banal, she reflected weakly, listening to her own voice, husky with the beginnings of fear, as though she were an outsider, standing away from herself and recording her own reactions.

'Let's just say a friend of yours sent me shall we?' he suggested mock-affably. 'Wanted me to give you a friendly warning, like.'

The cold lump of ice which seemed to have lodged somewhere in the pit of her stomach reached out freezing tentacles that Jaime was powerless to cut free from. 'Nice place, you've got here,' the rough voice ruminated. 'Must have cost a fair bit to get it like this. It would be a pity if something should happen to it, wouldn't it?'

'Happen to it?' Jaime didn't really need to ask the question. She was already fully aware of the meaning behind his threats, but what she didn't know was why they were being made. American films and stories of extortion flashed briefly through her mind. A branch of the notorious Mafia in Frampton? It seemed highly unlikely.

'Yes . . . an accident like. People can be like that you know, interfering in other people's property, poking their noses in where they aren't wanted.'

Immediately she *knew*, and the blood in her veins almost froze, the hair at the back of her neck literally standing up on end as she felt the slow freezing crawl of fear along her body.

'Are you talking about the Abbey?' she asked bravely. 'Is that why you're here, threatening me . . .?'

'Threatening? Just a pleasant little warning like. And there isn't just this place to consider is there? You've got a little kid haven't you? Pity if anything happened to her.'

'But why me?' Jaime said it piteously, barely able to comprehend what was happening to her. Outside the sun was still shining, casting beams which picked up the dusty motes of air inside. She could even hear the normal sounds of traffic along the main road, but inside nothing was normal, and she started to shiver convulsively remembering the acid hatred in Caroline's eyes and her determination to sell the Abbey. 'The decision to oppose the sale has been made by a committee. I'm only one member of it.'

'But you could persuade that solicitor friend of yours to stop pressing things so hard. Without his support the others will soon lose interest.'

What he was saying was true, but Jaime felt obliged to make one last attempt to discover why she was the one being threatened.

'Why pick on me?' she asked huskily, 'Why . . .?'

'Why? I don't give the orders. I just follow them.'

'And what are your orders in this case?' she asked bitterly. 'To destroy this place? To terrorise me through my child? You do realise I could go to the police?'

The moment the words were said she knew they were a mistake. The man's face hardened, the step he took towards her definitely threatening.

'Maybe you can, but you won't. Not if you value your kiddie's safety. You can't watch her all the time,' he told her, reading her thoughts, 'but we can . . .'

What on earth was she going to do? Terror-crazed thoughts swirled through her mind, gathering such momentum that she was in a fever to get home and find Fern. She had left the little girl with Mrs Widdows, who had promised to babysit whilst her mother was away on holiday. 'Just remember,' the man told her as he moved towards the door, 'all you have to do is to persuade your solicitor friend to drop all the opposition and everything will be fine.'

His final words were still filling her mind when Jaime drew up outside the cottage. Fern came running out to greet her, and squealed her protest when Jaime hugged her tightly. 'Mummy, you forgot to get the bread,' she remarked when Jaime thanked Mrs Widdows for looking after her. She forced a brief smile for Fern, wondering wildly if she could possibly close up the school and go away, taking Fern with her. Blake . . . Blake would know what to do. . . . It seemed natural to think automatically of turning to him, and without thinking proerly about what she was doing, Jaime bundled a protesting Fern back into her car and headed for the Abbey.

It was only when they were nearly there that she remembered Blake could well still be in London but, to her relief, as she approached the cottage, she could see his Ferrari parked outside.

As she got out of the car, telling Fern to stay where she was, her whole body started to tremble with relief. Blake would know what to do. He would help her keep Fern safe. Blake! She had never needed him more than she did now, and it never even occurred to her that she could not rely on him entirely.

As she walked past the sitting room, she saw Blake's dark head through the open French windows. He was sitting with his back to her and, rather than ring the bell, to save time, Jaime moved quickly and instinctively towards the open windows, only to freeze in dismay as she heard Caroline's sharp, complaining voice.

Caroline was with him? Why hadn't she thought of that? He had told her that it was merely a coincidence that he was Caroline's tenant, and she had believed him, because she had wanted to believe him, but now, watching them, she wondered if she had allowed herself to be duped. Blake had claimed that he wanted to get to know his daughter, but why had he waited this long? And why had she been foolish enough to believe him when she had known exactly how she felt about Fern even before she was born? Because she loved him, that was why. Because she loved him and was foolish enough to keep on hoping that one day a miracle would occur and he would love her too.

As she stood there in a daze, she heard Blake saying comfortingly, 'Well, I shouldn't worry too much about her now Caroline, that's all been taken care of. I've spoken to her myself, and I doubt she'll give you any more trouble.'

Jaime didn't wait to hear any more. Stumbling through the shrubbery, she headed back to her car, ignoring Fern's anxious, 'Mummy . . .' as she started it up and fled down the drive in a series of kangaroo leaps which showed how little her mind was on her driving.

No . . . she couldn't . . . she wouldn't believe that Blake was involved in this plan to intimidate her. And yet she had heard him with her own ears. . . . But he had said nothing about threatening her. Perhaps that was Caroline's idea. . . . Yes, it must be, Blake would never . . . Round and round went her thoughts, seeking the avenue that offered her escape from her doubts about Blake. No, she firmly refused to believe he would ever be involved in anything like that. She knew Blake. He was so honest and upright it was almost painful.

It was only when she got back at the cottage that she realised she was no closer to finding a solution to her problem. She couldn't really leave the village. Where could she go? Neither could she give in to any threats. She would simply have to stay, she thought feverishly. She would have to stay, and she would have to close down her school, either that or take Fern with her to classes. Logic told her that nothing could happen to her daughter in public and that, as long as they remained part of a crowd, they would be safe.

If only her mother wasn't away. If only there was someone she could turn to, but there wasn't. There was no one.

A week dragged past, and Jaime wondered if she was the only person to be aware of the unnatural calm that seemed to have settled over the village. Perhaps her fear had given her an unusual percipience, she didn't know. She only knew that she was constantly afraid, and the hot sultry weather seemed to increase her fear. Two meetings of the committee had been called. Blake had attended one, but he had left before the end, and Jaime shivered, wondering if she was a fool for believing that he couldn't know of the threats that had been made to her. If she really believed that, why didn't she go to him for help? Why didn't she trust her own judgment enough to tell him what was happening? Was it because she wanted to believe in him so much that if she found she was wrong it would almost destroy her completely?

Fern was getting niggly and impatient of the fact that she wouldn't let her out of her sight. A naturally independent child, she found Jaime's protectiveness irksome, and this led to outbursts of temper. Jaime felt it was the last straw the morning she received a postcard from her mother informing her that they had decided to extend their holiday by another three weeks. She could hardly write back saying, 'Come home—I'm frightened,' but that's what she wanted to do.

Every night she made sure the house was securely locked, grateful for the presence of the neighbours either side of her, and for the extension telephone upstairs. She had nightmares about waking up and finding the cord cut, and she knew the strain was making her lose weight. Despite her tan she looked ill, so much so that even Sally commented on it.

In the end, she had decided to continue with her classes, glad that the school holidays made it seem quite natural for her to have Fern with her. The little girl grew quickly bored with the day-to-day routine, and one morning when she disappeared Jaime thought the worst, almost sick with shock when she re-appeared with Sally, who had taken her down to the local park for a swing. Both of them had been surprised by her outburst Jaime knew, Sally's brown eyes faintly hurt. She was the eldest of four children, and well used to keeping an eye on the younger ones, and, although Jaime knew she was hurt by her apparent lack of trust, she couldn't confide in her.

After the second committee meeting Paul Davis arranged for them to be interviewed on one of his current affairs programmes. There was also an interview with someone from local government who pointed out the loss to the country and generations to come when properties such as the Abbey were destroyed.

Caroline and the builders were also interviewed. Caroline claimed that death duties and other large expenses made it necessary for her to sell to the highest bidder, and the builders claimed that their houses would provide homes for many more people than the Abbey had ever housed, and, moreover, that everything would be of the 'highest quality'.

'In other words,' Charles said bitterly, 'they intend to make as much money from the land as they can.'

It was three days after the second interview when the blow fell. Jaime had been expecting it, almost anticipating it, and the reality was in some strange way almost a relief, although the threat had been carried out in a different fashion than she had envisaged.

She had expected a secret, night-time attack on the school, but instead it was broken into in broad daylight by a teenage gang who had almost completely wrecked her main studio before the police managed to stop them.

They were demonstrating for jobs, they claimed, when they were interviewed. The sale of the Abbey to the developers would mean fresh jobs in an area where they were notoriously scarce; and not just temporary jobs, but houses, shops, a new school.

They had been drilled well, and Jaime knew with a sense of sick certainty that no one would guess from listening to them that their beliefs were anything other than genuine. She had been picked out as a target because she already had a thriving business; she did not suffer as they did through unemployment; she was living up in the clouds, ignoring reality.

That evening she couldn't settle at all. Several people had called round to commiserate with her, many of her pupils offering to help her to get things back to normal, but there had also been 'phone calls from some of the others cancelling their lessons, and Jaime wondered despairingly if she was witnessing the beginning of the destruction of all her hard work.

To make matters worse, Fern was being recalcitrant and irritable. Jaime could sympathise with the little girl. She was used to a certain measure of independence, and she chafed against the confinement of their new way of life.

'I hate you,' she had stormed at Jaime when she put her to bed. 'I hate you and I want to go and live with my Daddy.'

Apart from one brief glimpse of him at the committee meeting, Jaime had not seen him since his return from London. Why hadn't he sought her out? He had been quite determined about his intention of getting to know Fern better, but he had made no approach to her since then.

She had just made herself a mug of coffee and settled down in her favourite chair when she heard a car outside, swiftly followed by a sharp rap on the door. Although she knew no attacker would signal his arrival in this way, her nerves were so overwound with tension and fear that she literally cringed away from the sound, cowering back in her chair willing her visitor to go away.

Dusk was just falling, masking the identity of

her caller. Mrs Widdows would be installed in front of her television and the young couple next door had gone out to dinner, so there was no one to hear her call out. She glanced instinctively towards the telephone, and then tensed as the imperious rap on the door was repeated, accompanied by Blake's voice calling her name.

The relief was so great that Jaime felt almost light-headed with it, rushing to the door, and pulling it open, unaware of the way the light fell on her pinched features revealing the deprivations of recent weeks.

'Jaime! Are you ill?'

Ill? If one could literally be sick with fear, then that was what she was Jaime thought numbly, letting Blake follow her inside.

'Why didn't you come to the door before? Didn't you hear me knocking?'

What would he say if she told him the truth? That she hadn't answered his knock because she feared he had come to fulfil the latter part of another man's threat.

'I'm sorry. . . .' She started to shiver uncontrollably, glad of the warmth that flowed into her cold body from the fingers he clamped round her upper arms. He was frowning, his eyes dark as she remembered them from the days when she had challenged him with almost hysterical conviction of wanting some other woman, and she fought to pull herself together, her pride demanding that she didn't give way to her feelings, that she showed him that she was now fully adult and capable.

'I'm quite all right Blake,' she managed to stammer, as she pulled away, but he refused to let her go, his arms clamping round her as he pulled her against his body. 'No you damn well aren't,' he said brusquely, 'and no wonder. I'd have been here sooner if I'd known. I've been away. I only got back this evening. I had some business in London.'

'With your publisher?' she asked the question half drowsily, almost drunk on the warmth and comfort of his arms, and she wished she hadn't spoken when she sensed his faint hesitation.

'Er . . . yes . . .' he agreed. 'Caroline told me what happened when I got back.'

'Gloating over every word of it no doubt,' Jaime said bitterly, trying not to remember those words she had overheard the day she had gone to him for help.

'Where's your mother?' Blake was looking round as though he expected Sarah to materialise in front of him.

'She's still away.' Jaime explained that her mother was extending her holiday.

'You shouldn't be alone here.' Her heart leaped and then fell. Was he genuinely worried about her, as his expression and words seemed to hint, or was his concern all part of a carefully made plan to undermine her defences? Her instincts told her to believe the former, to lay her head on Blake's shoulder and pour out her fears; to have him hold her even closer, and tell her not to worry any more, but she dared not trust her instincts, in fact, she had to be wary of them because they

would always find in Blake's favour influenced by
her love for him.

'Mrs Widdows is next door on one side and the
Hargreaves on the other,' she said as lightly as
she could, disentangling herself from his arms
with a reluctance that was almost a physical pain.
'So I'm not precisely alone.'

'And Fern is sleeping upstairs, no doubt,'
Blake broke in roughly, 'ready to defend you the
moment those young ruffians decide to take their
"demonstration" a step further. I don't believe
you fully realise the danger you could be in
Jaime.'

If only he knew! She turned away from him so
that he couldn't see the indecision she was sure
was written plainly in her eyes. Once he did see
it, he would soon drag the whole story out of her,
and she couldn't risk finding out that he was
involved in it.

'I think you ought to stand down from that
committee.' His words surprised Jaime into
turning round. Blake was facing the empty
hearth, frowning. 'I realise you won't want to,
but I'm not sure you fully realise the potential
dangers here. Barrons are well known in the
building industry for their ruthlessness, and they
seem extremely determined to get the Abbey.'

'Even to the extent of ignoring a Government
Preservation Order?' Jaime demanded huskily.
On the face of it, Blake's suggestion was a
reasonable one; one she had even contemplated
herself, and yet. . . . 'In that case, perhaps we
ought to disband the committee altogether, after

all if they're as ruthless as you seem to be suggesting, we're all equally at risk, surely.'

'You may all be at risk, but not equally so,' Blake countered roughly. 'You're far more vulnerable than any of the others, Jaime, and if Barrons are behind this demonstration today, you can be sure they won't stop there. I want you to . . .'

Before he could get any further, there was another knock on the door. Charles, Jaime recognised, not knowing whether to be glad or sorry that they were being interrupted. Blake, however, seemed to know exactly how he felt. He was scowling darkly when she let Charles in.

'I thought I'd just pop round and see how you were,' Charles began fussily, breaking off when he saw Blake leaning against the fireplace, for all the world as though it were his own.

'As you can see, you were rather laggard,' Blake taunted him, his voice deep with disapproval as he added, 'As a matter of fact, I'm rather surprised that you allowed Jaime to return home alone, in view of today's events.'

'I got held up at the television studios,' Charles explained stiffly before Jaime could protest that she wasn't a child, and that she was perfectly capable of making her own decisions.

'Oh, I see.' Blake's tone was openly derisive, and Jaime saw a dark tide of colour sweeping Charles' face. Perhaps, she thought later, that was the reason for his next outburst—one which she was sure startled him as much as it did her.

'Look, Templeton,' he began heatedly, 'I'm

perfectly capable of looking after my own fiancée, and I'd be obliged if you'd go and leave us alone. I want to talk to Jaime privately.'

'Do you now?' In direct contrast to Charles' blustering, raised voice, Blake's was very cold and soft. 'Well, I'm afraid that's not going to be possible. You seem to have forgotten that the woman you're claiming as your fiancée is still my wife, and if anyone's going to be leaving, it's not going to be me, and what's more, if you really, genuinely cared about her as much as you pretend to do, you'd never have left her alone this evening, whilst you gave a television interview.'

'Jaime understands that we have to get our campaign the maximum amount of publicity.'

'Even to the extent of arranging today's débâcle? Oh, it has been known,' Blake continued icily before Charles could protest, 'although in this instance I'll acquit you of it, but as for Jaime understanding the importance of your campaign, right at this moment, I'll bet she's wishing she wasn't involved in it, and if you really cared about her, you'd make sure she wasn't. She's too vulnerable to be caught up in the sort of terror-tactics firms like Barrons use.'

'And that's precisely the reason we have to go on fighting against them,' Jaime found her voice for the first time since Charles' arrival, and it rang with a quiet conviction that brought Charles' eyes to her face in pleased approval and Blake's in wry acceptance.

'So you won't withdraw?' he said softly, 'I suppose I should have anticipated that. You always were a cussed little thing. I think it's time you left,' he said to Charles.

'Left?' he spluttered indignantly, looking to Jaime for help. 'But I've only just arrived.'

'Claiming my wife as your fiancée,' Blake drawled. 'Rather precipitate of you in the circumstances.'

For a moment Jaime wondered if Charles would defy Blake, but he didn't. At the door, he turned to her and said woodenly, 'I'll be in touch tomorrow Jaime.'

Jaime could tell from his expression that he had expected her to object to Blake's comments, but somehow she just hadn't had the energy. Blake had made her feel protected and safe and that sensation had lingered long enough for her to want to keep him with her as long as she could.

'It won't do, you know,' he said softly, when they heard Charles' car start up. 'You'll always have to fight his battles for him, Jaime, and you're not that sort of woman. . . .'

'What sort am I then?' she demanded waspishly. 'The clinging helpless type who needs a big strong man to protect her?'

'No. . . .' He moved, and came to stand beside her, looking down into her upraised face. Jaime knew she should move away, but she couldn't. 'No, you're a woman who's learned to stand alone; an intelligent caring woman who combines all that is so essentially feminine in her sex, with a dash of independence and individuality that add the necessary spice to a sweet mixture. Sometimes, you're a woman who's afraid to

admit to her femininity, who tends to hide herself
away behind self-erected barriers.' He removed
his leather jacket, and dropped it down on one of
the chairs. When Jaime followed the movement,
frowning slightly in non-comprehension, he
explained easily—'I don't feel happy about you
being here alone at night, Jaime, and as your
Galahad seems reluctant to take proper care of
you, I've decided to do it myself.'

'You mean you're staying here tonight. . . . But
you can't.'

'Why not? After all, we are still married, if
it's the moral aspect of my staying that worries
you. Don't forget, we still have to talk about
Fern.'

'Why not?' he had said, and Jaime tried
muzzily to summon to mind all the reasons why it
was not possible for him to stay in the cottage
with her, but all the time her heart was telling her
how much she longed to give in and accept his
suggestion, his protection.

'I'll sleep in your mother's bed, if that's what's
worrying you.' He was watching her closely, and
all she could manage to say was a feeble, 'But . . .
but, you've nothing to wear and . . .'

'I sleep in the raw, or can't you remember,' he
derided her, 'and as for the rest, it won't be the
first time we've shared a toothbrush will it?'

Jaime's face flamed. She knew what he was
alluding to. The night he had asked her to marry
him. The night she had insisted on going home
with him. The night they had first made love and
she had woken up in his arms and known that

that was where she wanted to spend the rest of her life.

'No more arguments?'

'I'll have to make up the bed. . . .'

'Well, you go and do that, I'll make us both a hot drink.'

Numbly, Jaime went upstairs, chiding herself for her weakness, for wanting to lean on him. She wasn't a child any longer; she was fully capable of taking charge of her own life, but, oh, the relief of knowing that tonight she wouldn't be alone, the sole guardian of Fern's safety! Her heart leapt and sang. Surely she had been right to believe that Blake wouldn't do anything to hurt either her or Fern? Unless of course he had been a party to the initial plan, but was now having second thoughts. No, she decided firmly, no, she wouldn't believe that about him. She wouldn't!

Half an hour later, drinking the mug of cocoa that Blake had made for her it seemed the most natural thing in the world that he should be sitting opposite her drinking his.

For the first time since she had left him, she felt safe and cared for, an illusion she would be wise to be wary of. Hadn't she taught herself in the intervening years that it was both foolish and selfish to rely completely on another human being, and that, by doing so, one was forging bonds which sooner or later, they would find so constricting that they would want to break them and find freedom? Her type of love was too intense, too overwhelming, as Blake had already taught her once.

CHAPTER FIVE

JAIME slept restlessly, waking up in darkness to discover that it was still only three o'clock. Whether because of the traumatic events of the day or because of Blake's disturbing presence under the same roof she found it impossible to get back to sleep. Her mouth felt dry and she craved for the unique comfort of a cup of tea.

Not wanting to disturb either Blake or Fern, she went downstairs in the dark, finding her way to the kitchen without too much difficulty. It was under Blake's bedroom and so she moved about as quietly as she could. It was just as she was taking a china mug from the cupboard that she saw what she thought was a human shadow moving stealthily through the garden. The mug fell from nerveless fingers, splintering on the quarry-tiled floor with a crescendo of noise which made Jaime forget about the intruder she may or may not have seen as she worried about whether the noise of the breaking china—so loud in the kitchen—could have woken Blake.

She was just sweeping up the shards when she realised that it had. He came into the kitchen, fastening his jeans as he did so. His hair was still rumpled from sleep, the bare expanse of his chest glowing golden under the electric light. Despite the fact that he had just woken up, his eyes were sharply alert, going from Jaime's pale face to the broken mug, and then back again.

'I wanted a cup of tea,' her voice sounded guiltily apologetic. It was *her* home, Jaime reminded herself, and Blake was an uninvited guest.

'You were making as much noise as an addict looking for a too-long delayed fix,' Blake growled in response.

'I'm sorry if I disturbed you.' The kettle was boiling, and Jaime moved across to it automatically. She had her back to Blake when she heard him say shatteringly, 'I was out of bed and half way downstairs before I realised what was going on. . . . My first instinctive response was that someone must have broken in. I'm not at all happy about you and Fern being alone here—not after what happened this afternoon.'

'And you think if I left the committee it would stop happening?' She couldn't look at him, and see her fears made fact by what she might read in his eyes.

'I certainly think it would help, but I doubt that you're going to stop campaigning against the sale of the Abbey. However, Barrons are very powerful opponents.'

'And you think they're the ones responsible for what happened at the school?'

He might genuinely believe the builders had arranged the demonstration but, on the other hand, if he and Caroline had been responsible for it, he would want her to think that. If only she had the courage to ask him the truth. Coward, she mocked herself, weak, stupid coward.

'I think it's a very strong possibility, although I doubt that you'd ever get proof. They're far too clever for that. Mind out . . .!'

His warning came too late as she almost trod on a sharp piece of pottery.

'Blake!' Her protest was smothered against his throat as he bent to pick her up and then strode into the living room with her, depositing her on the settee. Just for a moment, as he leaned over her, the warm male smell of him reminding her of countless other occasions when he had held her in his arms like this, Jaime wanted to beg him not to let her go. Instead, she struggled steadfastly against the warm pressure of his arms, wondering if he was as aware of the fact that her breasts were crushed against the naked warmth of his body as she was.

A familiar heat rose up inside her, the thin cotton of her nightdress clinging provocatively to her body as he released her. 'You stay there,' he told her curtly. 'I'll make the tea and clear up. What were you doing down here anyway?'

'I woke up and couldn't get back to sleep. I thought a drink might help.'

'I know the feeling, but I normally opt for something more alcoholic.'

Jaime watched him, through the open doors, tidy the kitchen, each movement smoothly economic. During the time they had lived together when he was at home, he had always insisted on doing his share of the chores. In some strange way then she had resented it, seeing it as yet more proof of how little he needed her. They had quarrelled about it, she remembered, and he had lashed out at her saying he didn't want her as a housemaid, but as a companion. He had offered her so much, she realised now, the sort of relationship every woman hopes for, but she had been too frightened, too insecure, and too reluctant to abandon her cherished dream of conventional marriage and motherhood to take what he had been offering.

'Hey, come back. Where were you?'

'I was thinking about Charles,' Jaime lied hastily, avoiding his eyes as she took the mug he proffered. It wouldn't do her any good at all if Blake guessed that *he* was the subject of her thoughts, him and regrets for her folly in the past.

'Oh, were you?'

Surely that wasn't rage she saw in his eyes. She knew that Blake didn't like Charles, but the dark, fiercely intent gaze he was turning on her now was that of a very jealous lover.

'You're still *my* wife, Jaime. . . .'

'But that doesn't mean I can't think about other men.' What on earth had got into her? She sounded almost provocative! When she saw the way Blake's tension increased, his whole body taut with it, she knew why she had reacted the way she had. She wanted to make him jealous.

'Doesn't it? He isn't worthy of you, Jaime. Stop thinking about him. Think about this instead.' His hand slid up into her hair, twining through the silky strands, and tugging gently until her throat arched. The thumb of Blake's

free hand stroked along her jaw, his eyes
registering the soft quiver that betrayed her,
before his fingers curled against the warmth of
her throat, imprisoning her so that she was forced
to witness the leisurely descent of his mouth,
without being able to do a thing to avoid it.

The anticipation of his mouth on hers was
almost unbearable, and even whilst she felt
resentment at Blake's openly 'dog in the
manger' attitude, there was a spiralling excitement and satisfaction in knowing that he
wanted to kiss her.

'Jaime. . . .' His mouth touched hers lightly at
first, as though he was trying to judge her
reaction, and then when he met no resistance, his
tongue stroked coaxingly along the tremulous
outline of her lips until they were pliant and
moist, already half parting in anticipation of his
kiss.

It was an explosion of pleasure within her, a
reaffirmation of all that she already knew she felt
about him. She moaned hungrily in her throat
when she felt the possessive pressure of his
mouth yield, arching against him in her need to
prolong his kiss.

Blake seemed to know how she felt, just as he
always had. His kiss deepened to match her need,
fuelling and feeding the growing hunger she
could feel inside her and then, easing slightly,
bringing her back down to earth by gentle
degrees until she realised that she was lying in his
arms, with her mouth swollen from his kiss and
his lips still warmly pliant against hers.

'Jaime, you're as hungry for me as I am for you.'

'No,' she moaned the denial out loud, but knew in her heart that Blake was right. 'What on earth do you see in that Thomson as a man? He can't satisfy you in any of the ways that a woman like you needs to be satisfied. He calls you his fiancée, but he isn't your lover.'

'How do you know that?' She moved restlessly in Blake's arms, aware of treading on treacherous ground and yet unable to deny herself the pleasure of being this close to him.

'Because, if he were, you wouldn't want me to touch you like this . . .' His thumb stroked softly behind her ear and down over her throat, shaping the line of her collar bone and drawing shivering frissons of pleasure from her responsive flesh. 'Or like this.' His fingers probed the low neckline of her cotton nightdress and found the swollen mound of her breast. At the first touch of his thumb against the vulnerability of her nipple, Jaime sucked in her breath, tensing her whole body, her heart pounding so heavily it seemed to echo in the silence between them. Deftly, expertly, Blake slid the straps of her nightdress down until Jaime felt that the mere vibration of her breathing would be enough to make the fine fabric fall free of her upper body, but it was Blake's hands that smoothed the cotton free of her skin and then shaped the full femininity of her breasts, his eyes following the line of tan that revealed that all her sun bathing had been done with the benefit of her bikini top.

'Blake, please, we mustn't.' She had to take hold of her common sense and stop him now before she was completely mesmerised by the desire glittering hectically in his dark eyes. It would be so easy to give in to her own need to be with him like this, to urge him to possess her body in the same way that he possessed her heart, but what about afterwards?

'No, Jaime, you're wrong. We must.' His voice sounded hoarsely unfamiliar as though he were fighting to retain some control over his feelings. Drawn by some impulse she knew she ought to repudiate, Jaime reached up to touch his skin. His collar bone gleamed golden in the light from the lamp and she felt the powerful surge of response that rippled through his body at her touch. It was headily exhilarating to know that she still had the power to arouse him. Desire isn't love, an inner voice warned her, but she chose to ignore it. She was too hungry for this intimacy, this magic that only Blake could work, to listen to any warnings.

'Jaime, if you continue to touch me like that I'm going to make love to you whether we must or must not. Your fingers are telling my skin that you want to touch me as much as I want to touch you.' He groaned suddenly as her nipples burgeoned into pulsating life in recognition of her physical response to his words.

'You *do* want me,' he said it with almost a fierce triumph, as though there had been a time when he had doubted her desire. How could that be? She had always been dotingly, almost embarrassingly, eager for his lovemaking, so much so, that she had practically trembled with anticipation every time he came near her.

She didn't draw her eyes away, suddenly made bold by the strength of her love for him, and then as though to underline her unspoken desire she ran her fingers lightly through the matting of dark hairs that covered his chest, following them downwards until she came to the barrier of his jeans.

Burying his mouth against her throat Blake groaned. 'Jaime, you witch, you must know how I've wanted you to touch me like that. You do something to me that no other woman can.'

His admission gave her a heady power that drove out fear and shyness completely. It was as though some wild, wanton part of her had suddenly taken control, knowing without words, simply by touch, how to please and torment the male body above her. Her lips, delicate as butterfly wings, touched along Blake's collar bone. The intimate male scent of him was instantly recognisable, heightening her responsiveness. Unlike in the past, when she had been content to let him take the lead, now Jaime wanted to share the same urgency that burned inside her. Her tongue brushed the strong column of his throat and felt the tremors shiver across his skin. She teased him again, feeling his muscles clench against her sensual torment, his hands sliding down from her breasts to her hips, anchoring her beneath him, his body surging helplessly against her.

Her fingers found his belt, but it was Blake who finished the task for her, throwing aside the jeans he had pulled on to come downstairs.

The nude magnificence of his body, coloured tawny teak in the glow of the lamp, made her catch her breath in awe. Almost wonderingly she let her fingers drift over him, drinking in the sensation of warm, male skin and sinew beneath finger tips and then palms, her touch an unconscious worship of his masculinity.

'Jaime,' Blake muttered her name in a thick protest jerked past tightly compressed lips, warning her that she was pushing him to the very limits of his control, but it wasn't enough to simply feel the warmth of his body beneath her hands. Love and desire mingled inside her, raising her senses to such a pitch that she yearned to communicate her feelings to him, to pour out her love in such a generous libation that it would be a gift he couldn't refuse. Her hand rested against his thigh and she could feel the tension the muscles were communicating to her. She bent her head and let her lips drift in wordless adoration over the flat plane of his stomach, feeling the sharply indrawn breath he held until her own lungs hurt in response.

'Jaime.' Her name was a hoarse protest on his lips, lost against her hair. His fingers twined in its midnight silk as he tried to lift her away, and then, tensed instead, pressing her closer to his body as he yielded to the intimacy of her caress.

A harsh cry, somewhere between pain and pleasure, filled the room as Blake writhed convulsively against her, his body hot with the desire she could feel pulsing through her, and then, suddenly, he was lifting her away; holding her immobile slightly above him, his mouth finding her breast and piercing her with sweet pleasure.

The almost languorous need she had known to show him her love was gone, and in its place was a fierce, almost savage, hunger. They were lying side by side, Blake stroking her body with roughly urgent movements that mirrored her own desire, his mouth fiercely possessive as it moved on her breasts, his hand at last reaching the juncture of her thighs and remaining there to coax from her body the restless spirals of pleasure she had begun to believe must just have been a figment of her imagination.

'My sweet Jaime, I've wanted this so much.' Blake's voice was raw with feeling, his body shaking as he stroked and caressed her into a mindless oblivion she knew could have only one ending. 'You want it too, don't you?' Blake's tongue flicked against one highly sensitive nipple, shudders rippling convulsively through her. Lean and powerfully muscled, his body was a welcome weight on hers, her mouth parting eagerly for his fiercely possessive kiss, her body responding blindly to the male thrust of his, welcoming the heat of him inside her, moving to the rhythm he had taught it, and which it had remembered ever since.

Somehow, they had rolled on to the floor—and if anyone had told her five days ago that she

would be here, making love with Blake, she
would have shaken her head in astounded
disbelief. But she was here: they both were, and
Blake wasn't making any secret of the fact that he
wanted her as much as she needed him. An
explosive climax gripped her body, and she cried
out his name, letting his mouth steal the sounds
from her and tell her of his instinctive male
triumph as his own body shuddered in paroxysms
of pleasure that left her sated and bonelessly
feline.

'Anyone would think we were two teenagers
without a bed to go to, never mind two to choose
from,' Blake muttered as he pulled her closer
within the circle of his arms.

'Mine's only a single,' Jame protested sleepily,
'nowhere near large enough for you.' Her sleepy
glance encompassed his lean, male frame, as
relaxed and supine as a jungle leopard's.

'You've changed,' Blake murmured, his hand
automatically cupping her breast in a gesture of
instinctive possession. 'Before, you never would
have taken the initiative. Never have touched or
caressed me as you did tonight.'

'I thought it was unfeminine—that you
wouldn't want me to.' She was glad that the
darkness hid her flushed face from him.

'Not want you to!' Blake groaned. 'My God, if
you'd only known. There were times when I used
to feel like going down on my knees and begging
you for just a tenth of the loving you gave me
tonight, Jaime. I know this isn't really the time,
but I have to say it. Leave that committee. I can

understand why you feel so strongly about the Abbey, but you don't know what you're tangling with. . . .'

'And you do?' Jaime demanded angrily. Her mood of peaceful contentment had completely gone, all her earlier suspicions rushing back. Had Blake made love to her deliberately, hoping to get her to change her mind, knowing how malleable and weak his lovemaking always made her?

'More so than you,' he said brusquely, 'and what I know, I don't like.'

What did he mean? That he *had* been a party to Caroline's threats, but that he was now having second thoughts? Perhaps he had even suggested them, she thought sickly, and suggested to Caroline that she approach Barrons with them, for their help. She was sure now that the man who had come to see her had somehow come from Barrons.

'Is that why you came here tonight? To persuade me to leave the committee?'

Blake had withdrawn from her, and she felt cold without the support of his arms. His withdrawal was almost symbolic of their relationship, she thought bitterly, as was her shivering reaction to it.

'No, it damn well wasn't,' Blake said bitterly, 'but of course you'll put your own crazy interpretation on my actions—you always did. . . . You always were full of crazy accusations. I thought you'd grown up, but I can see I was wrong. Well, just remember before you get up on your high horse, that it isn't just yourself you're risking. It's my daughter as well, and as long as you're still my wife, I mean to see that someone keeps an eye on the pair of you.'

'Then I'll just have to make sure I'm not your wife for much longer, won't I?'

She could have wept. Not ten minutes ago, they had been as close as two human beings could be, but now it was all gone. A lesson to her not to be deceived into thinking that desire could in any way compare with love.

'I think I know that what's supposed to mean,' Blake gritted at her through grimly closed teeth, 'but you seem to have forgotten something—for a divorce you need either my agreement or proof that we haven't cohabitated for over five years, and you have neither.'

'Why do you insist on keeping me tied to you like this?' Jaime cried out painfully. 'What's the point . . .?'

'The point is, my dear Jaime,' Blake responded cruelly, 'that it prevents you from marrying dear Charles and anyone else from marrying me. And now,' he announced, standing up, 'I'm going back to my room to try and get some sleep for what remains of the night. If you get lonely, don't bother coming looking for me, will you?'

With that last taunting remark he was gone. As she climbed the stairs in weary resignation, Jaime reflected that she would never sleep, but towards dawn she did.

When she woke up the first thing she saw was a cold cup of coffee on the table beside her bed. In her sleep-fogged state her first thought was that her mother had brought it up, but then she remembered and she coloured hotly. Why on earth should it make her feel so vulnerable that Blake had watched her whilst she slept, when not half-a-dozen hours ago, they had been lovers?

Through her open window she caught the sound of Fern's laughter wafting up from the garden. It had been so long since Fern had laughed. On the verge of a sigh, she tensed and leapt out of bed, rushing to the window, relief warming her chilled bloodstream when she saw that Fern was playing with Blake. Whatever his feelings about her, surely he would never countenance any harm coming to his daughter, and if he knew of the threats made against her, he must know of Fern's danger.

As she stood watching father and daughter playing together, Jaime forgot that she was naked. This was what she had dreamed of for herself, a father who would play and laugh with her child, and she had tried to impose her own desires on other people she now recognised. A sudden stillness from Blake warned her that she was observed, but before she could move back from the window his eyes had roved with careless thoroughness over the exposed curves of her breasts. Quickly, she withdrew, her cheeks flushed and her temper high. He had looked at her as though he were remembering their lovemaking last night and wanted *her* to remember it too.

She got downstairs just as Charles arrived on an unheralded visit. He was plainly disconcerted to find Blake so obviously at home in the cottage, although Jaime was sure that Blake had deliberately installed himself in the kitchen to reinforce that view. He even insisted on making her some breakfast, so that Charles was forced to sit at the table with her whilst Blake moved about in the kitchen beyond.

'I wanted to talk to you privately,' Charles hissed in an angry whisper, but Blake heard him, coming through to deposit a large plate of beautiful, fluffy scrambled eggs in front of Jaime, and saying, 'Whatever you have to say to my wife that's private can be said to me as well.'

'Your wife. . . .' Charles looked angrily from Blake's face to her own, and asked Jaime, 'What is he talking about . . .? You've been separated for so long that . . .?

'That I've decided it's time the separation was ended.' To Jaime's astonishment, Blake reached across the table, lifting up her left hand, and turning it palm up to his lips. The brief movement against the sensitive skin of her palm made her stomach lurch protestingly, 'To our mutual satisfaction,' he added in a husky, intimate tone that made Jaime colour up and curl up her toes to stop the response shivering through her body.

She had to wait for Charles to leave to take Blake to task. He shrugged powerful shoulders when she demanded an explanation.

'I was simply doing what any man would to defend his property,' he said lazily, without a trace of remorse.

'I am not your property!' Jaime flung back at him.

'No, but you *are* my wife, and as I said earlier, that's what you're going to stay. Face it, Jaime, you would never have been happy with him. He would never have been enough for you.'

'And you are, I suppose?' she demanded with bitter sarcasm.

'Perhaps not, but at least I come one hell of a lot closer to it than he does. I didn't notice any holding back in my arms last night,' he reminded her cruelly. 'Your response wasn't that of a woman who already had a lover who satisfied her, Jaime. In fact, I'd go so far as to say that since you left me there haven't been any other lovers at all.'

'Go to hell!' Jaime stormed at him, hating the soft laughter that followed her as she fled to the sitting room.

'I wish Daddy hadn't gone,' Fern complained an hour later when the two of them were alone. Jaime sighed as she smoothed her daughter's unruly curls. She and Blake had argued before he left. He had wanted her to leave the committee, but how could she? Already, several people had begun to show a marked loss of interest in the campaign, borderline cases who had promised their names for the petition the committee were organising and who were now saying that perhaps Barrons' estate would be a good thing, bringing in all those jobs for the young folk, and modern, attractive houses.

She was very low on bread and eggs—Blake

had used the last of them for her breakfast—and she debated whether it would be wiser to stop in the village or go to the nearest town. She was reluctant to leave the house empty for longer than necessary, and opted, in the end, for the village.

CHAPTER SIX

'JAIME, my dear, I've heard the news about those hooligans. How horrible for you!'

Jaime paused to accept the sympathy of the Vicar's wife, trying to keep an eye on Fern at the same time.

'Janice and the children are staying with us at the moment,' she continued, referring to her married daughter. 'Perhaps Fern would like to come round for tea one afternoon?'

The Vicar's twin grandchildren were approximately the same age as Fern, and, although Jaime was reluctant to agree, Fern was already so enthusiastic about the proffered treat that she felt compelled to accept.

'You look peaky, my dear,' Mrs Simmonds continued. 'When's your mother back? I wanted to ask her advice about a pair of candlesticks we've discovered in the attic.'

By the time she had chatted with the dozen or so people who had stopped to commiserate with her over the destruction of her studio, and Jaime was ready to start back for the cottage, it was quite late. She was just on her way to the car when she was stopped by Bill Smithers, who dashed out of his office to catch her. Bill was the local insurance broker and handled both Jaime's and her mother's insurances.

'Jaime, I'm glad I caught you! I've had a call from your insurance company. They're sending out an assessor tomorrow. He wants you to meet him at the school.'

Tomorrow! Jaime thought quickly. It was just as well that she had accepted Mrs Simmonds' invitation for Fern. She could hardly have taken the little girl with her.

'That's quick.'

'Well I told them that you would be pretty anxious to get started again. There's nothing to worry about. You're very well covered—which is more than I can say for some of my clients, and Rick Brewer is a pleasant chap.'

After agreeing a time, Jaime hurried Fern back to the car. When they reached the cottages, Blake's car was parked outside, with Blake sitting in the driver's seat. He got out as they drove up and Jaime felt her heart begin its familiar drum roll of reaction. He was frowning as he opened the car door for her, although he managed a smile for Fern when she ran towards him, calling 'Daddy . . . pick me up, Daddy, pick me up!'

Jaime hadn't expected to see him so soon, and she bent her head to hide the swift rush of colour to her face when she remembered their love-making. Mrs Widdows was watching from her window as they walked up the path, and she wondered what the old lady thought of Blake's constant comings and goings.

'What did you want to see me about?' Jaime marvelled at how calm her voice sounded.

'I don't like the thought of you and Fern being

here alone—not after what happened at the school.'

'So, what do you suggest I do?' Jaime demanded flippantly, 'Hire a bodyguard—I don't think my income will run to it!'

'I was thinking more along the lines of you and Fern moving in with me—at least until your mother gets back.'

Jaime stared at him, completely astounded. 'Stay with you—you mean move into the Lodge. Won't Caroline have something to say about that?'

The moment the bitter words were out, she wished them unsaid, knowing that they betrayed her jealousy, but Blake seemed to take them seriously. He frowned again and studied her.

'What could she have to say? I have rented the Lodge for the entire summer and you are my wife, Fern my child.'

'Blake, we can't move in with you,' Jaime protested desperately, 'This is a very small village. If I do, people will think. . . .' she floundered desperately.

'That we've decided to give our marriage a second chance. What does it matter what they think?'

His casual arrogance infuriated Jaime.

'It might not matter to you,' she agreed, 'but Fern and I have to live here after you've gone.'

'And you're frightened it will spoil your chances with Thomson? I've already told you, Jaime,' Blake said in a harsh voice, 'he isn't the man for you—he isn't man enough for you.'

'I can't do it, Blake. We can't simply move in with you.'

'Not even to protect Fern?'

Jaime's heart slammed to a full stop and then started beating again as the full horror of his words sank in. She *had* been right, not to trust her instincts. Blake *did* know about these threats, and that was why he wanted them to move in with him. Perhaps he had originally gone along with Caroline's plans and was now having second thoughts. Perhaps what had happened at the school had alerted him to the reality of their danger and now he was trying to protect them— or rather, he was trying to protect Fern.

'It's impossible,' she said it shakily, too sick at heart to try and conceal her reaction, 'and besides,' she added numbly, 'there's your work; you won't be able to concentrate on your writing with us around.'

'So who's going to watch over you, Jaime? Thomson?'

'At least Charles' motives are honest ones,' Jaime snapped back, stung by the contempt in his voice when he mentioned Charles' name. She straightened up from unpacking her shopping, just in time to see the thin cruel line Blake's mouth had become. His eyes glittered, green jade shot through with gold, a sure sign that he was in danger of losing his temper. She stepped back automatically, although there had never been a single occasion when Blake had ever hurt her physically, and as though the act of her cowering away snapped the final threat that held his temper in check, Blake advanced on her, grasping her shoulders and almost violently shaking her. 'Stop casting me as the villain of the piece, Jaime,' he demanded angrily, 'and don't cower away from me like that. God, I can almost understand why some men are driven to violence by women!' He looked down into her pale face and swore suddenly, his mouth covering hers before Jaime could utter the smallest protest.

It was a bitter travesty of the kisses they had shared last night, a cold, cruel method of branding her as his possesion, more effective than any blow, lacerating her pride and bruising her soft mouth. She tried not to respond; not to let her lips soften into submission beneath the hard pressure of his; but to her shame, they accepted his touch, knowing and wanting it no matter how contemptuous it was.

'Damn you, Jaime. You make me forget that. . . .' He broke off, and released her. 'I'm going now. If you won't come and live with me, at least promise me that you'll take care?'

Her pride still smarting from the angry kiss he had forced on her Jaime snapped bitterly, 'It's a bit too late for you to start worrying about us now, isn't it?'

For a moment, a white, haunted look subtly changed Blake's features so that she might have been looking at a stranger, and then it changed, angry colour burning along his cheek bones, his eyes as bitter as his voice.

When he had gone, Jaime sank down in a chair, burying her face in her hands as she rocked back and forth, trying to exorcise the pain tearing into her. It got worse, not better. Her body craved him as it might a drug, her heart yearned for him, and her mind feverishly tried to resist the claims of the other two and think only of Fern and how Blake had put his child at risk.

There was another meeting of the protest committee that evening, and Jaime forced herself to go. The young couple next door had returned and promised to sit in with Fern. Jaime felt happier about leaving her with them than with Mrs Widdows who would be able to do nothing to protect Fern if anything should happen. As she got ready, a small traitorous voice reminded her that, with Blake, Fern would háve been completely safe, but how could she agree to live with him, loving him as she did and yet suspecting his involvement with Barrons and Caroline?

Charles came to pick her up, his manner stiff and formal. Jaime knew she ought to offer some explanation about Blake's presence in the cottage, but the words simply would not come.

'We've got someone down from the Department this evening to talk to us about the problems they have to face. Do you know how many historic buildings have been deliberately destroyed this year alone?'

Jaime did not, and, since statistics were one of Charles' hobby horses, she listened with one ear to his outpourings, relieved when they finally reached the church hall where the meeting was to be held.

The first thing Jaime noticed was the drastic

reduction in attendance. There was no sign of Paul Davis, and Charles said, curtly, that he understood that the Barrons were substantial investors in the independent radio station that Paul ran.

'He's probably decided that it would be more diplomatic of him to withdraw from the campaign,' Charles told her.

So, gradually, Barrons were whittling down the opposition to their plans. It only needed her to convince Charles to withdraw and they would virtually have a clear field. Jaime shivered despite the warmth of the summer evening. Could she now expect their harrassment to increase? Both they and Caroline must be anxious to see a conclusion to the sale.

The speaker, an attractive and vigorous woman in her forties, spoke well and with great feeling about the problems their Department had to face. Their only means of punishing those who transgressed against preservation orders was the threat of prosecution, plus a large fine.

'And, of course, an unscrupulous building company always claims that the demolition or destruction is the fault of the contractors who acted contrary to instructions. Once a building has been destroyed, there is nothing we can do, and very often the profit element on whatever is built on the land is such that they can pay the fine and still show a substantial profit at the end of the day.

'I could list a dozen or more incidents where old and historically valuable buildings have been destroyed over a bank holiday weekend by a man with a bulldozer, acting on apparently "misunderstood" instructions. We believe he has understood his instructions all too well, but the problem is in tracting those instructions back to the company who stands to profit the most.

'Barrons is one of the companies we know to use these underhand methods, but we've never been able to prove it. The BBC are actually hoping to do an in-depth enquiry programme on just this sort of abuse, and if they do, we're hoping that it will highlight the problems we face.'

'Do you think Barrons will try to destroy the Abbey?' someone called up from the audience.

'I don't know. The owner is very keen to sell to them, but I understand there is another buyer—not offering quite as much, but someone who wants to keep the Abbey as a home and restore it. Obviously, as far as we and you are concerned, this would be a much more attractive proposition, but we can't entirely discount the fact that Barrons may insist that they have a prior lien on the purchase.'

The rest of the evening passed quickly. Charles drove Jaime home, in silence, speaking only when he had brought his car to a halt outside the cottage.

'In view of your apparent reconciliation with your husband, our . . . relationship will have to be terminated. I can't help wishing you had spoken to me first, Jaime,' he added in a pained voice. 'As your legal adviser, I should have been made aware of your intentions, and on a more personal note, you must have known. . . .'

'Charles, I do apologise,' Jaime interrupted, feeling obliged to mirror his formal tone, 'and, of course, I hope we shall stay friends.'

As she got out of the car she had to suppress a faintly hysterical laugh. They had both been so absurdly formal, like a couple out of a treatise on correct manners. As she walked up the path to the cottage door, she reflected that, at least, she could not now be expected to bring pressure to bear on Charles to quit the Committee. All she could hope was that whoever it was who was prepared to buy and live in the Abbey managed to persuade Caroline to sell it. That would solve all their problems.

Her neighbours greeted her warmly when she walked in, and assured her that Fern had been no trouble. Jaime thanked them for sitting for her and then, when they had gone, began her routine nightly check of the house. She had just finished when the 'phone rang. She stared at it with compulsive dread for several seconds before lifting the receiver.

'Jaime?'

Blake's voice sounded sharp.

'Blake. Is . . . is something wrong?'

'No, I just wanted to check that you got back safely. You did go to tonight's meeting, didn't you?'

'Yes.' Her voice dull and flat, Jaime gave her reply. Just for a second, she had been warmed by his concern; had wanted to pour out to him her hopes that the Abbey might have an alternative buyer, and then she had remembered his involvement with Caroline.

'That's all right then,' now his voice was as devoid of feeling as her own, 'I'll say "goodnight" then.'

The 'phone in the Lodge was in the hall and, just as she was about to replace the receiver, Jaime heard someone knock on the door, and then Caroline's voice reached her.

'Darling . . .' she heard her say, 'here I am, at last.'

She replaced the receiver, feeling acutely sick. Were Caroline and Blake already lovers? She had always known that Caroline was attracted to Blake, and Blake? . . . Blake had never refused an attractive woman's advances, surely she already knew that?

After another disturbed night, Jaime woke up late, but this morning there was no Blake to make breakfast for her. After eating a slice of toast and drinking a cup of coffee, she got Fern ready for her visit to the Vicarage, instructing her to play quietly in the sitting room while she changed for her appointment with the insurance assessor.

A tailored, soft yellow skirt she had bought the previous summer, teamed with a blouse in the same colour, decorated with pretty, self-embroidery, seemed appropriately formal without being too dressy. As she brushed her dark hair, Jaime debated whether to put it up and then decided against doing so. A touch of blue eyeshadow to emphasise the dark sapphire of her eyes, and the merest covering of soft pink lip gloss completed her make-up and then she was back downstairs, calling to Fern.

Mary Simmonds came out to the Mini when Jaime arrived, escorted by the four-year old twins, Simon and Mark. By the time Jaime was ready to leave five minutes later, having refused a cup of coffee, Fern was already expertly bossing the two little boys about, and they were her willing slaves.

'Don't worry about rushing back,' Mary Simmonds told Jaime when she explained where she was going, 'Fern can stay all day if necessary.'

An empty Ford estate car was already parked outside the school when Jaime arrived, and, as she locked her Mini, Jaime frowned faintly. She had noticed a certain sluggishness in her brakes as she drove to the school. The car had been serviced only recently, and she would have to take it back to have the brakes re-checked— another potential expense.

As she stepped into the school, a tall, fair-haired man came towards her, wiping dusty fingers on what had once been a pristine white handkerchief.

'I know,' he grinned, when he saw the look on Jaime's face, 'my mother will kill me. She keeps threatening to buy me only dark-coloured ones. I'm Rick Brewer,' he introduced himself, 'and you must be Jaime? Bill told me you were very attractive, but he didn't do you justice. You must be very upset about all this,' he added, gesturing to the room behind him. 'I doubt that any of the

fittings can be salvaged. Bill tells me you've had
to close your classes down for the time being.'

'I'm afraid so,' Jaime agreed.

'Well, you're fortunate in having Bill as your
broker. He's very thorough, and I believe you've
followed all the advice he gave you. You do have a
loss of earnings policy with us, as well as general
cover, which means that we will compensate you
for loss of earnings during the time the building is
out of commission. We shall need to see your
books, of course, to estimate just exactly what your
weekly takings are, and I should like to discuss with
you the sort of time scale envisaged for getting this
place sorted out. How do you feel about us
discussing things over lunch?'

Jaime accepted his invitation unhesitatingly,
and then explained that she kept her books at the
cottage.

'Fine, we'll go in my car and pick up the books
on the way back. I thought we'd eat at a place I
know near Dorchester.'

He told her the name, and Jaime recognised it.
The Belfry was a very well-known local restaurant
with a first-class reputation. She had only been
there once before—with Henry and her mother.

'Would you mind if I drove my own car?' she
asked him, quickly explaining about the brakes
and adding that the local dealer, from whom she
had bought the car and who had serviced it since,
was on the way to their destination.

'I can call in on the way back and leave the car
there, if you wouldn't mind giving me a lift back
to the cottage?'

'Not at all.'

They went inside, and Rick spent close on an hour walking round, inspecting the damage and making notes. 'There doesn't seem to be any structural damage fortunately, but we'll check that out, just in case. I wish everyone was as thorough about their insurance as you've been.' He frowned, and Jaime asked sympathetically, 'Are you worrying about somewhere in particular?'

'Yes, I shouldn't really tell you this, but the fire policy on the Abbey lapsed last month and hasn't been renewed. Of course, it is expensive to insure an old building like that, but it's taking a terrible risk not to have it insured.'

It was twelve o'clock when they left the village, Jaime following Rick's car as he drove towards Dorchester and The Belfry.

The car park was quite full when they got there. Rick explained that he had already booked a table, hoping that she would accept his invitation. 'This place is far too busy to leave getting a table to chance.'

As they walked into the restaurant Jaime was glad that she had taken the trouble to dress smartly for their meeting. All the other diners seemed to be very well-dressed, mainly older couples with a sprinkling of dark-suited businessmen. A couple of tables were occupied by farmers, looking uncomfortable in their tweed jackets and firmly buttoned shirts.

Then, as they were led to their table, a trio on the other side of the room caught her eye. She recognised Blake and Caroline immediately, but the third occupant of the table was unfamiliar to her.

'Ummm,' Rick commented, following her gaze. 'That looks like Guy Barron over there, but I don't know who he's with.'

'You sound as though you don't approve of him,' Jaime remarked, without telling him the identity of his companions. She was speaking automatically, not really caring what response he made as long as it helped her to blot out the pain of seeing Blake with Caroline and Guy Barron. So her suspicions had been correct. It gave her no satisfaction to know that she had been right not to trust her instincts, the instincts of a woman deeply in love who would defend the actions of the man she loved no matter what he might do.

'I don't. He had a policy with us—an old farmhouse he had supposedly bought for his own use. It burned down, and twelve months later he managed to persuade the local council to give his company planning permission for a small estate on the land. Not only did he get the profit from the houses, he also got the fire insurance as well. Of course, we couldn't prove a thing, but we had our suspicions. He's an extremely ruthless man, and not above straying on to the wrong side of the law if he thinks he can get away with it, or perhaps I should say that he's not above paying someone else to do the straying.'

Delightful though she was sure the lunch was, Jaime barely tasted it. All the time they were in the restaurant she was acutely conscious of Blake at the other side of the room.

Rick Brewer was a pleasant companion and she felt guilty because she wasn't able to respond to him as she ought. Her feeling of relief when they finally left was cut short by the emergence of Blake and his two companions at almost the same time. They all paused in the car park, not half a dozen yards from Jaime. Blake looked up and saw her, his eyes moving coldly from her to Rick before returning to his companions. He made no attempt to acknowledge her presence which, illogically, hurt Jaime more than anything else.

She watched as he and Guy Barron shook hands, and then ushered Caroline towards the Ferrari.

They must have made a detour into town for something, Jaime realised when she was halfway home, as she glimpsed the now-familiar outline of the Ferrari in her driving mirror, the black car gradually cutting down the distance between them.

Because of her concern for her brakes, Jaime did not want to push her small car, and she was conscious of Rick Brewer in front of her, matching his speed to hers. Blake would soon overtake them—he had plenty of opportunity; the road was straight and wide enough; and yet, for some reason, he chose not to do so. It was less than a mile to the garage, and Jaime heaved a mental sigh of relief. She wasn't at all happy about her car, not being a confident driver at the best of times. It was actually comforting to have

Blake behind her. He wasn't driving too close as so many drivers did, and she kept glancing into the mirror, comforted by the sight of the curved black bonnet behind her.

Rick had pulled out to overtake a stationary car, when it happened. Someone had parked at the side of the road, almost dangerously so, and Jaime followed his example, but, just as she was about to overtake, the rear door of the car was thrust open and a small child jumped out.

There wasn't time to think, only to act instinctively, and Jaime put her foot down hard on her brakes, appalled to discover that there was just nothing there and that she was on a direct collision course with the open door and the young child.

The other side of the road was clear, open fields beyond the hedge, and Jaime pulled hard on her wheel automatically, wincing at the sharp squeal of her tyres as she managed to pull the car round, and it careered uncontrollably across the road, heading straight for the hedge. Jaime tried to steer as best she could, hoping that her car would run out of momentum before it hit the hedge, but she had forgotten about the deep grass-covered ditch, and suddenly the front wheels dipped down and she was flung into the steering wheel. It hit her chest with an impact that knocked her breathless, her seat belt cutting painfully into her as her hands left the wheel and the car plunged to a standstill.

'Dear God, what happened?'

Jaime recognised the voice, but she couldn't put a name to it. Near at hand a child was crying, a high-pitched, keening sound. Fern . . . but no, it wasn't Fern.

'Come on, Jaime, move your legs.' She recognised the voice.

'Blake.'

She didn't realise she had croaked his name until she heard the other male voice exclaiming thankfully, 'She's come round.'

'And she doesn't seem to have broken anything. I'll take her back. She'll need to see a doctor—there could be concussion.'

'I can't understand what she was doing.'

That was Caroline, her voice annoyed. Jaime could just picture her petulant expression.

'She oughtn't to be on the road if she can't control her car better than that.'

'She told me that she was worried about her brakes. She said she was going to take her car in on our way back.'

Jaime could place the other male voice now, Rick Brewer, the insurance assessor. She struggled to sit up, to explain to him that something *had* gone wrong with her car, but something stopped her.

'Lie still.'

She opened her eyes, disconcerted to discover that she was lying full-length on the grass verge, her Mini a crumpled mess in the hedge. She shuddered, re-living the sickening impact, and then winced as she felt the pain in her chest.

'Just as well you're a law-abiding citizen and

you were wearing your seat belt . . .' Blake told her curtly. 'I'm going to take you home and get a doctor out to see you.'

Out of the corner of her eye, Jaime could see Caroline pout. Rick Brewer, too, looked disconcerted, until Blake explained tersely, 'Jaime is my wife.'

'Perhaps I can offer you a lift,' Rick suggested to Caroline. 'We could call at the garage and get them to tow the car away.' He frowned, very much the insurance official. 'They'll need to check those brakes. . . .'

'Leave the car,' Blake said curtly. 'I'll make all the arrangements that are necessary.'

Jaime wanted to protest, but her head was thumping, nausea driving out the ability to speak. She didn't want Blake having anything to do with her car. Did he suspect, as she did, that it had been tampered with? Was he hoping to destroy the evidence, in order to protect Caroline and Barrons, or, even worse, had he been an actual party to it? She didn't believe for one moment they had wanted her to have a fatal accident—just a fright, and if she hadn't had to brake so hard to avoid that child, probably the worst that could have happened was a bad swerve when she tried to cross the road to drive the car into the garage, where the same garage hand who had been bribed to make the brakes unsafe in the first place would no doubt have put them right, and she would have been a step nearer to withdrawing from the committee. How had they planned to work on Charles? Perhaps, by offering him a large slice of the Barron corporate business, she wondered cynically.

'Now, just lie still, and I'll try not to hurt you.'

She knew that Blake was being as gentle as he could, but even so she wanted to protest that she didn't want to go with him, that she didn't want to be alone with him, and, strangely enough, her feelings sprang not from a fear that he might hurt her but from a dread that, in her weakened emotional state, she might betray to him how she felt, but, before she could protest, a sharp pain knifed through her, stealing away her consciousness, wrapping her in a dense black cloud of oblivion.

CHAPTER SEVEN

'WELL, everything seems to be in working order. You'll need to keep an eye on her, just in case there is any concussion. You know what to look for.'

Jaime was dimly aware of Dr Philips talking to someone who stood in the shadows of the unfamiliar room as he bent over her, searching for bruises and abrasions. 'She's lucky she got off so lightly.'

'Yes.'

Jaime recognised the terse assent, and struggled to sit up.

'Fern,' she protested huskily, suddenly remembering her small daughter, 'she's with Mrs Simmonds. I must go and get her.'

'You won't be going anywhere—at least, not until tomorrow or the day after,' Dr Philips told her, with cheerful disregard for her maternal anxiety.

'Don't worry about Fern, Jaime. I'll go and collect her,' Blake interjected.

'Where am I?' Jaime lifted her throbbing head, and gazed round the unfamiliar bedroom. She was lying in a large double bed that almost filled the floor space. An old-fashioned wardrobe stood in one corner of the room, almost opposite the curtained window, the door hanging open. She could see men's clothing hanging up inside and, on the matching dresser, was a small pile of change and some masculine toilet articles.

'This is your room.' She whispered the accusation into the shadowy corner by the door where Blake stood. 'Why have you brought me here? I want to go home.'

'Now, now, Jaime. Stop making such a fuss,' Dr Philips soothed. 'Naturally, Blake brought you here. Who do you think could look after you and Fern if you stayed at home alone? Now just lie still. I'm going to give you an injection that will help you sleep. . . .'

'My car . . .' Jaime croaked feebly, knowing that, for now, she had no option but to give in to the combined male opposition of Dr Philips and Blake.

'Stop worrying so much,' Blake intervened roughly, 'The car's been taken care of. I'm having it towed to my garage where they'll give it a thorough inspection.'

'No!' Jaime wanted to shout her protest, but Dr Philip's injection was already taking effect, and the sound emerged as a pitifully small whisper. She wanted an independent garage to check over her car—someone she could trust. A forlorn tear trickled down her cheek as she admitted to herself how much she longed to be able to trust the man standing watching her with such apparent concern.

'Wake up, Mummy, I've brought you your breakfast!'

Jaime opened her eyes reluctantly, wondering why the window had changed places, and then she remembered. Fern stood just inside the door of what, Jaime felt sure, must have been Blake's room, beaming with excitement. Her small daughter's face looked scrubbed and clean, her curly hair neatly brushed, the soft pink cord dungarees and toning T-shirt all properly fastened.

'I dressed myself this morning,' Fern declared importantly, just as though she realised what Jaime was thinking. 'Well, Daddy did help me with some things,' she admitted, obviously feeling that she ought to share the praise. 'He told me a lovely story last night—all made up— and I had to sleep in a proper bed. I liked it. Today I'm going to play with the twins again. Daddy's going to take me when you've had your breakfast, because you've got to re . . . re. . . .'

'Recuperate,' Blake drawled laconically, emerging in the open doorway carrying a tray.

'Grapefruit, scrambled eggs, toast and coffee. I trust that is to Madame's liking?'

Jaime turned her head away so that he couldn't see her tears. That had been the breakfast he had always made her as a Sunday treat—on those rare Sundays when he had been at home.

'I must get up and dressed, then I can get back to the cottage. Fern and I have put you out enough. You really shouldn't have brought me here.'

'No? Then where should I have taken you?' Blake demanded, his face grim. 'To Thomson's?'

He saw her expression, and said harshly, 'You're my wife, Jaime, remember? And you're staying here until Dr Philips says you can go.'

'No,' Jaime fumbled awkwardly with the bedclothes, flinging them back, forgetting the brevity of her cotton nightdress as she swung her feet to the floor.

When she tried to stand up, it was just as though her legs were stuffed with candy floss. They completely refused to support her. She swayed sickly, and would have fallen if Blake hadn't put the tray down on the dresser and scooped her up in his arms.

'That settles it,' he said grimly, 'You're staying here. You're as weak as a kitten. For God's sake, Jaime. What are you so terrified of? That people might gossip? So what! We are married, and you're staying for your own protection, if nothing else.'

He broke off as he caught her faint gasp. So now he was as good as admitting it. Her body throbbed with pain, and she longed for the numbing sanctuary of Dr Philips' drug.

'Protection against what?' she demanded huskily, willing him to tell her the truth, but instead he merely placed her carefully back on the bed, tugging the discarded quilt around her. She could feel the clean warmth of his breath against her skin, stirring the soft hair at her temples, setting up a reaction that was a staccato thud of her pulses by the time it reached her bloodstream.

'Would you like more pillows?' Blake had piled

the pillows up behind her, propping her up with a solicitous care that, in other circumstances, would have had her breaking down in tears and begging him to take her in his arms.

'This is Daddy's bed,' Fern told her, climbing up to sit beside her. 'Simon and Mark's Mummy and Daddy sleep in the same bed. . . .'

Jaime didn't dare look up. She knew Blake was watching her.

'Lucky Simon and Mark's Daddy,' Blake drawled succinctly.

'If you're my Daddy, why don't you sleep in this bed with Mummy?' Fern pressed, the import of Blake's mocking comment lost on her.

It wasn't lost on *her* though, Jaime thought, knowing that her flushed face betrayed her response. As Blake leaned towards her with the tray, settling it beside her, she glimpsed the green glitter of desire in his eyes and her own pulses leapt in recognition. Their lovemaking had always been tumultuously passionate, and she knew already that Blake still desired her—just as he probably desired many attractive women. Desire on its own meant nothing.

'If Mummy wants me to share her bed, she only has to ask me,' Blake replied to Fern, his mouth curling in amusement as he saw the way Jaime's lips compressed. He had no right to torment her like this, using Fern's innocence.

'Well, Mummy?' he murmured huskily, his lips almost touching her temple.

'Perhaps, if Mummy had you to share her bed, she wouldn't cry at night,' Fern continued blithely, unaware of the reaction of both adults to her artless remark. Jaime had never realised that Fern had heard her crying at night. Sometimes, she wasn't even aware of it herself until she woke up with tears on her face.

'Don't be silly, Fern,' she burst out impulsively. 'You're imagining things.' She had to look away from Fern's small, worried face. How could she pretend that Fern was wrong when she knew. . . .

'Fern, why don't you go downstairs and see what the postman's brought?' Blake suggested softly, without taking his eyes off Jaime's pale face.

'*Do* you cry at night, Jaime?' he asked quietly, when Fern had gone.

'No, of course not,' Jaime denied, hoping that the faintly high-pitched, defensive tone of her voice wouldn't betray her. 'Like I said, Fern must have imagined it. . . .'

'And yet she has struck me as a rather pragmatic child. What's the matter, aren't you hungry?'

She had been, but all at once her appetite had gone.

'Blake, about my car. . . .'

If her intention had been to distract his attention, she had succeeded, Jaime thought seconds later as he walked away from the bed and leaned against the window, his powerful frame outlined by the sunlight.

'You should never have been driving it, Jamie,' he said severely, 'the brakes were in a very dangerous state. When did you last have them serviced?'

Either he genuinely didn't know the truth, or he was one hell of an actor, Jaime thought bitterly, and the awful thing was that she didn't really want to know which, in case he *had* known, so she said nothing about the car's recent service.

'Now I want your promise that you won't go back to the cottage—at least, not until your mother returns.'

What did she have to lose that she hadn't lost already? Her heart? That was already in his keeping. Her pride? Wasn't that already in tatters? Her safety . . . weren't she and Fern safer here with Blake than on their own?

'After I drop Fern off at the Vicarage, I'm going to Dorchester.'

He didn't say why, and Jaime didn't ask.

'I should be back later this afternoon. Dr Philips said if you felt up to it today you could come downstairs, but that was all.'

Anything was better than lying in Blake's bed. Perhaps her imagination was working overtime, but she could almost believe it still held traces of his unique male scent, and she couldn't lie here all day, remembering how it had been when they were married.

'I should like to get up.'

'Bathroom is the door opposite. Would you like me to carry you there?'

Jaime froze, tensing as he pushed broad shoulders off the wall, and came towards her.

'No . . . no . . . I can manage.'

To her relief, he didn't press the point and, although she had to grit her teeth to do it, ignoring the pain in her bruised body, Jaime did eventually manage to make her way to the bathroom. The warm caress of the shower helped to ease away some of the pain. The soap she found there reminded her of Blake, and she grew angry with herself for the erotic thoughts she couldn't dismiss as she lathered her skin.

'Jaime, you okay in there?'

The door was thrust open before she could call out, and she stood transfixed, all too aware of Blake's stunned green gaze slipping over her naked body.

He recovered from the shock faster than she could, surprise replaced by a smouldering sensuality that left her in no doubt as to his response to her nudity. Her skin was still slick with water, her nipples erect, and Jaime blushed hotly, knowing that they were mirroring the arousal suggested by her inner thoughts.

Blake made a thick sound in the back of his throat, breaking the spell which had held her motionless. Jaime made a clumsy grab for a towel, shielding her body with it, her breathing rapid and shallow.

'You're perfectly safe.' The green gaze flicked over her body again, but this time without desire—without any discernible emotion, as far as Jaime could see. 'I'm not going to pounce on you. I thought you might have fainted. Dr Philips told me to watch out for signs of concussion.'

'Well, you were certainly looking hard enough,' Jaime responded heatedly, trying to cover her response to him with anger, 'Where did you expect to find them?'

Blake took a step towards her. Another moment, and she would be in his arms, crushed against the powerful wall of his chest. Her heart started to beat in heavy anticipation. Her mouth went dry, and Jaime touched her tongue nervously to her lips.

'Daddy, when are we going . . .?'

The hand Blake had extended towards her dropped heavily to his side.

'Coming now, Fern,' he called back through the open door. 'Saved again,' he said mockingly to Jaime, his eyes narrowing suddenly as he added in a lower, taunting voice, 'always supposing you really wanted to be.'

Despite her protests, Blake insisted on carrying Jaime downstairs and settling her in a chair in his study within easy reach of the 'phone which he had brought in from the hall. He had also made her a fresh breakfast and practically stood over her while she ate it. A thermos of coffee had been placed beside her, plus an assortment of books.

'Now, don't move from there,' he ordered as he left, 'not one single step.'

As she heard Fern chattering excitedly to him as they headed for the Ferrari, Jaime was overwhelmed with a feeling of loneliness; the sensation of having been deserted and excluded. Surely, she couldn't be jealous of her own child?

Blake had only been gone half an hour when

Jaime ignored his instructions. None of the books he had left her appealed, but on the study shelves she recognised the dust jacket of what she realised must be his second novel. She had read his first one without recognising that the writer was her husband. His second hadn't been published in paperback yet. She managed to struggle out of her chair and across to the shelves, despite her stiff limbs, and within half an hour she was so deeply engrossed in Blake's novel that she no longer noticed her bodily discomfort.

Set in Central America, it was a gripping story for which he had obviously drawn on his own El Salvador experiences, and Jaime felt humbled by Blake's compassionate grasp of the feelings of the peasant army described in his book. His descriptions gave her a far deeper insight into the problems of the area than any newspaper stories had ever done. His heroine, the young, initially naive American reporter, sent out by her newspaper to get a 'human interest story slanted in favour of the United States' was so well drawn that Jaime found herself jealous of the character and wondered whom Blake had based her on. Obviously not her. She didn't possess a single jot of that girl's courage or intelligence. Her love affair with the guerilla leader made Jaime's heart ache in anguished sympathy as the girl was torn between what she saw as her duty and her love for a man so much removed from her culture and background. When, in the end, they were both killed in an ambush, Jaime felt tears sting her eyes. The love scenes between them had been pure poetry. How could it have happened that Blake had possessed this sensitivity; this intense well of emotion that he used so apparently effortlessly on paper, that she had never known was there?

When she had finished the book, Jaime dozed for a while. Mrs Simmonds rang to sympathise about her accident and to assure her that Fern was welcome for as long as Jaime wanted her to have her.

'And, of course, I can't say how pleased we are that you and Blake . . . (the Reverend Simmonds had married Jaime and Blake in the village church) . . . are back together again. I know your mother always hoped it would happen.'

Had she? It was news to Jaime, who suspected Mrs Simmonds was guilty of a little romantic daydreaming. When she replaced the receiver, she felt nervously tense. Although she knew Blake wouldn't have deliberately given the impression that they were reconciled, it was going to be very embarrassing explaining once he had gone. She would just have to say that the reconciliation hadn't worked out. Only *she* would know just how much she wished it might have been real.

She must have dozed off to sleep again because the next thing Jaime knew was that she could hear Caroline calling Blake's name. She came bursting into the study, coming to an abrupt halt when she saw Jaime.

'Where's Blake?' she demanded peremptorily.

Jaime noticed that her make-up wasn't as

immaculate as usual and her face seemed oddly flushed.

'Out, I'm afraid. In Dorchester. Caroline . . .' Jaime took a deep breath, coming to a sudden decision, 'I've told the police about the threats you and Barrons have been making. I know who was behind that attack on the studio—who arranged for the brakes to fail on my car.'

Caroline attempted to laugh . . . but her high colour betrayed her.

'All right, it's true,' she said defiantly, 'but you'll regret going to the police, Jaime, when they trace everything back to Blake.' She laughed victoriously when she saw Jaime's stricken expression. 'Blake's been in it right from the beginning,' she said triumphantly. 'He agreed with me that I ought to be able to sell the Abbey to whomever I wanted. It is mine, and I need the money.'

'Blake agreed. . . .'

'Agreed! It was his idea,' Caroline told her. 'Oh, I know you're still crazy about him, Jaime. That's what we counted on.'

Jaime felt dizzily sick. Never had she visualised this cruelty. She couldn't believe it of Blake, wouldn't have believed it, but Caroline's voice was telling her it was true.

'You'd better go back to the police and tell them that you made a mistake. Unless you want Blake to end up in gaol. Guy Barron's a very generous man, as both Blake and I have discovered. . . .'

Barrons had paid Blake. . . . No. She wouldn't

believe that. She tried to cry out a protest, but a thick, inky blackness was enveloping her.

'Jaime, I have to see Blake,' she heard Caroline saying urgently. 'You must tell him when he comes back that I want to see him . . . Jaime. . . .'

The world seemed to tilt forward as she tried to shake off Caroline's fingers, tipping her into an inky black sea whose waters closed suffocatingly over her.

It was the sound of the telephone ringing imperiously close to her ear that brought Jaime back to consciousness. She was slumped across Blake's desk and she reached automatically for the receiver, trying to clear her mind.

'Jaime?'

She recognised the anxiety in Mrs Simmonds' voice and knew instantly. She had heard the description, 'a cold fist clutched her heart', but had not known until then just what it meant. Something, some terrible, unbelievable fear had her heart in such a grip that its freezing touch almost burned.

'Jaime, it's Fern,' Mrs Simmonds said tearfully. 'She's gone, and we can't find her. One minute she was playing in the garden with the twins . . . the next. I've alerted the police. . . . Is Blake . . .?'

'He isn't here.' Her voice was an agonised croak. Where was Blake when she needed him? When Fern needed him? If anything, the paralysing grip on her heart became tighter. Was there some

special significance in his absence? Had he
known. . . . But no . . . no . . . Blake was Fern's
father. . . .

The moment Mrs Simmonds hung up, Jaime
dialled Caroline's number with tense fingers. As
she had half-anticipated, there was no response.
She stood up cursing the weak trembling of her
limbs. Where ' was the telephone directory?
Feverishly she searched under B, but there was
no listing for Barrons. Dear God, where was
Fern? . . . Where was Blake?

It was half an hour before she heard the sound
of Blake's car. Half an hour in which she cursed
her isolation and immobility. Where was Fern?
Where had they taken her? Jaime was in no doubt
that she had been kidnapped on Guy Barron's
instructions. Hadn't she already been threatened
by one of his men?

'Blake . . .' she was half hysterical by the time
she heard Blake's footsteps outside the study,
wrenching open the door, only to stand there,
white and shivering, as she looked from his bleak
face to the small bundle in his arms.

'No, Jaime. . . . She's all right; just tired out,'
he said huskily, correctly interpreting her
thoughts. 'She'd fallen out with the ' twins and
decided to come home on her own apparently,
only, of course, she got lost. The police used
tracker dogs and they found her almost straight
away.'

'Mummy . . .' the bundle in Blake's arms
stirred drowsily. Fern's small wan face appearing
from amidst the blankets. 'I went for a walk and

got lost, then this big doggie came and licked my face. Mummy, can we have a doggie?'

Torn between tears and laughter, Jaime knew that in that instant she would have promised her daughter anything, but Blake intervened.

'We shall have to see about that young lady. It seems to me that people who go off on their own when they aren't supposed to don't deserve to have a dog.'

Blake's firmly assured manner was what Fern needed right now, Jaime acknowledged. She herself was poised on the brink of too many powerful emotions to deal properly with the situation. Fern had obviously not suffered at all— unlike herself, but in many ways she was a sensitive child and Jaime did not want her to pick up on her own anxiety.

'Straight to bed with you, chicken,' Blake continued firmly. 'I'll take you up and then I'll bring you some supper.'

'Mummy, will you read to me?' Fern appealed tiredly, 'a story about a doggie.'

Her bruised legs had stiffened up too much for Jaime to follow them upstairs. 'Wait there,' Blake ordered tersely. 'I'll come back down for you.'

It was five minutes before he returned. Five minutes in which Jaime managed to convince herself that she wasn't dreaming and that Fern was safe and well.

'I would have rung you from the Vicarage, but I was anxious to get back with Fern. I knew how you must have been feeling. Mrs Simmonds had no right. . . .'

'To what? To tell me that my daughter was missing?' Anger flashed in Jaime's eyes. 'Then whom should she have told? Fern's father? The father who. . . .' She couldn't go on. Sobs rose up and choked back the words, and then she was in Blake's arms, her head pressed comfortingly into his shoulder.

'It's all right . . .' he was rocking her as though she were Fern's age. 'Cry it all out. . . . My poor darling, I know how you must have been feeling. It was enough for me when I arrived early to pick Fern up and discovered what had happened.'

Blake didn't know how she had been feeling, Jaime thought numbly. He didn't know that she had believed that Fern had been kidnapped, and had not really gone missing—he didn't know that she had thought him responsible.

'Come on. I'll carry you upstairs and then bring up something for Fern to eat. Children are amazing aren't they? Do you know, the very first thing she said to me was "I'm hungry, Daddy"?'

Blake was carrying her upstairs, speaking quietly and soothingly to her, his voice stroking gently over her jagged nerves, easing her away from the precipice of hysteria on which she had hovered. By the time they reached Fern's room, she was sufficiently in control of herself to smile wanly at her daughter.

Fern was tucked up safely in bed, fast asleep, but still Jaime couldn't bring herself to leave her bedside.

'Come on, I'll carry you to your own room, and then I'll bring you something to eat.'

'Blake, I'm not hungry,' Jaime protested. 'I couldn't eat a thing.'

'You must, you're getting too thin as it is. I notice you disobeyed my instruction this morning. My book,' he said dryly, 'I found it on the study floor. Not an indication of how you felt about it, I trust.'

'No . . . I loved it, especially your heroine,' she admitted half shyly. 'Who on earth did you model her on, or is she a figment of your imagination?'

'I only know one lady who comes anywhere near to approaching Helen for courage and intelligence,' Blake responded, but he didn't tell her who he meant, and Jaime wondered agonisingly if, somewhere in Blake's life during the time they had been apart, there had been a woman he had loved as he had never loved her, but who, apparently, had not loved him equally in return.

'The book must have fallen on the floor when Caroline called,' she told him.

'Caroline came here?' His glance sharpened. 'Did she say what she wanted?'

'Yes, she wanted to see you—quite urgently. I forgot about it completely when Fern went missing.'

'Then I'd better go and see her.' His voice was clipped, and Jaime wondered bitterly what it was Caroline possessed that could make Blake rush so eagerly to her side. Whatever it was, she didn't share it, she thought moodily.

Once Blake had gone, she felt too mentally exhausted to sleep. Fern. . . . She shuddered

deeply, forcing her aching limbs to carry her
from her own room to Fern's. Blake had left a
chair drawn up by the bed, and Jaime subsided
into it, watching her daughter's sleeping face
avidly.

Dear God . . . if anything had happened to
Fern. Gradually, the tension started to leave her
body. She knew she ought to go back to bed, but
the compulsion to stay where she was was too
strong. Her eyes closed, her breathing evening
out as sleep claimed her.

CHAPTER EIGHT

JAIME tensed, awareness returning as she felt someone touch her shoulder. It was her worst nightmare come true. They had come for Fern. She tried to get up, only to be attacked by a dizzying spate of pins and needles in her cramped legs.

'Jaime, keep still. I'm going to carry you back to bed.'

Blake! Reality returned, banishing her dark imaginings. Of course, she and Fern were with Blake at the Lodge, and she had fallen asleep beside Fern's bed.

Her thin nightgown was no protection against the chill night air, and Jaime shivered, feeling Blake's arms tighten around her in response.

'You're trembling.' His voice had an oddly hoarse undertone to it.

'I'm cold.' She was stiff as well, her bruised body screaming its painful protest as Blake put her down on the bed and her muscles refused to unlock.

'What's the matter? Did I hurt you?'

Blake knew the room well enough not to have needed to switch the light on, and now Jaime could see him in the soft moonlight flowing in through the uncurtained window. His hair was tousled, his face unusually drawn.

'I'm all right—just stiff,' she told him, and then, because she was reluctant to let him go, she added hesitantly, 'Did you see Caroline?'

His face became so shuttered that she wished she hadn't spoken. She had obviously intruded where she wasn't wanted.

'Yes.' His response was terse. 'I'll get you something for those stiff muscles; otherwise, you'll wake up later with cramp. Stay there.'

'As if there was the slightest chance of moving anywhere,' Jaime thought wearily, closing her eyes. They flew back open the moment she heard Blake's firm foot tread on the polished wooden floor.

'What is it?' she demanded suspiciously, as he approached holding a small bottle. 'Horse liniment?'

Blake laughed, the warm natural sound making Jaime realise anew how much she had missed his laughter.

'No, it's something I had last year when I pulled a muscle in my calf. It has to be massaged in. I'll do it for you.'

'He's just feeling sorry for you,' Jaime reminded herself as she felt the first, soothing movements of Blake's fingers against her skin. Her muscles seemed to relax in obedience to his comforting stroking, although Jaime did tense when he pushed aside the hem of her nightdress and gently kneaded the aching muscles of her thigh. She knew she ought to tell him to stop. There was too much potential danger in letting him continue. Already, she was acutely aware of him; already she longed to reach out and run her fingers down his spine, to feel his body clench in the familiar prelude to lovemaking she remembered so well.

'Better now?'

At the withdrawal of his hands, a surge of disappointment swept over her. What had she expected? That somehow the deft hands that had soothed away her pain would become those of a lover?

'Yes . . . yes . . . fine.' Her voice was muffled as she pushed back the covers and crawled into the cold double bed. She could hear Blake moving towards the door, and childishly closed her eyes, burying her face in the pillow so that she wouldn't see him go.

As she tried in vain to sleep, she could hear him moving about, going into the bathroom, the steady hiss of the shower tormenting her with a thousand vivid pictures of his nude body. She was so busy trying to suppress them that she didn't realise that Blake was back in her room until she glanced up and saw him standing by the other side of the bed, a towel wrapped round his hips. The moonlight outlined the powerful lines of his body.

'Move over,' he said casually.

Blake intended to sleep *here*, with her? On the verge of protesting, Jaime was silenced when Blake continued, 'It's no use arguing, Jaime. You need someone with you tonight, if only to keep the nightmares at bay. Perhaps we both do,' he added in a sombre undertone. So Blake remembered the night terrors that sometimes haunted her dreams! It had only happened on three or four occasions during their marriage. Irrational and terrifying nightmares containing the father she had never known—a father she was constantly trying and failing to reach.

Lost in her thoughts, it was several seconds before Jaime realised that Blake was calmly removing the towel.

'You can't sleep with me like that...' she protested thickly, wondering irrationally why she was the one who felt the hot flush of embarrassment, and dragged her eyes away. Out of the corner of her eye, she saw Blake's brief shrug.

'Don't be silly, Jaime. I always sleep this way, you should know that.'

She felt the bed depress as he got in beside her and held her body taut, creeping as close to her edge as she could without falling off; her breath held in her chest in a painfully tight ball.

Almost within minutes, Blake was asleep, the even rise and fall of his breathing calming the heavy thud of her heart. Beneath the covers she could feel the heat of his body reaching out to her, warming her chilled back. More than anything else on earth, she wanted to turn round and creep closer to him, cuddling up to him as she used to do. The harder she fought the compulsion, the stronger it grew, until, at last, with a small groan of self-contempt, she turned over, drawn inexorably towards Blake's warm back.

Some time later, Jaime was drowsily aware of

Blake turning over, in his sleep, his arm automatically curving below her breasts and round her back as he settled more comfortably against the contours of her body. Jaime knew she ought to move away, but the temptation to stay where she was was too great. Ignoring all the urgings of common sense which told her she ought to move while she still could, she nestled closer to Blake's warm body. The hand that had been supporting the small of her back moved to cup her breast. Jaime tensed as Blake moved in his sleep, her mind a complete blank as she tried to find an excuse to explain away her presence in his arms if he should wake. Panic stealing away her previous contentment, she tried to move, and found that she could not. Blake growled protestingly in his sleep, his hand closing more possessively on her body.

'Jaime?'

Jaime tensed as she heard the sleep-slurred question in his voice. 'Why on earth are you wearing this damned thing?' Blake continued. 'You know I like to feel you against me.'

He thought they were still living together, was Jaime's first agonised thought. Still drugged by sleep, Blake believed they were still lovers.

'Blake . . .' she protested uncertainly, 'Blake. . . .'

'Umm. I'm here.' He nuzzled the vulnerable arch of her throat, his free hand curling around it, his fingers stroking gently across her skin.

Tiny fires started to burn wherever he touched, and Jaime shivered in mute response, knowing she should wake him up properly and stop him, and yet, despairingly, knowing at the same time that she was too weak to do so. She was here, in his arms, where she had longed to be so often in the long years they had been apart, her body already craving more than the gentle drift of his fingers against her skin and the warmth of his mouth tracing lazy kisses along her jaw.

The fingers that had been tugging at her nightgown finally worked it free of her arm, and then returned to cup the smooth pale flesh of the breast they had exposed.

His touch was as light as a sigh, Jaime thought lost in a daze of pleasure, and as potentially dangerous as dynamite. She stretched out her hand, genuinely intending to push him away, but the moment her fingers came into contact with the smooth wall of his chest, the touch she had intended as a repudiation became a hesitant caress.

Beneath her fingertips she could feel his soft body hair, and, as though magnetised to it, her fingers stole downwards.

'Umm, that's good.'

Jaime tensed. Her senses responding against her will to the husky, male appreciation in Blake's voice. Confined by the warmth of his hand, she could feel her breast swelling yearningly, shuddering when Blake stroked his thumb softly against her nipple in recognition of her arousal.

'Touch me again, Jaime.' His voice seemed to come from deep inside him, a sensual purr that she could feel reverberating through his body. 'Let's get this thing off.'

Deft hands tugged the whole nightie off. Blake wasn't anywhere near halfway asleep now, and must know that they were no longer living as man and wife, but it was as though a spell had been put on Jaime's speech, preventing her from bringing it to his attention. Instead she gazed bemusedly up at him as he lowered her back against the mattress, gently holding her hands at her sides as she automatically tried to conceal her nakedness from him.

'No, let me look.'

His gaze was almost a caress in itself, leaving her pliant and trembling, feeling that her body was a precious sacrifice that she must yield up to him.

'Jaime.' Her name left his lips on a whisper, as he kneeled beside her, bending over her until his body blocked out the light, cupping her face gently in both hands as he kissed her.

The touch of his lips was almost tentative, searching, delicate, almost as though she were some timid woodland creature he was frightened of chasing away. Indeed, in many ways, his hesitant caress was more seductive than a more fiercely passionate demand because it gave Jaime the confidence to relax, to let her lips and body flower into ripe awareness, like a flower opening up to the sun.

Gradually, the pressure of Blake's kiss increased, but Jaime was barely aware of it doing so. All of her was concentrated on responding

in counter to the fiercely sweet music Blake
was playing. In concert, they seemed to move
together, her mouth opening, her tongue tasting,
her body yielding even before Blake touched it.

Gently releasing her mouth, Blake commanded
huskily,

'Open your eyes.'

Obediently, Jaime did so, meeting the green
depths of Blake's. It was almost as though he
hypnotised her; as though she were unable to
withdraw her gaze from his as he released her
face and slowly stroked his fingers down her
throat. Jaime raised her hands, automatically
wanting to touch him, but Blake shook his head
and said softly, 'Not yet.'

He had reached the valley between her breasts,
cupping them both. Trembling with tension,
Jaime followed his gaze down her body. His eyes
seemed to smoulder as he studied the twin pink
crests. When he bent his head and slowly
anointed each burgeoning nipple with the moist
warmth of his mouth, Jaime shuddered in
helpless reaction, her self-control splintering.

'Blake.' He made no move to stop her when her
arms tightened round him, her trembling mouth
pressing wild kisses against his skin. Where it had
simply felt comfortingly warm when she had
cuddled against him, now it burned. His mouth
scorched her skin as tenderness gave way to
passion, forcing her to cry out his name and be
granted the immediate surcease of the caresses
her body craved. Everything about him was
familiar, and yet achingly exciting. His hand

stroking her thigh made her arch and ache with pleasure, his mouth against her breast unleashing the husky cries of need he seemed so hungry to hear.

In a frenzy of arousal, Jaime mimicked his caresses. Her tongue found and brushed his flat, male nipples, her hand stroked the smooth skin of his belly, the kisses she placed there making him groan and reach for her.

'Dear God, Jaime,' Blake muttered rawly into her parted mouth, 'If this is what it results in, I'll have to arrange for Fern to go missing more often.'

If the earth had rocked beneath her, it couldn't have had a more cataclysmic effect on Jaime. Her body tensed, her voice hoarse with pain, she said thickly, 'Don't you mean "again"? I know all about it Blake,' she continued bleakly, 'all about how you agreed with Caroline; how the three of you worked out your plan. You wanted Charles to leave the committee, and you thought you could get him to do it through me, hence that attack on the school, my wonky brakes ... but to threaten to hurt Fern ... your own child. I know you never wanted her, but. . . .' She was crying, forcing the bleak words out between sobs, wondering how she had ever found Blake's body warm and secure. Now she could almost feel the icy cold coming off it, freezing through her.

'Say that again. . . .' His voice sounded completely flat, almost dangerous in some strange way.

'I know you never wanted Fern,' Jaime hiccoughed.

'No, not that.... All that rubbish about Caroline and me.'

'It isn't rubbish. I didn't want to believe it ... but Caroline told me the truth this afternoon, when I threatened her with the police.'

'And when Fern went missing, you thought. . . .' Blake began slowly.

'I thought that your threat had been carried out. That's what the man who came to the school told me ... but I couldn't believe. . . .'

'But you *did* believe, didn't you?' Blake said furiously angry. 'You believed I was a party to this harrassment of you ... that I would actually condone behaviour which could hurt my own child. No wonder you left me, Jaime,' he said bitterly, 'I never realised before quite how low your opinion of me was. Well, for your information, until now I had no idea you were being threatened.'

'You mean, you didn't know about why the school was attacked and my brakes tampered with?' Hope flared inside her, only to die as she saw Blake's momentary hesitation.

'I certainly had no part in it,' he said at last, but Jaime had not received the answer she had wanted. Blake *had* known, and knowing had done nothing to stop it.

'Blake, I think it's best if Fern and I go home tomorrow,' she said tiredly.

'No!' The sharp denial pierced through her. 'No, Jaime, you're both staying where you are, or are you frightened that I might do the pair of you further harm, poison perhaps. . . .'

'No . . . no . . . of course not. . . .'

'Right then, you're both staying here, at least until your mother gets back. You can hardly think I'd let any harm come to you under my own roof,' he added sardonically. 'Work it out for yourself, Jaime. If I am as involved with Caroline's machinations as you seem to think, then you're safer here than anywhere else.'

'And *are* you involved?' She held her breath, waiting for the answer. Only she knew how much she longed for him to deny it, but, to her anguish, he slid out of bed, leaning towards her.

'Have you so little faith in me that you need to ask, Jaime? Some wife you are . . . but then, you never did trust me, did you?'

'Because you never gave me reason to. . . .' Jaime cried out in pain.

'Trust shouldn't need reasons,' Blake responded bitterly. 'Like love, it should be given freely. I'll go back to my own room now. You needn't worry that I'll bother you again, Jaime.'

He spoke with such an air of finality that Jaime was confused. It was almost as though, in his eyes, he was the injured party, but how could that be?

The next day, Jaime barely saw him. She heard him outside with Fern, the little girl laughing as they played, but, apart from asking her if she was feeling well enough to be downstairs, he said nothing to her. Once she had assured him that she was, he abandoned Fern into her care and shut himself in his study. The closed door seemed in some way symbolic, and Jaime felt as though he had deliberately closed it against her, shutting her out of his life. In some strange way, she felt as guilty as though she had let him down, but, surely, he was the guilty one? Hadn't she given him every opportunity to deny his involvement with Caroline and Barrons? Trust should be given freely, as he had said, and Jaime had known he wasn't talking purely about the present, but, in the past, she hadn't had the self-confidence to trust in her own ability to keep his love. And neither had she trusted him to go on loving her. *Had* she been wrong? But no ... Suzy had made it plain that he had grown bored with her. He hadn't even loved her enough to give up his job and settle down, and yet no sooner had he come back from El Salvador than he had given up newspaper reporting. Too muddled to think any further, Jaime went out into the garden to play with Fern.

'I like living with my Daddy,' the little girl told her. 'Do you, Mummy?'

What could she say?

'I want to live with him for always,' Fern protested. 'Can we, Mummy?'

How on earth was she supposed to answer her daughter? How could she explain to her that Blake probably didn't want either of them?

Mrs Simmonds called round late in the afternoon, breathless and apologetic.

'You must have been frantic when I rang you about Fern. I was myself. They say these things come in threes don't they?' she continued. 'First your accident, and then Fern getting lost.'

Jaime shivered. 'Let's hope that this time they're wrong,' she said lightly, but she felt apprehensive nevertheless, and oddly glad that she had given in to Blake and stayed at the Lodge.

When six o'clock came and went, and Blake was still working, Jaime gave Fern her tea. She had found a chicken in the freezer and casseroled it, and now a tempting aroma filled the small kitchen. There had been enough gooseberries on the half-wild bushes to make a pie, and Fern's appetite did not seem to have diminished by her adventure because she ate well, which was more than she could do, Jaime reflected watching her.

Blake's portion she put on a tray, which she placed outside the study door, simply calling out, 'Food's outside for you, Blake,' and then walking away.

She was just putting Fern to bed when she heard a dull ominous rumbling. The sound seemed to fill the room, it almost seemed as though the Lodge was shaking to its foundations, rather like an underground thunderstorm, Jaime thought hazily rushing to the window. What could it be? Surely, not an earthquake? Chiding herself for being silly, she searched the sky for signs of thunder, but there weren't any. It was clear, soft blue, the sun just beginning to set. A band of parkland hid the bulk of the Abbey from her view and, although the sound seemed to be coming from that direction, Jaime could see nothing at all.

She was halfway downstairs when she heard the 'phone ring. The tray had disappeared from outside the study, but Blake was obviously still inside because he answered the 'phone almost straight away.

Seconds later, Jaime almost collided with him as he hurried out, pulling on his leather jerkin as he did so.

'I've got to get up to the Abbey,' he told her tersely. 'Stay here and keep the door locked until I get back.'

Before she could question him further, he was gone. Jaime was surprised to see him running through the garden, using the old track that ran from the Lodge to the house. If he was in such a rush, why wasn't he using the Ferrari? Obedient to his instructions, she locked and barred the old-fashioned door, checking that the French windows in the study were closed and locked. Fear shivered through her. What was happening? Why had he gone to the Abbey?

She had almost given up all hope of him returning when he eventually came back. She was sitting in the kitchen, and his brief rap on the door startled her.

'Jaime, open up, it's me, Blake,' he commanded tersely. When Jaime opened the door, she was surprised to see smudges of dirt on his face. His jacket had been torn, and there were more smears of dirt on his shirt.

'Make me a cup of coffee, would you?' he asked tiredly, dropping into a chair.

Jaime was longing to ask him why he had gone

to the Abbey, but pride put a guard on her tongue. As she handed him a mug of coffee she noticed that the skin across the knuckles of his right hand was split and bleeding. Her small gasp of alarm drew Blake's attention to his hand.

'What happened?'

'Nothing,' he told her brusquely, 'Look, I'm tired. I think I'll go to bed if you don't mind. I need an early start in the morning. I have to go to London.'

Never before had he rejected her so coldly. Jaime was still recoiling from the shock of it when he left the kitchen. Well, what had she expected, she wondered bitterly, automatically rinsing their empty mugs. That he would be so thrilled to find she had waited up for him so that he would take her in his arms and . . . 'Oh, stop it,' she urged herself. 'Stop hurting yourself. You know he doesn't love you.'

She was awake in time to see him leaving in the morning. It was the sound of the Ferrari that woke her, but, as she hurried to the window, it was towards the Abbey that he was driving—not away from it. Ten minutes later, the powerful black car reappeared, but this time Blake wasn't the only passenger. Caroline was sitting beside him.

A despair such as she had never known before overwhelmed Jaime. She couldn't stay in the Lodge a moment longer she decided. She would have to go home.

She was just on the verge of telephoning for a taxi when the sound of a car took her to the

window. An unfamiliar saloon car was pulling up
outside the Lodge. Someone was getting out. Her
mother, Jaime recognised on a wave of disbelief,
and Henry; and what was more, they were
holding hands and looking at one another for all
the world as though. . . . In a daze, she opened
the door.

'Darling,' her mother carolled, 'Guess what?'
She brandished her left hand, displaying the
brand new engagement and wedding rings.

'But. . . .'

'Let's go inside and have a cup of tea,' Henry
suggested practically, 'and we'll tell you all about
it. I must say, if I'd known the softening effect it
was likely to have on her, I'd have taken your
mother to Rome years ago.'

'You're married!' Jaime exclaimed stupidly, as
she filled the kettle, 'but. . . .'

'By special licence, my dear, no less,' Sarah
announced, grinning.

'Yes, once she agreed to marry me, I couldn't
risk her changing her mind,' Henry put in. 'I got
everything arranged as quickly as I could and we
flew into London yesterday. Just in time to tie
the knot.'

'We would have loved you to have been there,
darling,' her mother broke in, 'but when I
'phoned Blake, he explained how bruised and
battered you were.'

'You 'phoned Blake,' Jaime gasped, 'but. . . .'

'Well, at first, I rang the cottage, and then,
when I couldn't get any reply, I 'phoned Mrs
Widdows. She told me you and Blake were back

together, so naturally, I rang him. I asked him to keep our news a surprise though, so that we could tell you ourselves. Not that I'm the only one keeping secrets, and I can't tell you how happy I am about yours, darling. You were never somehow complete without Blake, and I always wondered if you hated him quite as much as you professed to.'

'Mother. . . .' Jaime tried to break into her mother's excited conversation to tell her the truth, but Henry forestalled her, dropping a bombshell which stunned her. 'Actually, we're rather glad about the reconciliation for selfish reasons. Your mother and I have decided to move to Bath. I have a friend there who's selling his antique business. It's a very good one, but rather pricey, but with what we'll get for ours, plus the sale of the cottage, we should have enough.'

Jaime just didn't know what to say. With one blow, she was losing everything, and Mrs Simmonds' pessimistic pronouncement came back to her. While she tried to recover from the blow, she was aware of her mother and Henry glowing like a pair of teenagers, no doubt waiting for her congratulations.

Pulling herself together, Jaime hugged and kissed them both, chiding herself for her selfishness. Of course, she was pleased to see them, it was just that she hadn't bargained for losing her mother and her home quite so unexpectedly. Another thought struck her. How could she tell them the truth about Blake and herself now? If she did, her mother would immediately realise that she had no home to go to. No, Jaime thought determinedly, she mustn't spoil their happiness. It would mean asking Blake to participate in the charade but, hopefully, not for very long. She would have to find lodgings for herself and Fern somewhere in the village eventually, which wouldn't be easy, and she would have to work even harder at the studio. Not for the first time, Jaime recognised how much she had relied on her mother's support, both moral and financial. What if Blake wouldn't agree? Jaime could hardly bear to think about it. He *had* to. He *had* to. All at once, she was in a fever of impatience for him to get back.

'Where is Blake, by the way?' her mother asked.

'In London—on business. . . .'

'Well, we won't stay. We just wanted to give you our good news. Henry wants to take us all out to dinner on Sunday—a post-wedding celebration. We're staying at the cottage tonight. . . .'

'I'll come round tomorrow then, and we'll have a chat,' Jaime responded. 'Most of our things are still there. . . .'

'Yes, Blake told me the Lodge was only a temporary arrangement,' her mother agreed, bending to kiss both Jaime and Fern who had been listening to the adult conversation with great interest.

'Are you now my grandpa?' she astounded them all by asking Henry as they prepared to leave.

'Do you want me to be?'

'Yes,' she said, with such simple enthusiasm that they all laughed. Henry picked her up until their faces were level, 'Then I will be.'

'Now I've got a daddy and a grandpa,' she exclaimed, with very evident relish, when Henry put her down.

The Lodge seemed unappealingly quiet when they had gone. Just what had she got herself into, Jaime wondered, in a fever of torment for Blake to return. If he refused to help her, what on earth was she going to do? How did he really feel about Caroline? He had not mentioned divorce, and yet he seemed eager to rush to Caroline's side at her slightest bidding. He had wanted her to stay at the Lodge, and yet he had not denied that he had been involved in those threats against her. Sighing, Jaime walked round the Lodge.

She had put Fern to bed, and now time seemed to drag as she waited for Blake to return. She wandered into his study and curled up in his deep leather chair, finding comfort in the faint scent of his body which clung to the leather.

CHAPTER NINE

'Jaime?'

Jaime opened her eyes muzzily. She could hear feet pounding down the stairs.

'In here, Blake,' she called out, stretching stiff limbs and glancing at her watch. Eleven o'clock! Could she really have been asleep that long? The handle of the study door turned, and Blake walked in. His eyebrows met in a heavy frown, a look she was unfamiliar with shadowing his eyes.

'I thought you'd left.'

'Without Fern? I was waiting up for you. . . .'

'How flattering.' He seemed to be in a strange mood, moving restlessly round the room, picking up and then discarding various articles.

'Jaime.'

'Blake.'

They both spoke together.

'Ladies first.' Blake made her a brief bow.

Now that the moment was here, Jaime just didn't know what to say. 'Blake, please let me live here so that my mother thinks we've been reconciled.'? 'Blake, my mother thinks. . . .'?

'Blake.' Her voice cracked over his, and she tried again. 'Blake, my mother came round this afternoon.'

He had been reaching for the decanter that stood on the shelf and now his hand stilled. 'Yes?'

The word was curiously without any depth of emotion, as though he was deliberately trying to give off a calm he was far from feeling.

Jaime took a deep breath.

'I know you know about her marriage. I'm pleased for them both, of course, but there are problems.' She risked a look into his face, and wished she hadn't when she saw the brooding darkness there.

'She . . . that is, they . . . believe that we're reconciled, and she wants to sell the cottage.' It all came out in a rush with Jaime nervously twisting her fingers together. 'Blake, I. . . .'

'And?'

Dear God, how on earth was she going to ask him? In the end, there was only one way. 'And I was hoping you would agree to let Fern and me live here with you—as though we *were* reconciled,' she added baldly, so that there couldn't be any misunderstanding, 'at least, until they sell the cottage. They need the money, you see,' she added desperately, 'they want to buy a business and move to Bath, but if mother thinks she has to be responsible for Fern and me. . . .'

'As opposed to thinking *I* am responsible for you, I suppose you mean. . . . Do you honestly realise what you're asking me, Jaime?'

'Yes.' How small and weak her voice sounded as she shrank beneath the biting lash of his voice.

'Yesterday, you couldn't wait to get away from me, and yet now you're telling me that you want to stay.'

'I realise it's an imposition, Blake.' Suddenly

her courage returned, 'But if you hadn't dragged me here in the first place, no one would have thought we were reconciled. . . .'

'And that being the case, it is incumbent upon me to see that the deception continues. Very well. . . .'

'You mean . . . you mean we can stay?'

'Yes.'

He had his back to her, and Jaime couldn't see his face, but his voice was as cold as arctic ice.

'And now, if you don't mind, I'd like my study to myself for a while. I've got some clearing up to do.'

Knowing that she was being dismissed Jaime walked out of the room on very unsteady legs. Blake had agreed to her request, but, instead of feeling relieved, all she could feel was an aching emptiness.

'Look, Mummy, a picture of Daddy,' Fern flung herself on to the bed, thrusting the local paper under Jaime's nose. She picked it up, reading the headline in disbelief.

'Well-known writer and local police foil attempt to destroy building of historical importance.' As her eyes slid over the printed lines, Jaime felt as though she had strayed into a completely unfamiliar world, one in which Caroline had apparently been intimidated by Barrons into agreeing to sell them the Abbey, only to change her mind and decide instead to sell it to another buyer—someone who wasn't named but who wished to keep the Abbey as a private home and preserve it. Blake had apparently played along with Barrons, pretending to support their plans in order to gain inside information on them.

The news that a bulldozer had been driven into the Abbey grounds had alerted the police to the fact that Barrons had decided to take matters into their own hands and force Caroline to sell to them by destroying part of the building. Blake, summoned by a terrified Caroline, had succeeded in knocking out the bulldozer driver, and preventing any damage, before the police arrived to take control.

Jaime put down the paper with a white face, scraps of conversation returning to mock her. 'Are you involved . . .?' she had said, and Blake had avoided answering her. 'Trust should be given freely,' he had said, and she had not understood, had not wanted to understand. Blake had known because of his self-appointed role, and, knowing, had tried his best to protect Fern and herself by taking them into his own home. That was why he had insisted on them moving to the Lodge, not because he particularly wanted them there.

As Jaime heard his footsteps on the stairs, shame washed over her, and then pride came to her rescue.

'I see you're quite a hero,' she announced gaily, as he walked in, carrying a mug of coffee.

'The local rag's made it all seem much more important than it was. I knew about Barrons' reputation from a documentary a friend of mine in television had been working on. As soon as I put Caroline wise, she began to have second thoughts about selling to them, especially as there was another . . . interested party, but she couldn't withdraw very easily. You weren't the only one to be threatened by Barrons' strong-arm team.'

'And the bulldozer?'

'A rather hackneyed method of getting rid of unwanted old buildings. Barrons no doubt thought that knocking down a wall or two would panic Caroline into selling to them, and then they could pull the whole thing down—get it listed as unsafe. It's been done before. All it needs is a greedy council official.'

'So that was that rumbling sound I heard the other night,' Jaime breathed, 'and your knuckles. . . .'

Blake caught the consternation in her voice and said coolly,

'The bulldozer driver came off much the worse of the pair of us—he was ten years older and running to fat. Strong enough to frighten a woman on her own, but something of a coward once he was removed from behind his machine.'

'Even so. . . .' She wanted to say that she had misjudged him dreadfully, and to beg his forgiveness, but how did one beg forgiveness for a sin, the enormity of which she was only just beginning to realise?

'Jaime, in view of all the publicity about this affair and the fact that Barrons are still bound to be feeling slightly raw, shall we say, I think it advisable for the three of us to go away—it won't

seem too unexpected in view of all the circumstances. After all, we have just been reconciled.'

Jaime winced, wondering if she was being
oversensitive to sense derision beneath the calmly
spoken words.

'Away?'

'Yes.' Blake wasn't looking at her. 'A friend of
mine owns a cottage in Pembroke. I've spoken to
him by telephone and arranged to rent it from
him for a couple of weeks. That should give all
this fuss time to die down.'

'Pembroke,' Jaime stared at him with tear-
sheened, disbelieving eyes, 'You mean the one
where we spent our honeymoon?'

'You remember it?' Blake's eyes were hard. 'I
am surprised. You left me with such unflattering
alacrity, I'm also surprised to see how senti-
mentally it affects you.'

She wanted to cry out and scream, but her
vocal chords were frozen in a paroxysm of pain.
How could Blake do this to her?

He had left the room before she could object,
coming back minutes later to add, 'We're leaving
tomorrow. I've arranged to hire a saloon car. It
will be more comfortable for the three of us than
the Ferrari.'

'I'll need to go back to . . . to the cottage, to pack.'

'I'll drive you there on my way to pick up the
hire car. Fern can come with me. . . . Unless, of
course, you're still frightened that I intend to
arrange her abduction.' He said it with such soft
savagery that Jaime went white with the cruelty
of the thrust.

'I'm sorry I misread the situation, but how was I to know any differently?'

'How indeed?' Blake's cold voice mocked her. 'Of course, it was only natural to assume that her father would lay her open to such danger; that indeed I should want to terrify and potentially injure you both. I suppose you even think I tampered with your brakes personally! Dear God, Jaime,' he burst out in a sudden explosive outburst, 'surely, you know I'd never. . . .'

'Not the car . . .' Jaime agreed in a stricken voice, 'but I think it was only meant to frighten me. If I hadn't had to brake for that child . . . and it was only threats where Fern was concerned . . . I just thought, when she went missing . . .' She swallowed hard, trying to control her shivering body.

'And yet you still let me make love to you,' Blake said softly.

'I. . . .' What on earth could she say to him, 'I couldn't help myself. I still love you . . .'? She shuddered, rejecting both explanations.

'No, don't tell me,' Blake intervened. 'I don't think I want to know.'

'Why did *you* make love to me?'

Jaime could hardly believe she had asked such a question. A curious expression crossed Blake's face.

'I don't think I can tell you the answer to that,' he said at last. 'It isn't very flattering to either of us.'

Hot colour scorched Jaime's face as he left the room. He meant that he had made love to her simply because she had been there, and she had not repudiated him, but, at least, he had not guessed her secret; he did not know that she still loved him.

Her mother expressed no surprise at learning they were going away. 'I think it's the best thing for all three of you,' she said calmly. 'You need time on your own as a family, and you're not likely to get it with everyone in the village wanting first-hand information about Blake's heroism.'

When Blake heard about the proposed dinner party he decided they would delay their departure until the Sunday.

'Good,' Jaime's mother pronounced when Jaime telephoned her with the news, 'That gives us time to go shopping on Saturday.'

'What on earth for?' Jaime asked her. 'I thought you bought plenty of new clothes before you went away.'

'I did,' she agreed, 'but you haven't. It seems to me that a second honeymoon, albeit with a small daughter in tow, calls for something a little more glamorous than the jeans and T-shirts that make up your wardrobe.'

'Pembroke is very quiet, Mother,' Jaime expostulated. 'We won't be dressing up to go out.'

'I wasn't thinking about when you go *out*,' her mother said mysteriously. 'I'll pick you up on Saturday morning. Blake can look after Fern.'

'Isn't it amazing how men change their minds about children once they arrive?' Sarah asked with a chuckle on Saturday morning as she and Jaime drove away from the Lodge. 'Fern can wind Blake round her little finger already.'

'Umm.' Jaime found she didn't want to talk about Blake's very obvious love for his daughter. She daren't allow herself to think about it because, if she did, she would have to face up to the problems there would be when she and Blake parted. In her eagerness not to spoil her mother's happiness she had completely overlooked the potentially devastating effects of her deception on Fern. Already, the little girl looked upon Blake as a permanent feature of her life. How would she feel when she realised that he wasn't?

'You're very gloomy.'

'Not really,' Jaime forced a smile and began to chatter enthusiastically about the coming holiday.

'Here we are,' Sarah parked deftly in front of a small shop Jaime had never noticed before. The window was decorated with a plain pink skirt and a toning silk-knit jumper.

'Italian,' her mother pronounced approvingly. 'This is my second time around wedding present to you, Jaime, so I'm going to choose.'

Half an hour later Jaime stood bemusedly by as her mother insisted on adding yet another pretty blouse to the pile of clothes already on the chair. There was a skirt like the one in the window, plus a jumper and several blouses; a pair of French-cut white trousers that flattered her slim figure; a soft, silky dress in pinks and lilacs, and, last of all, a whole set of delicate, shell-pink underwear, trimmed with écru lace.

'Oh no!' Jaime protested, 'They're far too expensive . . . and so delicate. I couldn't. . . .'

'You aren't doing,' her mother reminded her firmly, 'and I'm sure Blake will appreciate them even if you don't.' She and the owner of the small boutique exchanged grins while Jaime picked up the wispy briefs that tied in small bows over her hips. In addition, there was a bra, a camisole top and matching French knickers, a suspender belt, and an underskirt, as well as a frivolous, fragile silk teddy which the owner of the boutique suggested, without a blush, that she wore in bed rather than under her clothes.

'That's what the Americans do,' she informed them.

'Really? In my day, it was Chanel No 5,' Sarah announced irrepressibly. 'I used to fantasise about some gorgeous male buying me some— with the implied, but unspoken, desire that I should wear it in bed.'

As it was nearly lunchtime when they emerged from the shop, Jaime gave in to her mother's persuasion that they eat at a small wine bar in the centre of the town. On their way to it, they passed several shops, stopping to drool over shoes and matching bags in one of them.

'Jaime, just look at this,' her mother insisted. 'You must buy it—you can wear it tonight.'

'It' was the first of the new autumn fashions, a sapphire blue angora dress to match her eyes, with a tiny belted waist and a semi-circular skirt.

The dress had a boat neck and three-quarter sleeves, the back dipping in a low V.

'It's exactly the same colour as your eyes,' her mother pronounced. 'Let's go in.'

Although she had no intention of doing so, somehow Jaime found herself in a fitting room, trying on the dress. It fitted her perfectly, and she knew it suited her. The fine, soft wool hugged her breasts and narrow waist, the skirt emphasising the long length of legs. She knew she would have to buy it.

'Now, lunch, then we'll get you some shoes to match.'

Realising that her mother wasn't going to be swayed, Jaime gave in.

It was late afternoon before they got back to the Lodge. The saloon car Blake had hired stood outside in place of the Ferrari, and, as they drove up, Jaime saw Blake and Fern emerging from the drive that led to the Abbey.

'Everything's all right,' he told Jaime, when he saw her anxious face. 'I just wanted to have a word with the security guards.'

Jaime knew that two security guards now mounted a round-the-clock watch on the Abbey, and she wondered if Blake had engaged them on Caroline's behalf or if they were employed by the new owner-to-be. She hesitated about asking Blake any questions. He had become remote and withdrawn with her, only really behaving naturally when they were in the company of others.

Her mother refused her offer of a cup of tea,

explaining that she had to get back if she was to
be ready in time for their meal.

'It's seven-thirty, don't forget!' she called out
as she drove away, 'and don't forget to wear your
new dress.'

Blake's eyebrows rose, but he made no
comment. They might be living together, but
there was no real communcation between them,
Jaime thought despairingly.

Mrs Widdows was to have Fern for the
evening. She would sleep in her old bedroom at
the cottage, and they would pick her up on their
way to Pembroke in the morning.

Blake made no comment when Jaime appeared
in her new dress. She was also wearing her
sapphire engagement ring, something she hadn't
done all the time they had been apart.

'Still got that?' His eyebrows rose. 'I thought
you must have got rid of it.'

'No.' The shocked denial was out before Jaime
could silence it.

'Well, it can hardly have any sentimental value,
unless it's to remind you of the disaster our
marriage was,' Blake claimed acidly.

What could she say? That she had kept it
because she loved him, and that she hadn't worn
it because he hadn't loved her? All at once, her
pleasure in her new outfit was gone. What had
she expected, she wondered drearily? That a new
dress would somehow make her irresistibly
desirable in Blake's eyes?

'Daddy, you promised me a story,' Fern
reminded Blake on their way to the cottage.

'And you'll get one, never fear,' he assured her, as they all got out of the car.

'You're going to have to watch it, Jaime,' Henry joked jovially, when they were all on their way out, Blake having come back downstairs with the news that Fern was fast asleep, 'otherwise, you might lose your husband to your daughter.'

Blake laughed, 'Yes, I confess I'm rather smitten with Fern.'

'What's the matter?' he asked, when he and Jaime were in his car. 'Are you jealous of Fern?'

'No, just surprised that you should admit you actually care about her,' she replied in a brittle voice. 'After all, you never *wanted* her.'

She saw his hands tighten on the steering wheel, and wished the bitter words unsaid.

'I didn't want us to have a child because I didn't think our marriage was stable enough to provide a secure home for one,' he bit out at last, 'and I was proved right. . . .'

'That's a lie,' Jaime threw back at him, her body and voice shaking. 'You didn't want a child because you didn't want to give up your precious freedom, your job . . . even though you knew. . . .'

'My job was never the real issue between us, Jaime,' Blake said coldly. 'You just used it to mask your compulsive possessiveness and lack of self-esteem. If I didn't want us to have a child it was because I didn't think you wanted one for the right reasons.'

'No . . . that's a lie. . . .' Jaime gasped out the words, but, in her heart of hearts, she knew they held some truth. When she first discovered she was having Fern, hadn't she thought that, at last, here was someone who was completely and absolutely dependent on her—that she would be the strong one, the dominant one in their relationship?

'Just as you wanted me to give up my job because you weren't mature enough to accept that being away from you didn't mean that I didn't care about you. I knew when I married you that you were immature, but I hoped that you'd grow. . . .'

'Into someone like Suzy?' Jaime bit out. 'How disappointed you must have been when I didn't. If you had wanted the sort of open marriage Suzy approves of, you should have married her, and not me. I can't imagine why you didn't. . . .'

'Don't be so childish. . . .'

They were within a mile of the restaurant where they were to eat. Jaime was close to tears of rage and humiliation. Somehow she had to get control of herself before her mother saw her.

'Whatever happened in the past is the past, Blake,' she said as evenly as she could. 'I don't deny that I was naive, and, yes, too clinging. I can understand how that must have irritated you, but you see it was because . . . I always knew you married me partially because you felt sorry for me, because I was so inexperienced, and I was so terrified of losing you.' There was a huge lump in her throat and nothing could have made her look at Blake, but she had to go on. 'Every time you left I was frightened that you wouldn't come back; that you would realise you had made a mistake in marrying me.' She couldn't go on. 'We're here.'

Henry's car turned into the car park ahead of them. There wasn't time to say any more, and Jaime was glad of the protective dusk when Blake opened the car door for her. She didn't want to spoil her mother's evening, so she talked gaily, avoiding Blake's eyes, hoping she was deceiving the others better than she was deceiving herself.

Blake was unusually morose, barely speaking to any of them. Surely, her mother and Henry must notice something, she thought nervously, but they were so wrapped up in one another and their love that they didn't.

'Why don't you two go and dance?' Sarah suggested, when she and Henry returned from the small dance floor.

'No. . . .' Jaime murmured her refusal, but Blake was already on his feet, his arm curving round her waist.

The tempo of the music slowed slightly as they reached the dance floor. Jaime tried to pull away as Blake circled her completely with his arms, but he wouldn't let her. Often, in the past, they had danced close together like this, but then she had leaned her head against Blake's shoulder, her palms pressed flat against his shirt front. Now, she tried to hold herself away stiffly, not wanting the torment of his body brushing hers, but he misunderstood her tension and said thickly, 'For Christ's sake, Jaime, I'm not going to rape you in the middle of a dance floor. Try to relax. We're supposed to be enjoying ourselves.' His hands pressed against her spine as he spoke, forcing her against his body. She could feel the heavy beat of his heart and smell his clean, fresh cologne. Her hands had nowhere to go, other than his chest. The dance seemed to last an unendurable age, but, at last, it was over. By the time they were ready to leave, Jaime's head was aching with tension.

Once they got back to the cottage, Henry insisted that they all have a nightcap. Fern hadn't stirred, Mrs Widdows assured Jaime. 'Don't worry about her. She'll sleep until morning,' her mother chimed in, 'and you'll be able to get ready much faster without her. She'll love the beaches. I remember the first time I took you to the seaside. You rushed on to the sand and started building a sandcastle.'

'She hasn't changed much, then,' Blake pronounced dryly, 'She did much the same thing on our honeymoon.'

And afterwards they had made love in the dunes, on the soft car rug Blake had spread there, watching the sea eat into her creation. All at once, she wanted to cry, but tears would change nothing, nothing at all.

CHAPTER TEN

JAIME's head was still aching the next morning from the tension, and wine, of the night before, when she and Blake drove to her mother's cottage in an uncommunicative silence. As she knew from their honeymoon, it was at least a four-hour drive to the Pembroke cottage, and she was glad when Fern fell asleep after the first hour.

'Another hour, and we'll stop somewhere for lunch,' Blake told her, but Jaime shook her head. 'Don't bother unless you're hungry. I'm not, and Fern will probably sleep through until we get there now.'

Apart from a brief tightening of his lips over her ungracious response, Blake said nothing.

The countryside flashed by them, Jaime trying not to remember how it had been the first time she had gone this way with Blake. They had just been married, and she had still been dizzy with wonder because he had wanted her. She stifled a small sound of pain, and tried to follow Fern's example, leaning back into her seat.

'Wake up, Jaime, we're here.'

Blake's voice sounded very close to her ear. Jaime reluctantly opened her eyes, appalled to discover that she was leaning against his shoulder.

'You've been asleep for ages, Mummy,' Fern

accused from the back seat, 'but Daddy said I wasn't to wake you.'

It must have been the tablet she had taken for her headache, Jaime thought muzzily, fighting against a reluctance to lift her head from its solid resting place. Poor Blake, his shoulder muscles must be quite stiff after supporting her weight for so long. If they were, he gave no sign of it, calmly reaching across her to release her seat belt, and then freeing his own before turning to free Fern from her seat.

For a man who had claimed that he never wanted children, he made a very caring father, Jaime thought as she opened her door and stepped out.

The cottage was miles from anywhere, perched on the cliffs with the National Trust pathway, that ran the whole length of the Pembrokeshire coast from St David's, only yards away from the front door. Small and compact, it had been an ideal honeymoon retreat, and Jaime knew that Fern would fall in love with the tiny, secluded beach within easy reach of the cottage, just as she had done.

The nearest village was three miles away and, during their honeymoon, Jaime and Blake had walked there when they wanted to reprovision. This time, she doubted that there would be long, private walks or lovemaking in the seclusion of the wild headllands. Not that they had spent all their time alone; they had gone one day to Milford Haven, to watch the naval vessels, and another to Haverford West. They had also visited

Pembroke Castle. Castles were something Pembroke was rich in, but Fern was too young to want to do much more than play on the beach.

The cottage was very much as Jaime remembered, with one double bedroom and the two smaller interconnecting ones, into which she put her and Fern's things.

'Would you like me to unpack for you?'

Blake was outside, still unloading the car, and he nodded his head briefly at her question. How polite and formal they were being to one another, and yet Jaime felt as though their politeness was unnatural, like the ominous silence before a thunderstorm. Only Fern seemed relaxed, chattering eagerly as she followed Jaime from room to room. The cottage had no television, and Jaime wondered how on earth she and Blake would pass the long, light summer evenings once Fern was in bed.

As Blake had told her, the freezer in the kitchen was well-stocked, and she had brought with her a selection of Fern's favourite foods.

After they had eaten, Fern insisted on going down to the beach.

'I'll take her,' Blake offered, and Jaime wondered, watching them go as she tidied up after their meal, if this resentment was something all women felt when they were excluded from the activities of their men and children.

Half an hour later they were back, Fern clutching some small shells, her face wreathed in smiles. They had paddled in the sea she told Jaime, as Jaime got her ready for bed, and then Daddy had climbed on some rocks. . . .

Telling herself that she was a coward, Jaime went downstairs and told Blake she was going to bed. 'I've had a headache all day,' she said, with some truth, 'and I think I'll have an early night.'

'I need to stretch my legs,' Blake informed her when she had finished, 'I'll lock up when I get back.'

Although she strained her ears, listening for sounds of his return, Jaime fell asleep before Blake came back, and their first evening at the cottage set the pattern for the evenings that followed.

The weather remained hot and sunny, but with a sultriness in the air that promised storms to come. Every morning Jaime took Fern down on the beach while Blake worked, using the portable typewriter he had brought with him. They returned at lunchtime when Jaime prepared a light lunch. After lunch, Fern napped while Jaime worked in the cottage garden or walked to the village.

Sometimes, later in the afternoon, they went out in the car, although these expeditions were seldom successful. Jaime felt that Blake was accompanying them as a duty, and his presence was a constant reminder of how much things had changed between them.

In the evenings he disappeared—to the village pub, Jaime suspected, where he, no doubt, found more congenial adult company than that to be had at the cottage.'

Their fifth day was much as the others, although it was hotter, the sky a brassy yellow colour. During the afternoon it became so sultry that it was as though the entire countryside was holding its breath.

Fern was in a fretful and irritable mood that ended in a temper tantrum and tears; for once, she seemed to prefer Jaime's company to Blake's, even to the extent of wanting her mother to read her bedtime story, something Blake had done ever since they had come to the cottage.

When Jaime finished settling Fern and went downstairs, she discovered that Blake had gone out. The thought of another solitary evening was just too much to be borne. A restless urgency pulsated through her body, but, of course, she could not go out and leave Fern.

Thunder rolled ominously in the distance, and there was no sign of Blake when Jaime went to bed. He would probably get soaked on the return journey from the village, because he had not taken the car. 'Serves him right for leaving me here alone,' she thought crossly.

Jaime was dreaming. She lay trapped in a cold, dark cave, with water dropping on her from the moist, unseen roof. She felt clammy and uncomfortable, but no matter how much she tried to wriggle away, the dripping continued. She shivered and woke up to discover that the dripping had been no dream and that her bedding was saturated from a leak in the ceiling above her bed.

Outside she could hear the fierce sounds of a storm, her curtains billowed at the open window, and the temperature had dropped several degrees. Cold and wet, she clambered out of bed in the dark, searching for the towelling robe she used for journeys to the bathroom, stubbing her toe on the base of the old-fashioned bed and knocking over a chair as she hopped up and down on one foot.

Lights sprang on outside her bedroom, the door opening as Blake strode in frowning, 'What the devil's going on?'

Like her, he was wearing a towelling robe, which he was hastily tying, as Jaime indicated the damp ceiling.

'There must be a slate loose. I'll get someone from the village to look at it tomorrow. It's probably been loosened by this storm. What about Fern's room?'

'I've only just woken up,' Jaime told him. 'I'll go and check.'

Fern was sleeping soundly and drily. Jaime turned back to her own room. Blake was leaning over the bed, pulling off the covers and the mattress which he propped up on its side away from the damp.

'What are you doing?' Jaime demanded.

'Propping this thing up so that we can get it dry. Tonight, you'll have to share with me. You can't sleep here,' he pointed out when Jaime was silent, 'and I'm certainly not giving up my bed to sleep on that apology for a settee downstairs. It's barely four feet long.'

It was, Jaime knew. Even she would be cramped up if she tried to sleep on it.

'I'll sleep in Fern's room—on the floor,' she said coolly.

'Don't be ridiculous,' Blake was frowning. 'Why make a martyr of yourself when there's a perfectly good double bed available—but then, you always did enjoy that particular role, didn't you, Jaime? Come on, leave this lot, we'll get it sorted out in the morning. You're cold,' he added, frowning when he saw her shiver.

'And wet,' Jaime agreed, shivering again. The thought of a cosy, warm bed was extremely alluring. She stifled a yawn. She really was too tired to argue with Blake tonight, and, after all, what was there to fear? That he might try to make love to her? 'Would that he would!' a small, inner voice sighed mournfully.

She looked for a dry nightdress, and then remembered that she had washed her spare one that morning and that it was downstairs in the ironing basket. She grimaced distastefully at the thought of keeping on the damp, clammy one she was wearing, and then remembered the silk 'teddy' her mother had bought for her. Eyeing it wryly, she took it with her into the bathroom. It was no more revealing than the cotton tops and shorts she had been wearing all week; but it was decidedly more provocative, she reflected, when she had towelled some warmth into her cold body and slipped it on.

During the week her skin had tanned, and it glowed softly beneath the fine fabric. The silk clung lovingly to her body, caressing it almost, but it was all she had to wear other than her undies, and so Jaime pulled on her towelling robe, and comforted herself with the thought that Blake would probably be asleep by now anyway.

He wasn't. He was propped up in bed, reading some typed sheets with the aid of a bedside lamp, when Jaime walked in.

Apart from glancing up when she opened the door, he paid no more attention to her. Even so, Jaime kept her back to him as she stood by her side of the bed and quickly slipped off her robe. That way, all he could see of her, if he did look, was her back. She sat down on the edge of the bed and pushed back the covers, and it was then, as she glanced up, that she saw the long pier mirror facing her. In it she could see both her own and Blake's reflection. He was leaning, watching her, his head propped up by one hand, his work forgotten, and Jaime's face flamed as she saw the *way* he was looking at her.

'If you've quite finished, I'd like to get some sleep,' she said icily.

'Why wear it if you didn't want me to see you in it?' Blake drawled easily. 'Why not stick to those cotton monstrosities you seem so fond of?'

'Because I only have two of them with me,' Jaime seethed. 'One is soaking wet, and the other is downstairs, unaired. It was either this or nothing. . . .'

'I think I'll go for the second option,' Blake said softly, and, before Jaime could stop him, Blake was reaching for the tiny pearl buttons that fastened the front of the teddy.

'Blake, stop it!' she lashed out at him with small, tight fists.

'Shussh. Don't make so much noise; you'll wake Fern,' he warned, ignoring her attempts to stop him, and easily imprisoning her wrists in the iron span of his fingers, securing them behind her back.

'Umm, very nice.' His free hand had worked the first few buttons open, and the silk fell away to reveal the tawny rise and fall of her breasts. Jaime kicked angrily out at him, quivering with anger. How dare he treat her like this! She had completely forgotten that, not ten minutes before, a part of her had longed for his lovemaking. The punishing grip of Blake's fingers jerked her wrists back so that she overbalanced, her arms still pinned beneath her by Blake's hand.

'Now what are you going to do?' he mocked softly. 'I know what I'm going to do, and it's this.'

'This' was his fingers flicking open the rest of the buttons that ran down to her navel. She looked like some slave girl spread out for her master's delectation, Jaime thought disgustedly, catching sight of herself in the mirror. Her skin glowed tawny against the soft silk, the rise and fall of her breasts tightening the frail fabric through which she could clearly see the outline of her own nipples. Even the way she had fallen on to the bed when Blake overpowered her suggested a sensuality that angered her, her body a languid sprawl of sleek, tanned legs and provocative, pale silk.

'Blake, this is ridiculous. Let me go at once,' she protested.

'In a moment. When you've told me you don't want me to do this . . .' He bent his head, and his tongue delicately flicked aside the fragile silk that covered one taut nipple, 'or this . . .' The tormentingly light, moist circles his tongue painted around her pulsating flesh had Jaime tensing her whole body against the urge to cry out the need his touch engendered.

'Well . . . tell me you don't, and I'll stop.'

She wanted to. Oh, how badly she wanted to, if only for the sake of her pride, but her tongue seemed to have stuck to the roof of her mouth. Speech was impossible. There was only feeling— wave upon wave of it—as Blake turned his attention to her other breast, repeating the torment he had already inflicted.

'You always did enjoy this,' he murmured shamingly, studying her flushed face with knowing eyes. 'You want to deny it, but you can't, can you Jaime? This,' he touched his mouth to the pulse pounding at the base of her throat, 'betrays you. It's no use, Jaime,' he told her softly, 'I mean to have the response from you I know your body wants to give, even if it takes all night.'

'Blake . . . please, you can't do this,' Jaime protested, making a last-ditch attempt to sway him. 'You can't use me, just to slake a sexual hunger. . . .'

'Why not?' he countered smoothly, with a barely discernible edge of anger under the soft words, '*You're* using me to protect your mother. . . .'

When he said that, Jaime knew she could not argue against him. Without another protest, 'she forced her body to relax.

'All right, Blake,' she said numbly, 'rape me, if you must, but just . . . just get it over with.'

'It won't be rape,' Blake told her softly, 'and I promise you, Jaime, you won't want me to "get it over with", but to prolong every tormenting moment of pleasure. You always did.'

It was useless to deny what he was saying. They both knew it was the truth. He bent his head, tracing a line of kisses down between her smooth breasts, down to where the final button lay close to her navel. Jaime drew in a sharp breath and then tried to release it as his tongue investigated the small hollow. She tried not to move but her body betrayed her, quivering in heated response to Blake's expert caresses. His tongue drew a line along the barrier of silk, and Jaime moaned protestingly, tugging her arms free. Blake released her, as though he knew that, this time, she didn't want to hold him off

Her fingers stroked the smoothly compact muscles of his back, tracing the line of his spine, her body arching in helpless supplication to the sweet torment he was wreaking. When he lifted her hips to slide the silk free, Jaime sighed with pleasure, welcoming the sensation of skin against skin as the hard warmth of his thigh brushed against her. Now there was no question of her not wanting him to go on. Her whole body cried out for him, shamelessly telling him so, as it arched and seduced.

His mouth against her breast made her cry out with pleasure, her small teeth biting sharply into his skin.

'Jaime.' His hand rested possessively against her thigh, his voice commanding her to meet the hungry passion of his kiss. She gave herself up to it gladly, welcoming the hot invasion of his tongue, matching him in her need to convey her increasing need of him.

His fingers, caressing her intimately, transported her to a world she had nearly forgotten existed, her own hands reaching out to find the hard maleness of him.

Blake moaned his pleasure as her fingers stroked the throbbing tissue that told her of his desire, and Jaime knew that the moment of physical possession could not be delayed much longer, but she let Blake prolong the anticipation until it was almost a pain, kissing the moist warmth of his chest and then sucking the flat maleness of his nipples until his body shuddered in uncontrollable response, surging into hers with a fierce heat that satisfied the dull ache radiating from the inner core of her.

Their lovemaking was as fierce and elemental as the storm that raged outside, the powerful rhythm of Blake's body wringing from Jaime a shuddering response that made her cry out in a delirium only to find that, instead of reaching the peak of pleasure, they were still climbing; through the stars and into empty, dizzying space where Blake's mouth stifled her final cry of fulfilment, his tongue licking the tears of pleasure from her face.

Jaime fell asleep in his arms, her body still entwined with his, his arm a heavy weight against her.

When she woke up in the morning, Blake was gone. She could hear sounds of movement from downstairs, but, when she tried to get out of bed, she found her body lethargically uncooperative. She had just rescued the discarded teddy, when Fern burst into the room, closely followed by Blake.

'Breakfast,' he said calmly. 'I thought you might appreciate a lie-in this morning.'

Jaime could no more have prevented her brilliant flush than she could have flown. Blake's comment was as intimate as though he already knew of the love-bruises faintly colouring her skin and the pleasant ache still left in her body.

Half of her was relieved when he left her alone to eat her breakfast, and half of her disappointed. Where did they go from last night? Blake had never said he loved her, never mentioned permanency.... She would have to talk to him, Jaime thought despairingly. She couldn't go on sleeping with him, living with him, loving him as she did, while he ...'

When she went downstairs, there was a note in the kitchen from Blake to say he had taken Fern down on to the beach.

The storm had left the air much clearer, and the sun shone out of a soft blue sky. Jaime brought the damp bedding downstairs and put it in the washing machine, only to discover that she was out of powder. The car was outside, and it wouldn't take her long to drive to the village. It took her longer than she thought to get back. The village shop was busy, and it was over half an hour before she could set off back.

As she drove up to the cottage, Blake rushed out, his face white and set.

'Jaime!'

'Fern?' she exclaimed anxiously, 'Has something happened to her?'

'Fern's upstairs having a nap. Where have you been?'

'To the village, to get some washing powder.'

Was it her imagination, or did Blake relax slightly?

'Where did you think I was?' she asked curiously.

'I thought you'd left,' Blake's voice was completely flat. 'Jaime, it's time we sat down and talked. I've tried to be patient, to tell myself to take it slowly, to give you time, but I just can't take it any more. I thought when you first left me that, if I gave you time, if I didn't frighten you, you'd stop hating me and start loving me again. . . .'

'Stop hating you?' Jaime stared at him, sinking down on to the wooden bench outside the cottage. 'But Blake, I've never hated you.'

'That's not what you told Suzy when you told her you were leaving me. "Tell him I hate him, and that if he tries to see me I'll kill myself"— that's what you told her.'

'No, I told her no such thing,' Jaime protested. 'She told me that you had asked to go on an assignment in El Salvador, that you were tired of me, that . . . Blake . . .'

He had dropped to the seat next to her, his head buried in his hands. 'Oh my God,' he said indistinctly. 'Is that really true?'

'Of course, it is. Why should I lie? I always loved you, Blake,' she said softly. 'Surely you knew that?'

'I knew you were infatuated with me. I knew I ought to give you more time to discover what life was all about. I knew I ought to give myself more time to accept that our marriage would mean a whole new way of life, but I also knew how desperately you craved security, and I was terrified that, if I didn't give it to you, someone else would. I told myself that, within the security of our marriage, you'd mature; that our love would mature, and that you'd stop being terrified of losing me . . . I was terrified that security was all you wanted from me, and that, one day, you'd grow up and realise that for yourself. . . . That's why I tried to get you to cling less . . . so that you could realise . . .' he shook his head. 'That day, when we had the quarrel, I'd already told them I wouldn't accept the El Salvador assignment. I knew I couldn't go and do the job properly, because too much of me would be left behind with you, but the moment I started to tell you about it, you threw that temper tantrum. . . .'

'Because I suspected I was having Fern, and I was so scared . . . so terrified that, once you knew, you'd be so angry that you'd leave. No children you had said. . . .'

'Because I wanted you to want them for the right reasons. Not because you needed someone to love. Dear God, Jaime! Of course, I wanted you to have my child.'

'So, why didn't you answer the letter I sent you telling you about Fern, and asking if I could come back?'

'You did that?' He looked distressed. 'Jaime, I left the flat the day after you. I was so bitter, so despairing that I told the editor I'd changed my mind, and that I would accept the El Salvador assignment. It was the last one I did accept. Suzy was the photographer assigned to me—we'd been lovers once, you know, not in the emotional sense, but merely in a physical one, and, while we were away, she made it plain that she wanted to resume our old relationship. I didn't— couldn't. I wanted only you, and, rather than embarrass her by telling her so, I decided to quit. I wanted to by then anyway. I'd always wanted to write. I got in touch with your mother the moment I got back, but she said she thought you wouldn't see me.'

Jaime remembered telling her mother, almost hysterically, how much she hated Blake. If she had told her the truth, how different things might have been!

'She advised me to bide my time . . . to wait . . . and I kept on waiting and waiting . . . and then she wrote to me and told me about Charles. I knew then I dared not wait any longer in case I lost you forever; so I decided it was time to re-enter your life.'

'Was that why you rented the Lodge?'

'Yes ... but nothing turned out the way I'd planned. Almost from the word "Go" I found that you and I had mysteriously got ourselves on the opposite sides of an argument. When I heard that Caroline was planning to sell the Abbey to Barrons, I was really worried. I knew all about their reputation, but I knew that if Caroline knew I was opposed to the sale. . . .'

'So you pretended to be in agreement with it?'

'I didn't want to be thrown out of the Lodge, I needed to be near you,' Blake told her. 'Jaime, about last night. . . .'

'It was one of the most beautiful experiences of my life . . .' Jaime said quietly, taking her courage in both hands. 'Blake, I've never stopped loving you, never stopped regretting leaving you, never stopped wishing I hadn't behaved so childishly Every criticism you ever levelled at me was justified. I *was* immature, I *did* cling ... not because you offered me security, but because I couldn't understand what you saw in me. I could't believe you loved me. . . .'

'I told you you were short on faith and trust.'

'I thought you'd married me because you felt you had to—because I was a virgin,' she said simply.

She felt him draw in his breath and then release it, and then his hands were on her shoulders, turning her face to him.

'I married you because I loved you, because I

couldn't tolerate the thought of life without you, and then felt horribly guilty because I felt I'd used your inexperience to pressure you into a marriage you might later regret. We've both been guilty of confusing what is, basically, a very simple emotion, because, for different reasons, we couldn't bring ourselves to believe in it and one another.'

'Yes,' said Jaime sadly.

'I could wring Suzy's neck for lying to me, but I blame myself more. I should never have believed her, but you'd been so cold towards me those last few days. . . .'

'Because I suspected I might be pregnant, and I was trying to prepare myself for the loneliness I was convinced I would have to endure when you found out. I was sure you would leave me.'

'Never,' he averred softly. 'I still love you Jaime, and last night meant something very special to me, too. A chance to show you with my body, if I couldn't tell you the words, how much I still loved you.'

'And I love you. . . .'

'Which is just how it should be,' Blake grinned, teasing her, but there was nothing teasing in the warm pressure of his lips on hers, and Jaime responded to it joyously, letting the love she had struggled to conceal for so long show in her response.

'Now I know why you were so keen for us to come and live with you,' she smiled.

'Not entirely. I knew about Barrons' threats, and yet was powerless to do anything about them.

And there is one other complication you *don't* know about yet. You know the Abbey had another purchaser?'

Jaime nodded her head, puzzled.

'It's me,' Blake told her. 'I fell in love with it the moment I saw it. I couldn't help picturing you in every room, you and Fern, and the other children I wanted us to have, but I had to keep it a secret in case Barrons found out. The bulldozer episode was the the final clincher as far as Caroline was concerned. The very next day we signed contracts. If Barrons had known, they would have had even more reason to threaten you, Jaime. You'll never know how bitter I felt when I realised you thought I could harm so much as a hair on your head ... I wanted so much to tell you it all then ... but I was hurt, and I so wanted your love and your trust. ...'

'So you deliberately and sadistically allowed me to go on thinking the worst,' Jaime said softly, remembering.

'It's all over now,' Blake drew her head down on to his shoulder, 'and, if you agree, we'll move into the Abbey just as soon as we can. I intend to go on writing and, athough there'll be some travel, you can always come with me.'

'I've grown up now, Blake,' Jaime said gently. 'I'm strong enough to trust. You see, all the time I knew I should suspect you I didn't, because, in my heart, I still loved you. ...'

'Thank heavens for the leaking roof,' Blake murmured piously, just before he kissed her.

'Thank heavens indeed,' Jaime echoed

mentally, sliding her arms round him. From now on, there'd be no more separate beds, no more heartache or pain.

'Blake ...' she began dreamily as his lips moved seductively over her face, 'how do you feel about a brother or sister for Fern?'

'Do , you want me to tell you,' he asked wickedly, 'or show you?'

DARKER SIDE OF DESIRE

DARKER SIDE OF DESIRE

BY

PENNY JORDAN

MILLS & BOON LIMITED
Eton House, 18–24 Paradise Road
Richmond, Surrey TW9 1SR

*First published in Great Britain 1984
by Mills & Boon Limited*

© Penny Jordan 1984

*Australian copyright 1984
Philippine copyright 1984
Reprinted 1984
This edition 1988*

ISBN 0 263 76070 7

*Set in Monophoto Plantin 10 on 11½ pt
19-0488-56883*

*Printed and bound in Great Britain by
Cox & Wyman Ltd, Reading*

CHAPTER ONE

'DARLING, I'm sorry about this, spoiling what was supposed to be your holiday treat too.'

'Being with Uncle Henri is far more important than spending the day shopping with me,' Claire assured her godmother. 'It was just lucky that the hospital managed to get through to you before we'd left the hotel.'

'Umm.' A worried frown creased her godmother's forehead. 'Henri has had these attacks before of course, but . . .'

'You must go to him,' Claire told her firmly. Her godmother's second husband had suffered from angina for several years and Claire knew that her godmother was deliberately playing down her concern because she didn't want to spoil what had been intended as her birthday treat to mark Claire's twenty-second birthday.

'There's a flight back to Paris in just over an hour. I could be on it.'

'You *will* be on it,' Claire corrected. She glanced at her watch, surprised to see that it was still only seven in the morning. The call which had disturbed their sleep and altered their plans seemed to have come hours ago not a mere fifty-odd minutes. 'I'll help you pack and ring down to reception to tell them that we'll be checking out. I'll come to the airport with you.'

'No, Claire.' Susan Dupont spoke firmly. 'No, I

want you to stay on here and enjoy your day as we'd planned. You're looking so tired, darling,' she added softly. 'I wish I could do more to help you. If I could only pay Teddy's school fees for you . . .'

They had been through this discussion so many times before that she knew what her goddaughter's response would be before it came. Although Henri was a good and kind husband, she was solely dependent on him financially, and both she and Claire knew that if she did pay Teddy's school fees it would have to be without the knowledge and permission of her French husband, who, while he allowed her to spoil her goddaughter upon occasions, saw no reason why he should be responsible for that same goddaughter's brother's school fees, and this was something that Claire would not allow her godmother to do.

'Now promise me that you will spend the day shopping and enjoying yourself,' Susan Dupont pleaded. 'The room is paid for for tonight, and I'll speak to reception and have them forward the bill on to me.'

Claire smiled, signalling her acceptance. Two days in London staying at the Dorchester, all expenses met by her godmother, had been a delightful surprise birthday present, and even if she did not really have the spare cash to shop at the more exclusive stores she knew her godmother had visualised for the treat, she wasn't going to add to her distress by refusing to stay on at the Dorchester when her godmother left. She could easily fill in time wandering round the art galleries and museums, it would give her something to write to Teddy about when she next sent him a letter; and if she returned home all she would be doing would be moping about the small flat which was all she could afford at the moment.

Unconsciously she sighed. Life hadn't been easy since the death of her parents. Teddy had only been eight at the time, and because their parents lived and worked abroad, he had already spent two years at the exclusive and expensive private school their father had also attended. Ten years separated brother and sister. Claire had been on the point of starting university when her parents died. Like Teddy, she too had attended boarding school; her parents had been comfortably enough off for her to share in all the 'extras' the school provided, and she had not really given a thought as to how she would spend the rest of her life.

Then her whole world came crashing down around her. In six short months she had grown from a carefree teenager into an adult. Her father's generous salary ceased with his death, and apart from a modest insurance policy there had been no provision made for the future. There wasn't even a house to sell as her father and mother had lived abroad at his company's expense.

The family solicitor had tried to be as gentle as possible. Teddy would have to leave school, the man had told her, there simply wasn't the money . . . The proceeds of the insurance policy could be used to buy a modest house and provide a small income. But, rightly or wrongly, Claire had ignored his advice. His school and the friends he had made there were Teddy's whole world. If she took him away from school she would have to pay child-minders to look after him while she was at work and being taken away from his school so soon after losing their parents was bound to have a profound effect upon him, she decided, and so, instead of taking their solicitor's advice, Claire had used some of the money to pay for her own secretarial training, using the rest, carefully eked out over the years, to pay for Teddy's schooling.

Inflation had caused school fees to soar and over the last two years the money she had put aside hadn't been sufficient. A large part of her own salary went towards keeping Teddy at school. Her job was a good one, she worked for the Managing Director of an advanced electronics company based within half-a-day's drive of Teddy's school, but she didn't earn anything like enough to pay for six more years' schooling. Teddy was exceptionally clever, so his school told her, almost definitely Oxbridge material, and for the past few months the problem of how to raise the cash to keep him at school had constantly taxed her mind. She had no real financial assets. Her small Mini was already on its last legs, and the only thing she could think of was to try and get an evening job to supplement her daytime earnings.

This brief stay at the Dorchester was very much an unaccustomed luxury, but she was determined not to add to her godmother's problems by letting her see how disappointed she was that she could not remain with her.

'Now promise me you'll go down and have breakfast. Don't stay up here on your own,' Susan Dupont cautioned when her case was packed. 'Who knows, you might run into that gorgeous man we saw downstairs last night.'

Her godmother was an inveterate matchmaker, and

Claire subdued a small grimace. The gorgeous man her godmother referred to had done nothing for her. Oh, he had been gorgeous right enough—far *too* gorgeous with that thick dark hair, and those unusual green eyes. And despite the formal tailoring of his European suit there had been no mistaking his Middle Eastern origins. They were there in the arrogant pride of his profile; faintly cruel in a way which had sent shivers down her spine and made her think of herself as foolishly imaginative. She had disliked him instinctively. There had been something in the way he looked at her, a careless scrutiny that observed and dismissed with languid hauteur coupled with an unmistakable contempt that burned her pride.

She had seen him again later, in the restaurant, dining with a group of men. Unaware that her gaze had rested on him she had flushed uncomfortably when her godmother followed it and remarked teasingly, 'Mm, there's definitely something about those tall, dark, forceful-looking men, isn't there?'

To cover her embarrassment, Claire had replied acidly, 'He's probably the sort of man who thinks he simply has to dangle a diamond bracelet in front of a woman's eyes and she'll jump right into bed with him.'

Her godmother's rich chuckle had surprised her. 'My dear,' Susan Dupont had responded roguishly. 'I suspect that most women, if they thought such a gorgeous male creature was even thinking about taking them to bed, would be offering *him* the diamonds!' She had laughed again at Claire's shocked expression, noticing the sudden tightening of her lovely full lips with a faint sigh. She was full of admiration for the way Claire had shouldered her burdens since her parents' death, but it sometimes seemed to her that Claire was old before her time, not physically but mentally. There had been no time for fun, for the careless enjoyment of dalliance with the opposite sex, before the blow had fallen and now Claire seemed to concentrate all her energies and time on her job and her younger brother. If only Henri would allow her to help, but he had grandchildren of his own and Teddy was, after all, no relation.

'No, don't come to the airport with me,' Susan Dupont reiterated when Claire followed her out on to the steps in front of the hotel to wait for her luggage to be placed in the waiting taxi. 'Go back inside and have your breakfast.' As she got into the taxi she placed a cheque in Claire's surprised hand. 'This is the rest of your birthday present, darling. I want you to buy yourself something nice ... something ... sexy ...' she added with a twinkle. 'Something that would appeal to our friend from the restaurant last night.'

She was gone before Claire could protest. The cheque was a generous one and Claire already knew that she would not spend it on herself. She would use it to replace those items of Teddy's school uniform which most needed attention. Twelve-year-old boys grew so quickly ... She suppressed a small sigh.

It was all too easy to imagine the sort of 'something' that would appeal to the insufferably arrogant male nature she had sensed lurking below the warm olive skin and cold green eyes of the man her godmother had referred to. Rich silks and satins. Fabrics with a sensual appeal that would bring the glitter of sexual appreciation to those strange eyes. He would like his women supine and obedient, toys to be played with and then discarded when other, and more important matters took his attention. Unknowingly, her mouth hardened, and she was oblivious to the appreciative looks directed towards her by the hotel staff as she stepped back inside the foyer.

Slenderly built with fine bones, she had an air of fragility of which she herself was unaware. Silver-blonde hair which she wore in a shoulder-length bell because it was easy to maintain, framed a classically oval face. Long-lashed grey eyes surveyed the world with a cool aloofness that had been born the day she woke up and suddenly found she was alone with full responsibility for an eight-year-old boy. Always neatly groomed, her clothes were useful rather than alluring. Neat suits and high-necked blouses which she wore for work, bought normally in end-of-season sales. There were no 'pretty' clothes in her wardrobe, apart from the ridiculously expensive gifts she received from her godmother; beautiful silk undies, a cashmere jumper, things she never wore without thinking how much they cost and how that money might have been eked out on more practical garments. Of course she longed for nice clothes, for luxuries, and perhaps when Teddy eventually left university . . . She pulled a brief face. By then she would be in her thirties . . . It was a subject on which she refused to dwell.

There had been several men at work who had approached her for dates, but once they learned about Teddy their interest had waned sharply. And who could blame them? She was certainly not prepared to enter into any relationship which was one of mere sexual indulgence, and yet what man would want to marry her knowing she was responsible for a young brother? That problem was one she refused to dwell on too deeply. Of course she had had the normal feminine dreams. She had envisaged for herself a husband, a family, at some dim date in the future, after she had left university and enjoyed her freedom for a few years, but now she was resigned to the fact that she would probably never marry, and since she was not prepared to go from one affair to another, she had found herself coolly freezing off any male attempts to get closer to her, knowing in advance what would happen when they learned about Teddy.

Thousands of women lived alone these days anyway; she had a good job, a comfortable if small flat. When Teddy was qualified she would be able to travel . . . and yet somehow the picture of her future did not appeal. Although she enjoyed her job she was no career woman. Of course she did not want to batten on to a man simply to escape being alone. She wanted to love and be loved, Claire admitted as she headed for the lift. She wanted to share and enrich her life with another human being.

Her room was on the second floor, where the corridor was carpeted in a richly warm crimson and cream with a luxuriously thick pile. The room she had shared with her godmother was almost as large as her entire flat, and far more luxuriously furnished. Dressing in a soft tweed suit in mauves and lilacs with a toning grey silk blouse, she brushed her hair into its neat bell, applied a discreet touch of make-up and then picked up her bag and key. Over breakfast she would decide how to spend her day.

At first when she stepped into the dining-room she

thought she must have mistaken her directions and that she had inadvertently strayed into a private room. A large party of Arabs—all male—were seated together in deep discussion, and her own entrance occasioned an immediate and embarrassing silence which held her immobile on the threshold of the room until a waiter came forward and led her to a table.

All the way down the length of the room Claire was conscious of male eyes following her progress, studying her, assessing her, but the scrutiny she was most aware of was that which came from ice-cold green eyes that seemed to follow her every step, carelessly dismissing while still assessing her.

It was an unnerving experience, and she was dismayed to discover how much her hands trembled when she eventually sat down. She should have breakfasted in her room, but it was too late—and too obvious—to get up now and walk away.

As her composure returned she realised that she was not, as she had thought, the only female in the room. Several tables away a young Arab girl was trying to feed a small baby, strapped into a highchair. The child, a little boy, was protesting volubly, pushing away the proffered spoon, and Claire could tell that the girl was getting impatient with him. Twice she slapped the small plump legs, raising crimson marks, making the child cry loudly in retaliation. The girl was too uncaring to be the child's mother, and Claire guessed that she must be his nurse, but there seemed to be little sympathy between them, and she was aware, as she glanced up from her own breakfast, that the man with the green eyes was also studying the little boy and his nurse, with a frown.

When the proffered spoon was pushed away for the umpteenth time the girl lost her temper, forcing it into the small mouth. The result was inevitable. The child started to cry loudly, and his efforts to avoid the unwanted food dislodged the dish holding it, spreading it over the table and the floor. The girl threw down the spoon, smacking the chubby legs hard as she pushed away her own chair. Claire noticed that as she stood up she glanced at her watch, hesitated, and then saying something in Arabic to the gathered men, walked towards the door.

The baby was still crying, quite hard now, and against her will Claire felt herself sympathising with him. He had been naughty with his food, but perhaps if the girl had cajoled instead of forced he might have been better behaved. He was wriggling violently in his chair, and Claire gasped as she saw it tilt, rushing instinctively to steady it before it fell.

Close to the baby was enchanting, with soft olive skin and huge tear-drowned dark eyes. He clutched hold of her blouse, the crying stopping as he gazed up at her. He wasn't even secured properly in the chair, and Claire wondered a little at the child's parents, allowing such an inexperienced and uncaring girl to have charge of him. Was one of the men seated at the table the child's father? She glanced towards them and found herself pinned where she stood by the sharply cold glance of the man with the green eyes. What was the matter with him? she thought, unconsciously touching her tongue to suddenly dry lips. Did he think she was going to run off with the baby? His eyes dared her to so much as touch the child, and perhaps it was that, or perhaps it was the piercingly forlorn cry the baby gave as she started to move away that prompted her next action.

Almost automatically she turned back, smiling a little as the baby, sensing victory, lifted his arms. She half expected the man watching them to tear the baby out of her arms, but surprisingly no one moved. When she had been training to be a secretary she had often supplemented her income by baby-sitting and although it had been a couple of years since she had last held such a small child she found herself instinctively slipping back into the mothering role.

The olive cheeks were faintly flushed, his skin hot, and Claire guessed that he was probably teething. His clothes were obviously expensive but crumpled and stained with food. Suddenly realising what she was doing Claire moved to put him back into the chair. He cried protestingly, clinging on to her. Torn between common sense and an inborn instinct to comfort him she glanced across the room. *He* was still watching her and it was something in that look that impelled her towards defiance. Turning away from the chair and walking back to her own table, she soothed the complaining howls, murmuring soft nonsense which seemed to have the desired effect for the cries gradually ceased. She had just reached her table and turned when she saw the men enter the room.

Later she decided she could only have acted by blind instinct, because surely there hadn't been enough time for her to register the menacing appearance of the gun; the silent intent of the man pointing it towards the now empty highchair, and even as he sought her out she was pushing over the sturdy table and crouching behind it, cradling the baby as she heard the sharp splinter of china and another noise that chilled her blood.

Gunfire was something she was familiar with from television, but she had never before experienced it so close at hand. The silence that followed those staccato spurts of sound was, in its way, even more terrifying than what had gone before. Dimly she was aware of running feet, of doors being closed, of someone approaching, a dark hand resting on her shoulder. She knew she tensed, unable to turn and look up, her too-vivid imagination working overtime, so that when she was eventually able to move the first thing she saw was the gun, held casually in the hand of the man standing over her.

Fear thundered through her body, leaving her drenched in perspiration, and trembling so much that he had to drop the gun to pull her to her feet. She heard him mutter something she couldn't understand and she had a vivid moment's recognition of green eyes, no longer ice-cold but hard with a burning anger, as her head was pushed against his shoulder and her body, betrayingly, sank gratefully against solidly braced male muscles, taking the support they offered without paying the slightest heed to her brain's feverish command to resist and pull away.

Dimly she was aware of the doors opening, of hurried, staccato conversation; her eyes fluttered open, to discover that she was still holding the baby and that both of them were safe and unharmed.

The arms that had been holding her fell away and she told herself it was foolish to experience such an acute sense of loss. Dizzily she became aware of her surroundings; of the limp, lifeless dark-suited bodies lying on the floor; of the small, voluable middle-aged man who had erupted into the room, and whose features she vaguely recognised; but most of all of the man who had been holding her and who was now standing several feet away talking calmly to his plump, disturbed companion, both of them pausing to glance at Claire.

She only realised when the baby let out a protesting cry that she was holding him too tightly. Her head felt as though it was full of cotton wool. She seemed to have strayed into another world and she still couldn't take in what had happened. Now, only the overturned table and the smashed crockery remained to prove that it had been real, that she had actually taken shelter behind it while bullets flew about the room. Suddenly, desperately, she wanted to laugh—or to cry—and the only thought surfacing through the muddle of her brain was that if she had to pay for the broken china it would probably use all her godmother's parting cheque.

'Please . . . forgive me . . . I am so disturbed that I forget my manners.' Claire smiled vaguely at the plump bearded man. 'I am Sheikh Ahmed ibn Hassan,' he told her, introducing himself, 'and if you had not . . .' He tried to compose himself, shaking his head slowly. 'Allah must have been smiling upon us this morning, Miss . . .'

Dutifully Claire supplied her name. 'But, we cannot talk of this here. Will you come up to my suite so that I can thank you more properly . . .?' He saw her hesitation and smiled, warmth and charm lighting his rather heavy features, and in that instant Claire recognised him.

He was the head of a small Middle Eastern state and she had seen his photograph in the papers. He was in Britain on a state visit, although the Press had suggested there might be something more in it than that. His country would offer a strategic point for Europe and its allies in a military sense, and it was strongly hinted that this could be the purpose underlining his visit. Claire also remembered reading that his nephew and heir had recently been killed in an accident together with his wife, and there had been rumblings of a Soviet plot to instate a ruler of their choice with sympathies to them rather than to the West.

'I can ask the hotel management to vouch for me . . .' her companion was saying earnestly and Claire realised that he had misinterpreted her hesitation.

She shook her head and proffered a brief smile. 'No . . . no. I recognise you from your photograph in the papers, Sheikh.'

When they left the room they were followed by most of the other occupants, although Claire noticed that one man stayed behind and the mockery in his green eyes seemed to follow her as she walked out of the room, head held high, the baby still clutched in her arms, surrounded by what seemed like a phalanx of silent men.

The lavishness of the Sheikh's suite made her blink, and as she sat down Claire found herself wondering curiously about the child she was still cuddling. She couldn't blot out of her mind looking up and seeing that gun pointed lethally in the direction of the highchair.

'You must be wondering what is going on,' Sheikh Ahmed announced when she had refused a cup of coffee and his attendants had been dismissed. 'This child,' he looked at the baby on her knee, 'is the only son of my nephew, and will in time succeed me as ruler of our state. Today's events have proved beyond any shadow of a doubt that his life is at risk.' The baby started to cry and he frowned in concern. 'There is something wrong?'

Claire shook her head wryly. 'Not really. He is wet and hungry. His nursemaid . . . the girl who was with him in the dining-room . . .'

'I suspect she was a plant who had been paid to leave him unattended. He is normally guarded at all times, but Raoul tells me that the girl insisted that I had said he was to eat in the dining-room. This is not true, and if it had not been for your quick actions . . .'

'I thought we were both going to die,' Claire admitted, shuddering herself.

'And yet thinking that, you did not abandon Saud,' the Sheikh commented watching her. 'Raoul tells me that but for your quick thinking Saud would be dead.'

'Were you . . . were you expecting something to happen?' Claire asked, remembering the guns which had appeared as though by magic in the hands of the men in the dining-room.

The Sheikh shrugged fatalistically. 'Not so much expecting as suspecting. There is a faction in our country that does not approve of our ties with the West. It is not always easy to know friend from foe and one must always be on one's guard. Saud's nursemaid is an example of how easy it is to be deceived. I myself am widowed and have no female relatives close enough to trust with the child.' He suddenly looked tired and careworn. 'But I must not

burden you with our problems. I should like to reward
you for . . .'

'No . . .' Claire spoke quickly and automatically,
reiterating, 'no . . . please, I would rather you did not.
I simply acted instinctively.' She looked down at the
child now sleeping on her lap. 'Is there someone who
can change and feed him?' It seemed incredible to her
that this child, who was apparently so important,
should have no one to care properly for him.

'I had hoped to find a nanny for him while we are
here, but Raoul is opposed to it. He believes Saud
would be better looked after by one of our own race.'
He smiled. 'Perhaps because of his own dual blood,
Raoul is more opposed to Saud having a foreign nanny
than might otherwise be the case. He feels very deeply
the differences which set him aside from his peers.'

What relationship did Raoul have with the baby on
her lap, Claire wondered, but it was a question she
could not ask, she had no desire to pry into the
personal life of the man who had looked at her so
coldly with those too-seeing green eyes. Had they
registered her minute, betraying reaction to his
proximity? The momentary weakness which had had
nothing at all to do with her shock and had instead
sprung from an entirely voluntary response to him as
an intensely male man? It was humiliating to think
that they might, especially when she had on more than
one occasion seen the derisive dismissal of her as a
woman in his eyes.

'Er . . .' She paused, seeing hesitation and embarrassment on the Sheikh's face, intrigued because she
sensed it wasn't a habitual expression for him.

'Saud's room is through there.' He indicated a

communicating door. 'Would it be trespassing too much to ask you to . . .?'

'You want me to change and feed him?' Claire supplemented, hiding a small smile.

'We did not bring a large entourage; the boy's nursemaid was to have been sufficient. I feared to leave him behind unprotected, but now . . . I think what happened this morning will prove to Raoul that we cannot entrust his care to anyone lightly. The girl who had charge of him came extremely highly-recommended, and yet it is plain that she was part of the plot to kill him.'

Remembering how the girl had lost her temper with the child, and looked so pointedly at her watch before she left the dining-room, Claire suspected that he was right.

The Sheikh was charming and as she allowed herself to be manoeuvred into taking Saud into his own bedroom to attend to his needs, she repressed a small smile. This was most definitely not what her godmother had had in mind for her stay in London.

The baby was supplied with every luxury imaginable, from toys to silk and satin clothes, but there seemed to be scant love in his young life, Claire thought pityingly as she first fed and then bathed him. He was not a difficult baby really, responding affectionately to her when she cuddled and held him. She was just towelling him dry, laughing as he lay gurgling on her lap, when the door opened. She tensed automatically, unable to blot out the mental image of men carrying guns and the high-pitched whine of bullets.

Cool green eyes surveyed her speculatively. 'A very

domesticated picture. What a shame that it is me and not Ahmed who is witnessing it. What are you hoping for with this touching display of maternalism, Miss Miles? More than a diamond bracelet, obviously.'

Claire winced, recognising that he had overheard her conversation with her godmother the previous night, and then anger replaced embarrassment as she recognised the calculated insult behind his words. He was implying that she was motivated by materialism. Her full pink lips tightened ominously, and for a moment she considered thrusting the still damp baby into his arms and letting him finish the task for himself. That would soon destroy his sardonic dignity. A small giggle bubbled up inside her as she pictured his immaculately suited figure dealing with the squirming baby.

'Sheikh Ahmed asked if I would help, and I agreed,' she said calmly, 'but only because Saud was both wet and hungry, and too small yet to fend for himself. Sheikh Ahmed tells me that you are against his employing a European nanny for Saud.'

'You *have* been exchanging confidences, haven't you? What else did he tell you?'

'Nothing.'

'Liar. I'm sure knowing my uncle as I do that he also told you of my mixed blood, and now, no doubt, you are on fire with curiosity to know more.'

His arrogance provoked her into an instinctive anger. 'On the contrary,' she told him coldly, 'I have no desire to know the slightest thing about you. Why should I?' She finished buttoning Saud into clean rompers and got up, thrusting the baby towards him, a little surprised by how deftly he held the child, then swept out of the room before he could stop her, seething with fury, because he was right—she had been curious about him. Of course, he must be used to women finding him fascinating. That blend of East and West was a potent one, and he knew it, damn him!

She had always loathed arrogant, self-assured men, Claire reminded herself as she let the door slam behind her and hurried towards the lift, and if she had responded momentarily to the sheer male power of his body against her, it had been a reaction intensified by weakness and relief. After all, she would be a fool to think for one moment that those green eyes might burn with tenderness and passion for her, or that that hard, faintly cruel mouth might touch hers in need and hunger. A complete fool.

CHAPTER TWO

THERE was no reason for her to feel so dissatisfied. Her day had passed pleasantly enough, Claire told herself. She had visited the Tate to admire many old favourites, and then there had been a pleasant walk through the park. Now she was on her way back to the Dorchester to indulge herself with afternoon tea in the promenade room, so why should she feel this tiny feathering of restlessness that kept disturbing her? Perhaps it was because she was alone. She would write to Teddy, send him a postcard of the hotel. Thinking of Teddy reminded her of her ever-present worries about finding his school fees. Generous though her salary was, it couldn't cover them. She would have to find a part-time job. By her reckoning, she could just about manage two more terms with what savings they had left, and the present term's were paid.

'Afternoon tea, madam?' The waiter's voice broke into her reverie, and when she nodded he showed her to a comfortable padded chair, the small table in front of her set for two.

It was just gone five o'clock, obviously a popular time for tea, because most of the tables were taken, and Claire amused herself as she waited for hers to be brought by studying her surroundings. The room itself was long and rectangular with several sets of doors leading off it which she knew led to the restaurants. Decorated in soft buttercup-yellow with the frieze picked out in gold, the decor was an attractive one. Marble columns soared up to the ceiling, and underfoot was a soft patterned carpet rather like an Aubusson. Voices rose and fell mingling with the chink of china cups and the clatter of cutlery against plates.

Nibbling her dainty sandwiches, Claire continued her scrutiny. Expensively and elegantly dressed men and women sat at the small tables, couples in the main, although there were some family groups. All at once she felt very alone, the food she was eating turning to sawdust in her mouth. Pushing away her plate, Claire got up unsteadily, the events of the morning catching up with her. The Head Porter handed her her key when she asked for it, and also an envelope bearing her name. Unable to recognise the handwriting, Claire frowned as she headed for the lift, the small mystery solved when she opened the envelope and realised that the letter was from Sheikh Ahmed.

The lift came. She was the sole passenger and started to read her letter as she was borne upwards. Barely able to take in its contents before the lift stopped, she hurried to her room, unlocking the door with nervous fingers, sinking down into the comfortable chair by the window before unfolding the heavy, expensive paper and reading through the note again.

The Sheikh wanted to see her to discuss something with her. But what? The note was almost deliberately evasive, full of gratitude for what she had done and yet really telling her nothing of the Sheikh's purpose in writing to her. He would send someone to escort her to his suite, his note informed her. Obviously she wasn't going to be allowed to refuse.

Repressing a sigh, Claire found the card she had bought for Teddy and started to write to him. The summer holidays were coming up and she already knew that Teddy had been invited to join a schoolfriend on his father's yacht. She had been worrying about how she was going to pay for the clothes that he would need, but her godmother's generous cheque had solved that problem. It would also enable her to give Teddy some money of his own to spend while he was away and she was just writing to him to this effect when she heard the sharp rap on her door. Guessing in advance that it would be one of Sheikh Ahmed's armed men, she went to the door and opened it, suppressing a small stunned gasp of dismay when she realised he had sent Raoul.

'I'll just get my bag and my key,' she told him, surprised to find that he was following her into her room. Her key and bag were on the far bed and as she picked them up she was astounded to discover that Raoul was openly reading the card she had been writing to Teddy.

'Your lover?' he questioned, without a hint of embarrassment at being discovered.

'My relationship with Teddy is private,' Claire responded furiously. From the first moment she had set eyes on him something about this man had antagonised her, and it was plain that he shared her antipathy. He was looking at her with something that bordered on acute dislike.

'That will be something my uncle hasn't bargained for,' he murmured under his breath as he straightened up, but before Claire could question him further he was heading for the door, the small courtesy of opening it for her and then standing back so that she could precede him, drawing a thin, sardonic smile from his lips. 'My mother used to say that the thing that made her fall in love with my father was his good manners. My countrymen . . .'

'Believe in treating their women like possessions,' Claire said unwisely. 'No wonder your mother chose to marry a European.'

'You prefer European males to Eastern?' The dark eyebrows shot up. 'Why is that, I wonder? Because you know it is easier to dominate them? Are you then a modern, liberated woman, Miss Miles, who believes herself equal or indeed superior to my sex? A woman who chooses her lovers as her grandmother might have done a new gown and discards them just as easily . . .'

Trying to hold on to her temper, Claire responded briefly, 'And you? Am *I* to infer from what you have said that you prefer your women to be of a more biddable disposition; Muslim women, in fact, taught from the cradle to revere and worship the dominant male? How fortunate we both are that we can indulge our separate tastes without opposition.'

She had meant the words as a taunt, but had been totally unprepared for the look of dark, almost brooding anger that tightened every feature, his eyes almost black as they bored into puzzled grey ones.

'You might be able to indulge your preferences, Miss Miles,' he said at last, 'I am less fortunate. Muslim fathers are careful where they bestow their daughters, and like any child of a dual-race marriage, I am totally accepted by neither. Indeed, if it were not for the good offices of my uncle Sheikh Ahmed, I doubt I would even have a country to call my own.' He saw her expression and his face hardened further. 'You might find the thought of a marriage between East and West a romantic concept, Miss Miles,' he told her, correctly reading her thoughts, 'but my mother soon discovered to her cost that my father had no intention of keeping the promises he made when they became man and wife. In the East at least a woman has the comfort of her family if she should be deserted or ill-treated by her husband, in the West . . . My father married my mother purely for her wealth. Once they were married and I was conceived, he devoted all his spare time to other women and gambling. My mother died shortly after I was born. The shame of her husband's desertion was something she could no longer endure, and once my father discovered that he was not going to benefit from his marriage, he gave my uncle the option of either bringing me up himself or placing me in an orphanage.'

Why was he telling her this? Only this morning he had savaged her with the knife thrust of his contempt for merely betraying a brief curiosity, but now he was telling her the intimate details of his life, and in such a taut, bitter way that she guessed every word was a sharp thorn piercing an old wound. She couldn't understand it.

They were borne upwards in the lift towards the Sheikh's private suite. As before, the Sheikh was alone, his smile welcoming and she was sure sincere, as he waved her into a chair.

'Please, sit down, Miss Miles,' he glanced at his

nephew as Claire obediently sank into a plush chair. 'Has Raoul said anything to you of my purpose in asking you to join us?'

'I have told her nothing. You know my views.'

'But if she is agreeable you will . . .'

'I will do whatever is needed to protect the child, you know that.'

Alarmed by the harsh tone of his voice and the undercurrents she could sense seething between the two men, Claire glanced from Raoul's set, dark face to the Sheikh's kinder, but no less resolute one.

'You are alarming our guest, Raoul,' he berated mildly. 'My dear, there is no need to be afraid. Indeed we are the ones to suffer that emotion lest you should . . .' He broke off while Claire stared up at him in mystification. Neither of them struck her as men who would fear anything, especially Raoul. By his actions this morning he had proved that when it came to physical danger . . . She shuddered, suddenly overtaken by a vivid memory of the gunmen and the rapid sound of gunfire, the fear that had been pushed aside by the adrenalin-induced need to act now emerging to surge sickeningly through her veins. Only the knowledge that Raoul was watching her and would no doubt relish her weakness gave her the strength to suppress her feelings, her nerves as taut as fine wire as she waited for the Sheikh to continue.

'I have a proposition to put to you, Miss Miles,' he began quietly, and beneath the calm dignity of his manner Claire sensed a deep inner disquietude. 'Indeed, it is only because I sense within you a warm and sympathetic personality that I am able to speak of this matter to you at all.' He gave her a charming smile. 'You might say that I am taking an unfair advantage of your good nature, and I'm afraid that is true. This morning you risked your own life to save that of my nephew . . .'

'I acted entirely instinctively,' Claire told him, a faint warm colour staining her cheekbones. If the Sheikh had brought her here to offer her another reward, she was going to refuse it. But surely a reward would not necessitate Raoul's presence or be the cause of the uncertainty and agitation she sensed in the older man?

'Perhaps, but nevertheless, your first instinct was to protect Saud, and I myself have observed your care of the child. You like children, Miss Miles?'

'Yes, but . . .' Her voice trailed off as her muddled thoughts clarified. Could the Sheikh be going to ask her to act as Saud's nanny? 'I could not look after him full-time if that is what you are about to suggest. I have a job already, and then . . .' Then there was Teddy, but some inner caution made her say haltingly, 'I have certain commitments . . .'

'To your lover?' Raoul suggested sardonically. 'His should be the commitment to you, Miss Miles.'

'There is a man already in your life?' The Sheikh looked disturbed.

'Yes . . .'

'But you are not betrothed or married to him. There is no truly firm commitment?'

Her mouth had gone dry. Why hadn't she simply explained that Teddy was her brother right from the start? How on earth was she going to extricate herself from her own half-truths now? Anger came to her rescue. What business was it of either of these men what her relationship with Teddy was?

'Miss Miles and her lover are conducting a long-distance affair,' Raoul supplemented cynically. 'She was writing to him when I went to collect her.'

'So . . . Then it is possible that you would be free to return with us to Omarah?'

'As Saud's nanny? I cannot. I am not trained . . . I . . .'

'It is not as Saud's nanny that my uncle requires your services, Miss Miles,' Raoul cut in in a hatefully mocking voice, 'but as his mother.'

'His mother?' The room seemed to whirl dizzily in front of her eyes, 'but . . . but that is impossible.'

'Biologically yes, but . . .'

'What my nephew is trying to say, Miss Miles, is that in order to protect Saud it might be as well if we allowed those who instigated this morning's attack to believe it succeeded. No . . . please hear me out,' he begged when Claire would have interrupted. 'No one apart from ourselves and my guards, whose loyalty I know I can depend on, know the truth. Those sent to kill my nephew have themselves been killed, but if we return to Omarah with Saud there will be other attempts on his life, attempts which could easily prove to be successful, and then I fear my country will turn its eyes and heart to Russia. You know already of the divisions in my country.' He drew a sharp sigh. 'Had Raoul been the son of my brother rather than the son of my sister, I could have appointed him as my heir . . .'

'And that, I believe, is the only thing I can thank my father for,' Raoul interrupted grimly.

'I know you have no wish to step into my shoes, Raoul. Raoul is the head of our petrochemical

industries,' the Sheikh told Claire, and something in
the look on the former's face told her that this was no
sinecure post, and that Raoul was completely genuine
when he said that he had no wish to take his uncle's
place.

'And thanks to the insistence of my father I am also
a Christian,' Raoul added grittily. He saw Claire's look
of surprise and said cuttingly, 'Does it surprise you to
know that those of my uncle's faith are so tolerant
towards others? The Prophet himself decreed that it
must be so.'

Why, when he obviously felt so bitter about his
father, and had chosen to ally himself to the Arab
blood he carried, had he not changed his religion,
Claire wondered, trying to shrug her curiosity aside as
the Sheikh shook his head warningly.

'We digress Raoul. We have not appraised Miss
Miles of our . . . plan. Obviously, if we do allow it to
be known that Saud did not survive this morning's
attack, it would be difficult for us to take the child
back with us to Omarah. I did think at one time of
leaving him in your country where he could be
brought up in secret and, I hope, in safety, but . . .'

'But if you do that he will grow up a stranger to his
own country and its customs. The people would never
accept him in your place. He would be more European
than Arab.'

'This is true,' the Sheikh agreed gravely, 'which is
why, my dear, we are seeking your help. You see, the
only way we can take Saud back with us in safety is if
we take him as someone else's child. You can see, I am
sure, the dangers attendant on such a course. How
could we be sure that the couple we might choose

would be trustworthy? And Saud must be brought up as befits his station.'

'I am honoured that you should have thought of me as a candidate,' Claire responded truthfully, 'but surely, even if I agreed, people would think it strange that you should take into your family an unmarried European girl with a child. Surely they would suspect . . .'

The two men exchanged a look that made her blood turn to ice in her veins, a feeling that she had suddenly strayed on to very unsteady ground sending alarm signals rushing to her brain.

'I have not entirely explained, Saud would not just be your child, but . . . but Raoul's as well. It would be announced that you were married during our visit to your country, and . . .'

'Oh, but that couldn't possibly work,' Claire expostulated, refusing to dwell for the moment on the multitude of sensations assailing her and clinging only to the bare facts. Later, when she was alone, she would allow herself to think more deeply on the strange sensation stirring in the pit of her stomach at the thought of Raoul as her husband . . . her lover.

The look he gave her was bitterly sardonic. 'Well, it won't,' she said sharply. 'Everyone will know that we haven't been married long enough to have a child, and . . . and with a European woman . . . Surely . . .'

Finding no reassurance in Raoul's hard, cynical features, she looked wildly at the Sheikh, her heart sinking at what she saw in his calm, dark eyes.

'We have been into this, and if you are in agreement, our story will be that Saud was the result of an affair between you and Raoul. He spends a

considerable amount of time abroad, so that aspect
need not cause us any concern. Your child will have
been born illegitimately, and I will have coerced Raoul
into marriage with you, for the child's sake.'

The picture he was painting wasn't a very attractive
one and Claire found herself grimacing in distaste. 'I
suspect Miss Miles is thinking the proposition would
sound more attractive had I been the one to do the
coercing, Uncle,' Raoul interceded mockingly, 'but
you are not thinking clearly, Miss Miles. No one
knowing me would believe that I had willingly
married a European woman . . .'

'But they will believe that one bore your child?'
Their argument had personal undertones that bewildered Claire. Calm and even-tempered, she had
never allowed herself to be so provoked and disturbed
by any man. In fact, she had come to think of herself
as someone who could not be affected physically by
men, and yet this man with merely a look—a word—
had inflamed her temper to the point where she could
feel her self-control slipping dangerously away.

'I am a man who spends a considerable amount of time
away from my own people,' Raoul acknowledged,
shrugging as though dismissing her accusation as juven-
ile gaucheness. 'Naturally, it would not be expected
that I should live as a monk. It is also well-known in
our country that European women take lovers.'

'I cannot do it,' she said positively. 'I'm sorry, but
I . . .' She broke off as the door opened and a young
girl walked in carrying Saud. She was dressed in
the uniform of the hotel staff, the little boy was still
flushed and fretful. But he seemed to recognise Claire,
perhaps because of her fair hair, which was probably

unusual to him, Claire thought, unable to check her own response and he wriggled impatiently in the girl's hold, stretching out his arms to her.

The girl came over and handed Saud to her, saying something in Arabic that Claire couldn't understand, before leaving the room.

'She thinks you are Saud's mother,' the Sheikh pointed out quietly. 'I know it is a great deal to ask of you, but I beg you to reconsider. Saud's life is at stake ... We cannot protect him for every second of it. Another year and we shall have overcome our problems. Then you will be free to go. A year, that is all we ask.'

'And, of course, you will be well paid,' Raoul interjected swiftly, mentioning a sum of money that made Claire gasp. It was a fortune, more than enough to put Teddy through school and university and still leave enough for her to buy herself a small house instead of the poky flat she presently rented.

'But ... marriage ...'

'Our marriage will be a mere fiction,' Raoul assured her contemptuously. 'Why else do you think my uncle is at such pains to state that it will have been forced upon me? That way neither of us will be expected to play too false a part. We can live our separate lives ... I told you you should have offered the money first,' he said over her head to his uncle.

The contempt and ugly suggestiveness of his tone took Claire's breath away. She dearly longed to throw his words back in his face, and his money, but at that moment Saud started to cry, and by the time she had soothed him, rocking the small round body against her shoulder, enjoying the warm baby smell of him, she had

had time to think. Time to consider all that such a large sum of money could mean for Teddy. No more scrimping and scraping; no more having to do without the treats enjoyed by most of his fellow boarders. She suppressed a small sigh, knowing that she really had no choice. And then there was Saud. Already she was fond of the small child. There had been one attempt on his life, and she had to admit that the Sheikh's plan was an excellent one.

'I . . . I agree.' The words almost choked in her throat as she saw Raoul's cynically knowing eyes rest on her flushed cheeks. The Sheikh was thanking her profusely, but Claire barely heard him, she was still too shaken by the look of acute dislike she could see in Raoul's eyes. And this was the man she would have to live with as his wife for twelve months! It was on the tip of her tongue to take back her words, but before she could speak he forestalled her.

'I will have the arrangements put in hand. First we will fly to Paris. At the end of the week . . .'

'Paris?'

He saw her stunned expression and laughed sarcastically. 'Oh, don't worry, I have no intention of extending the farce of our "marriage" to include my French relatives, it is just that as my wife you will be expected to maintain a certain standard of dress and appearance.' His lips twisted bitterly as they surveyed her slender frame in the tailored tweed suit. 'While your clothes might be perfectly suitable for your present life-style . . .'

'My nephew is quite right,' the Sheikh interposed sympathetically when he saw her face. 'He is a very wealthy man, and it would not be fitting . . .'

'But surely, if everyone knows you have forced him to marry me, they will not expect . . .'

'What they will expect is for you to be dressed as befits my wife, even if I don't treat you as such.' He grimaced as he caught her brief flush, and added with infuriating accuracy, 'Oh come, surely you don't really suppose that I can't see what is running through your foolish head now? I will say this once and once only, Miss Miles. Even if you were the type of woman I find physically attractive, which you are not, the fact that you have another lover, and your very evident avarice, would undoubtedly be sufficient to kill any desire I might have for you.'

Claire went red and then white as he turned on his heel and stormed out of the room, leaving her alone with the Sheikh and Saud in a silence that seemed to thicken with every passing second.

'Try to forgive him,' the Sheikh said softly at last. 'His has not been an easy life. His mother, my sister, was forced to live almost as a servant in her own home when she returned from France. She had married Lucien D'Albro against my father's wishes, and when they parted . . .' He drew a faint sigh. 'You must understand that it is a matter of family honour when a woman parts from her husband, and my father was of the old school. To make matters worse, a marriage had been arranged for Zenobe. She died when Raoul was very young, but my father remained bitter about his birth to the end. As a child I remember Raoul desperately wanted to be accepted by my father, but he was a man of cruel pride. Raoul of all the family is most like him, and I think my father sensed this. Against his will he loved Raoul best of all his grandchildren. When he died he left him a considerable fortune, but nothing could wipe away the bitter loneliness of those early years. As a child, Raoul was taught to hate and deride his European inheritance. As an adult, he knows that this teaching sprang from my father's anger against Zenobe and against her husband, but Raoul is a complex character; a man who has suffered and still suffers great pain.'

He saw Claire's expression and assured her softly, 'You do not believe me, but I assure you this is so. Why else, now that he is an adult and free to adopt the Muslim religion if he so chooses, does he deny himself this thing that he wanted so desperately as a child? He is a man deeply conscious of the schisms within himself.'

Rather than reassuring her, the Sheikh's words only made her regret more than ever her folly in agreeing to accept the role of Raoul's wife. It might only be make-believe, but some deep inner instinct warned her against any sort of intimacy with Raoul, no matter how tenuous. He would hurt her if he could, she could sense it inside him. Saud stirred in her arms, and she glanced down at the olive face.

'Already he is attached to you,' the Sheikh said quietly. 'I should like you to remain here with us until it is time for you to leave for Paris.'

'I . . . I shall have to tell my employers.' And Teddy, she added mentally. She would drive down to his school to tell him—but tell him what? She nibbled her lip, worrying at its soft fullness, as she took Saud through to his own room and set about preparing his food. She knew that there were several Arab children at Teddy's school. If she told Teddy the truth, he might innocently mention it, and she felt it would be unfair to put the Sheikh's plans at risk. But what other alternatives did she have? She could hardly not tell her brother anything.

The problem worried at her mind as she prepared Saud for bed. Perhaps she ought to allow Teddy the fiction that she was marrying Raoul. She would say nothing of Saud, of course ... And then in twelve months' time? Marriages broke up all the time ... Dear God, what was she doing?

Panic swept over her, pushing aside all her sensible thoughts and decisions. She couldn't go through with it. She couldn't! She couldn't put herself in the power—no matter how briefly—of Raoul D'Albro. He would taunt and torment her continually. She had seen it in his eyes when they studied her with contempt and bitterness. But she had to go through with it. She had said she would—and then there was the money.

Her mouth twisted wryly. Oh, she had seen the look in Raoul's eyes when he mentioned it. He thought she had accepted through greed, but he was wrong—quite wrong. It was for Teddy's sake, not for her own personal gain. But he thought Teddy was her lover. As her feelings of panic subsided, Claire acknowledged that she was the one responsible for that error. But even if she could correct it, would she? Wasn't she safer while Raoul thought she was a greedy, avaricious female with at least one established lover?

But safe from what? Even if he knew the truth Raoul would not be interested in her. She wasn't his type. He had told her that. But the danger didn't come from him, it came from within herself, Claire acknowledged tiredly. Right from the very first time she had seen him it had been there, although she had fought against admitting it; she had told herself that he was everything she disliked and resented in a man.

And he was, but there was more to it than that; more to her feelings than mere dislike. And yes, if she were honest, she would have to admit to the faint, but unmistakable feelings of nervy excitement that his presence aroused. An excitement which she knew instinctively possessed the seeds of very great danger.

CHAPTER THREE

THE week seemed to fly past. Claire spent most of it with Saud, and found herself getting fonder and fonder of the little boy with every hour that passed. Fifty thousand pounds had been deposited in her bank account, and she had written to her employers, telling them that she was getting married, deeming this the wisest course in view of what she intended to tell Teddy.

Teddy. She gnawed anxiously on her lower lip. Yesterday she had told Raoul that she had someone she had to see before they left for Paris. From his cynical, taunting smile she knew he thought she referred to her lover, and she hadn't tried to correct him, but now, this morning, he had told her that a car and driver would be put at her disposal—in case she tried to run out on her agreement, she thought cynically. After all, with the money in her bank account . . . But no, she would never do that. She would keep her side of the bargain, for little Saud's sake if nothing else.

It would take about three hours to drive to Teddy's school, and somehow she would have to find a way of eluding her driver, just in case he discovered it wasn't a man she was seeing but a little boy! Perhaps she could persuade him to wait for her in the village. It was only a mile from the school. She could easily walk. Thank goodness she had had the foresight to telephone the school and speak to Teddy's headmaster. He had readily agreed to allow her to speak to Teddy, promising that he would warn her brother to expect her visit.

She had bought him a new watch, remembering that he needed one badly, and hoping that she had made the right choice. She was just studying it when her door opened and Raoul walked in. As always, she felt acutely ill at ease in his presence, her sense of anxiety increasing as his cool gaze slid over her slender body in its pale lemon linen suit. The suit was relatively new and fitted her body snugly, drawing attention to the slender curves of her hips and her slim length of thigh.

His mouth curled when he had finished his inspection. 'Very cool and correct. What are you hoping to do? Drive him into wanting the woman you have hidden behind the barrier of your oh so correct clothes?' His eyes sharpened as he saw the watch she was holding in her hand. 'What's this?'

'A farewell present,' Claire told him tautly, shivering beneath the icy glare of fury he directed towards her.

'You are giving him presents?' His mouth tightened ominously. 'Is the gift of your body not enough?' Anger gave way to contempt. 'Abase yourself as you wish, Claire Miles, while you bear your own name, but once you carry mine . . .' He broke off to study her contemptuously. 'Have you no pride that you must needs buy a man's affection with gifts? What does he give you, Claire, apart from satisfying you with his body? What manner of man is he?'

His mouth twisted with contempt, impelling Claire to retaliate, to wound his pride as he had tried to wound hers. 'What's the matter, Raoul?' she demanded, her voice husky with anger. 'Has no woman ever loved you enough to buy you gifts; to sacrifice her pride? Are you always the one who has to do the buying? Is that . . .'

'You will not speak to me like that.' He had closed the gap between them before she could move, his fingers biting painfully into the soft flesh of her upper arm, his eyes so dark that they seemed almost black, forcing her to stare helplessly into their mesmerising gaze as he dragged her against his body. She could feel the anger emanating from him, the taut control of his body bending hers like a bow.

She had pushed him too far. She could see it in the controlled fury of his face. In the tight muscles of his body as her own jarred against the hard impact; and now the cruel line of his mouth was approaching hers, hovering, waiting to punish. Something quivered through her, burning her skin, and her lips parted invitingly, her eyes soft and luminous. She caught Raoul's muttered imprecation and then suddenly she was free, dazed and bewildered to the point of shock.

'Oh no,' he was saying tightly. 'Oh no,' he reiterated with cruel softness. 'I'm not falling for that. What did you expect,' he added tauntingly watching her white face, 'that I would be deceived by your clumsy ploy? Enough to take you into my arms perhaps and from there into my bed? How much would I have had to pay for that dubious pleasure, I wonder? However cheap the price, it would be too much. You overrate your appeal and my need. Both would have to increase considerably before I would even contemplate such a course.'

'I . . .' Fury tied Claire's tongue in knots. And besides, how could she explain logically that momentary and totally bewildering impulse which had had her lifting her face to his, ignoring all the warning commands of her brain?

Humiliation scorched through her. Somehow she managed to stagger out of her room and into Saud's, picking up the little boy with arms that still trembled, hugging him as though somehow the warmth of his body would dispel the frozen bitterness that seemed to have invaded her every bone and muscle.

How could she go on with this charade, knowing how deeply and intensely Raoul despised her? But how could she not do it when she thought of what was at stake? And she wasn't thinking just of the money which she needed so badly. There was also Saud, of whom she had become very fond, and who she knew was daily becoming more attached to her. If Raoul's dislike and contempt was the only price she was asked to pay for Saud's safety and Teddy's future financial security, surely it was not too great a burden to bear?

It was just after eleven when she went downstairs to the foyer to find that her car and driver were waiting for her. The fact that the car was an elegant and brand-new Rolls caught her off guard and she stared uncertainly at it for a moment before approaching it cautiously. When the front passenger door was thrust open unceremoniously she eyed it uncertainly, gasping with shock and disbelief when Raoul's voice commanded her curtly to 'Get in.'

'You!' Sheer disbelief prompted the shocked protest, but to judge from the tightening of his skin

over the bones of his face, Raoul had read more than
disbelief into her brief exclamation.

'Did you honestly expect I would allow you to see
this man un . . .'

'Unguarded?' Claire supplied bitterly for him as she
slid into the plush leather seat and closed the door
after her. 'What's the matter? Are you afraid he might
persuade me to change my mind?'

The look on Raoul's face as he turned towards her
shocked her with its biting contempt. 'Hardly,' he
drawled, his eyes pitiless as they raked over her pale
face and slender body. 'A man who accepts expensive
gifts from a woman, who allows her to do all the
running and chasing, isn't going to be fool enough to
place her virtue and his honour above money.'

'Meaning, of course, that you would never stoop to
allow your women to do so,' Claire threw at him
angrily, torn between humiliation and searing fury.
How dare he judge her so contemptuously and on so
little evidence! A man who could do that must surely
hold the whole female sex in contempt.

Her mouth tightened. It was just as well she had
discovered this side of him from the start. That way
she was hardly likely to be dazzled by his handsome
face and masculine body. She checked, tensing, her
fingers on her seat-belt as the full import of her train
of thought sank home. Of course she hadn't been in
danger of falling for Raoul; he might be the epitome of
every girl's idyllic romantic daydreams, but she wasn't
stupid enough to believe those daydreams could be
translated into real life.

'My "women" as you term them, are content to be
what Allah ordained them to be.' Raoul's cold, soft

voice broke into her thoughts, sending icy shivers rippling over her skin.

'Meaning that they know their place and are kept in it,' she taunted back. 'Bought and paid for, so that they are easy to discard when you are bored with them, is that it? Or is it they who grow tired of pandering to your vulnerable ego, Raoul? It takes a very special sort of man to accept a woman as his equal in life, capable of thinking and functioning for herself; a man who can appreciate what a woman must give up when she . . .'

'Gives herself to her lover? In the East we have a saying that man and woman are food and drink, each enhancing the other. In my country a woman is not ashamed to be a woman. She is content in her own role and does not seek to usurp that of the male.'

They had joined the main stream of traffic and Raoul broke off to ask Claire for directions. She told him where they were heading and kept silent as he manoeuvred the large car through the ceaseless flow of traffic. He drove well, neither uncertainly nor aggressively, and his consideration for other drivers and pedestrians was something that surprised her. He had been so arrogant and contemptuous where she was concerned that she had expected him to betray the same traits towards others.

It wasn't until they had left the London traffic behind them and were heading out in the direction of Teddy's school that Raoul picked up the threads of their earlier conversation. 'As my supposed "wife" a certain standard of behaviour will be expected of you,' he began without preamble, and without taking his eyes off the road, 'and now is as good a time as any to speak of this. In the East . . .'

'A woman is a man's possession?' Claire interrupted furiously. 'But you are forgetting that you have been forced to "marry" me by your uncle. We will lead completely separate lives, or so you told me. Feeling the way you do, I'm surprised you aren't already married. To some dutiful, biddable Muslim girl brought up to think of her father and then her husband as her master.'

Dead silence filled the car, and a quick glance into Raoul's face showed Claire a look of such brooding bitterness that her heart quailed a little. It was too late now to regret her lack of tact, and she was surprised when, instead of changing the subject, Raoul said curtly, 'There was to have been such a marriage, but it required that I should change my religion.'

'And you would not? But why? You obviously consider yourself more Eastern than Western. You were brought up there.'

'Sometimes a man needs to be accepted for himself alone,' was all Raoul would say, but it gave Claire something to think about as the powerful Rolls gobbled up the miles.

His comment pointed to a far greater sensitivity than she could ever have imagined he would possess; a need to be accepted that gnawed at her thoughts as she tried to fit together the complicated pieces of the puzzle that went to make up the man seated at her side. The Sheikh had warned her that Raoul found his dual inheritance a difficult one and for the first time she began to appreciate what the older man had meant. To the casual onlooker, Raoul was completely of the East, but that was merely the outward covering; what about the man inside the tawny skin, the man whose father had so contemptuously rejected his mother—so much so that she had returned to her own people, taking her child with her?

It was only as they neared Teddy's school that Claire ceased tussling with the problem, turning her thoughts instead to Teddy and how she was going to stop Raoul and her brother from meeting.

She and Teddy were very close, a result of their parents' death, and Teddy was intelligent enough to suspect the truth if she did not take great care to hide it from him. She had no wish for her brother to grow up under the burden of knowing she had sacrificed her pride and self-respect so that she could pay his school fees, and so she had already decided to tell Teddy that she loved Raoul. There would be time enough later to worry about explaining to him why she had returned to England, her supposed marriage over, but that was something she wasn't going to think about right now. Her first problem was to get rid of Raoul.

In the end it was surprisingly easy to arrange her 'escape'. Raoul insisted that they stop for lunch five miles outside the village, at a hotel Claire remembered being taken to with her parents. It was a large country house set in its own grounds, and ordinarily she would thoroughly have enjoyed the treat of eating there, but on the pretext of wanting to tidy herself up she slipped away to telephone for a taxi, nervously dreading Raoul's appearance with every second that passed as she waited for it to arrive.

Only when she was finally inside it and speeding away from the hotel, did she expel a sigh of relief, hoping that the note she had handed in to reception would find its way safely to Raoul. In it she had told him briefly that she would be gone for a couple of hours. If he did not choose to wait for her she had sufficient money to get herself back to London and, feeing more confident than she had done since leaving London that morning, Claire settled back in her seat, watching the familiar countryside flash past.

Teddy's school had once been the country seat of a wealthy Victorian landowner, and Claire was warmly welcomed into the Headmaster's panelled study by that august gentleman. She had told him briefly on the telephone of the reason for her visit, and after exchanging pleasantries with her, he suggested that she might like to join Teddy in the small sitting-room off his study where they could have some degree of privacy.

Although it had only been Christmas when she last saw her brother, Claire was amazed at the way he had shot up. He badly needed new trousers, and it took her several seconds to get used to the unusual sensation of noting this without the sinking feeling of despair which normally followed such an occurrence. Teddy greeted her warmly, but with a boyish insouciance which brought home to her how quickly he was growing up.

'The Head told me you were coming. Said you'd got something to tell me . . .'

Both of them were remembering how she had been the one to break the news to him of their parents' death and Claire smiled reassuringly. 'Nothing to worry about. I just wanted you to know that I'm getting married.'

In order to avoid confusion, she had made up her mind that she would stick as closely to the Sheikh's story as possible, and so she explained to Teddy that she had recently met Raoul and that they were to be married abroad, all of which he accepted without too many questions, his main concern being whether he could come out to Omarah to spend some of his summer holidays with her.

'We'll have to see,' Claire hedged, deftly turning the conversation to other channels, asking him about his proposed trip with his schoolfriend, and handing over to him the money she had brought with her. 'You'll need some new clothes,' she added practically. 'I'll have a word with Matron before I leave.'

Because they had so many overseas boarders the school was perfectly accustomed to replenishing its boarders' wardrobes and Claire envisaged no problems in this respect. Before she left, two hours later, she had managed to fit in a brief discussion with Matron who had assured her that she could safely leave everything in her capable hands. A final goodbye and thank you to the Headmaster completed her afternoon's work, and Claire would have been surprised had she known his thoughts as he watched her walk down the drive.

A brave girl, and a selfless one who had shouldered the responsibility of her younger brother with a courage he wished more of his pupils could imitate. Dr Harwarden was a wise and knowledgeable man and he only hoped he was mistaken in his fears that this marriage, arranged so suddenly, was being entered into for the right reasons. Not that he doubted Claire's motives, but he was concerned that she might sacrifice herself for others. He knew there had been financial problems following her parents' death, and of the close relationship between brother and sister. Sighing a little, he turned his attention back to the mound of papers on his desk, telling himself that Claire was old enough to make her own decisions.

Wrapped up in her own thoughts, it wasn't until she drew level with the school gates that Claire saw the Rolls parked on the other side of them, Raoul lounging back in the driver's seat. Her footsteps slowed instinctively, apprehension feathering along her spine. How had he known where to find her? Did he know about Teddy? It was only stubborn pride that had kept her from telling him the truth herself. Let him think the very worst of her if he wished, she wasn't going to be the one to show him the error of his ways.

Instinctively, she knew if she told him the truth, his condemnation of her would be much less harsh, but the way in which he had immediately leapt to the wrong conclusion had stung her pride. Was that honestly how he saw her? If so, then let him, and as she approached the gates Claire knew that she did not want him to know the truth. She would rather he thought the worst he possibly could of her. It was as though his contempt of her was a protective barrier between them, although why she should need its protection she wasn't quite sure.

As he saw her approach, Raoul opened the car door and came towards her to unfasten the gate. His unfailing politeness set her teeth on edge, as though his actions were designed somehow to underline his contempt for her.

'How did you know where to find me?'

His eyebrows rose fractionally as she spoke. 'It

wasn't very difficult. I simply checked with the taxi firm. So your lover is a teacher. Is that why he doesn't mind you leaving him for a year, because it is difficult for the two of you to meet? What will you do with the money my uncle is paying you for acting the part of my wife? Help him to find more congenial employment?'

Expelling her breath on a faint sigh of relief, Claire refused to rise to his taunts. At least he didn't know the truth. 'I think that's my business, don't you?' she said loftily as she followed him back to the car, stopping in her tracks as Raoul suddenly came to a halt in front of her, grasping her chin with his fingers and tilting it upwards so that he could study her face.

'It must have been a very cool leave-taking,' he said slowly at last. His thumb brushed slowly against the fullness of her lower lip. 'Your mouth doesn't even look as though it has been kissed.'

Shock widened her eyes, her cheeks flushed as she wrenched herself free of his grasp. 'I don't think that's any of your business either, do you?' she asked icily, reaching for the door handle. 'Or is that the sort of thing that turns you on? Hearing about other people's . . .'

The ferocity of the expletive that left Raoul's lips cut across her words, and her body tensed automatically as she shrank away from him. 'Your innuendos are an insult,' he told her harshly, 'and no doubt the product of a silly, immature mind. Remember that from now on to all intents and purposes you are my wife, and you will be expected to behave accordingly.'

'By obeying your every word and abasing myself before you like . . . like a slave?'

The icy contempt in his eyes made her tremble at her folly in goading him. 'By remembering that I value my self-respect, even if you don't value yours, and that as my wife, my honour and good name *are* yours, and that any attempt to sully either will be swiftly punished.'

It was enough to keep her silent until they were well on the way back to London. Once or twice she stole a quick peep at his arrogant profile, each time reading a rejection and contempt there that reinforced her silence. If he didn't want to talk to her then he needn't. There was still much she would need to know about their life together; about his family, and how she would be expected to behave, but she wasn't going to beg to be told.

It was a relief to get back to the Dorchester, and the now familiar routine of caring for Saud. The little boy was openly pleased to see her, but Claire was conscious of Raoul's eyes boring into her back as she picked Saud up and cuddled him.

'Someone should tell your lover how good you are with children,' he murmured against her ear as she straightened up. She hadn't realised he was so close to her and Claire felt almost suffocated by the warmth of him against her back, a primitive flood of awareness burning through her body as it responded to the proximity of his. 'Or doesn't he care enough for you to give you the gift of his child?'

Only by pretending she hadn't heard him and keeping her back to him was Claire able to cope with the heat she could feel burning against her skin, unaware that she was still holding her breath in apprehension until the door closed behind him and she was safe to breathe out and relax.

'Would you care for a drink?' Claire couldn't help noticing that the air stewardess's smile for her was nowhere near as warm as it had been for Raoul. They were flying over the English Channel en route for Paris, Saud in between them, fast asleep. She had fought against this visit to Paris, but the Sheikh had gently pointed out the necessity of it to her. In their absence, the news of their marriage could be broken and would doubtless be picked up by the Press. Their trip to Paris would give Claire an opportunity to get used to her new role, and although she had protested that no man being forced into a marriage he did not want would take his new bride on a shopping spree in Paris, both Raoul and the Sheikh had overruled her.

'As my wife you will be expected to maintain a certain standard,' Raoul had repeatedly told her, adding sardonically, 'besides, you cannot really expect me to believe that any woman would turn down an opportunity to refurbish her entire wardrobe at a man's expense.'

'That depends on how she has to repay him,' Claire had retorted tartly, and as she relived the scene, she remembered how the Sheikh had smiled, half-secretly to himself as he listened to their quarrel. It was just as well that his plan did not call for her to play the adoring new bride, because that was something she was sure she would not be able to do.

Two hours later, installed in a luxurious suite at the George V, Claire was still trying to come to terms with the luxury of her surroundings. Unashamedly lavish, decorated with Flemish tapestries, sculptures, paintings and ormolu clocks, its magnificence took Claire's breath away. Delicate eighteenth-century French furniture, almost too dainty to use, furnished their suite. Her own bedroom could easily have housed a small apartment and the bathroom off it was a sybarite's dream. A cot had been provided for Saud and Claire's first duty was to feed and change the small boy. She was glad of the activity to take her mind off the fact that she and Raoul were now practically alone, Raoul having told his uncle that he thought it best that they dispensed with any retainers or guards for their trip to Paris.

'If we are to be accepted as a married couple it is necessary that we have a little time to ourselves to get used to the new role,' he had told the Sheikh, and trying to come to terms with her sudden elevation to the world of the unbelievably rich, Claire was glad that the Sheikh had allowed him to have his way. It was bad enough trying to behave as though such luxury was an everyday habit, without trying to cope with the curiosity of Raoul's retainers. Only a very few of the Sheikh's private staff were aware of the deception, mainly those men who had been in the dining-room when the murder attempt took place. It was fortunate that Saud was too young to talk yet, Claire ruminated as she changed him and placed him in the cot, otherwise the small boy might easily have betrayed them.

A member of the hotel staff was summoned to keep watch over the cot; as their child, Saud was in no danger, Raoul had told her, but even so, Claire knew a certain sense of misgiving when she joined Raoul in their sitting-room. For the flight he had worn a dark, formal suit, easily at home in European clothing, the white silk shirt drawing attention to the smooth dark texture of his skin. In the melding of East and West, he seemed to have inherited the best physical characteristics of both races, his features reminding Claire sharply of a Leonardo drawing or the purity of a Greek statue. He was almost too physically perfect, and in some ways it was no wonder he held her sex in contempt. He would have been hopelessly spoiled by it from the hour of his birth, even had fortune not favoured him with position and wealth in addition to good looks.

In silence she accompanied him to the lift and down into the foyer. In the taxi, Raoul spoke in fluid French, a sharp reminder of his parentage.

The rest of the day passed in a whirl of activity. If she had ever doubted the power of money, she did so no longer, Claire thought cynically as the staff of exclusive fashion houses fluttered round her like bees to honey, praising her slender figure, and the silver blondeness of her hair as they vied with one another to provide the sort of trousseau her new husband's wealth demanded.

Claire wasn't entirely surprised to learn that wealthy Arab women made up a large proportion of their clientele, but she firmly refused the ornate and lavish gowns that several of the couturiers told her were favourites with Middle Eastern women. Her own choice was for simple, well-cut clothes, and she was surprised to discover that Raoul seemed to share her taste. When she protested that she was hardly likely to wear half of the clothes he had selected, he cut her short, telling her curtly that contrary to her apparent belief they would be invited to many social events and that she would be expected to be dressed accordingly.

'As Finance Minister for our country I often have to entertain foreign dignitaries. As my wife, you will be representing our country on those occasions.' But that did not entirely soothe her conscience, especially when Raoul presented her with jewellery which must have cost a minor fortune. Emeralds and diamonds comprised a suite which would cover every occasion, the deep glow of the gems enhancing the colour of her eyes as they widened in awed disbelief over the glittering stones.

Exhausted long before the afternoon was over, it was only pride that kept Claire from pleading that they finished their shopping another day. Her feet ached and her head buzzed as she tried to assimilate all the differing experiences. It was like trying to digest too much rich food all in one go, and when Raoul took her elbow and escorted her into yet another discreetly expensive boutique, Claire was almost too numb to glance at her surroundings. It was only the sudden realisation that it was underwear that was being displayed for her consideration this time that jolted her out of her exhausted lethargy.

Delicate bras and briefs in finest silk and lace were displayed for his inspection; cool pretty cottons and openly seductive silk-satins in soft misty pastels and rich darker fabrics. The *vendeuse* barely concerned herself with Claire's opinion. A tall, elegant Frenchwoman in her thirties, all her concentration was centred on Raoul. And why not? Claire thought bitterly, he was the one paying the bills, buying for her the most intimate of clothes with a casual experience that spoke volumes on his knowledge of her sex.

'These, I think,' he ordered, indicating a camisole and matching french knickers in pale aqua silk-satin, lavishly trimmed with blonde lace. 'The colour will suit my wife's pale skin . . .'

'The fabric may not be suitable for a hot climate,' the vendeuse pointed out, glancing briefly at Claire. 'Cotton . . .'

In response Raoul picked up the silk-satin he had pointed out, letting the material slide smoothly from his fingers. 'Cotton does not feel like this,' he said coolly, his eyes registering the hot colour stealing over Claire's skin. An inner voice reminded her that for all his Eastern outlook he was a man who was part French; a sensualist, she guessed, no matter how much he might keep that side of his nature sternly controlled. Just for a moment she was tormented by an image of those lean, dark fingers against her skin, stroking it with the same appreciation with which he touched the silk, and then the vision was banished, her body trembling in acute reaction. How would she feel right now if Raoul was in fact her lover, was in fact buying her these clothes because he wanted to enjoy the warmth of her skin beneath its satin covering?

'Raoul, I don't need those . . .' she began jerkily, trying to dismiss her unruly thoughts, but her protest was ignored, and by the time they left the shop she felt she had enough new clothes to last her the rest of her life. She ought to have hated Raoul buying her such intimate items of clothing, but instead she felt almost excited, a strange, tense sensation invading the pit of her stomach.

What on earth was the matter with her? Raoul despised her. She must never allow herself to forget that fact. Raoul despised her and was simply playing a part.

By the time they returned to their hotel, Claire was so tired that she could only nod her head when Raoul suggested that they dine in their suite. Her meal tasted like sawdust as she envisioned all the lonely months ahead when the silence between them would stretch into what was becoming a familiar tension, or when she would be left completely alone while Raoul pursued his business interests. But what else did she expect? She was doing a job for which she was being paid extremely well and that was all there was to it. It was foolish to feel regret because Raoul evinced no desire for her company, or chagrin because he excused himself as soon as he had finished eating, retiring to his own room where she heard him lift the telephone and then talk into it in harsh Arabic.

Tired though she was, it seemed hours before sleep finally claimed her, her dreams a jumbled mixture of events from which she was glad to wake when the maid brought her a tray of tea and some small, plain biscuits, English and French newspapers on her tray.

Their marriage was mentioned in both; a discreet paragraph in *The Times* and something similar in its French equivalent. The gossip columns of the English tabloids gave a little more detail, including a mention of Saud. Unwittingly, Claire sighed. It was too late to back out now. For the next months at least she was, to all intents and purposes, Raoul's wife and Saud's mother.

Movements from the cot at her bedside reminded her of Saud's presence and she reached him just as he started to make his protest. His face was faintly

flushed, the gums he exposed to Claire in a wide grin
betraying the fact that another tooth was on the way.
Sitting on the side of her bed with him, Claire rubbed
his swollen gum consolingly. She would have to try
and buy him a teething ring. It constantly amazed her
that such a wealthy and important child should be so
lacking in the most basic comforts. If his mother had
lived things would have been different, and she told
herself that if nothing else, at least her presence would
benefit Saud.

She was so engrossed in watching him that she
didn't hear her bedroom door open, only becoming
aware of Raoul's presence when he was halfway across
the floor. Already up and dressed, he made her feel
acutely vulnerable in her thin cotton nightdress, her
hair still tousled and her face completely free of make-
up.

'You've seen the papers?' Claire nodded, still trying
to comfort Saud. 'What's the matter? Is something
wrong with him?' Raoul asked her, glancing down at
the child in her arms. Saud wriggled on her lap, his
movements tightening her nightdress until the soft
swell of her breasts was clearly visible beneath it.
Raoul's glance lingered only briefly on her body, but it
left Claire's acutely aware of her near-nudity.

'He's teething,' she replied huskily. 'I think perhaps
I'd better stay with him today . . .' She didn't look up
at Raoul.

'We'll both stay with him,' he surprised her by
saying. 'Or rather we'll take him with us. Don't forget
you'll need to equip a nursery for him before we leave
Paris, and we've only got a couple more days.'

He bent down, one lean finger touching Saud's hot

cheek, his knuckles accidentally grazing her breast. Her response was instant and electrifying, awareness flooding her body. All Raoul's attention focused on her as he studied her flushed cheeks, his eyes slowly dropping to her breasts and lingering there for several seconds. It took a considerable effort of will-power to keep her breathing steady and even; to busy herself with Saud as though she was completely unaware of the way Raoul was looking at her, or her body's immediate physical response to it.

'I'll get Saud dressed. If we're getting short of time we'd better not waste any of it.'

It was amazing that she managed to sound so calm, when her whole world had been jolted off its axis. No man had ever aroused such a reaction within her. If Raoul had leaned forward and stripped the nightdress from her body, she wouldn't have made the slightest move to stop him. And if he had touched the flesh where his glance had lingered ... A wave of heat burned through her. What on earth was she thinking? She was glad that Raoul had turned away and had not witnessed that betraying tide of colour. Her reaction must have had something to do with the tenderness she had seen fleetingly in his eyes as he bent to touch Saud. Yes, that must be it! His affection for the little boy had caught her off guard.

Feeling relieved that she had managed to find an explanation for her unusual reaction, Claire waited until the door had closed firmly behind him before moving from the bed. A glimpse of her own reflection in one of the room's many mirrors arrested her, fresh colour storming her cheeks as she realised how transparent the fine cotton actually was, every line of her body revealed through it. What was she worrying about? Raoul was hardly likely to be aroused by the sight of her naked form. Hadn't he already told her how much he despised her? And he was hardly likely to be short of admiring female companionship.

For some reason the thought was a depressing one, but Claire didn't pause to analyse why. She was growing adept at avoiding unpleasant issues, she recognised wryly, as she bathed and dressed Saud, forcing her mind to turn to Raoul's plans for the remainder of the day.

CHAPTER FOUR

THEIR shopping spree finished, the purpose of their presence in Paris achieved, Claire found her thoughts turning again and again to the country which was to be her home for the next twelve to eighteen months. Rather than ask Raoul about his country, she had secretly managed to buy some books about the Middle East from a book store selling books in both French and English and she pored over these, alone in her room after Saud was asleep.

Omarah, it seemed, was one of the most forward-thinking of the Gulf States and reputedly one of the most beautiful, with a long coastline along the Persian Gulf and a wild hinterland behind it where the nomadic life of its desert inhabitants was preserved and protected. Careful forward-thinking had resulted in a diversification of business interests. Omarah was the centre of the Middle Eastern banking world, with a university that prided itself on the number and excellence of its science graduates, and technological progress had been carefully matched by a retention of Muslim values and the tolerance on which all Muslim races prided themselves towards adherents of other religions. Unlike many of the other Gulf States, Omarah possessed a capital that had its roots in antiquity. That Belthar had been a port of renown when Baghdad was still a village was a common boast, or so Claire read, and her senses were stirred by the photographs in her guide book, depicting, as they did, scenes she felt could not be rivalled by Hollywood's most lavish Arabian Nights fantasies.

On the last night of their stay in Paris, Raoul surprised her by announcing they would dine in the hotel's most exclusive restaurant. Claire wanted to refuse, but Raoul coolly overrode her objections.

Among the clothes he had bought for her was a Dior model lavishly designed; a swathe of off-white satin covering her from throat to ankle at the front, but dipping down to her waist at the back. The fabric enhanced her pale colouring, drawing attention to the size and depth of her eyes. With it Claire wore the diamond and emerald earrings Raoul had bought for her, the diamonds throwing out tongues of fire when she studied her reflection in her mirror. The slender sheath of silk made her look taller and somehow fragile, her hair a silver veil curving down on to her shoulders. She was just slipping into high-heeled sandals when she heard the knock on her door. Expecting the maid who was to watch over Saud, she called out 'Come in,' sudden tension infusing her muscles as the door opened and Raoul walked in.

Dressed in formal evening clothes, he projected a devastating image of male beauty; the same sort of beauty possessed by a mountain leopard, Claire thought, shuddering slightly; a beauty that engendered fear and gave birth to a curling sensation of pain cramping through her lower stomach. He studied her without comment, and she had to bite back the childish desire to demand if he was satisfied with what he saw. Everything she was wearing he had paid for, and as he watched her she felt a bitter impulse to tear off the silk dress and the fine underwear she was wearing beneath it and to fling them at his feet, together with the priceless gems adorning her ears, and to tell him she would rather go naked through the streets then wear clothes paid for with his money. But she quelled the impulse, telling herself she was being stupid. Like herself, he was simply a pawn in a very dangerous and difficult game. There could be no personal relationship between them, they were simply actors, each playing a part.

The feeling that she had somehow strayed into an extravagant play was accentuated when they walked into the restaurant. For a moment, Claire was dazzled by the sophistication of the other diners. Women glittered with expensive jewels, their bodies wrapped in *haute couture* gowns. Conversation rose and fell in dizzying waves and although she was loath to confess it, Claire was glad of the elegant length of Raoul's body alongside her own. Dangerous and lethal as a black cheetah he might be, engendering fear and awareness in every part of her body, but he was also a protection against the battery of curious eyes studying her, observing their progress across the room.

'Raoul!'

Claire came out of her panic-stricken reverie to register the scrape of a chair being thrust back and the husky, vaguely familiar masculine voice exclaiming Raoul's name as its occupant got to his feet. Only slightly less tall than Raoul, the resemblance between them was so marked that Claire knew without even considering the matter that she was looking at Raoul's father. His companion had also got to her feet. She was young, about her own age, but Claire barely had

time to register the avid look of appreciation in curious
brown eyes before Raoul's father was reaching out to
embrace her, not casually as he might have embraced
an acquaintance, but intimately as befitted a true
daughter-in-law.

'I read that you were in Paris, and that you were
married. If I read the papers aright, you have made
me a grandfather.' Speculative grey eyes rested
thoughtfully on Claire's flushed face. 'Forgive me if I
seem surprised, *mon cher*, but somehow from what I
had read I expected your bride to appear much less
. . . innocent.'

Something flashed briefly in Raoul's eyes, whether
anger or contempt Claire could not be sure, and for a
second she held her breath, wondering if he would
look at her again, and see in her face what his father
had.

'It seems your sins have caught you out, my son,'
the Frenchman was continuing. 'Ahmed always was
strongly morally motivated . . .'

'A fact of which you were undoubtedly aware when
you seduced my mother and implanted her with your
seed,' Raoul grated back. 'I hope you are praying to
Allah that Ahmed might be granted a long life, Father,
for once he is dead you need not look to me to
continue the generous allowance he permits you.' His
mouth curled contemptuously as he looked past Claire
to the brunette standing by his father's side. 'How will
you pay for your little diversions then, I wonder?'

'How easy it is for you to condemn. But then you
have never gone hungry, never felt the gnawing ache
that springs from poverty. You are more my son than
you will ever allow yourself to admit. There was only

one woman who mattered to me. Your mother knew that. I was always honest with her on that score. My little Marie was killed, killed by the Germans just before Paris was liberated. Your mother knew of my love for Marie. I made her no excuses for what I was, no apologies for loving Marie more than I loved her. Your mother was a spoiled child, Raoul, and I was lonely and bitter enough to think that what she could give me might be some sort of compensation. One day you will love a woman as I loved Marie, and then you will understand.'

When he had finished speaking there was silence. Claire had expected to dislike him, but instead she felt moved to a reluctant pity. She glanced into Raoul's face, shocked by the bitter contempt she saw there.

'I might feel more charitable about your denial of my mother, and of myself, if it were not for the fact that you have lived off us both for so many years.'

'No, you hate me because I couldn't love you as a man should love his son,' his father said calmly. 'I cannot lie to you, Raoul, nor put right an old wrong. From the moment of your birth you were your mother's son, a child of her heritage. I confess I was surprised when I read that Ahmed had compelled you into this marriage for the sake of the child you had conceived. Knowing you as I do, I thought you would rather have cut off your right arm than deny yourself to your own child, especially a son, but then perhaps there is more of me in you than you wish to admit.'

Raoul's face was bone-white with fury, his eyes glittering almost black in the mask of bone and skin, and Claire reacted instinctively, speaking almost without thinking as she sought to defuse the situation.

'Raoul didn't know about . . . about the baby,' she interceded huskily. 'We quarrelled and I didn't tell him . . .'

'But somehow Ahmed found out, and now you are married? She is very loyal to you, this wife of yours, Raoul, more loyal than your mother ever was to me. She couldn't wait to run home to her family to complain that I didn't love her as she believed I ought, even though I had told her what our marriage would be.'

'Lucien . . .' The brunette pouted, bored with a conversation which excluded her, and Claire shrank from the contempt in Raoul's eyes as they moved from his father to the pouting girl at his side.

'You insult the memory of my mother to speak her name in the company of such a . . . *putain* as this, and if you were not my father . . .'

'You would what? Have me stoned to death? There is little of the Frenchman in you, is there, my son? Take care that fierce pride of yours does not blind you to what you really want from life. You are very like your mother. Had she listened properly to what I told her, our life together could have been a comfortable one . . .'

'With both of you living on her wealth?'

'We made a bargain, she and I. Which is the greater dishonour I wonder? To renege on one's word or to live off one's wife?' With a sudden switch of mood that startled her, Raoul's father turned to Claire and said courteously, 'When you have finished dining perhaps you will allow me to dance with you, always supposing, of course, that my son permits?'

'I . . .'

'We are newly-married, *mon père*. Tonight Claire will be in no one's arms but mine.'

Raoul's fingers on her arm urged her forward before his father could add anything further, and although he seemed to be completely in control of himself, Claire was painfully aware of the biting grip he had on her arm and knew that in the morning her skin would bare bruises from his touch.

The altercation with his father had taken away what little appetite she had had, and she shivered as she tried to study the menu, stunned when Raoul took it away from her.

'I am not hungry and neither, I suspect, are you,' he said abruptly, 'we will dance and perhaps our appetites will return.' He made no other reference to his father, and Claire was reluctant to bring the subject up. Neither did she particularly want to dance with him, but she sensed that to refuse him would be like a torch applied to dry tinder, igniting the temper she could sense he was struggling to control.

He was an excellent dancer, but she was too acutely conscious of the proximity of his body to hers to relax completely. The top of her head barely reached his shoulder and she was strongly aware of the warm, musky scent of his body, of the tautly controlled anger he was banking down. He bent his head and she had a momentary glimpse of something approaching deep pain in his eyes, before he banished it. Her heart ached with a tender pity and an insane desire to comfort him.

Was she completely mad? It would be like trying to comfort a wounded cheetah, and she would be mauled agonisingly in the process. His experiences with his parents had left him emotionally scarred and defensive, so much so that she doubted that any human being could get really close to him, and those foolish enough to try would receive the full force of his raging anger.

Across the room Claire's eyes instinctively searched for Lucien D'Albro. Did he realise how severely his rejection had damaged his son?

'What's the matter? Wishing you were with my father?' The bitter savagery of his taunt caught Claire completely unawares. 'I know you were speaking about him,' Raoul continued before she could speak. 'He has the reputation for being a first-rate lover.'

'Unlike you,' Claire retorted scathingly, hating the way he was looking at her, with a cynicism that bordered on complete contempt. 'Making love with you would be like . . . like being mauled by a . . . a wild animal,' she flung at him without bothering to weigh her words, realising her danger only when his lips parted in a feral smile that froze the blood in her veins.

'I think we will finish this conversation in the privacy of our suite.' It was impossible for her to resist the pressure of his fingers curling round her arm as he practically dragged her bodily from the floor. Pride and pride alone kept her from crying out in protest as he propelled her into the foyer and towards the lifts.

By the time they got upstairs he would have got his temper back under control, he was furiously angry with her now but it wouldn't last. He didn't even desire her, Claire comforted herself as the lift bore them upwards and he retained his savage hold on her. In a thick silence he pushed her into their sitting-room. All the protests and objections she had prepared mentally died on her lips as he dragged her through the sitting-room and into his own bedroom, locking the door behind them. It was only when he pocketed the key that she realised the extent of her danger and how far she had underestimated his mood. Black, terrifying rage simmered in the depths of his eyes as he released her arm, and laughed mirthlessly as she fled to the locked door.

'Oh no, you won't escape that easily,' he taunted her. 'Downstairs you sympathised with my father, didn't you?'

'I always try to see both sides of a story,' Claire palliated.

She had hoped to soothe him, but fear raced through her as he smiled coldly, his voice chilling her skin as he said softly, 'Oh good, then you'll understand why I want you to fully appreciate my mother's. Tonight it seemed to me that you were distinctly unsympathetic towards her—a young girl, the wife of a man who neither loved nor respected her. By tomorrow you should be much closer to appreciating her position.'

He took off his jacket and started to unfasten the buttons of his shirt with a slow purposefulness that mesmerised her. 'Of course, she was an innocent virgin, while you are a woman of the world, but then by all accounts my father is a far more considerate and appreciative lover than I. What was it you said . . . it would be like making love with a wild animal? I shall try not to disappoint you.'

This couldn't be happening to her, Claire thought wildly, closing her eyes to blot out the terrifying image of Raoul slowly and deliberately removing his shirt, his eyes pinpoints of black ice in the taut sleekness of his face. Her fingers tugged ineffectually at the locked door, panic stirring deep inside her, threatening to overwhelm her, in a primitive and helpless bid for flight. She wouldn't add to the futility of what was happening by running from him like a terrified animal trying to escape the talons of its captor. She would try to retain the remnants of her self-control, to . . .

A small sob escaped her as she felt ungentle hands on her shoulders, quickly turning her, seeking the fastening of her gown and sliding it from her shoulders. As Raoul turned her to face him, she crossed her hands over her exposed breasts instinctively, her eyes opening wide as she heard Raoul's acid exclamation, overriding her small cries of protest as he pried her protective fingers away from her body, forcing her hands down to her sides as her gown slid in a silken heap to the floor and his gaze roamed boldly over her naked curves. No man had ever seen her like this, nor studied her so intimately, and a deep flush of shame seared her skin.

In the lamplit room, Raoul's skin gleamed soft bronze, a tangle of dark hairs revealed by his open shirt. His flesh so dark in contrast to hers transfixed her gaze, her mouth suddenly so dry that she had to touch her tongue to her lips to moisten their contours. Dark eyes followed the intimate gesture, the fingers which had been clamping her arm to her side moving slowly over her body, stroking the curve of her hip which the brevity of her silk briefs did nothing to conceal. Tremors of reaction coursed through her body, the silken intimacy of Raoul's fingers against it triggering off strange waves of sensation. The soft pink areolae of her nipples seemed to swell and harden, and cool brown fingers were leaving the curve of her waist to investigate the rosy peaks.

'How very responsive you are, an enticement any man would find hard to ignore.' Without her being aware of it, Raoul had moved closer to her. His tongue brushed the soft outline of her lips, her eyes widening in astonishment as her body registered its response to his light touch. His tongue moved over her mouth again and Claire found her lips parting, wanting against her will a deeper contact. Her near nudity was forgotten as Raoul's mouth moved lightly against her own, teasing and tormenting until without being aware of it she was moving closer to him, like a moth attracted to the flame; realising too late, when she was helpless, held fast in his arms, his mouth plundering the innocence of hers with a bruising pressure that shocked and frightened her, what she had done.

Her breasts were crushed against the hard wall of his chest, his mouth enforcing his dominance over her, his fingers tightening on her hip bones as he moulded her against his body.

'Raoul, please don't do this,' she begged in a panicky voice when his mouth finally released hers. Her lips felt swollen and bruised, her voice unfamiliar even to her own ears, edged with fear and hysteria.

'Pleading with me, Claire? You should know better than to plead with a wild animal.' His voice possessed a hypnotic quality that held a deadly fascination, and despite the warmth of his room Claire shivered, gasping in shock and outrage when his hand spread possessively against her breast. His thumb stroked slowly over her nipple and the dark head bent. Fierce shafts of pleasure seemed to jolt through her body, a crazy, mindless frenzy taking possession of her. 'Claire . . .'

The shrill command of the telephone cut through the heavy silence, and Raoul released her almost instantly to go and answer it. He spoke into the receiver in Arabic, frowning as he turned and saw her, her gown still on the floor, her arms wrapped round her body. Murmuring something curtly into the receiver, he put it down and came towards her, taking the door key out of his pocket.

'Saved this time from the mauling of the wild animal.' The anger had gone completely from his expression. 'Is that relief or disappointment I see in your eyes, Claire?' he added mockingly as she edged away from him. 'Your body is quite intoxicatingly responsive. Your lovers must have taught you well . . . or is it simply frustration that made you so hungry in my arms?'

He picked up the receiver before she could retaliate and tell him that she had felt nothing in his embrace apart from fear and loathing. He had treated her as though she were a rag doll incapable of feelings and her pride was as bruised as her mouth. He was an animal, a dangerous animal she would be wise not to tangle with again if she valued her self-respect and her safety. She had always sworn that when she did share the pleasure of intimacy with a man, it would be with a man she respected and trusted as well as loved, and yet she was forced to admit that she had come dangerously close to forgetting all the tenets by which she had previously lived her life when Raoul held her in his arms. Those light teasing kisses had inflamed her to the point where nothing else had mattered other than the hard possession of his mouth, and without the brutality of the kiss he had forced upon her she doubted that she would have been able to break free of the spell he seemed to have woven round her senses.

Safe in her own room she dismissed the maid and then locked the door behind her, telling herself that it was just as well she had found out what manner of man lurked behind the urbane exterior Raoul showed to the world. Now there would be no danger of her falling prey to his potent maleness. But as she lay on the verge of sleep she was forced to admit that there had been excitement as well as fear in her reaction to him; that her body had responded overwhelmingly to his touch and that she would have to keep a stricter guard over her emotions.

'Welcome to Omarah!'

They had flown Concorde to Omarah in less than half the time it would have taken on a normal flight, and Claire inclined her head slightly towards Raoul as she followed him down the gangway, her body trying to adjust itself to the intense heat of the Gulf afternoon. Heat lay in a haze of dust over the city beyond the modern airport; minarets and mosaics vying with skyscrapers, the mingling of East and West an assault on Claire's senses as she tried to assimilate the contrasting cultures.

A Mercedes limousine was waiting to ferry them from the airport to what was to be Claire's home for the duration of their stay. She knew that Muslim families lived together, and had somehow expected that she would be sharing the woman's quarters of someone else's home but Raoul announced, as their driver negotiated the narrow streets of the souk, and then open, gracious boulevards, that the Sheikh had put one of his palaces at their disposal. 'It is on the gulf, away from the city. The air is more healthy there for Saud.'

It was disconcerting to learn that they would be living alone together. When she had visualised her life in Omarah Claire had envisioned a life shared in the main with other women, rather than with Raoul who she had imagined would have as little desire for her company as she had for his, but her doubts and fears were forgotten as the city was left behind and they took the coast road along the gulf, past sugar-icing places, Moorish in concept, decorated with iron grilles.

They had gone several miles before they turned off the main road and bumped down a narrow track which came to a full stop in front of a pale pink palace, its narrow slit windows staring haughtily in the direction they had just travelled. As though by some magic signal, two doors opened in the high wall surrounding the palace and the Mercedes purred silently inside.

They were in a courtyard enclosed by the high wall on one side and a row of what seemed to be garages and outhouses on the other. In the distance, Claire could hear the sound of water, and the brilliant sunshine cast harsh shadows over the coloured pavings. More utilitarian than decorative, the court-yard was faintly disappointing. She had expected something more exotic.

Raoul was climbing out of the car and coming round to open her door for her, a courtesy she hadn't expected, bearing in mind the much-publicised superiority of the Middle Eastern male. The heat of the afternoon struck her like a blow after the air-conditioning of the car, and a wave of faintness swept over her. Her body shrank from even the most accidental contact with Raoul's, her eyes darkening as she remembered the savagery of his assault on her body. If the phone hadn't rung when it had . . .

She shivered suddenly, forcing down her fear. If Raoul had been savage it was because he had been angry. Meeting his father had opened old wounds and he had reacted instinctively, wanting to hit out and hurt as he had been hurt.

'Are you all right?' He asked the question automatically and Claire nodded her head.

'Just tired, that's all.' She leaned into the car to take Saud, as always finding comfort and strength in holding the child. A link had been forged between them the day she had saved Saud from death, and in some strange way it was almost as though he *were* her child.

A door opened in the palace wall, and taking a deep breath Claire followed Raoul towards it. She was now in his country, and would be judged as his wife; the woman who had borne his child outside marriage and who he had been forced to marry by his uncle. For Saud's sake she must play her part perfectly. Head held high, Claire followed him into the cavernous darkness waiting beyond the open door.

CHAPTER FIVE

'IF the Sitt would come with me.'

As her eyes accustomed themselves to the darkness, Claire saw that she was being addressed by a girl in her late teens. Pretty and slender, her dark eyes regarded Claire rather anxiously, but her smile was warmly welcoming, and Claire was too tired to do anything other than follow her up what seemed to be an everlasting spiral of stone stairs, narrow slit windows giving her the occasional glimpse of sea and land spread out below them. By the time they reached the top, Saud had become a heavy weight in her arms, but mindful of the real reason for her presence here in this palace which made her feel totally alien, she was reluctant to let him go.

At last they stopped climbing and her companion indicated an arched doorway decorated with a fretted frieze of stylised flowers and symbols. Claire already knew that it was forbidden for a Muslim to copy directly from nature, but the intricacy of the detail of the frieze had a beauty all of its own. The heavy wooden door slid open under her companion's touch, and at first Claire was almost blinded by the brilliance of the sunset flooding the enormous room. Tall arched windows looked out across the gulf, the scent of sandalwood hung evocatively on the evening air. A large low bed on a raised dais caught her attention, its gauzy hangings moving lightly in the air-conditioning.

Brilliantly hued silk and satin cushions were heaped on the bed and on the divan just below the windows.

It had been decided when Claire accepted the Sheikh's proposition that she would have almost sole care of Saud. 'It will not be thought of as unusual since you are a European,' the Sheikh had told her, 'and it will make the task of guarding him much simpler.'

After her companion had introduced herself as Zenaide, and had explained that she was to be her personal maid, she turned to the wall opposite the windows and opened a door set into it indicating that Claire was to follow her.

A narrow corridor lined on one side with floor-to-ceiling wardrobes opened out into a small square room with three doors off it. One of them led into a sumptuous bathroom, the huge sunken bath in the middle of the room making Claire draw a rather shaky breath. Two people could easily fit inside it, and hard on the heels of that thought came a vivid and tormenting mental image of Raoul, naked, his tawny skin gleaming with water as a dark-eyed, doe-like houri bathed his body.

More disturbed than she wanted to admit, Claire hurried out of the bathroom, heaving a faint sigh of relief as Zenaide opened one of the other doors and she realised that she was in Saud's room. Nearly as large as her own it was rather bare, apart from a cot and a highchair, but once the furniture they had chosen in Paris arrived it would look much more cheerful. She would have liked to suggest having a mural painted on the walls—woodland creatures, scenes from *Jungle Book* and *Winnie the Pooh*, but guessed that it would not be permitted. Saud was, after all, a Muslim child, but perhaps once she had got to know Zenaide a little better she could discover from the girl how they could make the room look more attractive and stimulating for the baby.

When they emerged once more into the small, square ante-room, Claire glanced curiously at the third door, but Zenaide made no move to open it, and when Claire asked her what lay behind it she blushed a little and murmured, 'It is the room of the Lord Raoul. Once many years ago this was the suite of the Sultan's favourite woman but Sheikh Ahmed has given instructions that this suite was to be prepared for the Lord Raoul and the Sitt.'

From Zenaide's stumbling explanation and obvious embarrassment Claire divined that it was not the custom for married couples to live so closely together, and indeed her reading had given her to believe that she and Raoul would live completely separate lives. For a moment a *frisson* of fear touched against her spine as she remembered Raoul's bitter passion in Paris, but she banished it quickly, reminding herself that on that occasion he had been under severe provocation and that now it was necessary if they were to protect Saud properly for them to have as much privacy as possible. Indeed, it was comforting to know that Saud's room could only be reached through her own or Raoul's.

Shifting the sleeping weight of the little boy on to her other arm, she followed Zenaide back to her own room. What did the Arab girl think about her and her marriage? Was she shocked that the 'Lord Raoul', as she called him, had married a European girl, or was it already common knowledge in Omarah that the Sheikh had compelled Raoul to marry her for the sake of 'their' child? Zenaide struck her as a kind, gentle girl, and perhaps once they had got to know one another better they might be able to talk as friends.

'If you will allow me to take the Lord Saud,' Zenaide began when they were back in Claire's room.

'No. No, it's all right, I prefer to look after him myself,' Claire told her, robbing the words of any unkindness with a warm smile. 'He's not really used to strangers yet.'

'You are lucky to be able to care for him yourself,' Zenaide told her. 'My own sister, who is married to a second cousin of the Sheikh, has three sons, but their nursemaid will not allow her to care for them. Poor Yasmin would like to dismiss her, but if she does the girl's family could starve. The Sheikh is trying to educate all our people so that all can find work, but it is not always easy.'

It couldn't be, Claire agreed mentally. Superstition and custom were always barriers to education. People treated change with suspicion and fear, clinging on to what was familiar. As she glanced out of the window and saw the waters of the gulf dyed crimson by the setting sun, she shivered briefly, startled by the unfamiliar and mournful sound of the muezzin, and watched as Zenaide gracefully obeyed the summons of her religion. As an instinctive mark of respect she too remained still and silent until the eerie sound had died away and Zenaide was on her feet once more.

While Claire bathed and fed Saud, Zenaide unpacked her cases, openly admiring the things Raoul had bought her in Paris. One of the new silk nightgowns was carefully laid out on the large bed, and watching Zenaide's hennaed hands gently smoothing the fragile fabric, Claire wondered what Zenaide really thought about her—a woman who had borne a child out of wedlock and who, because of that child, had been forced to come here to a strange land and live among a race who prized female virtue above all things.

When Raoul did eventually marry, what manner of woman would he choose? Not a European, she thought immediately. No, he would choose a girl like Zenaide, innocent and obedient; a girl who would worship him from afar, grateful for whatever crumbs of affection he gave her. Had he ever been in love? He had mentioned an arranged marriage to her, had he loved her, a girl forbidden to him because of their differing religions?

A tap on the outer door startled her, and Zenaide went to open it, a pretty jewelled moth in her floor-length caftan with its glittering embroidery. A man stood outside, tall and robed. He murmured something to Zenaide in Arabic, his teeth white in his tanned, bearded face.

'That is Ali, the Lord Raoul's body-servant. The Lord Raoul has sent him to tell you that it is time to eat. Ali will escort you.'

Time to eat? Claire glanced helplessly at her creased suit. She had been so busy with Saud that she hadn't even had time to wash her hands and face, never mind change her clothes. And who was she supposed to eat with? Raoul? Surely she had read that in the East men and women ate separately, men first and then the women afterwards?

Guessing from Zenaide's anxious expression that it would be a mark of disrespect to keep Ali waiting, Claire hurried to the door, puzzled to see that Ali averted his face from her as she did so, until she remembered that it was forbidden by the Prophet for a man to look into the face of a wife of another, and that this was the reason women wore the all-covering burnous.

Ali led her back down the stairs she had come up with Zenaide, pausing after three flights to indicate the door which lay beyond the small hallway with its rich Persian carpet and decorative wall-hanging.

The room beyond the door looked out over the sea like her own, but darkness had fallen with the swiftness of a deep blue velvet cloak studded with diamanté during her short journey down the stairs and the room was illuminated with the soft glow of many lamps, secured on the walls.

At first as the door closed behind her Claire thought she was alone in the vast chamber. A divan ran the length of the window, heaped with silk cushions, three other divans were arranged close to the long low table in the centre of the room. Priceless silk rugs adorned the floor, the smell of sandalwood once more tantalised her.

'If you would care to sit down, I shall instruct Ali to serve our meal.'

Raoul's voice reaching her from the shadows startled her and she swung round, her eyes widening as he came towards her. Gone was the urbane, dark-suited businessman and in his place was a stranger dressed in a soft white robe, moving as silent and sure-footed as a mountain lion as he came towards her, cynicism curving a deep line on either side of his mouth as he observed her astonishment.

'When in Rome do as the Romans do, is that not a familiar saying to you? We of the East have learned that it is easier to do business with the West when we accept its mode of dress, but you will not see many men wearing pin-striped suits walking the streets of Omarah.'

More than ever Claire wished that she had had the opportunity to wash and change. Compared with Raoul, she felt grubby and travel-worn and she wondered if he had arranged matters deliberately so that she would feel at a disadvantage.

'Should we be eating alone together like this?' she challenged, wanting him to know that she wasn't completely ignorant of his country's customs.

'It is known that you are not of the Muslim religion or of our country and allowances will be made. Besides there are matters we still have to discuss. Please sit down.'

She did so awkwardly, trying to tuck her legs beneath her as she subsided on to one of the divans and watched as Ali opened the door and their meal was brought in. Saffron rice, and other delicacies Claire could not recognise were placed before them, Ali watching hawk-eyed to make sure that everything was in order. When the food was set out and the servants had withdrawn, Ali also left the room, closing the door behind him. Raoul, who had been standing by the window, came and sat down on the divan opposite her, his supple body easily accommodating itself to the narrow, low furniture, increasing Claire's awareness of the awkwardness of her own limbs.

'What are you waiting for?' Raoul drawled when Claire continued to sit without moving. 'Or is it that you fear our food will be offensive to your westernised palate?'

He was mocking her, Claire suspected, because the saffron rice and sweet-smelling lamb both looked delicious. 'I thought it was the custom for the man to eat first,' she reponded calmly. Raoul's eyebrows rose.

'Yes, at a formal banquet, or in an old-fashioned household; indeed in times gone by a man might feed his falcon before he fed his favourite houri, but I have no intention of starving you, Claire. My uncle has given us this palace as our home because it is relatively easy to guard,' he continued, changing the subject. 'As you will have observed it faces the sea and is protected on all other sides by its own wall. It was once the stronghold of what in Europe would have been called a pirate. Those rooms you share with Saud have in their time housed many a stolen European beauty destined for the Sultan's bed.' He laughed harshly when Claire shuddered. 'Times change, and now there is no need for us to use force to compel Western women into our beds; they are only too anxious to be there, and so have lost much of their value.'

'I can't believe that all Muslim women are as pure as the driven snow,' Claire countered, impelled to defend her fellow European women.

'Perhaps not, but they are the product of centuries of women who know how to please a man and make it their life's work to do so. You are happy with your rooms?' he asked once again changing the subject.

'They have been very well chosen,' Claire agreed.

'The only way anyone could get into Saud's room is through mine, or . . .'

'Mine? Yes. I am sure that no one suspects the truth, but it is always wise to take every precaution. While you are living here as my wife a certain standard of behaviour will be expected of you. Ramadan is behind us now and you may expect to receive bride visits from the female members of my uncle's family. Zenaide will help you if there is any point on which you are in doubt.'

'And you? Will you be . . .?'

'Will I be what?' Raoul taunted. 'At your side like a duitiful caring husband? You have forgotten surely that this "marriage" has been forced upon me for the sake of "our" son. There are business matters which compel me to spend time in the city, but you need not fear, the palace will be guarded at all times.'

Why did she feel as though she was suddenly being deserted? Raoul meant nothing to her, and yet unbidden her fingers pressed lightly on her lips, as though she could still feel the pressure of his mouth on hers. It came to her then, on a jolting shock wave, that she *wanted* to feel his mouth against hers again and the food before her was forgotten as she stared blindly towards him, shaken by the discovery but knowing it was something she had held at bay from the first moment she saw him.

She had been attracted to him then although she had fought against admitting it, and when he had kissed her there had been part of her that revelled in the hard, bruising contact of his mouth on hers, that yearned for the touch of his fingers against her skin.

'Is something wrong?' The green eyes narrowed,

skimming her too-pale face. Another second and he would surely guess the truth, Claire thought in panic.

'No . . . no. I'm just tired . . . I should like to go back to my room.'

Raoul inclined his head. 'If you wish. I shall have Ali escort you there. Tomorrow I must go to the palace. My uncle will have returned and we have much to discuss.'

Back in her own room Claire discovered that she was in truth tired. Zenaide was waiting for her, and despite her protests, insisted on helping her to undress and on bathing her. How different it would be if it was Raoul who was with her, caressing her perfumed skin while she caressed him. Clamping down on the feverish intensity of her thoughts, Claire dismissed Zenaide, assuring the concerned girl that she was quite well, merely suffering a little from jet lag and exhaustion.

On her way back to her bedroom, she paused outside Saud's door, and pushed it open. He lay on his back fast asleep, breathing evenly. When the new cot arrived from Paris perhaps she would ask Raoul if he could sleep with her in her room. She had grown dangerously fond of the little boy and already was dreading the parting that must eventually come.

Just thinking about it made her want to bend down and lift him out of his cot. It was the sudden rush of air that warned her that she was no longer alone and she straightened immediately, protecting the cot with her baby, her eyes wide and frightened in her pale face, the exposed skin of her shoulders and arms suddenly chilled by the air-conditioning. On dismissing Zenaide she had simply wrapped one of the large, plush towels around herself sarong-wise, but now she felt acutely vulnerable, her eyes searching the darkness beyond the open door as they sought the intruder.

'Claire!'

She sagged in relief on recognising Raoul's voice. 'Raoul, you frightened me.'

He came further into the room, a rather puzzling expression on his face, and Claire realised that although she had not at first been able to see him, he had quite clearly seen her in the glow of the lamp above Saud's bed.

'Yes, and yet your first instinct was to protect Saud.'

'An automatic reaction,' Claire told him shakily, not wanting to admit to the powerful love she had felt for the little boy ever since she saved his life. 'A piece of universal female programming.' As his eyes swept slowly over the cot and then shifted to her body she became acutely aware of how little she was wearing.

'You are cold?' Raoul frowned, his fingertips brushing the goose-bumps on her arms, 'or is it something else that causes your skin to react like this?'

Danger signals flashed from her body to her brain as his fingers became caressing, smoothing over her skin.

'I . . . I don't know what you mean.' How husky and uncertain her voice sounded, as well it might. She knew exactly what he meant and his smile told her that he knew it too.

'I mean desire, Claire,' he told her softly, 'and why should you not feel it? You are a woman used to the caresses of a man. I knew that in Paris. Your response was not that of a woman who is still unawakened.'

His fingers had reached her shoulder now and were

caressing the smooth roundness of her bones, somehow propelling her closer to him. Her nostrils were full of the clean warm male scent of him, mingling with the wool of his robe.

'Raoul, please stop this,' she protested achingly. 'You do not desire me, you told me that . . .'

'I did not,' he corrected, 'but hunger has a way of stifling our more fastidious mental urgings, and all I know now is that my body is aroused by the cool paleness of yours, just as yours yearns for the possession of mine.'

'No!' She croaked the denial between stiff lips, horrified by the weakness invading her body. How could she still feel this way about him when with her own ears she had heard him callously describe how he felt about her? He still despised her, that hadn't changed, but now his body wanted her. As hers wanted him, she acknowledged inwardly, but it wasn't simply his physical possession she wanted. She wanted more.

For a split second it seemed as though her heart had stopped beating. A panicky, suffocating sensation washed over her. No, no, it couldn't be true. She wasn't in love with him! She started to tremble, gasping aloud as she felt the warm abrasiveness of Raoul's robe pressed against her skin. His arms were round her, holding her against him, letting her know that he hadn't lied when he said she aroused him. She could feel the heat coming off his skin, the fierce compulsive pressure of his thighs and the unmistakable hardness of his body against hers.

His hands tugged at her towel, urging it away from her body, his mouth exploring the vulnerable curve of her throat, his tongue brushing delicately against her ear until she was mindless with hazy pleasure, her arms around his neck, her fingers luxuriating in the feel of his thick dark hair. The golden glow from the lamp bathed her body, but she was no longer conscious of her nudity, only of Raoul's hands moving across it, travelling the length of her spine. He murmured huskily as she arched instinctively against him, the fierce throb of his body pounding out a siren song she was unable to resist, and which echoed in the heated rhythm of the blood coursing through her body. Her throat arched in mute pleasure beneath the warm exploration of Raoul's mouth, capturing and feeding the frantic pulse beating there until she could hear the blood roaring in her ears, and her body felt as supple and as pliable as a length of silk.

'Claire.' He murmured her name against her lips as his tongue teased their moist curves; her fingers were trembling as they investigated the opening of his robe, following the shape of his shoulders, lost in a daze of mute pleasure. She had never dreamed that the mere touch of skin beneath her fingers could convey such a kaleidoscope of delight. Raoul's mouth brushed against her own, and finding it softly closed, hardened demandingly, his teeth nipping at her bottom lip, his tongue stroking persuasively against it until her mouth opened and fierce sparks of pleasure shot through her body as his tongue slid moistly against hers, exploring and enticing, until she was moaning softly into his mouth, half delirious with the pleasure he was giving her.

The reason she was in his arms was forgotten, her body offering its own incitement as it arched and stroked against him. The low groan that came from deep in his throat as his hands swept upwards towards her breasts offered further excitement, her body abandoned in its response to the desire she could feel building in his. Once again Claire felt her breasts swell and harden beneath his touch, but this time it wasn't just the hard pad of his thumb that brushed her sensitive flesh. His mouth lifting from hers, Raoul bent his head, the lamplight revealing to her the dark flush staining his cheekbones and the feverish glitter in his eyes. His tongue touched her breasts lightly, almost exploratively, but Claire could feel the build up of tension in his body which ignited the smouldering fires already burning in her own.

With almost feverish intensity she pressed herself against him, her fingers curling into the dark hair covering his chest, her lips raining tiny, hungry kisses against his throat, her whole body convulsing with fierce pleasure as she felt the cool breath he expelled against her breast and almost simultaneously the shudder that racked his body, his mouth opening over her taut nipple.

A shiver of ecstasy surged over her, her small white teeth biting into the tanned smoothness of his skin, as she sought to communicate the need building up inside her. He tasted faintly of salt, the musky scent of his body increased her arousal. When his hand slid down to her thigh she welcomed his touch, every nerve-ending in her body urging her on towards fulfilment.

Somewhere in the distance she was dimly aware of a sound trying to penetrate the fog of desire blanketing her. Gradually the sound became louder, and she recognised it as Saud's crying. In the same moment as she tensed, Raoul released her and she dropped back to earth with a humiliating thump, hastily reaching for her discarded towel and wrapping it quickly round her body before turning towards Saud.

Her thoughts a jumble of confused impressions and fears, she reached automatically for the crying child, barely noticing that Raoul had gone until she turned round. It took her fifteen minutes to soothe Saud whose teeth were still troubling him, and by the time he was asleep all she could think of was how much she hoped she never had to set eyes on Raoul again as long as she lived.

What must he think of her? Her face stung with scarlet colour. She knew what he thought of her. He thought her an experienced woman of the world who thought nothing of satisfying her physical need with whatever man happened to be handy. But if they had continued to make love, he would have discovered for himself that she had had no previous lover.

She started to tremble, and as she hurried to her own room she tried to convince herself that it wasn't disappointment that made her limbs feel as weak as water and her pulses thud with a pagan need. What was the matter with her? Was she honestly naive enough to believe that once Raoul discovered her innocence he would fall madly in love with her? That sort of scenario belonged to love stories, not real life. Somehow she had the lowering feeling that if Raoul knew the truth he would be at great pains to avoid her. All he wanted was simply to assuage his own physical need and she had happened to be there.

And yet she couldn't help thinking about what

would have happened if Saud hadn't cried; if Raoul had taken her to the privacy of his own room, his body as naked as hers against the silk covers. She shivered suddenly in the darkness, perspiration springing up on her skin, a dull ache she refused to give a name to pulsing through her lower body. If she was wise she would keep her distance from Raoul from now on. Now only *she* knew she loved him, but if he should ever make love to her and discover the truth he would know how she felt about him. How contemptuous he would be. He felt nothing for her, and nor would he ever do so. He had chosen to follow the ways of his mother's people, and if he ever loved it would be a doe-eyed slender girl like Zenaide, not a pale-skinned blonde who couldn't even sit on a divan without getting cramp.

'The Sitt has a visitor.' Zenaide came quickly into the room, excitement sparkling in her eyes. Raoul had been gone for two days, and much to her amazement Claire had not felt either bored or lonely. This morning she had taken Saud down on to the beach, much to Zenaide's disapproval, but the little boy had thoroughly enjoyed the experience, and as the small bay could only be reached from the palace, Claire judged it private enough for safety.

'A visitor? But I don't know anyone,' Claire commented before she remembered Raoul's comments about 'bride visitors'.

'It is the mother of the Sheikh,' Zenaide told her importantly, her eyes round as saucers. 'Ali has put her in the salon that looks out over the main courtyard.'

Claire had discovered in Raoul's absence that the

palace had several inner courtyards, the most beautiful of which was the main courtyard with its mosaic-tiled floor and tranquil fish pond. Overlooked by what had once been the women's quarters, the courtyard was a small peaceful oasis of escape from the burning heat of the sun. Peach and fig trees provided cool splashes of green, their leaves carefully sprayed daily by the gardeners. Gleaming carp swam leisurely beneath large lily pads and Claire often brought Saud down to the courtyard when it was too hot to take him to the beach, enjoying his pleasure in the swift movement of the fish through the calm waters.

There was only one person in the large, formal salon, wrapped in black from head to foot and half a head shorter than Claire herself, with dark, alert eyes searching her face as she stepped into the room.

'So, you are Raoul's wife and the mother of his son.' The dark fabric was withdrawn from her visitor's face and Claire found herself looking at one of the wisest and most serene human faces she had ever seen. All that there had been in the Sheikh's mother's life was written in her face, both good and bad, and Claire knew instinctively that here was no dutiful Muslim woman content to be a mere cipher in her family's life. She exuded an air of wisdom and great serenity. She had known great love in her life and great pain too, Claire sensed, as she returned her greeting. She had Saud in her arms, and had brought him down thinking that her unexpected guest would want to see him.

'And this is Raoul's child.' Before Claire could stop her she had lifted Saud out of her arms, studying him thoughtfully, an expression Claire couldn't read darkening her eyes. 'He has little of you in him,' she said at length, 'and much of my son. Raoul will not be pleased by this marriage my son has forced upon him. As a child he always swore that he was more of the East than the West. Had he been allowed free choice he would have married his second cousin. All that was required was that he should change his religion, but Raoul has always been proud—and stubborn.'

She smiled briefly, her teeth still white and even in the dark olive of her face. How old she was Claire could not tell, but she had a bone structure that was ageless, and must have been very beautiful in her youth. Raoul was like her, Claire realised with an aching pang, and like her he would age well. 'His father had made his mother promise that she would bring him up in the Christian religion. That was the price she had to pay for deserting her husband and Raoul has continued to pay it for her.'

'If Raoul hates his father and his French inheritance so much, why has he not become a Muslim?' Claire asked.

'Perhaps because he wants to be accepted for what he is. It is always hard for a child torn between two cultures. Zenobi, Raoul's mother, was accepted back into her father's home, but she was never allowed to forget her sin in marrying outside her own faith and race, and it is always hard for a child to come to terms with the apparent rejection of a parent, although in Lucien's case . . .'

'He told Raoul's mother that he did not love her before they married.'

'So you know about that? Lucien was working here when they met. I liked him, but it was obvious that Zenobi could not see beyond her besotted adoration of

him. What man could resist such a gift—a rich,
adoring bride?' She shrugged fatalistically. 'I have
always thought Lucien more sinned against than
sinning, and one day Raoul too will accept this. He has
already proved that he is not totally opposed to all
Westerners,' she added dryly, smiling when Claire
flushed. If only she knew the truth! If anything Raoul
destested her even more than he disliked his father.

'I am honoured that you have come to visit me,
Princess,' Claire murmured, trying to get the
conversation back on to more mundane lines.

'Not just to visit you,' the old lady said calmly. 'A
hundred miles is a long way for a woman of my years
to travel without a purpose. For a long time now I
have been looking for someone to continue my work
after I am gone. The women of my family have their
own concerns and much less freedom than I in my
time.'

She saw Claire's look of astonishment and chuckled.
'I was born in the desert. My people were nomads and
I knew no home but the desert until I married my
husband. My bride-price was the strip of desert where
Omarah's oil-wells are now situated.' She chuckled
again. 'Poor Khalid, there were times when he wished
he had taken a tame dove to wife rather than the wild
kestrel that he called me. I was not used to the
formality of the Sheikh's palace. My life had been one
of freedom. I was the only child of a prince of the
desert and proud of my heritage. Many of my tribe
still roam the desert and it is my self-appointed task to
help them. What we know as civilisation encroaches
further into their homeland with every year that
passes, making it harder and harder for them to

survive. They are offered pieces of land on which to
build homes and settle down, but what nomad can
ever live in one place for long and not pine for shifting
sands beneath his feet? But civilisation does have its
benefits—medical care, education—and it is these that
I try to bring to the women of the desert. They accept
me because I am one of them, and today I intend to
drive out to a small oasis where I know they will be
encamped. You seem to me to be a woman of spirit,
Raoul's English wife, I should like you to come with
me. Remember,' she added cryptically as she realigned
her all-enveloping robe, 'nothing that is worth having
is ever easily won. Now, do you come with me?'

'Yes ... Yes, I would love to,' Claire assured her
eagerly, 'but I shall have to take Saud with me.'

Once again she saw a strange look flit across the
older woman's face. 'It is a foolish man who seeks to
part the lioness from her cub,' was all she said,
standing up and walking towards the door.

Zenaide was nowhere in sight, but Claire found her
maid waiting for her in her bedroom, placidly
straightening the silk cushions. 'I will come with the
Sitt,' she pronounced firmly when Claire told her
where she was going, calmly producing two enveloping
hooded cloaks similar to the one the Princess had
worn.

It was a three-hour journey to the oasis and Claire
stared overtly at the black tents pitched beneath the
shade of the palms. Small children played noisily in
their shadow, and several men were grooming the pale
cream Arab horses which Claire knew were among the
nomads' most prized possessions. The moment the
Princess's car stopped it was surrounded, both men

and women abasing themselves before her as she
stepped out. An old, gnarled man whose proud
bearing proclaimed him the leader of the tribe came
forward and escorted them to the largest of the tents.
Inside it was far more luxurious than Claire had
dreamed, hung with silk tapestries, priceless rugs
adorning the floor. The leader of the tribe departed
and almost at once the tent became full of chattering
women, as inquisitive as magpies as they stared at
Claire's pale hair and skin, laughter gleaming in dark
eyes as they spoke to one another.

'They are saying that when you lie with Raoul it will
be like the sand caressed by the shadow of night,' the
Princess translated with a brief smile. Claire coloured
hotly at the smile, her embarrassment provoking
another wave of amusement. 'Now they are saying that
your cheeks are as pink as those of a maiden before she
knows a man and that no one would think you had
borne Lord Raoul's child.'

Hennaed fingers stroked and caressed Saud's plump
baby limbs, and the small boy bore the caresses
stoically until he was returned to Claire's arms. A
maidservant came in carrying a huge samovar while
another produced delicate bowls for coffee. As guest of
honour, the Princess was served first, Claire next. The
coffee, although fragrant, was too strong for her taste,
just as the sweetly sticky sweetmeats were too rich for
her stomach, and she winced to see how many were
pressed upon small Saud, but was reluctant to
intervene and possibly cause offence.

'You are thinking that too much rich food will make
him sick,' the Princess murmured astutely to her. 'It is
difficult for us to explain to them that it is better to

give their children fresh fruit, and we can only make progress very slowly. The Badu are a proud people, fiercely independent, and to shut them away in a reservation of the sort they have in America and Australia for their native people would be to offer them a slow, tortuous death. However, children must be educated if they are to fit into our modern world. They trust me and I do what I can. They like you, wife of Raoul, and it pleases me to think that when I am gone you will continue my work among them. You have much compassion, I think, and not just for your own.' She touched Saud's head as she spoke and Claire wondered how much those wise eyes had seen. Had she guessed the truth about Saud? If so, the Princess would keep her own counsel, Claire was sure of that.

It was late when they left the oasis, dusk falling swiftly on the heels of the flaming sunset, wrapping the landscape in darkness. Claire was still fascinated by the glittering intensity of the stars in the desert sky, and peered out of the car window at them, Saud a warm and heavy weight in her arms.

The place was bustling with activity as their car swept into the courtyard. An unfamiliar black Mercedes made Claire's heart thump. Raoul? Had he returned? Refusing her offers of hospitality, the Princess explained that she had an appointment in the city which she wished to keep. 'We will meet again, wife of Raoul, and until then I pray that Allah will watch over you.'

In silence Claire and Zenaide climbed the stairs to Claire's quarters. She was tired and hungry, but still alert enough to freeze when she heard the sound of footsteps coming down the stairs towards her, angry determined footsteps which she was sure could only belong to one person.

As Raoul turned turned the angle of the stairs, he saw them, a bitter oath splintering the silence and making Zenaide tremble as she clung to Claire's side.

'So there you are! What happened, did you have second thoughts?'

'Seconds thoughts?' Unable to comprehend what he was talking about, Claire stared up at him. He turned to Zenaide.

'I wish to see your mistress alone. Return to your quarters. Come with me,' he ordered Claire. 'I want to know exactly where you took Saud and why. Did you think to double-cross us? To claim a large reward for Saud's safety? Is that why you stole away from here with him this afternoon?'

CHAPTER SIX

'STOLE away?' Anger and astonishment battled inside her, anger suddenly getting the upper hand. 'I am not prepared to talk to you about your absurd suspicions on the stairs, Raoul,' she flung over her shoulder as she walked swiftly past him. 'I am not a servant to be berated on an open stairway.'

'No,' Raoul agreed ferociously. 'What I have to say to you is better said in private, and think yourself lucky if I content myself with mere words. What I would like to do . . .'

'Is what? Torture me? Murder me? And all because I accepted an invitation from your grandmother to accompany her on a visit to an oasis?' Triumph edged under her calm voice, but she turned away so that he wouldn't see it. All at once she wanted to punish him, wanted to humiliate and hurt him as he had hurt her with his accusations and lack of trust. 'Perhaps I shouldn't have taken Saud with me, but I thought he was safer with me than left alone, and I wasn't sure if it might be construed as an insult if I refused the Princess's invitation.'

'This is true? You have been out with Faika? But she takes no one on her trips to the desert.'

'She took me,' Claire told him defiantly, 'and you are perfectly at liberty to check with her. She is on her way back to the city at the moment. Of course, if you do check with her she will guess the truth, perhaps she might even think you have given me reason to flee from you, taking our "son" with me.'

'I—I owe you an apology.' He had his back to her, but Claire could see how hard it was for him to say the words. 'When I came back and found you both missing, my first thought was that somehow someone had discovered the truth, but when Ali told me that no one had been admitted to the palace I thought you must have left alone.'

'And knowing of my greed, of course you knew immediately what had happened?'

She watched in mute fascination as the dark tide of colour swept up over the back of his neck. Proud, the Princess had called him, and Claire could well appreciate how difficult he must be finding that he was in the wrong.

'You were the one who changed her mind when she was offered fifty thousand pounds,' he reminded her arrogantly, turning round to face her for the first time, the familiar coldness back in his eyes. 'Naturally, once I had assured myself that you and Saud had not been the victims of some kidnap plot, my first thought was . . .'

'That I had been the one doing the kidnapping,' Claire supplied bitterly for him, refusing to accept the validity of his explanations. Saud was his responsibility and a very heavy one as the natural inheritor of the Sheikh's titles and powers. 'Had I known you were likely to return, I would have left a message with Ali.'

Her gibe had gone home, she could see by the sudden tightening of his mouth, but if he chose to come and go at will, he could hardly expect to find her waiting patiently while he did so. 'As you can see for yourself, apart from having been fed with too many sweetmeats, Saud is quite well.' She held up the sleeping baby, his face still sticky and slightly grubby. 'Whatever you might think to the contrary, I do take my responsibilities towards Saud seriously,' Claire added on a quieter note, unable to bring herself to tell this hard, unyielding man how much she loved the little boy, so much that it was almost as though he were her own child.

'You have consistently shown a remarkable fondness for him,' Raoul agreed aloofly, spoiling it by adding cynically, 'but then when he is the heir to many thousands of millions of pounds, it is not hard to understand why.'

Anger made the colour bleed slowly from her face, leaving her as white as Raoul's robe. 'You think that,' she whispered painfully. 'You think me as vile and avaricious as that?'

'I think you are a woman whose devotion was bought for a mere fifty thousand pounds,' Raoul jeered at her hatefully. 'Oh, and by the way, I have a letter for you. From your lover no doubt. It was delivered to our Embassy in London and flown out with the rest of the mail. While you are living here as my wife, you will not receive letters from other men,' Raoul told her white-lipped, the sudden surge of anger she could see beating up behind his eyes frightening her with its intensity.

'What did you tell him when you wrote to him, Claire? That your bed was lonely and that you missed his caresses, so much so that you were quite prepared to take to your bed a man who is little better than a cross-bred mongrel, possessing the worst traits of both his parents? Oh yes, I know what is said about me,' he added tightly. 'Small children never spare the sensibilities or the pride of their peers.'

For one crazy moment she wanted to lean forward and smooth away what she was sure were lines of pain from beside his mouth, to hold him in her arms as she might have done Saud and comfort him, dispersing the hurt she could sense inside him, but the moment was destroyed as he flung her letter down on to the divan and walked through her room to the corridor that connected it with his own.

On this occasion there was no Ali to request that she join his master for dinner, and telling herself that she preferred it that way, Claire dismissed Zenaide when she had bathed and fed Saud, telling her maid that she was quite capable of preparing herself for bed. Zenaide still looked chastened and Claire hoped she had not been chastised for not telling Ali where they were going. Like an injured animal she wanted to retire to her lair to lick her wounds in peace.

How could Raoul have thought her so despicable? Surely he knew she would never do anything to hurt Saud? And as for his allegation that she might be deliberately fostering the child's affection for mercenary reasons ... Her mouth tightened and then relaxed as unbidden a memory slid into her mind of Teddy shortly after their parents had died. They had still been living in the old family house. She had spent the morning filling packing cases and Teddy was supposed to be playing outside in the garden. She had gone downstairs to make lunch and, on finding the front gate swinging open and no Teddy in sight, panic had exploded inside her. She had been on the point of calling the police when he had turned up three hours later, muddy and astonished that she should be so concerned. And yet instead of relief, all she had been able to feel had been a searing, blinding anger. She could well imagine Raoul's reaction to the news that they were both missing and perhaps his suspicions were understandable if one took the logical view.

Sighing faintly, Claire went through to the bathroom, filling the large marble tub with water scented with rose petals and relaxing into it while she read Teddy's letter.

Matron had taken him to buy some new clothes and he was to spend half-term with his friend 'Porky Rogers'. However, when she reached the final paragraph of his letter, Claire started to frown, a small gasp of dismay escaping her parted lips. Teddy wanted to know if he could spend part of the summer holidays in Omarah with her.

No! What on earth was she going to do? Having kept his existence such a secret from Raoul, she could hardly ask him now if her younger brother could come and stay with them. And Teddy was very astute for his age. She had allowed him to believe she had married for love. It wouldn't take Teddy long to discover what little regard Raoul had for his supposed wife. Hating to disappoint her brother but knowing there was little alternative, Claire tried to think of an adequate excuse. Perhaps she could tell him that she didn't have enough money for his flight. Yes, that would do it. She was always so chronically short of money that he would never suspect the truth. She would write to him later, and keep her fingers crossed that he wouldn't be too upset.

Back in her room, dressed in one of the soft silk

nightgowns Raoul had purchased for her in Paris, her hair a silver cloud on her shoulders, Claire found her thoughts returning to the scene in her room when they had returned from the oasis. Perhaps she ought to go and apologise to Raoul, and assure him that there was no question of her absconding with Saud. She could also tell him of her suspicions that his grandmother had suspected the truth. Not for one moment did she doubt the old lady, but it paid to be extra careful.

Before she could change her mind, or investigate her reasons too deeply, she shrugged on the soft peach negligee which matched her nightdress, unaware of how the silk-satin clung to her body, moulding itself lovingly to her curves, the soft peach fabric emphasising the silky pallor of her skin.

She knocked briefly on Raoul's door and hearing his voice pushed it open, puzzled when she saw that the room was empty, until she realised he was in the bathroom beyond. She heard him call out something in Arabic and as he emerged from the bathroom, a towel draped across his hips, his surprise at seeing her very evident as he frowned and pushed his fingers into the damp tangle of his hair.

'When I heard you knock I thought you were Ali. Is everything all right? Saud?' He sounded so formal and distant that Claire found herself wishing she had never been foolish enough to come to his room, on what she realised now was the flimsiest of pretexts and born more of her own need to be near him than any more logical motive.

'Saud's fine,' she assured him, dismayed by the husky, uneven pitch of her voice, dragging her eyes away from his gleaming torso, and the droplets of water still coursing hypnotically over his skin, darkening the tangle of hairs arrowing down over his flat belly. 'I just wanted to tell you that ... that I'd never do anything that might endanger him,' she managed, before panic overwhelmed her and she turned instinctively back towards the door, cursing the foolish impulse that had brought her into Raoul's presence.

'A pity you don't extend those sentiments to include yourself,' Raoul murmured softly, somehow reaching the door before her and leaning against it, blocking her exit, his mouth curling in a smile that increased her agitation. 'Because by coming to my room you have definitely endangered yourself, Claire, or is that what you had in mind? Did reading your lover's letter awaken a longing inside you that only a man's possession can assuage? This afternoon when I returned and found you gone, I wanted to seize your slender body in my arms and break it in two. But now my anger has found other channels and when it mingles with the desire I feel whenever you are close to me there is a dangerous alchemy between them. I want you, Claire,' he said softly, 'and by coming to my room you have admitted that you want me too.'

'No.' Her denial was a strangled protest which he ignored, smothering the sound with the raging heat of his mouth which told her that he hadn't exaggerated the dangerous chain reaction she had set off inside him. His tongue forced her lips to part, hotly exploring the hidden recesses of her mouth, compelling her to give him the fervid response his kiss demanded, and by doing so feed his desire.

'Too many times I have wanted you like this,' he muttered thickly, sliding his fingers into her hair and curling the silver strands round them. 'My desire for you is like a leech sucking at my life blood and my reason, and until I assuage it I cannot be free. You arouse me to a lust I heartily despise,' he continued, each word a poisoned barb in her heart, 'but I know if you tried to leave this room now I would come after you and drag you back to my bed, and even perhaps enjoy doing so. Strange that such a pale, golden beauty should arouse the darker side of desire.'

The darker side of desire. Claire shuddered deeply, trying to wrench her mouth away from the renewed possession of his, telling herself that she would despise herself to the end of her days if she gave in to the tug of sensation she could feel exploding through her now. He had told her quite plainly what he wanted, how he felt about her, but if she aroused dark, dangerous passions in him, he aroused a blind need in her that would not listen to reason or logic, and her fingers, encountering the hard smoothness of his body, could no more be stopped in their wanton exploration of his skin than her heart could be prevented from beating.

He quickly disposed of her negligee, stroking the liquid softness of her body until she was shivering delicately in his arms, welcoming the fierce, almost brutal urgency of his kisses, even though his hunger bruised her mouth and through her delirium a small voice warned that there could be only one outcome. It was with relief that she felt him remove her nightgown and carry her to his bed, her body stretched languorously on the silk covers as he stood over her, shrugging aside his towel. His body was totally male, his stomach flat and his lean hips narrow; her fingertips automatically followed the path of her eyes down his body, the hard tautness of his buttocks and the muscled solidity of his thighs, darkly shadowed with soft hair. He turned and she caught her breath, half-awed and half-dismayed by the aroused maleness of his body as he moved towards her, his fingertips drifting upwards over her body with far more assurance and knowledge in their touch than she felt she could ever possess.

'You want me. Tell me it's true,' he urged, as he came down alongside her, taking her in his arms, his mouth finding the vulnerable area behind her ear and teasing it until she was trembling against him, gasping out that she wanted him more than she wanted life itself.

'As bad as that?' He almost seemed to purr with satisfaction and alarm shot through the haze of sexual need engulfing her. This was wrong. She might love him but he most certainly did not love her, and worse still she suspected he was going to be very angry when he discovered that she was still a virgin. It occurred to her that she ought to tell him, but his hands were doing such delicious things to her body, his mouth and tongue were inciting such a fevered response from her that she felt incapable of discussing anything at all, much less something that would surely put a stop to his expert love making.

'Still want me?' His tongue teased her erect nipples and she raked her nails protestingly across his back, the tempo of his lovemaking suddenly changing as his body tensed against her, his mouth now avid in the demands it made on her body as his hands slid to her hips and his knee parted her thighs.

The intrusion of his body was unexpectedly painful, making her tense, her eyes widening in shock, the deep kiss she had been enjoying broken as she pulled instinctively away. But Raoul was still holding her hips and his possession continued even though she cried out to him to stop, her world turning from pleasure to a pain she fought instinctively against.

Something was different, but what? Slowly, Claire opened her eyes and then closed them again as reality hit her like a bath of icy water. She was still in Raoul's bed. She moved gingerly, feeling his body close to her and winced as she remembered his anger. Mercifully, she had passed out before he had been able to give full vent to it. He was asleep now, if she turned her head carefully she could see him. The lamp which was still illuminated threw dark shadows across his face. Even in sleep he looked hard and unyielding and she shuddered sickly, remembering what had happened.

Dear God, how could she have been so ... so stupid? No wonder he had been angry. She bit her lips, her face flaming as she remembered some of the comments he had flung at her. She had wanted to leave then, she rememberd, but as she had sat up the room swayed muzzily round her and he had pushed her back unceremoniously telling her to lie still. And that had not been the worst. Even though her mind shied away from it, she forced herself to remember how he had left the bed and come back with a sponge and some towels and had made her lie there while he soothed away the worst of the pain. She didn't think she could forget until her dying day how grim and furious he had looked. Never, as long as she lived, would she ever endure anything quite as humiliating. That at

least was something to be thankful for, she told herself
drily. She had acted like the heroine out of a Victorian
romance, swooning away because a man had . . .

'How are you feeling?'

Raoul was awake! Colour burned up under her skin.
Why, oh why had he insisted that she remain here
with him? Still, she would have had to have faced him
some time. Perhaps it was as well to get it over and
done with now.

'I . . . I'm fine, thank you,' she said quickly, edging
towards the edge of the bed. 'In fact, I think I'd better
go back to my own room, Saud might wake.'

'No.' His hand shot out, his fingers imprisoning her
wrist. 'Not yet. I've been lying here waiting for you to
wake up.'

He had? Misgivings smote her. Why? So that he
could lecture her again? Hadn't it all already been
said?

'I'm sorry.' Heavens, why was she apologising? He
ought to be the one doing that. But then, of course,
men did not expect to find themselves with an
inexperienced virgin in their bed these days.

'So am I,' Raoul agreed evenly, 'but what's done is
done. You must have been missing your boy-friend
very badly, although he'll hardly be gratified to learn
what form your frustration took.'

Claire had to bite down hard on her lip to stop
herself from crying. 'I . . . I must go back to my own
room,' she protested again. She suddenly felt weak
and shaky, and wanted to put as great a distance as
possible between Raoul's powerful body and her own
frailer one. As though he read her mind he turned
towards her, cupping her face with his free hand.

'I'm sorry if it didn't live up to all your maidenly expectations. It was quite a shock for me too, you know.' He saw her expression and laughed derisively. 'Oh yes, it isn't exactly a turn-on to find the woman in your arms is crying with pain and not pleasure. Not unless you're a sadist, that is, which I am not. Do you still want me?'

Claire could only stare at him, her disbelief showing openly in her eyes. He laughed again, his thumb rubbing slowly along her jaw. 'But you did want me,' he reminded her softly, 'you told me so, and I wanted you.'

'But that was . . .'

'Before I hurt you?' He bent towards her and Claire could see the smoky flames burning in his eyes. 'What happened was unfortunate, but it needn't be a tragedy. I suppose I should have guessed, but your response to me was so complete that I took you for an experienced sensualist.' He bent his head, capturing the frantic pulse beating at the base of her throat, and stroking his fingers along her flesh as though he enjoyed the vulnerability of her skin beneath them. 'No . . . keep still,' he told her when she tried to struggle. 'I'm not going to hurt you.'

She moved, and anger suddenly blazed in his eyes. 'Damn you,' he swore suddenly, 'have you any idea what it was like to see the fear and pain in your eyes? Why didn't you tell me, you stubborn little fool? But I will see pleasure in your eyes, Claire,' he added softly, 'and before dawn pearls the desert sky. You will melt beneath my touch and murmur your pleasure against my skin.'

He pushed back the covers he had heaped over her, exposing the full length of her body to his probing gaze, his hands moving slowly over her skin. She wouldn't respond, she couldn't respond, Claire thought numbly. What was the point when it would only end in pain? But against her will his touch communicated a wanton need to her nerve-endings, his slow caresses stimulating a desire she was surprised she could still feel.

'Touch me, Claire,' Raoul murmured against her ear, nibbling the lobe with sharp teeth. 'Wouldn't you like to touch me as I am touching you?'

Of course she wouldn't, but somehow she was, the tension expelled from her body on a soft sigh as his coaxing fingers drifted against her breast, stroking the rounded flesh gently so that Claire found it impossible to tell where acceptance ended and need began. So gradually that she was barely aware of what was happening, her body began to respond until it was no longer enough simply to lie in Raoul's arms letting him caress her, she wanted to touch him too. His skin burned strangely beneath her lips, moist with a perspiration she hadn't expected. The small satisfied sounds of pleasure he made as she touched him gave her the courage to go on, touching him more intimately, letting her tongue brush teasingly over his flat male nipples, half-exultant and half-shocked by his immediate response.

'I think I was right first time,' Raoul mutterd hoarsely, pulling away from her. 'You are a sensualist.' His fingers touched her thigh, moving along the tender inner flesh, his eyes locked on hers as he witnessed her involuntary response before she remembered her earlier pain and tensed in panic, trying to push him away, her heart thudding erratically until he moved, soothing her with light kisses until her fear was lost beneath a rising tide of need. Something was happening to her, something she hadn't believed possible when she opened her eyes less than half an hour ago; and when Raoul's hand returned to her thigh she only tensed momentarily, her fear forgotten as his tongue teased her nipples until her fingers tightened in his hair and she was abandonedly urging his mouth against her, her hands leaving his hair to clasp the smooth muscles of his back as he tugged gently on the aching peaks of her breasts.

Suddenly it wasn't enough simply to feel the contraction and expansion of his muscles under her fingers, she wanted to touch and taste every part of his body. A wild, heated urgency flooded out fear, even when Raoul's fingers stroked upwards, touching her intimately, making her gasp and tense and then relax beneath their knowledgeable caress. Her small teeth bit urgently into his skin, feeling his shoulder muscles clench and his body harden, pleasure banishing fear as she strove to communicate to him the delight he was giving her.

'Touch me. Kiss me, Claire,' he muttered thickly, punctuating his words with hard kisses, taking her hand and placing it against his body, kissing her fiercely as a shudder of pleasure rippled through him.

Fear left her completely, the soft kisses she pressed against Raoul's body eliciting a response that surprised and awed her.

'You don't even begin to know what you're doing to me, do you?' he demanded rawly, holding her slightly away from him. 'This began as an exercise in showing you that making love doesn't go hand in hand with pain, but when you touch me my body forgets you're only one step away from being a virgin and knows only that the softness of your hands and lips against it is a sweet form of torture.'

He kissed her again, more deeply this time until she felt as though she were sinking into soft warm darkness, the coaxing stroke of his fingers against the most vulnerable, intimate part of her body making her tremble and ache, her hands making feverish forays against his skin until he groaned and pressed himself against her, his flesh hot and damp, his skin tasting salt beneath her tongue. But it was only when his caresses had elicited a rhythmic unfamiliar reaction from her body that he gave in to the urgent need she could feel in the hard thrust of his body against her, this time drawing her slowly against him, teasing her breasts with light tormenting kisses as his body moved fluidly against hers, slowly possessing it, urging her to touch and experience the pulsating life force of him, until her touch became surer and communicated to him the same rhythmic welcome as her body, his mouth closing hotly over first the hard peak of one breast and then the other as she moaned and moved urgently beneath him, encouraged by the soft words of praise he murmured in her ear and then by the hard demand of his mouth as he relinquished his control, abandoning it to the driving force of his body.

His fierce cry of pleasure was an unfamiliar and yet elemental sound exploding around them as she dissolved into a whirlpool of pleasure, unaware that she was calling his name until he kissed and soothed her, unaware of anything other than the experience they had just shared.

CHAPTER SEVEN

WHEN Claire woke up she was aware of having slept well and deeply. She was alone but still in Raoul's bed, and she leapt out, hurrying into her own room, her cheeks darkly flushed as she saw Zenaide waiting patiently for her, playing with Saud.

'The Lord Raoul said to let you sleep,' she said easily, 'he also gave instructions that I was to prepare you for a journey. See . . .' she indicated a case on the bed. 'I have packed what he instructed.'

Claire's eyes widened in appalled comprehension. Raoul was sending her away! She had betrayed her love to him and now he was sending her away from him. But what about Saud? Perhaps if she pleaded with him he would allow her to stay. What had happened was not entirely her fault. Her skin flushed delicately as she remembered her abandoned response to him. But he was the one who had encouraged that response. He had wanted her as much as she had wanted him, but now he was obviously regretting that wanting and wished only to be rid of her.

Saud beamed up at her, holding up his arms, and she bent down automatically to pick him up, tears suddenly blinding her as she realised that this was possibly the last time she would hold the little boy. What would the Sheikh say when he learned what Raoul had done? How would Raoul himself explain away her absence? But then it was easy for Muslim men to divorce women they no longer wanted, wasn't it? Tired, muddled thoughts chased one another through her mind. Too proud to go to Raoul and beg him to allow her to stay, even for Saud's sake, she numbly allowed Zenaide to bully her gently into getting bathed and dressed, glad that she had sent the younger girl to look after Saud when she saw the beginnings of dark bruises staining her skin—the unmistakable signs of the passion which had over-whelmed Raoul at the height of their love making.

Shivering suddenly as she wrapped her body in the thick fleecy towel Zenaide had provided, Claire wondered a little about that love making. The first time she could understand. Raoul had been bitterly, furiously angry and she was not so naïve that she couldn't appreciate how quickly desire could spring from the loins of anger, once at least. But afterwards, when his anger had had time to die down ... He had still wanted her, Claire reminded herself bleakly, and he had decided to assuage that want, desire at that particular moment in time being more important to him than anything else. But later, with his hunger appeased, he would have thought differently. Besides, if she was honest with herself, he had never wanted her to partner him in this charade and she, fool that she was, had given him the perfect excuse to be rid of her. What would he tell his uncle? That she had fallen in love with him, and he found her love embarrassing?

'If the Sitt is ready, Ali is waiting to drive her to the airport.'

Heeding Zenaide's calm warning, Claire dressed quickly, donning the clothes Zenaide had put out for her—soft, pure silk underwear in warm cream and a silk dress in the same fabric with a matching unstructured jacket. The ensemble was a sophisticated one, a little too dressy to travel in, but she felt too weary and miserable to change it. When she walked back into her bedroom she saw on the bed the perky hat that went with the outfit. In the shop she had loved it, but now . . . However, Zenaide was placing it with the rest of her luggage. If nothing else, she was better off by an exclusive brand-new wardrobe, she reminded herself cynically, trying to ignore the inner voice adding that she was also coming close to having a broken heart. She loved Raoul. She couldn't deny it any longer. With one last kiss for Saud, her lips were trembling badly as she turned to embrace Zenaide. 'You will look after him, Zenaide, won't you?'

'The Lord Raoul has arranged everything,' Zenaide assured her. 'He will not be left alone for so much as a moment.'

In that, at least, she had faith in Raoul. He would never let anything injure Saud. But what of love? Would the little boy have that?

A servant placed her case in the car. Raoul was so eager to get rid of her that there hadn't been time to pack everything, but doubtless the rest of her wardrobe would be sent on after her. Just before she left she had slipped in to Raoul's room, trying not to look at the large bed as she placed the jewellery he had given her beside it.

All the way to the airport she was fighting for self-control, trying to force back the tears that, once started, wouldn't cease until she had cried herself dry. As before, there were no passport formalities to endure. Ali escorted her through the departure hall and out on to the tarmac where a streamlined jet plane waited, bearing the colours of the Omarah royal family. Her mouth twisted in a bitter smile, Claire mounted the stairs. Raoul was so anxious to get rid of her that he wouldn't even wait for the twice-weekly Concorde flight, and she shuddered to think how much it would cost to transport her back to London in this expensive rich man's toy.

A steward showed her to a seat. Unlike a commercial plane, this one was furnished more like a luxurious living-room with deep lush seats and a separate section which he told her contained a bedroom and bathroom.

They were airborne almost immediately, the blue waters of the gulf left behind below them as the plane levelled out. The steward had disappeared and yet now, when she had the privacy to cry, Claire found that her pain went deeper than mere tears. She wanted to cry but it just wasn't possible. Instead her body ached with feverish pain, her mind crawling round in circles as she tried to rationalise the agony of mind and emotions threatening to swamp her. She heard a door open, and anticipated the return of the steward, but instead it was Raoul who stood over her, bending down to speak to her, his face stern and somehow older as he said something that seemed to reach her through a dizzy haze. He turned away then and she closed her eyes thinking he must be a mirage conjured up by her yearning mind, but there was nothing illusionary about the brandy he forced her to swallow, or the anger she could see glittering bleakly in his eyes as he returned the glass to the hovering steward.

'Claire, are you all right now?'

'Perfectly,' she lied in a thin, little voice. 'It was just that seeing you gave me such a shock. But then I suppose I ought to have guessed. I suppose you're here to make sure that I actually leave ... I'm tired, Raoul,' she lied again, turning her face towards the window. 'I think I'll try and get some sleep. Wake me up when we reach Heathrow,' she finished sardonically.

'We aren't going to Heathrow.'

The quiet words were like a douche of cold water. 'Not ... Then ...'

'We're flying to Paris, Claire,' Raoul told her in the same cold emotionless voice, glancing at his watch, the gold strap glinting in the light, as he added, 'where we shall be married at five o'clock this evening. Everything is arranged. I have your passport, and I have checked with your Embassy. Since I possess dual citizenship and have retained my Christian religion, there is no bar to our civil marriage being performed in Paris. I have arranged matters with as much discretion as possible. Officially, we are travelling to Paris because my father has been taken ill, and you, in your capacity as my wife, have persuaded me to be reconciled with him.' His mouth tightened a little. 'My father has, of course, had to be included in my plans. He expressed himself most willing to participate in my charade ...'

'Married? You and I? But ...'

'Surely you did not think there could be any other outcome after what passed between us? Even now you might be carrying my child. Do you honestly think I would allow him to be brought up as I was, not knowing the love and care of his father?'

'Your child? But . . .'

'But what?' he asked sardonically. 'But it is not possible? On the contrary, Claire, it is all too possible! And our marriage need not be without its compensations. Sexually, at least, we are compatible, even if you do love another . . .'

Claire's head was reeling. Did he honestly still think she loved someone else, after what had happened between them? Even if he did, she suspected it would not be long before he guessed the truth, and dredging up every last ounce of her courage, she said firmly, 'No, Raoul, I will not marry you.'

'And I say you will.' His eyes had darkened to jade and Claire felt a *frisson* of fear as she looked into their obsidian depths. 'And I mean what I say. You will marry me, even if I have to drug and bind you to get you to the altar. Is that the way you want it, Claire?'

He wasn't lying. He had every intention of carrying out his threat if she didn't agree, and all because of a slender chance that she might be carrying his child.

'It seems a rather drastic course of action to take simply because we've been lovers,' she pointed out drily. 'We don't even like one another . . .'

'And I am the one to blame for this state of affairs because I gave in to my physical need of you, is that what you are trying to say?' His face darkened, the skin melding itself to his hard bones. 'You, Claire, are you not equally responsible? Do you think for one moment that if you had told me that you were still a virgin I . . .'

'But you did,' Claire reminded him hotly, his angry words unleashing her own temper. 'Afterwards you . . .'

'I am a man, not a boy, Claire,' he cut in jeeringly. 'What did you expect me to do? Carry you back to your own bed when every part of me still clamoured for release? But what is done is done and we must now think of the future. Our future and that of the child you might be carrying.'

There was no way she could make him listen to reason, Claire thought despairingly, and bearing in mind the traumas of his own childhood, was it so hard to understand why he was so determined that they should marry? He was, after all, right; impossible though it felt at the moment, she could be carrying his child. Taking a deep breath, Claire made up her mind what course of action she must take.

'Very well, Raoul, I will marry you,' she agreed with a calm she was far from feeling, 'but only if you give me your word that until we know whether I am pregnant or not, we live ... separately, and that if I am not carrying your child you will divorce me.'

'And if you are carrying my child?'

'Then ...'

'Then you will still want a divorce, even knowing you must leave your child with me, is that it? How you must love him, this man who holds your heart, even though it is I who have possessed your body. Very well,' he said tautly, 'it shall be as you wish, with one further stipulation. There will be no divorce until Saud is out of danger. Do you agree?'

Saud! She had almost forgotten him in the trauma of more recent events. 'And if I do will you ...?'

'Allow you to sleep alone in your own bed?' His eyebrows rose. 'You are letting your imagination run away with you, Claire. What happened between us last night happened, but you have my word that while you live under my roof, whatever hungers and appetites I might have, I will not seek to satiate them in your bed. Does that reassure you?'

Numbly she nodded her head, turning away so that he wouldn't see the pain in her eyes. Of course, she should have expected nothing more. Raoul was a man of the East, accustomed to satisfying his physical desires with women who would be pliant and accepting in his arms. She had been nothing more than a brief aberration which already he was regretting.

Please God, don't let there be a child, she prayed mentally. If she was to bear Raoul's child, how on earth could she bring herself to leave them; and how could she stay, falling deeper in love with Raoul every day and knowing that her love could never be returned? Perhaps even one day being forced to witness his love for someone else? Had he loved the Muslim girl he had nearly been betrothed to?

They were married quietly and discreetly later that afternoon in a suburb of Paris. Not the wedding she had always envisaged for herself. As they had stepped off the plane, Raoul had turned back and then reappeared, handing her the large box in which Zenaide had placed her hat as they stepped into the waiting car.

'It is perhaps not the bridal array you might have expected, but I asked Zenaide to pack it for you.'

As he had asked her maid to put out the cream suit, Claire wondered, stealing a brief look at his shuttered profile, before taking the hat from its box. It was true, it did make her look more bridal, but her heart was heavy when the car came to a stop outside the small town-hall where the wedding ceremony was to be performed.

Now it was over and they were man and wife, Raoul's gold ring glittering on her finger. Outside their car still waited, the engine purring almost soundlessly. The brief ceremony had taken little more than fifteen minutes, and as Raoul replaced their passports and marriage certificate inside his jacket, Claire stared numbly ahead. Fifteen minutes. That was all it had taken to change the course of her life. Automatically her hand crept to the reassuring flatness of her stomach.

'Praying your body is not cherishing my seed?' Raoul demanded harshly. 'Try to look on the bright side, Claire. If you are carrying my child you may be sure that you will be generously recompensed for the . . . inconvenience.' His lip curled disdainfully, and Claire was overwhelmed by the need to lash out and hurt him as he had wounded her.

'That's your answer to everything, isn't it?' she stormed at him. 'Money . . . Well, there are some things money can't wipe out. I don't want your money, Raoul. I don't want anything of yours!'

'Especially not my child.'

The words lay between them like a gage, but Claire was too bitter to back down now. 'Especially not that,' she agreed, watching the anger die out of his eyes to be replaced by a cold, blank dislike.

He leaned forward and said something to their driver, then settled himself back in his seat without another word. Claire longed to ask him where they were going and how long he intended them to remain in Paris. Already she was missing Saud. Her hand covered her stomach again. What would it be like to have Raoul's child? In other circumstances, if there was the merest chance that he might return her love, there was nothing that would bring her greater happiness, but as it was she dreaded the prospect of finding herself pregnant. For the rest of her life she would be torn in two. Torn between wanting and loving her child, and knowing that if she stayed with it she would be risking the untold anguish of living in proximity to Raoul, thirsting more and more with every day that passed for his love, like a man separated from an oasis by a thick glass wall. How could she possibly endure it?

Their car slid to a halt, jerking her out of her thoughts. They were outside a hospital, and Raoul got out, politely opening Claire's door, his hand on her elbow as he escorted her inside.

'We are in Paris to visit my father, remember?' he murmured as they walked into a tiled reception area decorated lavishly with flowers. The receptionist greeted them with a smile, her eyes widening fractionally as she looked at Raoul. No matter where he went, he would always draw those looks of appreciation from her sex, Claire recognised, the ache in her heart increasing. They were directed down a corridor and Raoul paused outside the room they had been told was his father's.

Lucien D'Albro was sitting up in bed reading a book, and he greeted them both with a smile. 'I had not realised that being in hospital could be such a pleasant experience,' he said to Claire, his eyes twinkling. 'One has every comfort. Indeed one might almost be in the most luxurious of hotels, and then of course, there is the added bonus of the nurses. So,' he turned to Raoul, 'it is done?'

'Yes.' Raoul kept his back to his father and walked across to the window. 'I have not yet thanked you for the part you have played in this. Time was short and there was no one else I could ask . . .'

His voice was low, the words terse and bitten off, but Claire was facing Lucien and was able to see the pain in his eyes as he said quietly, 'Is it so very hard to come to me when you need help, Raoul? I am after all your father . . .'

'Genetically, yes,' Raoul agreed harshly, 'but as a child . . .'

'It was your mother's wish that she return to her people. She wanted me to go with her, but my work, my life, was here in Paris. I explained that to her when we married. My tour in Omarah was only a brief one. She knew that once it was over I would be returning to France. I did not want to let you go, Raoul, but she reminded me how much more her people could give you than I. Our name is an ancient one, but financially . . .' He spread his hands. 'It was no secret that I married your mother for financial security. I had intended to use her dowry to restore the family château. It had been the dream of my father,' he sighed.

'You are lying,' Raoul interrupted angrily. My mother told me how you used her dowry—in gambling, escorting other women, living the life of a wealthy playboy.'

'No. You are wrong. That is how I made my *living*.'

There was a tense silence, and Claire wondered if she ought to leave them alone. She had a feeling that what was about to be said in the privacy of this room was something between father and son alone, but even as she made a move to leave Lucien grasped her wrist.

'No, Claire, please stay,' he said gently. 'If what Raoul tells me is true it could well be that you carry my grandchild.' He smiled when she blushed. 'I must confess I suspected all along that you were not the mother of Saud. You looked too innocent . . . and far too unknowing to have been the lover of a man like my son. I hope you will learn well from my mistakes, Raoul. I should never have let your mother take you, but I was tired of having her wealth thrown in my face. When she left I made a vow that I wouldn't touch a penny of her dowry and I haven't. Shortly after she had gone, I became ill and I lost my position in the Ministry. When I recovered I had to make a living somehow. I had always been lucky as a gambler . . .'

He shrugged his broad shoulders. 'You know the rest. The château still stands, but only just. I have willed it to you, together with your mother's money. Both are, after all, yours by right. Perhaps in time you will bring my son to Paris again, Claire, this time with the true purpose of effecting a reconciliation between us. Never let pride stand in the way of your happiness, my son,' he said quietly to Raoul.

They left the hospital in silence, Claire not daring to look at Raoul. How had he taken his father's revelations? That Lucien had spoken the truth Claire did not doubt, but it would take more than verbal explanations to cure the wounds of the past that still went very deep with Raoul.

They stayed once more at the George V, occupying the same suite they had had before. When Claire asked uncertainly if it was possible to telephone the palace to check up on Saud, Raoul glanced at her curiously. 'One might almost suppose you were genuinely fond of that child . . .'

'Why shouldn't I be?' Claire responded bitterly. 'Oh, I know you think my affection for him springs from avarice, but you are wrong. I was instrumental in saving his life,' she said almost to herself. 'I feel almost as though he is my child . . .'

'And yet feeling like that you are prepared to desert your own child, because he is also mine?' he threw at her harshly. 'How you must hate me, Claire. Why? Because I took from you that which you were saving for another? Or is there more to it than that? Is it not simply that I took, but that I gave too, more pleasure than you can ever hope to find in the arms of your cold English lover, who does not even want you enough to storm the citadel of your virginity . . .'

He had gone before she could think of a fitting enough retort to silence him, and it was well after midnight when Claire heard the door to their suite opening quietly. Where had he been all evening? With someone else? The thought was like a knife thrust in her heart.

Two days later they were back in Omarah, but this time she was in reality Raoul's wife. 'Saud has missed you,' Zenaide told her. 'He will be glad that you are back.' There was a small piece in one of the French papers about Raoul's visit to the bedside of his supposedly sick father, which Raoul pointed out to her one evening after he had returned from the city.

His business responsibilities kept him very fully occupied. Claire learned from Zenaide that it was Raoul and the Sheikh who had been responsible for the intensive reorganisation of the education system, so that girls as well as boys could benefit from the wealth that oil had brought to the small state.

A conference in London necessitated his leaving for that capital at the end of their first week of marriage, and as she watched him leave, Claire couldn't help wondering how he would spend his nights when he was away. She had no illusions. Any number of beautiful women would be only to glad to sleep with Raoul, even without the added allure of his wealth.

As yet there was no evidence that she might be carrying his child, and Claire was glad that she had stipulated that they were not to live as man and wife. Raoul was cynical enough to be perfectly able to make love to her without caring about her, but her frail spirit was already too overburdened to be able to take the strain of a relationship with too much love on one side and none on the other.

After a morning spent on the beach, Claire returned with Saud to the palace for lunch and then a sleep. She had found herself falling into the pattern of sleeping in the afternoon when the sun was at its hottest, and today she felt particularly tired. It was a steep walk down to the beach, and as she walked back up she visualised Raoul's Moorish ancestors carrying their human prizes back up to the palace—young European girls destined for the slave markets of the East, vast amounts of gold and precious jewels from

Spanish galleons, fair-haired, fair-skinned girls stolen from the English coast. How would she have felt had she been in their shoes?

She shuddered, putting Saud down as a wave of dizziness made her cling to the solid support of the cliff face. She must have walked up the path too quickly, she chided herself when the world had righted itself and Saud's plaintive cries reminded her of his presence. He beamed when she picked him up, proudly displaying his two new teeth. Poor Saud, who had lost both mother and father, and who for all the wealth he would one day inherit was a pauper indeed when it came to the riches of love.

There had been no more visitors to the palace, and Zenaide had explained that it was normal to leave newly-weds alone for one full month after the marriage ceremony.

'Blessed is the bride who can tell her family at the end of that time that she carries her husband's child.' She blushed rosily, glancing at Saud who lay kicking on the bed, revelling in the freedom from his nappy, and Claire guessed what she was thinking. Zenaide, at least, did not doubt that Saud was her child.

Once again Claire ate alone. She had found her appetite diminishing since their return from Paris. The heat seemed to sap her energy despite the efficiency of the air-conditioning installed in the palace. She was often lethargic and dull. She needed some activity to occupy her mind, she acknowledged. If she had really been Raoul's chosen wife she could have approached him with the problem. There must be many areas in which she could help. He had mentioned entertaining various representatives from other countries and Claire knew from Zenaide that he had an apartment in the city in one wing of the Sheikh's palace. She was not used to inactivity.

She picked up the letter she had received from her godmother, wincing as she read of her pleasure in her marriage. If only she knew the truth! Sighing, Claire folded the thick paper, suddenly remembering Teddy's unanswered letter. Where on earth was it? She must write to him telling him that it would be impossible for him to come out and stay with them. She would do it first thing in the morning, she thought to herself as she prepared for bed.

The night was hot, even the thin silk of her gown uncomfortable against her skin, sleep somehow eluding her as she tossed and turned in the wide bed. Where was Raoul now? Who was he with?

She tensed as she heard Saud cry. He didn't normally wake up during the night, and Claire listened to his cries for several minutes, warning herself that it would be foolish to go into him, but when they persisted she flung back the covers of her bed, pulling on a silk robe and hurrying through into Saud's room.

The panda which was his favourite toy was on the floor and Claire bent to pick it up guessing that it had been the cause of the commotion. Saud had seen her and crawled eagerly to the bars of his cot, grinning at her in the darkness. It was as she knelt in front of him, the panda in one hand, the other steadying herself, that Claire first heard the noise. No more than a soft slither, it sent such a shudder of dread through her that she couldn't move. Saud chuckled, obviously thinking he was participating in some new game, his chuckles turning to wails of protest when she didn't move.

The room was so dark. If only she had switched on
the lamp when she came in, Claire thought feverishly,
trying to shush Saud, her ears stretched for that
slithering sound which she prayed and hoped had
been nothing more than a figment of an overworked
imagination. But no . . . There it was again. Louder
this time, closer, relentless. Perspiration broke out all
over her body. Dear God, there was a snake
somewhere in the room with them. Numbly, she tried
to remember what Zenaide had told her about local
snakes. There were several varieties, one particularly
deadly, but how could she remember which was
which? She couldn't even see it and even if she could,
she was so panic-stricken that she doubted she could
have told the difference between a rattlesnake and a
common grass-snake.

Saud was trying to drag himself to his feet using the
cot rails, and Claire froze as she heard the sibilant
slither again. The thing was in Saud's cot, tangled up
somewhere among his covers. A scream clawed at her
throat but she suppressed it, her whole body
trembling as she straightened slowly, not knowing
where the danger lay, expecting with every second to
feel sharp fangs biting into her skin—hers or Saud's!
He was sleeping dressed only in a nappy because it
had been so hot, and Claire felt as chilled as though
she had been standing in an Arctic wind as she
visualised the thing in the cot with him. Even now as
he struggled to stand, beaming at her in the semi-
darkness, it could be positioning itself to strike.

The pictures conjured up by her mind were too
much for her. Not giving herself time to think,
Claire darted towards the cot lifting him out. He

whimpered in fright as though sensing her terror and as she clasped him against her, Claire heard another blood-freezing sound from his cot. It was too much. Trembling all over, she opened her mouth and started to scream, weak tears of terror pouring down her cheeks. The bedroom door was flung back on its hinges, the light blinding her as it snapped on.

'Claire . . .'

Raoul's voice roused her from her panic, her eyes opening and noting the dark trousers he was wearing, and the shirt unbuttoned almost to the waist as though she had interrupted him on the point of undressing. She hadn't realised he was back, but as he took a step towards her, his forehead pleated in a deep frown, she remembered what had happened and called out, 'No, Raoul . . . don't come too close. I think there's a . . . a snake in Saud's cot.'

She shuddered as she spoke, closing her eyes as she averted her face from the pretty blue and white cot they had bought in Paris. Never would she be able to look at it in the same way again. 'I heard him crying,' she added huskily, as Raoul continued to stare from her to the cot as though unable to believe what she was saying. 'I came in, and . . . and I could hear something moving. It seemed to come from the cot.' She was white and shaking with reaction, her frenzied, 'No, Raoul, please don't . . .' halting him on his way towards her. 'You might get bitten,' she added hoarsely as he looked at her.

'You come here to me then,' he said compellingly, using the same soothing tone he might have used to a terrified child. He didn't believe her, Claire thought sickly, as she took first one and then another step past the cot.

A sudden movement froze her, an angry hiss, and the dark, reed-like body emerged from the sheets, poised, watching, mesmerising her with its dark, glittering eyes. Dimly she heard Raoul curse, and then move, almost knocking her off her feet as he pushed her away, plucking the thing from the soft blue cotton. It squirmed through the air, landing on the floor, and Raoul's shoe crushed down on the back of its neck. Sickened but unable to tear her eyes away, Claire watched its dying writhing, its poison sacs emptying on to the floor, all movement slowly going.

'It's over,' she heard Raoul saying quietly. 'It's over Claire. You're both quite safe now. Come . . .'

Numbly she walked towards him, letting him take her hand and lead her back into her own room, feeling all the time as though she were sitting on the sidelines outside her body, watching its slow movements.

Her false calm broke when Saud started to cry, fierce tremors seizing her body. She was aware of Raoul taking Saud from her, the little boy finding comfort in the hard pressure of his arms; and then it was her turn, her face was pressed against the hard warmth of his bare chest as he put Saud down and comforted her.

'It's all over now, Claire. You're both quite safe,' he repeated, but Claire didn't feel safe. She felt distinctly vulnerable, her body aching with pain and need, her body treacherously conscious of Raoul's proximity, of the satiny feel of his skin beneath her trembling fingers, the dark hairs crisp against her palm, his heartbeat a reassuring thud against her.

'How could it have got in there?' she begged, her teeth chattering with reaction. 'Raoul, someone must know about Saud. Someone tried to kill him . . .' Her voice started to rise and she felt Raoul's fingers at her nape, urging her to relax against him.

'Perhaps,' he agreed, 'but maybe not. Whichever the case, it was fortunate that you went in to him.'

'He had thrown his panda on the floor,' Claire told him stupidly, knowing that she was simply talking to hold at bay the terrible fear still stalking her. 'I was just going to give it to him when I heard it. Oh Raoul, he could have died. I could have gone in there in the morning and . . .'

Her stomach heaved and she shuddered in his calming embrace. 'Shush . . . you mustn't torture yourself with too-vivid imaginings. It is true that it could have happened, but it is also true that it didn't. Allah must be over Saud.'

He said it half-humorously, but Claire wasn't in the mood to be amused. She glanced fearfully at her own bed, and correctly interpreting her fear, Raoul released her, carefully stripping it and then remaking it. Not until he had searched every inch of the room and assured her that it was safe did he return to her.

'If you would like me to stay with you for tonight . . . I should prefer what has happened to be kept a secret between us. If it was a deliberate attempt to kill Saud, then whoever made it will try again. I don't want to panic them into going into hiding. If we say nothing it might lull them into a false sense of security. Curiosity to discover how their plan misfired, if nothing else, should draw them out into the open.'

Did she want him to stay with her? If only he knew

how much, Claire thought wildly. There was nothing she wanted more right now than the security of his arms round her, his body shielding hers. A slow heat started to burn through her, amazing her that she could so easily feel desire alongside her fear. It wasn't merely for security and protection that she wanted Raoul beside her, she thought bleakly. She wanted the passionate possession of his body as well, his hands and lips against her skin, hers against his. She became acutely conscious of the warmth of his skin, of the thinness of her silk gown and her breasts hardening perceptibly beneath it, aroused by their contact with his body. Trying to disengage herself, Claire said wildly, 'I didn't think you were coming back tonight, I . . .'

'My business was completed earlier than I expected,' Raoul told her tersely, adding with a cruelty that hurt, 'besides, where else would I want to be other than with my wife; the woman who might bear my child?'

His hand covered her stomach, heating her skin until she felt fluid and boneless, his lips brushed hers lightly until they parted voluntarily.

'Go to sleep, Claire,' Raoul told her harshly, releasing her with an obvious rejection that stung. 'Otherwise I might forget my side of our bargain and take you to my bed.' He saw her expression and laughed sardonically. 'What's the matter? Do you find it offensive when I remind you of my frustration . . . my physical needs? Do I shock you with my blunt admission that I want you? Go to bed, Claire,' he reiterated, turning towards the door, and it struck her that he looked tired, and more than that, defeated. But there was no reason for him to suffer the demons of sexual frustration, she told herself bitterly. There must be women aplenty who would delight in his lovemaking.

Too exhausted to dwell more deeply on his comments Claire crawled into her bed, but she didn't sleep well. Almost every half-hour she was awake and checking on Saud, who Raoul had insisted she return to his cot, which he assured her was now quite safe. The snake had also been removed, but she couldn't pass the spot where it had lain without shuddering with fear and nausea. If she hadn't heard Saud . . . If Raoul had not returned . . .

Over and over her mind kept playing back to her the sound of the snake's soft movements, her throat gagging with fear, until sleep at last claimed her in a stifling, thick embrace.

CHAPTER EIGHT

NIGHTMARES tormented her uneasy sleep—muddled images of the dining-room at the Dorchester, men with guns which turned into writhing snakes—and Claire woke up, her heart pounding, her body bathed in perspiration, a sudden movement in the shadows by the door making her tense and call out in fear, 'Who's there?'

'Only me.' Raoul detached himself from the shadows. 'I'm sorry if I startled you, but you were crying out in your sleep.'

Shivering, Claire admitted huskily, 'Every time I close my eyes I keep hearing that snake, I keep remembering what happened in London . . .' She shuddered and then tensed in disbelief as Raoul walked towards her bed, casually pulling back the bedclothes. 'What . . . what are you doing?'

For the first time she thought she saw a certain grim humour gleaming in the darkness of his eyes as he surveyed her pale features and tense expression.

'Since you cannot sleep properly because of your nightmares, and I cannot sleep for the sound of your fear, we might as well share what is left of the night together.' He was in bed beside her before Claire could protest, and treacherously an inner voice whispered that the warm weight of his body in bed beside her was comforting.

'Come.' When his arms came round her, pulling her

against his body, a different kind of fear raced through her veins, but the heat of his body pressed against hers was too compelling to resist. She wanted this, Claire admitted drowsily, she wanted this close union of their bodies, this comfort Raoul gave to her standing between her and her fears. But merely being held in his arms possessed its own form of torture and Claire was relieved when she felt sleep stealing over her, drowning out her desire to touch the taut male flesh against which her head was pillowed, to press soft kisses into the curve of his shoulder and feel his body harden with desire, in the same need she could feel stirring deep inside her.

When she woke again it was morning and Raoul was gone, the only evidence of his occupation of her bed the shallow indentation of his head in the pillow next to hers. She turned her face into it hungrily, breathing in the trace of his body scent, feeling her body tremble with longing. She heard Saud cry and was instantly jerked back into reality. They couldn't rule out the possibility that someone had discovered the truth, Raoul had said last night, and a sudden wave of nausea invaded her stomach.

That was the first time that fear had actually made her physically sick, she thought, minutes later, standing in her bathroom shaken and dazed by the intensity of her emotions.

Too lethargic from her broken night to want to make the long trek down to the beach, Claire told Zenaide that instead she would take Saud down to the main courtyard. 'It is quite sheltered down there but open enough for him to get some fresh air.' She knew that Zenaide was looking at her disapprovingly

because she hadn't eaten her breakfast. Not even the
delicious fresh fruit Zenaide had brought had been
able to tempt her. Say nothing to anyone, Raoul had
said, but the burden of keeping to herself what had
happened was a heavy one. She couldn't suspect
Zenaide, who was always so gentle and caring, nor Ali,
but someone had been responsible for that snake . . .
there was someone in the palace they couldn't trust.

By the time she reached the courtyard her head was
throbbing, her headache a legacy of her fear. Even
Saud seemed to lack his normal vitality, crying to be
picked up and cuddled rather than employing himself
busily with his toys as he normally did. How on earth
were they going to keep him safe?

Because she had been concerned about his diet,
Claire had brought with them a large supply of baby
food which she prepared herself. Poison was a
favourite method of murder in the East, so she had
read, and she shuddered thinking of someone
administering it to her small charge. She must not
think about it, she told herself, she must get a grip on
her emotions. Already Saud seemed to have picked up
on her nervy, fearful mood and was reacting to it.
Perhaps Raoul would be able to discover something, to
find out who was the culprit. From Zenaide, she knew
that he had gone to the city; Ali had not driven him
and Claire wondered if he had deliberately left the
other man behind to watch over them.

She managed to eat some lunch—a little of the
delicately flavoured rice Zenaide brought out to her,
and some of the fresh fruit—but she was shudderingly
reluctant to return to her rooms, especially with Raoul
absent, even though common sense told her that

whoever had put the snake in Saud's room was hardly likely to attempt the same thing twice. She could only hope that Raoul was right when he said that by saying nothing they might be able to lure the would-be assassin out into the open.

She was just on the point of returning inside when Zenaide came hurrying into the courtyard, her normally smooth forehead puckered into a frown.

'It is the Princess Nadia, Sitt,' she exclaimed anxiously. 'She has called to see you.'

'Princess Nadia?' Claire too frowned, wondering if she ought to recognise the name. Raoul had mentioned various members of his family to her following the Princess's visit, but had added that his family was so large and its members so numerous that it was pointless her trying to remember them all.

'She is second cousin to the Lord Raoul,' Zenaide told her, still looking anxious. 'Shall I tell her that you are resting?'

For some reason her maid did not like the Princess Nadia, Claire observed, but that was no reason for her to deny herself. She had no wish to offend any members of Raoul's family and so she smiled calmly and asked Zenaide to bring the Princess to the courtyard and to arrange for coffee and almond cakes to be served to them.

Not sure of the correct protocol, but guessing that the title 'Princess' meant that her visitor was of superior rank to herself, Claire stood up as she heard footsteps approaching the courtyard, frowning a little as she caught the impatient tap of very high heels. She had been expecting a woman of middle age, but the girl stalking arrogantly towards her, the *abba* which had been covering her from top to toe as she rounded the corner discarded, was only half a dozen years or so older than herself. With swift dismay, Claire registered the haughty, almost petulant expression, the clothes that shrieked Paris and clung seductively to her lusciously curved body. Eastern her visitor might be, but her hair and make-up quite definitely came from the most elegant Western salons. This was no shrinking flower of the desert, but a sophisticated woman of the world whose elegance did little to conceal a nature which Claire guessed to be both hard and avaricious.

Her deeply-glossed lips parted in the coolest of smiles as she approached, dismissing Zenaide with a few curt words.

'So, you are the woman Raoul married instead of me?' were her first devastating words, accompanied by a taunting smile and a narrowed assessing glance. 'You have not deceived yourself that he cares for you, or ever will, I hope?' she added insultingly, carrying on before Claire could draw breath to retaliate. 'And this must be the child who is the cause of your hurried marriage. The Sheikh, my uncle, is well-known to disapprove of mixed marriages. Indeed it was he who advised my father to forbid my marriage to Raoul.' She shrugged and added, 'I must confess I was glad. As a lover Raoul is superb, but as a husband . . .'

A shrug of elegantly clad shoulders mocked all Claire's previous conceptions of what Raoul's intended bride had been like.

'A husband is only to be tolerated when he remains in the background, and provided, of course, he is very rich. Raoul is far too possessive ever to make a complacent husband. The insecurity of his childhood, of course. I hear he was most reluctant to make an honest woman out of you, Miss ... but, of course, Eastern men are renowned for the importance they place upon their eldest sons. How old is he?'

Desperately trying to hold on to her temper, Claire responded. So this was the woman Raoul was to have married, and who, if she was to interpret her remarks correctly, was still his lover. A wedding ring gleamed on her hand, so she must be married and, no doubt, used her marriage to protect her from any censure regarding her wanton behaviour. Muslims were very strict guardians of the morals of their women, but the Princess Nadia seemed to make her own rules.

Did Raoul love her? A quiver of jealousy burned through her at the thought, so tormenting her that she missed her unwelcome visitor's next question, and had to have it impatiently repeated, feeling very much like an ignorant schoolgirl being chastised by her teacher.

'Raoul, where did you meet him? It must have been when he was working at our Embassy in London. That was just after my marriage. My father asked the Sheikh to send him there. Poor Raoul, he took my marriage very badly. A hungry man will take whatever is available, is that not so, Claire? And a clever woman knows how to make the most of whatever opportunities come her way. A girl of your station in life cannot have had many. Raoul is very attractive as well as a very wealthy man, and you were clever enough to know exactly which bait to use to hook him. Is this his child? He does not look very much like him. I should have thought he would be much fairer skinned. Where was it you said you met?'

Saud had been pulling himself up on to his feet, and fell over, suddenly starting to cry. Claire went instinctively to pick him up, realising only as she straightened that Raoul had returned and was striding towards them. Nadia had her back to him, and Claire wondered if she had the courage to endure Raoul's reaction to the other girl's presence. But a little to her surprise, when Nadia did turn and see him, there was nothing but polite calmness in Raoul's eyes.

'Raoul . . .' Her arms went round him, the glossed lips pouting for his kiss. Claire averted her eyes, hating the fierce pangs of jealousy storming through her, fighting to appear calm and controlled.

'Princess Nadia was just asking if we met when you were working at your London Embassy, darling,' she managed to enunciate gaily. She wasn't sure where they were supposed to have met. Let Raoul do his own lying and his own explaining if Nadia should cross-question him afterwards. As they were lovers and apparently had been for many years, she would naturally expect to know about any other women in Raoul's life, although it was patently obvious that she did not consider Claire to be any sort of competition.

Her eyes dropped to Saud. He didn't look like Raoul, Nadia had said, and she had also commented on his olive skin. She started to worry at her lip, and was startled to hear Raoul saying curtly, 'It was the Paris Embassy at which I worked for a term, not the London . . .'

'Of course, Raoul,' Nadia was quick to intervene. 'That is what I said, Claire must have misunderstood me. It was just after I got married, wasn't it? I remember we visited you there when we were on our honeymoon. So where did you meet? You still haven't told me.'

'At a party given by a friend,' Raoul responded indifferently, surprising Claire by bending down to pick up Saud, who gurgled his pleasure, waving small fists excitedly in the air. Raoul must have been watching her, Claire thought dazedly, because there was nothing hesitant or awkward about the way he handled the child, and surely no one watching him would doubt that Saud was his. Claire had dressed him in cool cotton rompers, and the small chubby legs kicked enthusiastically. He had a small birthmark on his left thigh, and it caught Claire's attention as he wriggled in Raoul's arms. Nadia was looking at it too, and for a moment it seemed to Claire that the temperature in the warm, shaded courtyard suddenly dropped—enough to raise goose-bumps on her exposed arms, and to bring back the terrors of the night.

Raoul noticed immediately. 'You are not well?' he asked sharply.

'I'm . . . I'm fine.' How could she explain the *frisson* of terror which had just shivered through her? There was no logical explanation, but she was glad when Nadia eventually exclaimed that it was time she left, waving aside the coffee and almond cakes Claire offered.

'Far too fattening,' she pronounced, and Claire was sure it was no accident that her painted fingertips moved seductively down the curve of her body, drawing Raoul's attention to every enticing curve. Compared with Nadia, she was a pale snowdrop put against the beauty of a deep red rose, and she suffered by the comparison.

When Nadia had gone, Raoul announced that he had brought some work back with him that he wanted to finish. Claire wanted to talk to him, to tell him that she suspected Nadia might have guessed that Saud wasn't their child, but perhaps Raoul himself had told Nadia the truth. But surely in that case she would not have raised the subject? It was too taxing a problem for Claire to unravel. Her broken night was beginning to catch up with her, and when Zenaide came in to ask what she wanted to have for dinner, she told the little maid that she wasn't hungry and that she had decided to have an early night.

Saud, fortunately, seemed to have recovered his normal good spirits, laughing and gurgling when Claire bathed him, splashing her with the warm water as he played with his ducks. She grew more and more attached to him with every day that passed and knew she would feel the wrench when she had to leave. If she felt like this about Saud, how would she feel if she had conceived Raoul's child? Could she bear to leave him with his father?

She hadn't conceived a child, she was sure she hadn't, Claire told herself fiercely. She didn't feel any different than she had before. But it was early days yet, an inner voice warned her, far too soon for her to know one way or the other. As she prepared for bed, she found herself praying again that there would be no child. Hadn't she already endured enough heartbreak?

She was just walking through from her bathroom to her bedroom when the outer door opened. Thinking it would be Zenaide she paused, but it was Raoul who walked in, causing her nerves to quiver in mute reaction.

'Zenaide tells me you are not eating.'

'I ate some lunch,' Claire corrected.

'You are not feeling well?'

She flushed as she realised he was probably thinking along the lines she herself had been earlier, and probably with as much regret. If he wanted any woman to bear his child, it must be Nadia. 'Just a reaction from last night, that is all . . .'

'I wanted to talk to you anyway. It occurred to me this afternoon that we ought to have some sort of story prepared. Nadia will not be the only person to question you about the past.' He frowned as though remembering something. 'I cannot think why you should have thought she said I was posted to our London Embassy. Nadia of all people should . . .'

'Know that it was to Paris you were sent when she was married?' Claire said tautly. 'She did say London, Raoul. A slip of the tongue, no doubt, but she lied when she told you I had made the mistake.'

'Lied?' His eyebrows rose. 'Why should she do that?'

'Perhaps because she resents my presence in your life,' Claire said with a calm she was far from feeling. 'Anyone who loves resents the presence of someone else in the life of their lover.'

'And does your lover resent my presence in yours?' he asked softly. 'He has not written to you recently. Have you written to him, Claire? Have you told him that you might be carrying my child? That we have been lovers?'

'No . . . no, I haven't told him anything,' Claire whispered truthfully. Raoul's softly-spoken words were conjuring up images she would far rather forget.

They had far too disturbing an effect on her composure. She glanced up and found him looking at her, probing the pale silk of her robe, reminding her how intimately he knew the curves that lay beneath. A hot languor spread through her veins; a tormenting desire to go up to him and press her body against his, wantonly offering herself to him, feeling him respond.

'And nor will you do so,' Raoul muttered arrogantly. 'You are my wife now, Claire, mine!'

She wasn't sure which of them moved first, she only knew that somehow she was in his arms, breathing in the warm male scent of him, feeling her pulses leap in exultation. She wasn't even going to think about what had brought him to her, what had sparked off his desire. He bent his head, and her lips parted eagerly, welcoming the probing invasion of his tongue, all her earlier insistence that there should be no intimacy between them forgotten as her body's craving overruled the fragile control of her mind. Her senses reeling wildly, she responded with all the banked down hunger inside her to the hungry dominance of his mouth, groaning with pleasure when his hand cupped her breast, stroking roughly over the thin satin barrier which separated his fingers from her flesh. Opening to him as eagerly as the furled petals of a flower to the sun, Claire drank in the touch and scent of him, sliding trembling fingers inside his robe, pressing her palms flat against the moist heat of his skin, thrilling to the hard possession of his mouth when her thumb rubbed lightly against the hard flesh of his nipple.

He dragged his mouth away from hers, plundering the soft scented skin of her throat, pushing aside her

robe, copying the caressing movements her fingers had
made against him. Shivering waves of pleasure crested
and broke over her, her body the receptacle of
sensations so acute that she thought she might break
apart under the pleasure of them. Her tongue touched
the strong column of his throat, feeling the muscles
strain as he swallowed an involuntary moan of
pleasure, urging her closer to him, his hands sliding
down to her hips, and round to spread against the
rounded curves of her buttocks, pressing her against
him.

He was already hungrily aroused and the knowledge
thrilled and excited her, her hips moving in instinctive
enticement, her teeth nibbling delicately at the warm
flesh between his neck and his shoulder. Raoul had
taught her that love-making could be a sensual feast
and now he was encouraging her to make for herself a
banquet she knew no other man could ever rival. She
wanted him as much, if not more, than he wanted her.
She knew that male arousal was not as subtle as
female, but her longing for him swept aside any
rational doubts that might have made her think twice
about what she was doing. When her body became
impatient for his possession, she slipped out of her
robe, pausing when she saw the look in Raoul's eyes.
They glittered almost black in the dimly lit room and
the hand he stretched out to her betrayed a fine
tremble.

The drift of his fingers along the outline of her
body, no more than a butterfly touch, was excruciatingly arousing, but some inner sense, some instinctive
urge to respond to his rhythm held her still beneath it,
her throat closing on a hungry moan of impatience as

his fingertips brushed briefly over the curves of her breasts. Surely he could see what he was doing to her? How much she needed the solid contact of his body against hers? But again something prevented her from moving, from taking the few steps necessary to bring her against him.

'Claire.' He said her name thickly, picking her up and carrying her the short distance to the bed, removing his own robe before lying down beside her.

Her whole body trembled with an acute ache, her eyes closed so that he wouldn't see the depths of the hunger in them as he bent towards her. Disappointment shivered bitterly through her as she felt his brief kiss on her lips, his tongue stroking gently over them, when what she wanted was the fierce intensity she had felt in him earlier. His lips drifted gently across her skin, his tongue touching, arousing, and then withdrawing, all down the length of her body until she felt she might explode beneath his tormentingly tentative caresses. He paused when he reached her breasts, stroking their pointed aching tips briefly with his tongue, but when Claire reached up to him, her whole body surging beneath the caress, compelled by a fierce need to urge him to intensify the contact, his fingers locked round her wrists, forcing them slowly down to her sides, his tongue returning to stimulate her throbbing flesh, until Claire felt she could stand it no longer and her body began to move wantonly, perpetuating an ancient rhythm.

Almost instantly the gentleness left Raoul's touch, replaced by the hunger she had earlier yearned for, explosive in its unbridled demands; the searing touch of his mouth against her body wanted an intimacy that made her gasp and tense until he showed her how he wanted her to respond, and all her previously held ideas of what desire should be between a man and a woman were overturned in a storm of pleasure too intense to allow hesitancy or withdrawal.

When at last Raoul moved over her, her body quivered ecstatically in response, glorying in the surge of pleasure fusing between them as she arched to welcome his body into hers, her fingernails digging deep into the muscles of his sweat-slick back, the fierce sound of pleasure emitted from his throat echoing the elemental urgency she could feel soaring deep inside her.

All the delight in the universe seemed to be concentrated inside her; their bodies were no longer two separate entities, but one united whole, seeking and finding together the pleasure which was the nearest the human race could ever come to savouring eternity.

Afterwards she slept, deeply and dreamlessly, waking with the dawn, drowsy and satiated with satisfaction, her body as sleek and supple as a mountain cat's—until she turned her head and found that at some time during the night Raoul had left her.

CHAPTER NINE

IT was Zenaide who told her that Raoul had gone to see his uncle, the Sheikh, and that he had left a message to say that he might be gone for several days. His uncle—or Nadia—Claire found herself wondering bitterly. He might have made love to her, but that didn't mean that he loved her. Her hand brushed against the flat curve of her stomach as she remembered the feeling of nausea she had experienced earlier, and her haunting fear that she might be carrying Raoul's child returned. Up until now she had managed to keep it at bay, reassuring herself that she could not possibly be pregnant, but now she wasn't so sure. And there was Saud to worry about as well. How could Raoul leave them now, after what had happened? And moreover leave them so that he could be with Nadia?

He had been gone three days before Claire could bring herself to admit that she was pregnant. Her persistent sickness and the growing fullness of her breasts made it impossible for her to hide from the truth, and she was sure that Zenaide too had guessed. On one front at least, though, she could not accuse Raoul.

She had noticed how closely Ali stuck to both Saud and herself, remaining in the vicinity even while they were in the courtyard, and Claire had become particularly careful about Saud's food, making sure that no one apart from herself had access to it.

The knowledge that she was to have Raoul's child pushed aside some of her overwhelming anxiety for Saud, her mind grappling with new problems and fears. How could she leave her child behind with Raoul when they were divorced? But how could she stay, even if Raoul were to permit her to do so? The ideal solution would be for her to leave before Raoul guessed that she was pregnant, but that would mean deserting Saud. Her problems seemed insoluble.

On the fourth day of Raoul's absence, Claire woke to the familiar nausea striking her as she tried to leave her bed. She had learned to move more gingerly, taking her time in dressing and leaving her breakfast until she was sure the sickness had subsided. She was down on the beach playing with Saud when she heard the sound of feet crunching along the path. Tension feathered across her nerves instantly, the fear of danger to Saud never far from her mind, but it was Raoul who was striding towards them across the sand.

It was only when she shaded her eyes from the sun to study him properly that Claire saw the glitter of anger darkening his eyes. Fear trembled through her as she wondered at the cause of it. Was he angry because they had made love? Had Zenaide perhaps said something to him that had made him realise she was pregnant? She hadn't intended to tell him yet, not until she was properly sure, but his first words drove all thoughts of the baby out of her mind.

'I am surprised to find you still here when your lover has been so anxious to contact you—even to the extent of contacting our London Embassy. Have you any idea how I felt,' he continued bitingly, 'when I was summoned from an important meeting to be told that someone had been making urgent enquiries about you?'

Someone? Fear struggled with incomprehension, until the truth dawned. Teddy must have been trying to contact her, or someone on his behalf. Had he had an accident, was he hurt? Anxiety took the place of fear, her emotions mirrored clearly in her eyes as she struggled to her feet.

'Teddy . . .' she began urgently, only to fall silent as Raoul said thickly:

'So it's true, you do love him, so much so that I merely have to mention his name and you are filled with concern for him.' A muscle beat spasmodically in his jaw. 'I wonder if he will still feel the same about you once he learns that you have given yourself to me . . . abandoned yourself to me would be a better description,' he added softly, 'because there was total abandonment in the way you offered yourself to me, wasn't there, Claire?'

What could she say? She was too worried about Teddy to bandy words with him. 'I must go back to the palace,' she mumbled unsteadily, her mouth feeling as though it were full of marbles. 'I must ring . . .

'Teddy?' Raoul interrupted viciously. 'By all means, if only to tell him that he will make no further attempts to get in touch with you while you are living here as my wife. Indeed, I shall be surprised if he wishes to once he knows the truth, and you *will* tell him Claire, otherwise I will do it for you.'

With that threat ringing in her ears, Claire followed him blindly back up the path to the palace. Saud was balanced easily in his arms, chattering away in his as yet indecipherable private language, unaware of the tense atmosphere existing between the two adults.

Mentally checking the time difference, Claire worked out that she ought to be able to get through to Teddy's school. She knew the number, but because of the language difficulties she was forced to ask Raoul to ask the operator for it. He had told her she could make the call from his study, and although she had never been in the room before, apart from noticing that it was furnished functionally rather than anything else, she paid little attention to her surroundings.

She had expected Raoul to leave once he had requested the number, but to her dismay after handing the receiver over to her, he lounged on one of the divans, watching her twisting the telephone wire in nervous fingers. Willing him to leave, Claire turned her back on him. Why was he staying? To make sure that she told her 'lover' about her marriage? Dear God, how was she going to be able to speak to Teddy properly with Raoul there?

At last, when she was on the point of giving up, someone answered the phone. A voice she dimly recognised as belonging to the headmaster's secretary spoke into it, and haltingly Claire asked for the headmaster, too pursued by fear for Teddy now to worry about what conclusions Raoul might draw.

'Ah, Miss Miles,' she heard the headmaster saying calmly. 'I'm so glad you've got in touch, and you must excuse me for not using your married name by the way, but I'm afraid I don't recall what it is . . .' He sounded so normal and calm that Claire felt a little of her tension easing away.

'Teddy,' she blurted out. 'Is he all right?

Someone's been trying to get in touch with me, I believe . . .'

'And you thought something was wrong? I'm so sorry my dear. Teddy is fine. No, we've been trying to contact you about the holidays. Teddy wrote to you, I believe . . .' He broke off and murmured something which Claire didn't catch, her mind recognising with appalled dismay that she had never replied to Teddy's last letter. 'Look, I'm getting him to come to the phone. I know you'll feel more reassured if you speak to him yourself. He badly wants to come out and see you,' the headmaster was continuing, 'and if it's at all possible, I should strongly recommend it.'

'But . . .'

She was about to protest when the receiver was put down and then she heard Teddy's familiar voice, weak tears of relief pouring down her cheeks at his, 'Hi, sis. You've remembered that I exist at last, have you? Look, can I come out and stay with you?'

'Look, Teddy, I don't think it's a good idea,' she managed to interrupt before he could continue. 'It's terribly difficult getting out here, and . . .' She broke off as the receiver was wrenched out of her hand.

Raoul was towering over her, his face almost white with rage. Before she could stop him, he muttered thickly, 'I told you what to tell him and what I'd do if you didn't . . .' And then as he raised the receiver to his ear, Claire distinctly heard Teddy's reedy voice exclaiming anxiously, 'Claire? Sis, are you still there?'

For a moment there was deadly silence, Raoul's eyes locking with hers. Claire trembled, knowing that he too had heard what Teddy said, and then he was speaking into the receiver, his voice oddly warm and reassuring as he intoned, 'Teddy? This is Raoul speaking, Claire's husband.'

Teddy must have said something, because there was a silence from Raoul's end, and then he was saying, 'Of course you can come out. Yes, that's right, there can be problems with flights, but we'll organise something. Yes, I'm looking forward to meeting you too . . .' He handed the receiver back to Claire. 'He wants to say goodbye to you.'

Numbly she spoke to Teddy, letting Raoul take the receiver from her when she had finished. Again a tense silence filled the room, and then Raoul said quietly, 'I think we'd better have a talk, don't you? No more lies, please, Claire,' he continued curtly when she would have spoken. 'You can't honestly expect me to believe that your supposed lover is a boy with his voice still unbroken, who calls you "sis". And I can't understand why you should have allowed the misconception in the first place.'

'Can't you?' Her voice was bitter. 'Perhaps it just seemed easier to let you go on thinking the worst about me. You'd already made your mind up . . .'

'And you didn't care enough to change it?'

Why should he sound so tired? Honesty compelled her to admit a little of the truth. 'It wasn't that. I just thought it would be easier . . . safer . . .' He looked at her and she forced herself to meet the look in his eyes.

'Safer? But it wasn't, was it, Claire? Do you honestly believe if I had known that, I would have . . .'

'Made love to me?' she ventured with a brave smile.

'Among other things. But what's done is done, and now I want the truth. All of it,' he added implacably.

Slowly she told him, taking a deep breath and

speaking in a low, husky voice.

'So the money was for Teddy's school fees?'

Claire hung her head. 'Yes . . . I would have helped without any sort of payment . . . I wanted to help because of Saud, but you were so cutting and unkind, and I'd been worrying for months about how I was going to afford to keep Teddy at school. It's almost his home to him, you see,' she added unconsciously, pleading with him to understand. 'Since we lost our parents he's been so insecure. I wanted to provide him with all that he would have had if our father hadn't died.'

'And what about you, Claire?' Raoul asked huskily when she finished. 'Was there no one who could have lifted the burden from your shoulders? You were what when you lost your parents? Seventeen? Eighteen?'

'Eighteen,' Claire admitted, swallowed hard, hardly able to believe that it was tenderness she heard in his voice. 'I . . . I was just about to start university, but of course that was impossible. My godmother helped as much as she could, but her second husband has a family of his own . . . She often gave me little treats . . . That visit to the Dorchester . . .'

'Foolish, selfless Claire,' Raoul murmured over her downbeat head, 'so ready to deny herself for the good of others. I will arrange for Teddy to come out and stay with us, and you need no longer concern yourself with his school fees.' His mouth tightened when he saw her expression. 'No, Claire. Teddy is now my responsibility.'

'But . . . but our marriage is only temporary,' Claire reminded him breathlessly, 'and he can't come out here. I had to tell him something,' she reminded him. 'I couldn't just disappear, so I went to the school and

I told him we were getting married, but ...' She licked her lips, suddenly frightened to admit to Raoul the lie she had told Teddy.

'But?' he prompted, frowning. 'You didn't tell him you were marrying a man of mixed race, is that what troubles you? The shock he will have when he sees me?'

'No!' Her protest was vehement and instantaneous. 'Of course not. Teddy wouldn't worry about a thing like that. No, I told him we were in love,' she admitted miserably. 'I didn't want him to worry, or suspect anything you see. There are several Arab boys at the school and if I had told him the truth, he might have let it slip and it could have endangered Saud ... Raoul, what's wrong,' she asked uneasily, watching the slow tide of dark colour creep up under his skin. 'I shouldn't have lied to him, I know, but it seemed the most sensible thing at the time. Are you ... very angry?'

'Only with myself,' he told her in a voice tight with pain. 'I was judging you by my own standards, Claire, and I find it humiliating to see how ignoble they are compared with yours. Of course Teddy must come out to see you, he has been anxious about you. You haven't replied to his letters.'

'I forgot,' Claire agreed, gnawing her lip gently, thinking how wonderful it would be to see her brother—and how impossible. Surely Raoul could see that?

'I'd love to see him,' she admitted, 'but we, I ... we can't, Raoul. He's not naïve. He's bound to realise that ... that ...'

'We aren't in love?' Raoul supplied for her. 'I think

you are worrying far too much. Children tend to accept things very much at face value. Once he knows that we are sharing a bedroom as do other married couples, I doubt he will give the matter another thought.'

'But we aren't,' Claire protested, 'I mean we don't share a room.

'No, but for the duration of his stay we shall do so. He can have my room and I shall share yours. No more protests, please, I assure you I shall not take advantage of the opportunities such intimacy will afford me. You are quite safe, Claire, you may accept my word on that.'

'And Saud?' Claire pressed. 'What . . .?'

'Leave that to me. I shall explain to him that Saud had been orphaned and that as I am his legal guardian he will be brought up by us. In fact, I have been thinking . . .' he glanced at her and smiled mockingly. 'Poor Claire, you have far too soft a heart, how are you going to deny the claims of your three "children" when the time comes to leave me and make your own life?'

'Three? But . . .' Her heart started to thud erratically, her hand going protectively to her stomach. Surely he didn't know?

'But we do not know yet that you have conceived my child?' Raoul taunted. 'Ah, Claire, I am hoping that you have.' He saw her thunderstruck, disbelieving expression and laughed. 'I want to keep you with me, Claire, and I will use every means I can to do so. You already love Saud, you can't deny it, and I have been thinking that even when it is safe to reveal his true identity he could have no safer or more secure home than one presided over by you. And your brother. He is how old? Twelve? He will need your care for many years yet, and not merely financially. And lastly there are our children, Claire. If you give them one tenth of the love you shower on Saud, they will indeed be fortunate . . .'

'I am surprised you want me as the mother of your children,' Claire said bitterly. 'You were betrothed to Nadia . . .'

'Who is of a different religion, and a world away from the warmly maternal creature that is you, Claire. Nadia leaves her sons to be brought up by others. I suffered from that myself and have always sworn that I would not allow a child of mine to be torn in the way that I was. That is why . . .' He broke off, and said instead, 'My uncle, the Sheikh, will approve. He has liked you from the start.'

'And because of that, and two children, you expect our marriage to continue? You don't even . . .'

'Even what?' he taunted. 'Want you? You know that is a lie, Claire. My body finds a pleasure in yours that heats my blood just to think of it, and you are not, I think, indifferent to me. It need not be a bad life. You will be financially secure always, you will have the love of your children, and the . . .'

'Desire of my husband?' Claire demanded bitterly. 'At least until he tires of me and turns back to his mistress. Oh, you need not deny it, Nadia told me that you were still lovers . . .'

'You are overwrought, and now is not the time for us to argue. Think about what I have said, Claire.'

'But are you sure you want it?' she murmured, almost beneath her breath. 'I thought you loathed me and that you couldn't wait for me to leave.'

He bent his head, his breath fanning her temple. 'If that were the case, would I have sought to ensure that you remain with me?' His hand pressed against her stomach as he brushed his mouth across her surprised lips, making his meaning quite clear. 'The first time I must admit I did not think of the possible consequences until it was too late. But the second . . .' He smiled teasingly, stunning her with the amusement she read in his eyes. 'Ah, the second time, I must confess that I hoped your womb might be receptive to my seed and that there might grow in it the child who would keep you here at my side.'

Later, alone in her room, Claire found herself dwelling on what he had said. There had been no mention of love, and her heart ached over that, but it was tempting to think he might be right when he said they could build a life together—Saud and their own children growing up, perhaps some tenuous emotion growing inside him for her once she was the mother of his sons . . . And wasn't it too late anyway to make any conscious choice? She was already carrying his child and she sensed that once he knew that he would never let her go. In his way he was to be admired, because he wasn't just denying her love, he was denying it to himself as well, and she sensed that, while Nadia would always hold his heart, as his wife he would accord her respect and outward support. But did she have the strength to settle for that? Did she have any choice?

After that the day slid lazily into one another, and although nothing more was said Claire knew she had made her decision, and that Raoul was aware of it. She still hadn't told him she thought she was carrying his child. They were due to collect Teddy from the airport at the end of the week and Claire intended to ask Raoul if it was possible for her to see a doctor at the same time.

He had not been able to discover who was responsible for the snake in Saud's cot, but no other attempts had been made to injure the little boy, and Claire was beginning to wonder if it had been merely an unfortunate incident after all.

The day before Teddy's flight was due, Raoul walked into her room unannounced, frowning heavily. 'I have to go away for a few days. It can't be helped, unfortunately,' he told her. 'There's been an uprising in one of the remote villages on the border. Someone's been stirring up political problems, casting religious doubts on the new education plans and I have to go and see if it can't be sorted out.'

'Is it . . . is it the same poeple who tried to kill Saud?' Claire asked dry-mouthed, suddenly filled with dread.

'Possibly,' Raoul was cautious, deliberately casual, but Claire wasn't deceived, he was going into danger. She could so easily lose him!

'Raoul, you will be careful, won't you?' she begged, watching his frown deepen slightly as though he couldn't understand why she should be so concerned. Careful, she warned herself, another minute and he might guess the truth. If there was to be any dignity in the life she would share with him her love for him was something he must never suspect.

'I think I'm having your baby . . .' she told him huskily, knowing with deep feminine intuition that this was her strongest weapon, her greatest chance of keeping him safe. For his child's sake he would take fewer risks, think more carefully. 'I was going to ask you if I could visit the doctor when we go to collect Teddy. It's early days yet, but ... but I'm nearly sure.' She couldn't stop herself from blushing as he looked at her and then came towards her, sitting on her bed, pulling her down on to his lap.

'So my prayer was answered,' he said softly. She was wearing a soft cotton dress that buttoned down the front and before she could stop him he was deftly unfastening the buttons. His palm felt warm against the bare skin of her stomach, still ridiculously flat. But the evidence was there in the fuller curves of her breasts as he unfastened her bra and exposed them to his warm gaze, his thumb gently probing her peaking nipple. 'My child.' There was something almost reverent in the way he breathed the words touching her breasts with tender lips; a curious fluttering stirred in her stomach as he pushed her back on the bed, his head lying gently against her stomach, his face turned into the warm skin. 'My child.' He said it again, his breath soft against her body, the tender way in which he kissed her bringing an aching lump to her throat and weak tears to her eyes.

He couldn't have been more adoring if he had actually loved her, and for the first time she realised how important his child was to him. She had glimpsed it with Saud, in the tender affection he had for the little boy, and she was overwhelmed by a feeling of humility, a great surge of love that compelled her to put her arms round him, cradling him against her body, feeling the awe and the vigorous sense of achievement in him because his body had proved itself so potently virile.

'You must take care when I am gone,' he murmured, slowly releasing her. 'I shall take you to see a doctor when I get back. And I shall come back, Claire,' he assured her. 'My child will not be brought up without its father or its mother. They will all be our children,' he added, as though he had looked into her mind and seen what she was thinking. 'Teddy, Saud and this . . .' he dropped a brief, hard kiss against her stomach, 'and this as yet unknown, growing within the protection of your body. We shall love and succour them all.'

When he left she was almost glowing with happiness. His things had been moved into her room, and he had reassured her yet again that he would not be absent for long. But her fragile bubble of happiness burst disastrously the following morning when Zenaide came in to say that Princess Nadia had arrived to drive her to the airport.

Raoul had said nothing about Nadia coming to drive her, but perhaps it was as well that this had happened, Claire decided miserably. At least it served as a reminder to her as to where his feelings really lay. He was glad now because she was carrying his child and would be a tender, caring father. But he would never love her as a woman—as he loved Nadia.

CHAPTER TEN

TRYING not to betray how dismayed she was that Nadia was driving her to the airport, Claire checked her appearance in her mirror. The pale buttermilk linen suit she had chosen looked chic and attractive, her skin betraying just the barest suggestion of a tan. Saud was going with her—Raoul had suggested that she take him—and as she went downstairs to meet Nadia Claire couldn't help wishing that Raoul was there to go with them instead.

Nadia, as before, was expensively and elegantly dressed, her eyebrows rising slightly as she ganced at Claire's suit.

'Chanel?' she questioned unhesitatingly. 'But then Raoul always was very proud and he would scarcely want it to be said that he could not afford to keep his wife decently clothed. He said to tell you that he might be delayed, by the way,' she threw casually over her shoulder as she led the way to the car, and Claire had to bite down on the exclamation of dismay which sprang to her lips. When had Nadia seen Raoul? He had promised to telephone her and she had stuck close to the palace all day waiting for his call. He could not find time to telephone his wife, but he did have time to talk to Nadia, or so it seemed.

The interior of Nadia's Mercedes was comfortably air-conditioned, the fine leather seats contoured to provide the utmost comfort, but Claire wasn't in the mood to appreciate the quality of the car's German engineering and attention to detail. Nadia said something to her chauffeur before closing the panel that separated the front of the car from the rear, leaning back in her seat and lighting a cigarette.

'So. You have a brother, Claire, and Raoul has discovered that he has another responsibility. It seems you have also been able to effect a reconciliation between Raoul and his father. You know I find that very hard to believe. Not even our uncle, the Sheikh, has been able to make Raoul overcome his bitterness towards his father—and it isn't even as though Raoul cares in the slightest about you. Oh, come,' she drawled when Claire would have spoken, 'you and I both know the truth. Raoul might have turned to you in a moment of physical need . . .' she shrugged elegant shoulders, 'that is only to be expected, but he does not love you Claire.

They had been driving towards the city and Claire frowned as they suddenly veered off the main road, heading for the desert. 'A short cut,' Nadia drawled languidly, noticing her reaction. 'It will help us to avoid the congestion of the souk. Have you been there yet, Claire? Most Europeans find it interesting. Has Raoul told you that had he been born of the Sheikh's brother and not his sister our marriage would have been permitted? That would have meant that in time Raoul would have succeeded the Sheikh.' She spoke almost absently and yet Claire had the feeling that something important was hidden in her words. 'In the East, the only way for a woman to wield power is through her husband. My husband is third in line to the throne. He was fifth in line until my cousin was killed, a most unfortunate accident, and then his baby son too was murdered, in London as it happened. He would have been about the age of your Saud. Indeed, I believe there is also a certain physical resemblance, although I must admit that I only saw the child twice. But then, of course, they are related. Why, Claire,' she commented, watching her, 'you have gone quite pale. Are you quite well?'

'It is nothing,' Claire assured her, driven by some impulse to inflict her own wounds by adding casually, 'The early weeks of pregnancy can sometimes be uncomfortable. You have two children of your own Raoul tells me, so you will understand . . .'

'You are carrying Raoul's child?'

Something had gone wrong, because there was triumphant delight in the dark brown eyes instead of the angry jealousy Claire had expected to see, and when she glanced out of the window Claire was disturbed to see that they were surrounded by desert, with the city nowhere in sight.

She glanced at her watch, frowning as she realised the time.

'My brother's flight——' she began urgently.

'Unfortunately you will not be there to meet it,' Nadia interrupted with ill-concealed venom. 'You are far too trusting, Claire, and have played right into our hands. Hasim was right to guess that you would be our most powerful weapon. You and Saud, who we both know to be the son of my cousin, my dead cousin,' she repeated, 'and not Raoul. Oh yes, it was a clever move, and for a time you had us fooled. We truly believed that Saud had perished as he had been intended to, but Hasim was suspicious

about this marriage between you and Raoul, and
about the child you were supposed to have borne
him. Raoul is a clever man, but not clever enough.
He forgot about this.' She touched the birthmark on
Saud's leg mockingly. 'This is something Saud
inherited from his mother. She was my half-sister.'
Her mouth curled in mocking contempt. 'She was
also my father's favourite. I was too much a rebel,
too greedy for power and riches—like Hasim. Has
Raoul told you nothing of Hasim, my brother?' she
added. 'It was Hasim who urged my father to forbid
the marriage between us. Raoul, like the Sheikh, is
far too philanthropic. If it were left to them all the
wealth we derive from our oil would be wasted on
coaxing the desert to flower, on educating ignorant
tribes people, but they will not be allowed to do so.
Now that we have Saud we can force the Sheikh to
abdicate and Hasim will take his place on the
throne. We have turned too much to the West in
recent years, but once Hasim is in power things will
be different.'

Nadia's brother was the leader of the rival faction?
Did Raoul know of this?

'Raoul, of course, suspects nothing of this. No one
does,' Nadia continued, almost as though she had
guessed Claire's thoughts. 'Hasim has been at great
pains to remain in the background, but soon the day
will come when he can take his rightful place as leader
of our country, and you have helped us, Claire. With
Saud in our hands my uncle will refuse us nothing,
and I am sure that Raoul will also pay us well for the
return of his wife, especially as she is carrying his
child.'

'I thought you loved him.' The words escaped stiff lips as Claire tried to come to terms with what Nadia had told her.

'Loved him? A man who considered his pride more important than me? He could have changed his religion as my father directed but he refused, and humiliated me with his refusal, and I swore then I would be revenged upon him. Of course, he does not know how I feel. It is very easy for a woman to conceal her true feelings from a man, isn't it, Claire? I believe you love him, don't you?'

Averting her profile, Claire stared out of the window. Ahead of them she could see a fringe of palm trees against the horizon and bleakly remembered the oasis she had visited with the Princess. As they travelled along the straight road, the palm trees grew larger and Claire saw that they were indeed heading towards a small oasis, although whether it was the same one she had visited earlier she could not tell. Half a dozen black tents stared blindly at them as the Mercedes swept past in a cloud of dust. Nadia laughed tauntingly as she saw her expression. 'Ah no, I'm afraid there will be no opportunity for escape nor for rescue . . .'

'But Raoul will know the truth, he will know that I left for the airport with you.'

'By that time it will not matter. Once we let the Sheikh know we have Saud, we shall no longer need to preserve any secrecy.'

Although she talked glibly about ransoming her, Claire suspected that neither she nor Saud would be allowed to live, and as she looked down at the small boy asleep beside her Claire thought wretchedly how she had let him down—and not just him but Raoul as well. Her hand fluttered towards her stomach, the gesture arrested by Nadia's mocking laughter. 'Poor Raoul, he will be beside himself with concern when he learns what has happened, won't he, Claire? Not concern for you, of course, but for the child you carry. You can only be in the very early stages of pregnancy, an acutely vulnerable time . . .'

She wasn't saying anything that hadn't already raced through her own mind, and Claire turned her face back to the window, pushing down the hood of her burnous as she stared through the tinted glass with burning hot eyes. She wouldn't give Nadia that satisfaction. A cloud of dust on the horizon caught her attention, and Nadia grimaced as the Mercedes swiftly overtook a small cavalcade.

'Badu! The Sheikh and Raoul seek to educate them—when Hasim is in power money will not be wasted on such folly.'

'If your brother does turn towards Russia, do you honestly suppose you will be allowed to retain your wealth?' Claire asked quietly. 'A communist country would never . . .'

'I shall not stay here.' Anger flashed in the dark eyes. 'Hasim has promised that when this is over I can live wherever I wish. The world shall be my oyster, Claire.'

'And your brother, does he honestly believe he will be able to retain control of the country?'

'Hasim is clever. He has the support of a certain religious faction which is against our present progress. Omarah is too far away from Russia to be strictly controlled, and we have the wealth to protect ourselves.'

So Hasim would use Russian aid to gain control of the country and then once he had he would betray his former allies? Somehow Claire did not think he would be allowed to get away with such treachery.

It was growing dusk when eventually the Mercedes came to a stop at a small oasis. A cluster of tents crouched by the waterside. 'Out,' Nadia commanded, thrusting open the door, and wrinkling her nose fastidiously as they were enveloped in a cloud of sand. A small, squat man, heavily robed, approached the car.

'Well, brother dear, I have brought them to you as I promised,' Nadia called out gaily, 'and it is even better than we hoped. She is carrying Raoul's child.' She cast a taunting look over her shoulder at Claire. 'So we shall have to be extra caring of her welfare. Any news from the others?'

The man she had addressed as her brother switched into harsh Arabic, and both of them ignored Claire as she stood swaying in the darkness, overcome by heat and exhaustion, Saud a heavy weight in her arms. They were miles from anywhere and even as the thought of escape occurred to her, she was forced to admit that there was nowhere for her to escape to.

'You will be pleased to know that your husband is busy trying to vanquish the rebels,' Nadia taunted her, reverting once more to English. 'But my brother's men are skilled guerrillas and it will be some days yet before Raoul is able to return. By that time we will already have been in touch with the Sheikh.'

Before Claire could stop her, she picked Saud from her arms, showing him to her brother, pointing out the tiny betraying birthmark.

'We lost three valuable people in London. As well as paying for you, Raoul will have to make reparation for them. I hope he values his child-to-be highly, Claire, for if he does not ...' She laughed when she saw Claire's expression and tormented, 'Oh you need not worry, we shall not hurt you, you will simply be set free ... The desert has its own methods of punishing intruders.'

She was taken to a tent, far less luxurious than the one she remembered from before, and a surly girl brought food and water. Saud was fretful and remembering how cold desert nights could be, Claire wished she had something to wrap round him to keep him warm.

Although she had been sure that she would never sleep, she did so, so heavily that it occurred to her when she woke, cramped and cold just before dawn, that her food must have been drugged. Her main fear that Saud would be taken from her had not been fulfilled. As their chances of escape were nil, it was probably easier to allow her to continue looking after him, Claire decided, trying to coax him to drink a little of the water she had been brought by the same surly girl who had served them the night before.

She could hear sounds of activity from outside, and then the flap of the tent was thrust aside, and Nadia strolled in. 'Farewell, Claire,' she drawled. 'From now on Hasim will take care of you. I am returning to the city—to see how the Sheikh reacts to our demands. I doubt we shall meet again ...' She was deliberately trying to frighten her, Claire knew, but she refused to give in to the insidious tug of fear spreading swiftly through her veins.

'You will never be able to get away with this,' she retorted with more assurance than she could feel.

'You think not? Who is there to stop us? Raoul will never discover where you are. Never!'

Claire knew that she was probably quite right. After the tent flap was dropped in place behind Nadia, she heard the Mercedes purring away and then silence, punctuated only by brief outbursts of Arabic. Apart from the same girl who had brought her food earlier Claire saw no one all day. She tried to keep her spirits up by playing with Saud and by forcing herself to take some simple exercise—walking up and down her tent—but the relentless tide of fear she was constantly trying to hold at bay wouldn't relinquish its cruel grip.

Another night passed, another dawn was heralded by the now familiar sounds of the camp, then disturbed when Claire heard the sound of a vehicle arriving and a staccato burst of conversation. Had the Sheikh responded to their threats already? She was being foolish to hope, Claire berated herself, Hasim would never allow them to go free. While Saud lived there would always be another contender to the throne. Instinctively her arms fastened tightly round the little boy as she heard impatient footsteps approaching the tent.

They were taken outside and forced to sit beside the oasis as Claire witnessed tents being taken down and placed in sturdy Land-Rovers, and heard shouted, muddled instructions on the cool morning air. As the sun gradually rose, all signs of occupation of the oasis were swept away. They were obviously going to move on, but why? Had the Sheikh somehow discovered where they were? Hope flamed in Claire's heart, only to be doused when Hasim approached her. He was flanked by two men, both carrying rifles, and Claire stiffened automatically, remembering the scene in the breakfast-room of the Dorchester.

'Thanks to the ingenuity of your husband, we are forced to move on to a more secure place. Oh no, you are not to come with us,' he murmured, when Claire moved towards the nearest Land-Rover. His eyes rested on her body and he shifted uncomfortably from one foot to the other. 'Is it true that you are carrying his child?'

When Claire nodded her head, too weary and terrified to lie, he grimaced. 'You will not survive to bear it, I fear, but as any man who takes the life of a woman with child is thrice cursed by Allah, I cannot do as Nadia would no doubt insist and use these,' he indicated the guns carried by his men, 'to bring your life to an end. You have two choices. Either you leave the oasis now, taking the child Saud with you; or you remain here, where you might survive until you are found, but we shall kill the child before we leave.'

It was no choice at all and he knew it, Claire thought bitterly. How could she even contemplate saving her own life at the cost of Saud's? Once they walked into the desert they might as well be dead, she knew that, but she also knew that she would not even think of trying to save herself by sacrificing Saud.

'I choose the desert,' she said proudly, lifting her head to meet the cold dark eyes, 'and I give thanks to Allah that he gives special care to women in my condition.'

'Personally I care nothing for these old superstitions,' Hasim told her callously, 'but my men have learned of your condition and would doubtless react adversely if I killed you or instructed them to do so, and until I have taken my uncle's place I shall need their support. Now . . . walk . . .'

Refusing to give in to the urge to look behind her, Claire did as he instructed. With every step she half expected to hear the whine of bullets behind her, but it seemed Hasim had spoken the truth when he had said that his men would not kill her.

'Walk and keep on walking for two hours,' he called after her. 'If you attempt to return to the oasis before that time is up, Saud will be killed.'

And if she kept walking for two hours, the oasis would be lost from her sight, Claire thought bitterly. It had taken six hours for them to reach the oasis—in a car—and although she was following the road, she knew quite well that she would die, of thirst and heat, before she could reach safety. Feverishly she tried to think. Perhaps if she only walked at night. It was colder then . . . but how long could she exist without water? How long could Saud exist? Already he was a heavy burden for her to carry, and already the horizon was wavering in front of her. She stopped and turned. Hasim was standing watching her, rifle slung casually over his arm. No, her only option was to go on . . . and on . . . her mind thought drearily as two hours melted into three and she had no clear idea of where she was going, the road a dark ribbon where it wasn't obliterated by sand.

Saud was awake, demanding to be put down. Surely it wouldn't hurt her to stop for a brief rest? Three hours. Hasim would have left the oasis by now. She could turn back, but as she did so, Claire was attacked by swirling dizziness. She forced herself to walk back, counting her footsteps, forcing herself to concentrate, unaware until she found herself ankle-deep in sand that she had somehow strayed off the road. It was a physical effort to keep her eyes open, her skin burned, her body flinched from the scorch of the sun. She had to sit down and rest . . . and it didn't matter really if she did. She had plenty of time . . . all the time in the world . . .

Someone was speaking, dimly Claire recognised the harsh Arabic sounds. She forced her eyes to open, her lids feeling like heavy weights. Someone was leaning over her, a man robed and wearing a head-dress, his features concealed by the thickness of his beard. Vaguely she was aware of deep-set dark eyes, and the curved arrogant blade of his nose, and then everything started to slip away from her. There was something important she had to say, but she couldn't remember what it was. She roused herself again and this time she was aware of subdued, high-pitched chatter that she remembered from somewhere. She must have made a sound because the chatter stopped. Someone was offering her water, and she gulped at it greedily, suddenly remembering.

'Saud . . . Saud . . .' she cried weakly, but there was only silence, and the memory of burning hot sands and clear cloudless skies from which a relentless sun burned down.

Claire opened her eyes. She felt as though she had been asleep for a very long time. Her body felt unfamiliar, heavy and tender, her eyes gritty.

'Lord Raoul, the Sitt is awake.'

Zenaide. Claire recognised her voice, and yes, this was her room in the palace. Had it all just been a dream, then, that searing heat, that sense of fear, that walk with Saud . . . Saud . . . She struggled to sit up and was instantly restrained by Raoul's arm.

'Saud,' she protested weakly.

'He is fine.' She heard Raoul bite off an expletive and then turn to Zenaide. 'He is perfectly well, Claire, Zenaide will bring him to you. There is someone else waiting to see you, too.' He was watching her closely, and Claire wished she could remember properly. Something eluded her, tugging at the edges of her memory, but she could not summon it up. 'It's Teddy,' Raoul pressed. 'Your brother. Remember, you were to meet him at the airport.'

The airport. Nadia! She must have said her name out loud because Raoul's face tightened.

'That is enough for now, Raoul.' Another voice spoke close by her, and a man moved from the shadows. 'She is still tired and must be allowed to recover. Without you beside her, my friend,' the unfamiliar voice continued, although it seemed to Claire that it held compassion. 'There is nothing more you can do. Punishing yourself will achieve nothing.'

Punishing himself? Why should Raoul do that? Because of Nadia? Because the woman he loved had helped to try to murder Saud? Did he know about that? Thoughts too exhausting to be sustained flooded through her tired mind, and then something else surfaced.

'Raoul.' She clutched at his arm. 'My baby . . .' A

look of bitter sadness filled his eyes, and her own clouded with tears. 'Raoul, my baby . . .'

'Your baby is quite safe.' It was the other man who spoke, smiling down at her, his fingers feeling for the pulse in her wrist with a professionalism that put her fears to rest. 'But that is more than can be said for you. You must sleep now if you are to recover your full strength. Later you can talk.'

'Saud,' she pleaded, 'I must see Saud . . .' She saw Zenaide coming into the room, Saud in her arms, and she expelled her breath on a thankful sigh, gladly submitting to the sleep stealing slowly through her veins.

When she woke again Teddy was sitting on the end of her bed, watching her. 'Good. Dr Naud said you would soon be awake. I would have to miss all the excitement,' Teddy continued, obviously aggrieved. 'Boy, when I tell them about it at school. It must have been really ace . . . to be kidnapped and then . . .'

'I am sure your sister found her experience anything but "ace", Teddy,' Raoul's voice said drily from the door. Teddy scrambled off the bed as Raoul approached.

'But it was ace how the Badu found her and looked after her, wasn't it?' he probed. 'Boy just imagine being able to track like that . . . and recognising her too when Nadia drove her past the oasis. "Lady of the golden hair" they call you,' he told a bemused Claire, grinning a little. 'Just think if they hadn't seen you and sent word to Raoul . . .'

'That's enough, Teddy.' Raoul's calm firm voice cut through Teddy's excitement. 'Ali has prepared your dinner.'

'But what about you?'

'I will eat up here with your sister.' Teddy looked ready to protest, but something in Raoul's expression must have changed his mind because he went off without another word. 'Oh for the recuperative powers of the young,' Raoul said lightly when he had gone. 'When we first learned that you were missing he was inconsolable.'

'You know everything?' Claire whispered. 'By 'everything' she meant Nadia's treachery, and Raoul nodded.

'Yes, and I cannot see how we could have been so blind. In so many ways it was obvious, but because Hasim remained out of the country for long periods we never thought to connect him with the left-wing faction in the country, even though he is the Sheikh's heir after Saud.'

'What happened?' Claire pressed. 'I . . .'

'Let me tell you from the beginning.' Raoul perched himself on the end of her bed, and Claire looked away from him, wishing he would come closer, take her in his arms perhaps.

'As Teddy has just said, you were recognised as Nadia drove you through the Badu encampment—that was her main mistake. Nadia and her family are well known for their contempt of the Badu, and Ali ben Durai's curiosity was aroused enough for him to send some of his men out after you. He knew, in the way that the Badu always seem to know what is going on, that your brother was due to arrive and that you were to meet his plane. He also knew that I was away, but when his suspicions were confirmed, he sent messages both to me and to the Sheikh telling us that he feared you had been taken captive. One of the men on the Sheikh's staff here at the palace was a spy—the same one who placed the snake in Saud's cot, I suspect—and he managed to send Hasim a warning that we were on our way.'

'So that was why he broke camp.' Claire shivered. 'They were going to kill us, but because I was carrying your child . . .'

'I know it all.' Raoul looked grim, and Claire wondered if he was thinking about Nadia. 'Hasim was most impressed with your courage, Claire. You risked your own life for Saud, choosing almost certain death rather than safety. If you had opted to remain at the oasis you would at least have had water and would have been found in due time, even if we had not known where to look, but instead you braved the desert.'

'They meant to shoot Saud,' Claire said unsteadily. 'I knew that we probably wouldn't survive the desert, but I couldn't . . . couldn't . . .' Tears started to burn her eyes and she turned away, too soon to see the movement Raoul made towards her. As she turned from him as though in rejection his arm dropped to his side, his expression suddenly grave.

'You are tired and the doctor has ordered that you must rest. When the tribesmen found you they feared it was already too late. They sent word to me and took you back with them to their camp.'

'And you brought me back here,' Claire finished for him. Now that Saud was safe, would he still want her to stay? Would he still want them to live together as a family, or had he changed his mind? There was something different about him, she knew that.

'My father sends his love,' Raoul told her as he

stood up, watching her eyes widen as he spoke the words. 'When he worked here—before he met my mother—he made a survey of the desert. I telephoned him to check that the oasis was where the Badu tribesmen had described. We couldn't afford to waste any time.' He sighed, pushing his fingers into the thick darkness of his hair, and suddenly looked tired and defeated. 'When I was a child, my grandfather constantly told me how my father had deserted my mother, how he had taken her money and left her, insisting that I was to be brought up as a Christian, and I hated and resented him. But the story he told me differs from that of my grandfather. Perhaps the truth lies somewhere in between, I don't know, but suddenly it no longer seems so important. What is past is past, and I too now know what it is to feel bitter corroding regret for my own actions.'

He turned, leaving her, and Claire's heart ached. Was he talking about Nadia? Wishing he had not been too proud to change his religion; thinking that if he had, his love might have saved her from becoming involved in Hasim's machinations?

By the end of the week the doctor was pleased enough with her progress to allow her to get up and spend the pleasant hours of the morning in the main courtyard, Teddy and Saud keeping her company. When she mentioned to Zenaide one day that more than anything else she would like to go down to the beach, Raoul appeared as though by magic and insisted on carrying her down to the soft fine sand. He swam in the azure sea with Teddy. She watched him coming out of the water, his body sleek and bronzed, her memory replaying disturbing scenes inside her head as she stared helplessly at him, sick and aching for the touch of his skin against hers.

Raoul mistook the reason for her pallor and cursed himself for allowing her to get overtired. There was no point in her objecting when he insisted on taking her back to the palace. He was treating her as though she were made of Dresden china, and sometimes she thought she couldn't bear it. What had happened to the man who had told her so arrogantly that he wanted her, that they would build a good life together? The strangeness she had sensed in him grew, and towards the end of Teddy's holiday she learned why.

He sought her out in the courtyard one morning when she was playing with Saud. Pregnancy had brought a soft glow to her skin, a warm ripeness of which she was unaware as she laughed at Saud's attempts to walk.

'I have booked Teddy's return flight,' Raoul told her, bending dexterously to catch Saud as he fell. His face was turned away from her, his voice perfectly even as he said, 'If you wish, you can be on that flight, Claire. No, say nothing now,' he urged when she wanted to protest. 'Think about it and then tell me what you wish to do. I think perhaps it would be for the best if you were to go.'

He left then, while she was still trying to come to grips with the enormous pain. Because of her weakness after her ordeal, Raoul had not shared her room as they had planned, but had slept in another on a separate floor. He was so distant and aloof these days that there seemed no way Claire could reach him. Why had he changed his mind about continuing their marriage?

Because of Nadia? But what about their child?

Anxiety and pain made it impossible for her to eat, and telling Zenaide that she no longer needed her Claire made up her mind what she must do. Raoul seemed to be at pains to avoid seeing her alone, but how could she talk to him—how could she make him see that he owed it to their child to allow her to stay? She wasn't going to give in easily. Now, when she was faced with the reality of leaving him, Claire knew that she would fight to be allowed to stay.

She entered his room without knocking and found it empty. For a moment she thought he must still be working downstairs, but then she heard the sound of running water from his bathroom and she curled up on the divan beneath the window, knowing that if she remained standing she wouldn't be able to stop herself from pacing nervously about the room.

When he walked in from the bathroom he didn't see her at first. His hair was damp from his shower, his body gleaming beneath the soft Moorish lamps whose diffused light Claire had come to love during her stay. And then as though some sixth sense alerted him to her presence he wheeled round, his body tensing almost as if in expectation of a blow.

'Raoul, I had to see you,' Claire told him before he could speak, 'and this seemed the only way. Do you . . . do you really want me to go back to England with Teddy?' she asked him before her courage could desert her.

'It seems the wisest course.' He wasn't looking at her, reaching instead for the towel he had dropped on the bed. Against the brief one he had fastened round his hips, his body glowed the colour of warm honey, the muscles in his back as fluid as ripples of water on the surface of the gulf as he started to dry himself.

'But our child,' protested, refusing to heed the dismissal in his voice. 'You said . . .'

'Forget what I said.' Suddenly his voice was harsh, his eyes darkening to jade as he turned to her. 'Do you *know* how close you came to losing your life?' He looked so bitter, so caught up in whatever emotion it was that brought the deep-carved lines bracketing his mouth and the emptiness to his eyes, that for a moment Claire was lost for words.

'But I didn't lose it,' she reminded him. 'I'm safe and so is Saud. Oh Raoul, do you honestly want your son to be brought up as a stranger to you, as you were to your father?'

For a second Claire thought her impassioned speech had burst through the wall he had built around himself, but then he smiled with a return of the old mockery she remembered. 'My son? You are so sure then that this child you carry will be a boy?'

'Son—daughter—both have a right to your love, your presence in their lives,' Claire told him, wondering if he was aware of how much she was gambling, of how fast her heart was racing.

'You make a very convincing advocate, Claire,' she heard him say at last. His voice changed suddenly, full of bitter yearning as he added roughly, 'Do you really think you need to persuade me that I want both you and my child here with me? Do you have any conception of how hard it is for me even to contemplate letting you go? And that is even when I take into consideration how close you came to death, and all through my fault. If I had seen through Nadia earlier . . .'

'How could you when you loved her so much?' Claire said softly, wanting to take the look of burning pain from his eyes.

'Loved her?' He stared at her. 'Loved Nadia? What game are you playing now, Claire?' he demanded curtly. 'Nadia was once to have been my wife and would have been had I changed my religion. But I was too proud to do so, and for a while I told myself I was bitter because my religion set us apart, blaming my father because he had insisted that I was brought up as a Christian. But I tell you this, Claire, were religion all that stood between me and gaining your love I would gladly change it ten thousand times over. My father was right when he warned me against pride,' he continued, before Claire could draw breath. 'I thought I could compel you to remain here with me. I knew, you see, that you could never bring yourself to desert your child, not when you could hardly bear to be parted from Saud, and . . .'

'And yet now you want me to leave,' Claire stormed at him. 'You say you want my love and yet you want to send me away; and I don't even know why you should want it, you have never once . . .' She broke off in confusion when she saw the way he was looking at her. Never before had she seen such a look of burning intensity in his eyes, a look that was a complex blend of tenderness and intense desire.

'Never once have I what?' he asked her. 'Told you that I love you?' Self-mockery darkened the already deep colour of his eyes. 'I have not perhaps mouthed the words, but there are other ways, Claire, ways that rely on a touch . . . a look. Many, many times I have looked at you with all the love I feel for you, but you have never noticed it, and every time I touch you it is the touch of a man deeply in love. Why else do you think I want to send you away? I cannot expect you to stay here after what happened. No matter how much I personally want and need you by my side. Even if your love for me was as great as mine for you. Are you so blind, Claire?' he asked whimsically. 'Do you truly believe, knowing what you do about my past, that I would even contemplate you bearing my child if I had not fallen so deeply in love with that merely being in the same room, breathing the same air, is the most acute pain. I think I loved you from the very first, although I managed to hide my feelings even from myself. I told myself that you were greedy, avaricious; that you could not be the warm, loving person you seemed, that your love for Saud must be faked, that your responsiveness in my arms was only hunger . . .'

'If it was, then it is a hunger that only you can satisfy,' Claire managed to get out tremulously, her legs threatening to collapse beneath her as she stumbled towards the bed, swaying slightly so that Raoul was forced, almost against his will it seemed, to catch her in his arms.

'Oh, Raoul, please let me stay. Please tell me it's true and that you do love me.' The hesitant touch of her lips against the naked skin of his shoulder provoked a smothered groan of protest, his fingers biting deep into her slender arms.

'Do you really know what you are committing yourself to, Claire? Omarah is a very new country, and a great many years separate Saud from the maturity to rule it. Be warned that if you give yourself to me I will never be able to let you go. Already my nights are tortured by the memory of you in my arms, your body against mine. I thought we could build a life here together, until Nadia kidnapped you, and then I knew that no matter how much I loved you I could not risk your safety ever again.'

'Raoul, all that was at risk was my life,' Claire told him huskily, 'and without you in it, it is as arid and worthless as . . . as the desert without water—a vast expanse of nothing.'

'As is mine without you,' Raoul muttered hoarsely, his strong body trembling beneath the teasing kisses she was placing against it. Behind her was the vastness of the Sheikh's bed, and Claire felt no guilt or restraint about allowing her body to slip down on to it, enticing Raoul's to follow, her arms outstretched to welcome him. The faint sigh he gave as he did so was half surrender, half impatiently stifled desire, telling her that there would be no departure from Omarah for her, not unless Raoul was at her side.

'Tell me again that you love me,' he demanded arrogantly as his lips brushed hers. 'I want to hear you say it.'

'Of course I love you,' Claire responded mischievously. 'Are you not the Lord Raoul, keeper of my heart, guardian of my virtue . . . father of my child.'

'Worshipper of your body,' Raoul murmured as he feathered warm kisses across her skin. 'Lover of your heart.'

Beneath her the coverlet of silk shimmered in soft, rich blue waves, the evening breeze stirring hangings which had once graced the bed of the Sultan himself, but Claire was unaware of her surroundings. She had all that mattered safely encompassed within her arms, and the murmured words of love Raoul whispered in her ear were sweeter music by far than the soft desert breeze whispering through the silent courtyard outside.